# THE COLORED GARDEN

by

O. H. Bennett

# THE COLORED GARDEN

by
O. H. Bennett

Laughing Owl Publishing, Inc.
Grand Bay, Alabama

**The Colored Garden**
Copyright © 2000 By Oscar H. Bennett. All rights reserved.
Printed in the United States of America. No part of this book may
be used or reproduced in any manner whatsoever without written
permission from Laughing Owl Publishing, Inc. except in the case
of brief quotations embodied in critical articles and review.

Library of Congress Cataloging-in Publication Data

Bennett, O. H. (Oscar H.), 1957-
    The Colored Garden  /  by O. H. Bennett — 1st ed.
        p.  cm.
    ISBN 0-9659701-9-1
        1.    Afro-American families—Southern States—Fiction.
2. Storytelling—Southern States—Fiction. 3. Family—Southern
States—Fiction. I. Title.

PS3552.E54747 C65 2000
813'.54—dc21

                                                            99-056321

FIRST EDITION First Printing, 2000

Front cover photo by Aleta Boudreaux
Back cover photo by Oscar H. Bennett

Laughing Owl Publishing, Inc.
12610 Hwy 90 West
Grand Bay, AL 36541
www.laughingowl.com

# Acknowledgment

Not too many things of any substance are accomplished alone and the making of this novel is no exception. Help has come from many directions and I hope if I've done anything right I've diligently expressed my gratitude to those who've given me support and assurance.

I must, however, recognize Oscar and Bettina Bennett, who've never failed me; Muriel Donald of Laughing Owl, who gave her time and valuable advice; my grandmother Katherine Hale, who baked rolls and told me her stories; and my friend Tiffany Lach, who helped keep the dream alive.

# PART ONE

# I

## Meeting the Gardener

In the middle of Kentucky farmland where a cornfield of withered brown stalks meets the grass of a cow pasture there is a tiny huddle of stones. They are surrounded by a knee-high picket fence and canopied by two old oaks just outside the weathered pickets, though one oak has not borne leaves for a few seasons and stands only out of stubbornness. The stones still stand too—straight, most of them—enduring the sculpting of rain and the whittling of wind. Here is a formation of good and loyal soldiers stiffly awaiting inspection. Here are ancient, spindly teeth, much gnashed, jutting up from green gums. Here is a quiet orchard of red-brown rock and chalky stone, whose messages of remembrance are only faintly visible.

Beneath the markers are the sleepers, neither fitful nor troubled. Most were strangers in life, but now have become a close and enduring family. They are connected and settled through decades of repose. They belong to that growing thing of the land that is black earth and searching roots and crawling life. They are part of the very land they once toiled upon for these are the souls of slaves and the souls of sons of slaves. They were buried at a time when the gates of heaven kept separate and unequal entrances. And there are more here than the stones will testify to; they were laid to rest without markers or their wooden crosses have long ago rotted away. But even those souls whose names are not etched anywhere on this earth have an unmistakable presence in this small corner of a cornfield. On summer days, years ago, I could see them, the vibrant, palpable spirits of long ago ancestors.

Today, I see them again, black skin made blacker by the sun, full Negro lips pressed together, wearing worn, ill-fitting clothes. They make little note of me, except to say, isn't that the boy who many times came visiting with Ruth? So, perhaps my presence has served to heighten their anticipation for the one who has guarded them and tended them for decades. The whites of their eyes betray their anxiousness and they press near the fence to gaze down the narrow, dirt trail. They listen for the soft steps of their sister, Ruth Standard.

Something in me wants to avoid this confrontation; this is not a new feeling, but the desire to resist it is certainly new. The strong wind at my back prods me forward, goading me to leave, but when I step out onto the trail that leads gradually uphill to the barn, I stop and hold my ground even as my heart quickens. I resolve to wait with those whom I know best, stealing courage from them. My family won't think to look for me here after all this time. This isn't where I'm supposed to be. Kenneth Willis has made a career of that: being someplace else.

My suit and my tie would testify that I made an effort. I always try. On high school graduation day eight years ago, I tried to come here. I stood in cap and gown, proud of my accomplishment, though I numbered near the very bottom of the class of '82. There was no one to cheer me on, except the new Mustang my father the Colonel had promised me, the carrot he had dangled at my nose for four years. An IG inspection had kept him away, he said. I honestly did not mind at all, relieved not to feel the pressure of his disappointed expectations.

By the time I arrived home from the auditorium, I had concocted an unexpected plan: I would leave. No good-byes, no questions, just go. I would drive up to Kentucky to see my grandmother Ruth. I packed haphazardly, leaving many things behind. I gave no thought to informing the Colonel. By that, I mean, I didn't even think of it. I paused only in the living room, in front of his little two-stool bar, behind which he kept decanters and flasks of all sizes. But my release from school and the mechanical power of my new car had me feeling free and strong. I bypassed the row of bottles.

I hit the open highway feeling giddy with freedom. No more

Colonel, no more teachers and counselors. I had a little graduation money for gas and food, and no one who knew me had any idea of my whereabouts. At first, I saw nothing but the road and its white painted dashes that fired like bullets at the front of my car. My radio rocked anthems to my freedom and my left hand tapped the beat on the car's side. I left the windows down so I could feel and hear the rush.

I went for miles on that high, over the hills of northern Georgia. Somewhere along the stretch of a two-way road, I began to notice the countryside: dilapidated, weather-beaten barns, a rusting cultivator in the middle of a field, rows and rows of crops. All of this made me think of the Standard farm, and the first summer I lived there; without being conscious of it, I eased off the gas, the white bullets on the pavement elongating and coming at me more slowly. I realized I didn't want to go where I was headed, and I didn't want to turn back either. My car drifted to a stop, coughed and died in the middle of the highway. I couldn't have sat there for more than a few seconds, but I'm not certain. I stared at the speedometer, but I thought of Mama, and Julie, and Gramma Ruth and her garden. I saw the car coming from the opposite direction, yet thought nothing of it. The blast from the semi-trailer's horn behind me woke me up. He was charging up on me fast and the oncoming car prevented him from going around. I remember seeing the truck's great, chrome grillwork, and have made myself believe I saw the shocked expression on the tractor driver's face when he realized the car in front of him wasn't moving. I turned and started my car, heard the hiss and growl of air brakes and the truck's tread biting at the pavement. The horn blared right at the back of my head. I stomped on the gas pedal and pulled off the road just as the gusting wind of the passing trailer shook my car and slapped at my face. The driver still laid into his horn and its loud anger only faded with distance.

I fought to get control of my heart, and stayed for a long time on the shoulder of the road. When I finally continued my trip to the Standard farm that day I was much more sober, and I did not feel so much free as just alone. I made it to the farm that day, but not to here. Not to the cemetery. I make up for that day now.

The first day I came here was in late May or early June fifteen years ago. I met Mrs. Ruth Standard, my eccentric grandmother. I was an unhappy nine-year-old who'd just left his father in Germany and flown across the Atlantic, then bussed across half of the United States.

"It's up to you to look after the women, Kenny," my father had charged me at the airport. He picked me up, stood me on a waiting room chair so that we were almost eye to eye. "That's why I'm giving you a field promotion to Sergeant."

"Yes, sir. Thank you, Major."

"Oh, no, Daddy, he was hard enough to live with when he thought he was a corporal," Julie said.

"At ease," I told her. My father moved to hug me, but I gave him a trembling salute, wanting to cry but wanting to be a good soldier too. The Major came to attention smartly and returned my salute.

He hugged Julie, who began to cry immediately. Then he hugged my mother as Julie and I watched. Even at that age, I could tell from the hug alone—it wasn't tight enough, it wasn't long enough—that something was wrong. I knew life was changing for me, but not how or why. The flight over the ocean that I had convinced myself to look forward to was a bore. I had argued with Julie for a window seat only to see an unbroken floor of white clouds. The bus trip from the East Coast to the hills of Kentucky proved to be little better. Still, I hardly slept during the two-day journey. I was worried; the way little boys worry, becoming confused and ill tempered. Frequent glances at my mother's face told me nothing. I wasn't afraid to ask her what was going on, but I was afraid of the answer. I stayed quiet, kept my forehead pressed against the Greyhound's cool window, and watched the cow barns and billboards fall away.

Mama had a real hug for the big man who greeted us at the bus station. "This is your grandfather, kids."

"I know," Julie said and the old man kissed her on the cheek.

Timidly, I shook his hand. He had long fingers and dirty nails.

I climbed in the back of Grandpa Standard's pick-up with the luggage and finally enjoyed a part of the trip. With warm wind blowing the smells of farms, wet fields and livestock into my face, the truck turned down one narrow road after another until we crossed an open field along a gravel trail and pulled into the Standards' farmyard. Chickens scattered in front of the truck and a dirty-nosed collie crawled from underneath the porch of the Standards' big house.

Julie jumped from the cab of the truck. "This is where you grew up, Mama?"

"The very place," Mama answered, following Julie out of the truck. She looked around for a long while and the man who was my grandfather smiled watching her. "The very place," she repeated. "Dad, where's Mom?"

I remember thinking how strange it was to hear my mother call other people Dad and Mom.

Grandpa Standard scowled. "She'd be running full throttle out the house by now if she were there so you know where that leaves. Dang woman does it to aggravate me. Julie, run behind the barn, pick up a dirt trail and follow it on out to your Grandma. Fetch her back."

"Okay, Grandpa. Come on, Kenny." And then Julie said sweetly to the dog, "You can come too. What's his name, Grandpa?"

"Don't have no name. Fool dog just trotted in here a couple of weeks ago and made himself at home."

Julie and I raced to the barn calling the dirty-nosed dog and he followed after us. We found the trail down the hill from the barn. It ran between a field of corn, with stalks as tall as I, and a fence overgrown with vines and blackberry bushes. But the berries were small and green.

"Julie, are we going to live here?" I asked her. She said nothing and kept running.

When we came to a clearing where the rows of corn and the shaggy, green fence both turned away from the trail, only the dog kept running, bounding over a low, white fence and into a graveyard. Julie and I came to a complete stop. An old woman kneeled near one of the headstones, and I could hear the snip snip of fast-moving clippers. The dog ran in between and around the stones then stopped to smell one with concentrated interest.

"Zeke, don't you dare." The woman threw something at the dog who took off running toward us. Her gaze followed him out of the cemetery and right to Julie and me. "Lord sake," she said, beckoning us. She pushed herself to her feet with the help of the nearby stone. "Well, come on. You can move faster than I can."

Julie stepped forward and I followed. "This is spooky weird," I whispered.

She hugged Julie and after a moment Julie hugged her back. Then the old woman, who was only old to the eyes of a nine-year-old, ran her fingers through Julie's hair. "Such nice hair," she said. "You get that from our side of the family." Then she turned her attention on me.

Grandma Standard was an older version of my mother, though smaller. Her hair was dark, though on each side of her head strands of white-gray were tucked behind the ears. "This is my Kenneth?" She smiled with the little wrinkles around her eyes. "You were a baby last time I saw you. Now you're a—"

"A sergeant!" I told her.

Julie rolled her eyes. "Daddy promoted him."

"I see." She laughed. "Well, Sarge, will you give your Grandma a hug?"

I shook my head quickly.

"Kenny!" Julie scolded.

"That's all right, Julie. The Sarge here and I are strangers. After he gets to know me he might want to give me a hug. And after I get to know him, I might not want one." Julie and Grandma Standard laughed. And even though I was the butt of her joke, I laughed too. I stopped when I remembered where I was.

"Are you in mourning, Gramma?" Julie asked. "You're not wearing black. Grandpa sent us to fetch you."

"Dogs fetch sticks," she said. "That's about all the fetching that gets done around here." She picked up her basket of tools. "And there's no mourning done in this cemetery. This is a garden of good souls at rest."

Flowers decorated the sides of most of the headstones and

along the fence in orderly files as bright and rhythmic, with their heads bobbing in the wind, as a uniformed band. The grass grew low, green, and even. Some graves were outlined with rocks painted white. Many of the markers were uncut stone pointing at various angles at the sky. The true headstones were thin, chalky and rough edged, and their inscriptions were faint and fading. Two small crosses mingled in with the pack of stones and one small monument, newer and more ornate than the rest by far, had a stone baby with wings perched atop it. I read the stone nearest me.

*Hattie May*
*Born 1790? Died April 20, 1863*
*When the roll is called up yonder.*

"Kenny, don't stand on the grave. The ghost will haunt you!" Julie said.

I jumped quickly to the side and apologized to the stone.

"Hattie wouldn't mind, Sarge." Grandma Standard told me. "Young boy like you, she'd put right in her lap and sing you a song."

Julie and I looked at each other, but said nothing.

"Come on, children, I want to see my little girl now." Grandma led us from her garden of resting souls.

"You have a little girl, Gramma?" Julie asked.

"Your mother. Your mother is my little girl."

Julie and I giggled.

"Grandpa said that dog didn't have a name," I said pointing to the dog that ran a little way in front of us and turned every now and then to make sure we were following.

"Everybody, everything's got a name. That collie came around about a month ago. Asked if I'd name him Zeke, so I did."

I looked at this woman who was my grandmother, and I wondered if she believed that or if she just expected me to believe it.

"Gramma, do you know anyone buried in that graveyard?" Julie asked.

"I know everyone buried there," she said.

I believe I became an observer of people right then, specializing in grown-ups. I discovered that what I could see—like my parents' hug at the airport—would always tell me more than what people were willing to say. I would try to figure out why people acted the way they did. My mother and hers, Gramma and her little girl, stood behind the barn, facing each other, not four feet apart, and just looked at each other, as if they were afraid to get close. But then I realized they were just savoring the moment, like when you eat a slice of pie real slow. Finally, they hugged and began to cry as women do from time to time; the tears weren't sad ones or happy ones, but a bit of both.

Everyone asked me how I liked my room, so I knew we were going to be there awhile. I became moody and wanted to be left alone.

"Let's let Sarge look around on his own," Gramma said. Seemingly, she noticed my mood before Mama had. "Come on, Julie, let's go look at where you're going to stay."

My room seemed huge to me then; actually, it was quite small and cozy. The room was on the top floor of the big house and had a sloping ceiling and two dormer windows. A big, round rug with multi-colored, concentric circles covered nearly the entire floor, leaving only bare wood corners. A double bed with a book shelf headboard covered the length of one wall, opposite an old, nicked bureau with claw feet, and under one of the windows sat a chest with a padded lid doubling as a bench. I had decided; that was my spot. Many purple evenings were spent sitting at that window watching the hills and the fields, lost in the thoughts and wonder of youth. That evening I sat there for the first time with the window open just enough to let a cool breeze slip in. In the front yard, Zeke rolled on his back, grumbling. The corn plants waved their leaves in mass with the wind and even from the window the gently rustling rows could be heard. The stalks were not yet tall enough to hide the cemetery. The stones were white and glowing. Mystery lurked there, and my boy's mind preferred to attribute the glow of the headstones to less prosaic causes, to unknown, supernatural forces rather than the last rays of a setting sun.

The eeriness of the graveyard added to my lost, rootless

feeling; I felt like the uncomfortable guest of strangers. This was not my bedroom. Mine was across the pastures that lie beyond the cornfield and across an ocean. My Dad would not come in here tonight for "routine bed inspection" before ordering light discipline. I felt I had abandoned him. The Major was alone and that wasn't right. I had made a terrible mistake. Julie should be with Mama, but I should've stayed with the Major. And then I thought, he was waiting for me to volunteer to stay behind and I didn't. I had disappointed him.

"Zeke," I heard from outside. Grandma Standard stood in front of the house with a pan of water. The dog came running. He began lapping up the water with a vigorous sloshing sound even before she'd finished setting down the pan. "Getting in mischief is thirsty work," she said to the collie. "How do you like the boy?" she asked as if an answer would be forthcoming. Zeke did stop his drinking momentarily and look at her. "Hope you two get along, if not you're back on the highway where I found you." She turned to go back inside and I ducked from the window so she wouldn't spot me.

Of course, I liked Zeke; I liked almost everything about the farm, and Grandpa Standard and Gramma. I felt guilty about liking it and resisted the feeling. The Major wouldn't want me to give in so easily. That night I climbed into the biggest bed I'd ever had to myself, tossed and turned a little while, then fell asleep.

*

In the days that followed, we fell into the routine of the Standards. The day started before the sun rose and the smell of baking biscuits even floated up the two cases of stairs to my bedroom. Grandpa Standard assigned a few chores to me such as feeding Zeke and the chickens, collecting the eggs with Julie, keeping the tool shed orderly, and helping him fix all kinds of things.

Grandpa ate breakfast alone and was out and about before we'd get to the table. He ate quickly, not wasting the time to talk, following each bite of food with a gulp of black coffee. It was only when I awoke earlier than usual that I'd catch him at the breakfast table. Every chore had urgency for him. He moved from one to the next just like he moved from the eggs to the grits, quickly. Grandpa, Charles Standard, wearing his tee shirts riddled with holes that Gramma could not get him to throw away, was a serious, almost humorless man. But now and then, he had a joke or just a wink of the eye at the right time that always seemed funnier than it really was because of its rarity.

I soon noticed that Grandpa and Gramma did not chat. I mean they didn't have conversations like Mama and Dad used to have. Grandpa would inform Gramma the fuel pump on the tractor needed replacing, and she'd warn him the TV called for rain by late afternoon. That was usually the extent of it, at least that I heard. This would be a big, quiet house, I thought, if not for Mama, Julie, and me.

A grass-and-dirt-stained apron hung at the back of the kitchen door. When it came off its hook, everyone knew where Gramma was going. Grandpa Standard would roll his eyes on those occasions when he was around to see her reach for it. "Can't harvest rock," he'd say, "It's just a waste of time."

Gramma didn't seem to notice. She'd tie her apron on, humming softly to herself all the while, then head for the tool shed leaving Grandpa to present his case to whoever was in hearing distance. "There she goes, off to talk to people who been dead a hunnert years. S'pose to let them rest in peace. But that woman won't let nothing rest. Nothing."

Dad called after we'd been there a week. Mama spoke to him first, but only for a short time. I got angry. Julie talked next and she made it seem like everything was going just great. I got angry with her too. When my turn came, I was afraid, and Julie had to push the receiver into my hands. I knew the Major would be disappointed in me. This was my chance to volunteer to return home, but everyone was around. I knew Mama would not let me go back.

Dad's voice, tiny in my hands, called for me.

"Speak, honey," Mama urged. "This is long distance."

I placed the receiver to my ear. "Yes, Sir."

"How's my sergeant?" the Major asked. "Give me a full report."

"I'm sorry, Daddy." The words spurted out, I dropped the phone and ran from the house, ignoring Mama's calls.

My sister came hunting for me, zealously, no doubt sent by my mother. I hid beneath an old sawhorse covered with plastic tarp in the barn. Julie called, "Kenny, you'd better get back in the house; Mama is ticked off. You're going to get it this time."

I would not surrender. From my vantage point, I saw her stamp her foot. "I hope she wallops you good," she said over and over before giving up the search.

The barn smelled of moldy hay and fresh hay, animals, and old wood. I crept out and sat outside, my back against the peeling red barn and hidden from the house. I don't remember how long I sat there drawing in the dirt with my finger and hoping the Major wasn't mad at me and that Mama wasn't too mad at me.

"Who taught you to waste time like this?" Gramma stood over me. She wore her green stained apron and carried her tray of tools, which she set down next to me. "Make yourself useful," she said and started down the hill toward the cemetery. I followed several feet behind her, wondering when she would mention the phone call, and not wanting to return to that spooky graveyard.

The stones waited, casting small shadows on the graves. Bees were humming, dancing from flower to flower, from pink to purple, shopping. "Hello," Gramma Ruth said entering her garden, and I wondered if she spoke to the bees, or the flowers, or the stones. "Come along, bring my things." This she said to me.

I had seen a movie once where a long line of black, shiny cars with yellow headlights burning came rolling into a cemetery. The cars stopped and the people stepped out, all in black, all blank faced and quiet. They fell silently into procession behind the pallbearers who carried a casket as black and as shiny as the cars. The coffin was lowered while the gathering, crowded on the very edge of the open grave, watched its descent. The undertaker began to shovel in dirt that thudded and scattered across the casket top, marring its shiny, perfect surface. The mourners remained even as the casket was completely covered. Suddenly, the fresh dirt erupted; a clawing hand shot up, grabbing a black hem. The mourner was dragged protesting into the grave.

Gramma asked, "What's holding you up?"

I moved forward maybe an inch. "Graveyards are spooky," I said.

"Says who?" She looked at me, smiling. "Are you scared? You weren't afraid the other day, when you first got here. Come see my irises." She held out her hand.

I looked from her hand to the graves. There were no signs of eruptions. "Not 'fraid of nothing," I told her and walked into the cemetery.

She took the tray from me and went right to work. "You should have seen my azaleas, bright as peacocks. Everybody loved them. But you'll be here for the marigolds and the zinnias. They show off. I'm going to plant some around Hattie May's marker. She'll like that, Sarge. Do you want to help?"

"No." I stood over a grave without a marker, but outlined in white painted rocks all about the same size and same oval shape. End to end they formed a neat rectangle in the far end of the cemetery.

"I notice you don't do much that you don't want to do. Mighty strange for a soldier who's supposed to follow orders." She spoke as she worked, sitting on the ground near the stone. "I'll take this grass up and start it over in a brown spot near the fence." Again I wasn't sure to whom she spoke. "Sarge, why didn't you talk to your Daddy? What are you sorry about anyway?"

There. I knew she'd ask and she did. But what business was it of hers? At least she didn't press. I shrugged my shoulders, but, not sure she'd noticed, said, "I don't know."

Gramma pulled herself up, again with the help of a headstone. She stood next to me, then bent down to adjust one of the white rocks. I couldn't see a difference between how it was before and how it was after she quit moving it.

"This is the Chief's grave," she said answering a question moments before I asked it. "I can't pronounce his real name, but all the other slaves just called him Chief. You knew this was a cemetery for slaves didn't you, Sarge? Our place and the

Hendersons' and the Tates' and most of the MacEacherns' used to be one big plantation. Grew tobacco mostly. The simple folk resting here are the ones who did all the work. Hattie and Nettie, Anna and Mark Littlejohn, and Cakes and Tillie, and her sister Twilda. Lot more. Chief isn't alone in this plot. Course, Chief didn't work much. But it wasn't from laziness, it was pride. He was a war chief of the Wolof and labor was beneath his dignity, you see."

I hadn't thought about dead people being lazy or proud or slaves or anything except the bogeys of movies and ghost stories. But Gramma knew their names and what they were like.

"Poor Chief," Gramma said, and she picked a bright purple and white flower and laid it in the middle of the Wolof's grave. "Most of the other slave men didn't like him because he wouldn't do his fair share of the work. The women took care of him though, saved some greens for him. Chief spent the last three years of his life manacled hand to foot." Gramma looked at me and smiled. "I need some water for my marigolds. Would you fill the pail in the tool shed and bring it to me?"

"Tell me more about the slaves, Gramma. Is being a war chief like being a major?"

"More like a general. Bring the water and we'll see about more stories."

Half the water had sloshed out onto the hard dirt of the trail by the time I returned.

"Tell me about the Wolof general," I said.

Gramma took the pail from me. "It's your turn to do some talking now, Sarge. Why didn't you want to speak to your daddy?" This time she waited for an answer.

So I told her how he was probably mad at me because I didn't volunteer to stay behind, and now he was probably double mad because I didn't talk to him. She listened to me as I talked to the ground, looking up at her only now and again to see how I was being received. "I think I'd better go back home to Munich," I finished.

"Well, I see your point, Sarge," she said and began watering the plants. She moved from grave to grave, rationing the water to the flowers that adorned them. "I confess," she was saying, "that I hadn't really thought of your situation quite that way, but you do have a point. Could be he's powerful mad at you."

I began to fidget.

"But one question comes to mind, Sarge. Why in heaven's name did he promote you? Julie said you got a promotion. How do you figure that?"

I hadn't. "He wanted me to stay," I asserted.

"What did he say when he promoted you?"

I remembered back to the airport, my salute, Julie crying, strangers with bags looking on as they hurried by, the Major's face. "He said that I should look after the women," I said and realized at the same time.

Gramma smiled. "Hard to do from Munich if they're just outside Louisville."

I hugged her.

"Now you want a hug," she said, and hugged me back. "Tell you what you do. Write a nice letter to your daddy. Tell him about everything, and that you're going to carry out his orders."

I nodded, very much relieved and eager to start my letter.

"Well, go on," Gramma said. "I'll be along in a little while."

I took off toward the big house leaving Gramma, not alone, but with Hattie, who sang songs to little boys, and Chief, the proud Wolof, and the rest.

*

They were arguing in whispers, Gramma and Mama. I could hear them, but not their words. Whispers are shadows of real words and demand more attention than a shout, especially to a young boy. To my mind, whispers had to be the truth because that's when people said things they didn't want you to hear. I had been heading downstairs when I heard the harsh, hushed voices coming from Mama's room at the end of the hall on the second floor. I immediately got down on all fours and crept like an ungainly spider, butt thrust in the air, toward the partially opened door. I had made up my mind to pretend I was searching for a dropped marble should they step out quickly and catch me spying. I even fished a marble out of my pocket and sent it rolling ahead of me. Thing is, it kept rolling.

"I don't think happiness is foolishness," were the first words I heard plainly; they were Mama's.

"Keep your voice down," Gramma said. "It's just that the children have been through enough changes. Poor things."

The marble bounced up over the flat doorsill and rolled like a herald of Caesar into the room.

I could see them now, part of my face and one eye peeking in the opening. Both were around the bed holding clothes. Gramma was folding. Mama was balling them up. And the marble was still rolling.

"Then why are you helping me pack if you're dead set against this, Mom? I can do it myself."

The marble came to a rest between Mama's feet. I couldn't see her face, but Gramma's face looked sad or maybe tired. She said, "I know you can, Connie. You can do everything by yourself, always have." She took a breath. "I'm just saying if I were you, I'd wait and see how Stephen feels."

Mama stepped toward her bureau, leaving my field of vision. Her shoe grazed the cats-eye, sending it toward Gramma. "Quit telling me what you would do, Mom," my Mama was saying and it wasn't a whisper at all now. "Can't you see I'm trying my damndest not to do what you would do!"

Gramma looked shocked. Her eyes opened, and her mouth, but she said nothing. I saw her bend over. I felt sorry for her and wondered why Mama would say a mean thing like that to Gramma. The room was quiet after that. Gramma finished folding a sweater and laid it gently on the bed. The line of her mouth was set tight now and she nodded. She moved out of my sight and before I could figure out where she headed, the door opened wide and she looked down at me.

"Have you seen my marble?" I managed.

"It'll work out, Mom," my Mama said. Neither of them seemed to care I was there.

Gramma nodded again, but didn't turn around to face Mama.

She held my marble above me then dropped it into my hand. "Laying on the floor is a good way for big-eared boys to get stepped on, Sarge." She spoke without her usual smile and went down to the kitchen.

I was ready for Mama's "conference" by the time she called it that evening. I'd warned Julie that Mama was leaving, that I'd seen her packing, and we would be staying on the farm. Mama told us Daddy and she had decided it wasn't good for the family to be traipsing all over the mid-east and Europe. She said they thought it would be better for us to go to American schools and start establishing long-term friendships. She said she was going into Louisville to look for work, and the Major would join us once his tour of duty ended. I didn't believe her. I did not look into her eyes or listen to the rest of what she had to say. Julie believed her, believed it all. I thought, tomorrow I'll go exploring with Zeke or maybe go with Gramma to her garden.

The next day Grandpa took Mama into town and Julie went along for the ride. I stayed behind with Gramma, so Mama gave me a goodbye hug on the porch. I gave her one too, much like the one she'd given the Major at the airport.

## II

## The Color of Fried Corn Cake

As each day warmed and grew longer, a new routine developed on the Standard farm. Gramma would reach for her apron and I, just as automatically, would race to the tool shed to get her tray and fill the bucket.

The corn grew taller and the blackberries swelled and ripened. "You'll be picking blackberries not too much longer, you and Julie," Gramma said. "I'll bake you some pies. When you pick the berries watch out for the chiggers; they'll eat you alive."

In spring, the garden outshone every other place on the farm. The cemetery was cooled by the shade of the two oaks, and dazzling bright with flowers of all colors and types like fireworks frozen just as they exploded. The air was sweet, and the grassy earth, as soft as carpet. I'd sit, usually with my back against Hattie May's marker, feeling very content and cajole Gramma to tell me stories of the slaves that slept below.

One stone, with the stone cherub on top, made me particularly curious. It was newer and more ornate than the others and its inscription much more mysterious.

*Kate*
*Born and Died the Same Week*
*1931*
*"Budded on Earth to Blossom in Heaven"*

No month or day was etched there, just the line, "Born and Died the Same Week." There was tragedy in that line, conveying, simply, a callous unfairness done to the tiny sleeper below. I could

not, just nine years old, describe the feeling I had from reading the
stone, but I must have sensed some of the pain and frustration of
those who buried the diminutive coffin, who witnessed the birth,
the struggle, and the death all in one short, life-long week. *Kate.*
There was irony in this name, cut in stone, yet never called or
answered to.

"Kate probably never knew her own name, huh, Gramma," I
said one day.

Gramma pruned a small shrub near Kate's marker. "I'd expect
not," she answered. "Least not on this earth."

I waited for her to say more, then finally I asked, "Tell me her
story, Gramma."

"I don't know a story to tell you about baby Kate, Sarge." She
stepped to the stone. "Though I'm certain that Hattie, and Tillie,
and Twilda have looked out for little baby Kate. They probably
dote on her something awful." Gramma Ruth looked sad. "I don't
know a story to tell about Kate," she said again and laid a hand
upon the head of the cherub as if by doing so she might divine
some secret knowledge about the infant sleeper.

"That's okay, Gramma," I said. "Tell me about that one," and
pointed hastily to the next marker back, a chipped, weathered
cross that read,

*Cakes Huntley*
1857

Gramma's smile returned. "Cakes was a misunderstood man,"
she began. "He was tall and high yellow, and because of the color
of his skin, he got into a lot of trouble."

I settled back in Hattie May's lap, ready for another of
Gramma Ruth's stories.

"You see, Sarge, not too long ago color was more important
than it is now. It's still too important, but times were when it meant
everything. Even Cakes's name meant color. His mother named
him after the golden yellow of a fried corn cake."

Gramma became lost in her stories and she took me with her.
She told the story in whispers and roars. Her voice was gruff for

one character and soft for another. Her face and eyes and hands told as much of the story as her words, and completely captivated me. No television show or movie could wind such a spell as Gramma could amongst the stones and flowers of that gentle resting ground. I did not think about my mother or the lies she had told me. For a little while it did not hurt that the Major was so far away. I met new people like the lonely and confused Cakes Huntley. Without Gramma Ruth's expressiveness it loses a bit of its energy and life, but this is the story of one of my childhood companions, Cakes, as well as I remember it, and as best I can tell it.

The night Cakes's mother was birthing him, her man Tommas Huntley waited outside the one-room shack in the slave quarters alone, fidgety, and afraid.

Gramma Ruth pointed across the cow pasture where a group of sycamores now stood. "I think the slaves quarters, a little circle of small shacks, used to be right where those shade trees stand. I've found an old pot and nails rusted to dust over there."

Somewhere, just outside the circle of shacks probably, Tommas waited alone, not wanting any company. He was a tough, squat, hard- muscled man as black as the middle of the night. The other slaves looked up to him and that's why he didn't want them to see him frightened and shaking. He came running though, when he heard the first cries of the baby. He jumped through the doorway just as Cakes drew his first breaths with the women in a tight circle fussing over him. Tommas glanced at his woman, spent and sweaty on the bed, then went to the baby.

"Now, Tommas," one of the women said, "All babies darken up after they's born."

He had lived this moment before, maybe even a thousand times. He'd seen himself grab the wet, slick baby just as it was born and look straight into its open, tiny eyes. In his vision, only he and the baby existed. And the baby always stared hard back at him as if it were the one doing the examining with fiery eyes that were first brown, then blue. The nightmare vision had been born the day he returned from the field, much earlier than expected, and saw his owner, Masta Charlie, leaving his cabin, hitching up his suspenders.

He called his woman, who had been showing for a little while, on it immediately. "What's Masta Charlie been doin heres? How long this been goin' on? Why didn't you tell me?"

She just began to cry real loud and Tommas swung at her but missed and she kept crying and instinctively he had the answers to all his questions except one.

I remember Gramma paused at this point in the story and looked like she just realized something. "I don't suppose I should be telling you this part of the story. Do you understand these things between men and women, Sarge?"

"The Major told me all about that sex stuff, Gramma," I answered. Actually, at the time, I didn't understand the entire significance of Master Charlie hitching up his suspenders. But I did enjoy being told a story by Gramma. And I also guessed, even then, that Gramma wasn't telling the story just for me anyway. It was more like she knew the stories and so they had to be told. She gave me an appraising look, then continued.

His woman's crying told Tommas everything he had feared, that Masta Charlie had been visiting her for some time while Tommas worked in the fields, and that she'd been too afraid to say anything about it. Anger wrenched Tommas tight, the kind of anger he couldn't show outside of his little shack.

"Who's the papa?" he said and kicked at her legs, and she fell to the hard, dirt floor. "Who's the papa?" he said again and again and kicked her in the stomach. And when she curled up into a ball, he kicked her back and her legs until she scrambled wildly on the floor trying to get away and he booted her out the door.

When she came back hours later he wouldn't let her in, nor would he let any of the other slaves take her in. She stayed outside for three days until Masta Charlie—his full name was Charles Marshall Enright—heard about it and told Tommas to let her back in the cabin. "Now, Tommas," Masta Charlie said. "You know I don't usually come between a fella and his woman. And I know women can be a might exasperating can't they?"

Tommas answered, "Yassuh."

"Even Mrs. Enright can get to my bad side now and again."

Masta Charlie smiled when he said this and held his index finger to his lips conspiratorially as if he were sharing some secret between men with Tommas.

Tommas realized he should be flattered. "Yassuh."

"Besides," Masta Charlie said and shook that same finger at Tommas, gently chastising the boy he had taken a bullwhip to five times in the past. "Some of the other gals tell me she's with child. We don't want her out in the wet, morning dew now do we?"

"Nawsuh."

Tommas took his woman back in that evening, put his arms protectively around her and led her back in the shack. He hugged the trembling girl and kissed her face. "From now on you come out to the field with me," he said and gently touching her belly added, "And soon we sees who be really more de man."

And Tommas waited for the moment and lived with his vision that came to him every time he saw his woman's swelling belly, or saw Masta Charlie, or looked down the long rows of young tobacco and especially when he shut his eyes trying to keep it all out. But the moment came just like all moments we dread finally do.

In the vision it was just him and the baby and that's probably the way it seemed. He forgot about his woman on the bed, took the baby from the circle of women and they disappeared from his view too. He held the baby up and away from him, examining it by oil lamp light, looking into its eyes, but Cakes's little slits were shut tight and his tiny legs squirmed in Tommas's tight grip.

The anxious women stood near at hand, their hands outstretched ready to grab or catch the infant whose dangling umbilical cord had yet to be tied off. "All babies darken up after they's born, Tommas," one of them repeated.

But it wasn't the pale color of the newly-born that Tommas saw. It was Cakes's face. It was that narrow, tapered nose and thin, pursed lips that betrayed paternity. This single, quick moment Tommas had dreaded and lived with for months defeated him entirely; it broke him as the whip had never done. The snap came from inside and something within the great muscles of his arms, his back, and his legs collapsed on itself. He felt it. Utterly beaten, he handed the baby back to the relieved midwives, an act of resignation.

Only then did he look again to his woman. Completely exhausted, she still raised her arm and held out her hand toward Tommas. Shaking his head, he stepped back and out of the cabin.

Cakes grew up under many sets of watchful eyes. The most assiduous eyes were his mother's. She was very protective of him and constantly rushed from her cabin to rescue him from the rocks and fists of the other children. "They are jealous of what you are." She would console him and wipe his tears. She would tell him how special and different he was, but avoided telling him the identity of his father. The eyes of Mrs. Enright would watch him too, from the white trellises of her columnar porch.

When Cakes was just a month old she had come down to the slaves' row for her traditional visit to all newborns. She saw it as her duty as lady of the manor and brought with her blankets, and strawberry preserves—that the slave women themselves had made the previous season—and sometimes a little money, maybe a dollar or two. Mrs. Enright made a big show of her generosity and all those slaves who weren't out in the fields would gather around when she came down. In Tommas's cabin, she sat in a chair after laying one of the blankets across its seat.

She talked incessantly. "Babies are so wonderful, so wonderful," she'd said and, "We must all do our bit to increase the population of Enright Farms," she'd added. "So," she said to Tommas's woman, "Let's see your new pickaninny." Cakes was handed to her.

Something had caught in her throat when she first laid eyes on him. She didn't take the baby, but clutched at her throat instead and all the brown, dark eyes watched her blue ones grow to twice their size. There were those who wanted to help her, but all knew full well she shouldn't be touched; to do so would be a terrible familiarity. She jumped to her feet, upsetting the chair and tumbling her deliveries from her lap. She suddenly felt out of place—her colorful silk and crinoline, their stained and tattered cotton. She found herself, not the lady of the manor, but a white woman, surrounded by night-dark faces whose shocked expressions scared her. Still clutching her neck, she ran all the way back to the mansion. The gathering dispersed quickly, fearing someone would be blamed for whatever just happened. The house slaves reported that the relationship between Charles Marshall Enright and Mrs. Enright became strained after that day.

There were other eyes that looked upon the high yellow boy with soft, curly, brown hair with the same growing enmity the mistress of the manor possessed. Those eyes belonged to Tommas. His hatred for the boy festered deep within him in ways he didn't understand and tried to deny. But Cakes's very presence reminded Tommas of what he was and what he was not. He broke off his relationship with Cakes's mother and she and the boy moved into another shanty Masta Charlie ordered built not two doors away.

Masta Charlie would look at the increasingly undeniable resemblance between Cakes and himself with much amusement. Cakes was "his little nigger" he was heard to say on many occasions and sometimes he would throw his head back and laugh aloud in the boy's presence as if sharing a good, private joke.

Cakes wasn't any darker than a white man who spends his days working outside. He knew that everyone watched him, and talked about the color of his skin. He was different and he didn't need his mother's constant reminders to tell him that. And he knew different was good. Different meant being one of the only colored children allowed to play with Masta Charlie's nephews and nieces when they came to visit. And that meant no work, and it meant eating some of the same treats they received and even learning to read—a little bit. "You're not very much of a nigger," Masta Charlie's sweet smelling niece had said to him one day while the two waded in a creek. She was looking at his nearly white legs that stuck out of his rolled up trousers. Cakes glowed at that and nodded.

Different made life easier for Cakes, he thought. One day that hateful, black Tommas Huntley dragged him to the fields. "You're old enough ta' be workin. An' maybe out here in de fields you won't meet up with dat trouble dats waitin' for you."

Tommas set him to work clearing a field with the other slaves. Cakes gathered rocks and broken branches and pulled up stones under a baking, white hot sun. The slaves were scattered across the field, bent over, tugging at rocks or fat, stubborn roots; the men's bare backs glistened like coal, and together they looked to Cakes like a herd of demented beasts grazing on rocks. He did not want to be a part of them, not now nor in the evening when they'd gather about a fire to eat, laugh, and dance like living silhouettes around the flame. Cakes pulled up another stone, more like a boulder, and carried it to the trail where other blacks loaded the wagons. He moved slowly feeling the weariness in his back and legs. The jagged edges of the stone cut into his forearms as he cradled it. He stumbled to the wagon and dropped the rock, jumping his feet clear. Tommas, arms crossed in front of his chest, glared at Cakes, and Cakes's eyes met his.

"You can't do this to me," Cakes said. "You can't." The big black didn't say a word.

The second day started out worst than the first for Cakes. He ached everywhere. He felt wronged as if he were convicted to hard labor for a crime he did not commit. He felt angry and helpless. He felt like a slave. But Cakes had an appeal.

Masta Charlie came riding down the trail in his buckboard and Cakes let his load of rocks drop and raced across the field waving his arms and calling, "Masta! Masta!" He ignored Tommas's shouts and kept running. Tommas chased after him angry to the bone. Masta Charlie saw them coming and held up his team. They both arrived at the wagon at the same time and out of breath.

"See here, what do you boys want? What's the fuss?" Masta Charlie asked them, but he looked right at the exhausted, sweating Cakes. He smiled.

"Cakes here don't want nothin', Masta," Tommas said, and Cakes glared at him, still trying to catch his breath.

"You want anything, Cakes?"

"Yeahsuh, Masta. Ah was wantin' to work up at de house if Ah could."

Masta Charlie laughed. Tommas braced himself for trouble. "Don't much like field work, huh, boy? Well, the Mrs. picks the house help and I don't reckon you being up there would be my brightest ideer. Climb in the back. We'll take you over to the stables an' see if you don't like workin' around the horses."

Cakes grinned. "Thank ya, suh. Thank ya, suh!" He scrambled into the back of the wagon. He waved to Tommas as the buckboard pulled away, grinned and made funny faces. I am different, not one of them, Cakes thought. His delight didn't fade even as the wagon followed the trail up a hill and away from the field.

Cakes did get to work in the stables and he liked the horses. It was hard work too, but a far sight better than being in the field with that nigger Tommas watching over him. This was when Cakes really started to dream. He worked within sight of the mansion and saw the comings and goings of the Enrights and their guests whose horses he would water and tend while they visited. He never got to see these fine people close up because Masta Charlie had told him not to see to the horses until the guests were well inside the house. And Cakes, always eager to stay on Masta Charlie's good side, did exactly as he was told. He did see enough of the ladies and the gentlemen to know that their world was where he belonged.

He wanted to wear a top hat and step from a carriage with a lady as clean as snow, wearing lace and silk, holding on to his arm. His dream was that Masta Charlie would send him away to a school so that he could be educated and return a gentleman. He would show everyone where he belonged. Masta Charlie was, of course, the key, and Cakes would bend over backwards to please him. When Masta Charlie returned home from a business trip in town or from overseeing the planting in the fields, Cakes would run to him before he called and take his horse away. He worked meticulously in the stables, kept everything orderly, and was always excited by one of Masta's inspections and the praise he would receive afterwards. Cakes jumped at the first word out of Masta Charlie's mouth. He saw that Masta Charlie liked him and he knew the day would come when he could ask to be sent to school and to become a gentleman.

The other blacks on the plantation no longer shook their heads at Cakes's fawning, nor did the young ones tease him any longer. As the seasons went by his behavior was easily dismissed. "That's just Cakes," they would say. He was not a part of their community.

On one particular day, Cakes was awakened from an afternoon nap in the stalls—where he lived, mostly—by Masta Charlie's shouting. Cakes scurried to see what the commotion was all about. Outside, Masta Charlie was pushing a colored boy in front of him. Cakes recognized the boy, usually cocksure and smiling, who had bullied him when they were younger.

The boy, older than Cakes by a year or two, maybe sixteen at the time, kept falling to the dust in front of Masta Charlie who shouted, "Get up, lazy nigger," only to shove the boy down again when he rose slowly, shakily to his feet. In this manner, they progressed between the curing sheds, around the stable, and into the front yard.

A group of slaves—including Tommas—drafted as witnesses followed behind Masta Charlie not saying much; some of the women held their hands to their faces. The boy began whining now, promising to work harder from here on out, but red-faced Masta Charlie wasn't listening.

"Tie him up and take him to the tree, Cakes," he said and tossed Cakes some leather thongs.

Cakes moved as quickly as ever; grabbed the boy's wrists and bound them together.

"He gonna wear out my hide," the boy said to Cakes.

The tree, a fat sycamore, dominated one end of the yard with a steel ring embedded in it about seven feet up its trunk. Cakes pulled the boy to the tree, and, after a bit of trouble that caused Masta Charlie to holler at him—much to Cakes's alarm—tethered the boy to the ring.

There were clean streaks on the boy's dirty face where his tears had run down. "It's all right, Cakes," the boy said to him. "Ah knows you hafta do whatcha tol'."

Cakes stepped away from him, puzzled, having been forgiven without committing a crime.

"Tear his shirt away," Masta commanded.

For the first time, Cakes moved slowly to obey. He ripped the shirt open, revealing the boy's smooth, vulnerable back. The crack of the whip came immediately, almost catching Cakes. A sprinkle of blood dots made a line across Cakes's face, and the dark flesh of the boy opened red as he screamed. Cakes scrambled away and hid himself in the cool darkness of the stable. But the thunder snap of the whip and the screams were in there too, and Cakes began to cry. He wished the boy were different so that this wouldn't have to happen. He wished the boy was different like he was. Then he wished everyone were different.

Cakes came back out when the whip was quiet. A group of blacks took the torn up boy away and some of the girls were crying. Masta Charlie stood in the middle of the yard, exhausted. The anger had been worked out of him and the whip hung limply from his hand to coil like a resting snake at his feet. Sweat poured from his face. On reflex, Cakes ran quickly to the well and brought Masta Charlie the water bucket and a cup.

Charles Enright labored to catch his breath and he gulped greedily at the cup of water much like a weary field hand would. "Damn, my arm probably feels worse than that boy's back. Lazy nigger. Now he's gonna be laid up a week and I'll get no work from him a'tall." He dipped the cup in the bucket and drained it again, and only then did he appear to notice Cakes. "Thank you, Cakes, water's just what I needed."

The master smiled at Cakes. "I swear, boy, you're all right. You ain't no lazy nigger." He patted the boy on his head. "You're a good nigger," Masta Charlie said, then dropped the cup in the bucket and headed to the house.

Cakes ran the bucket back to the well, smiling on both sides of his face. Masta can see that I am different, he thought; surely he'll send me to school now.

The glow of Masta Charlie's compliment—as Cakes saw it— had him skipping along. When he rounded the corner of the stables, whap! Something exploded against the side of his face, dropping him seat first to the dirt. He was lost in a hazy, painful white blindness and it took several seconds to focus his eyes. When he finally did, he saw the big, black face of Tommas looming over him, blocking out the sun. Tommas's open right hand was reared up, ready to take another swing at the startled Cakes.

"A good dog," Tommas said, "still gets bare bones, still sleeps in the cold, still just a dog!"

\*

Perhaps if Cakes had worked in the fields with Tommas things would've turned out differently for him. But he worked at the stables in view of Mrs. Enright's window whose curtains parted when the high-yellow boy, with Charles Enright's nose and lips duplicated on his face, would run by. It was more than she could stand. So when Masta Charlie went on an extended business trip, she made her move. She really wanted to get rid of Cakes, but was too afraid of her husband to try that. Instead she sold Cakes's mother. One of the house slaves, it could've been Hattie May—she worked in the kitchen during this time—heard Mrs. Enright talking to the buyer and hurried down to the shacks to tell Cakes's mother. Cakes was with his mother when the news came and she cried out and clung to him like a drowning man would hold onto a log. "Gather up your thangs, theys is comin' right after me," the kitchen girl said. But Cakes's mother couldn't move, so the girl put things in a sack for her.

Everything happened so quickly and all Cakes could think was if the Masta were here this wouldn't be happening. "If only the Masta were here," he said.

"You tell Masta soon's he git back, boy," his mother said. She put her hands on either side of her son's face. "My pretty, pretty boy," she said. "You stay with Masta Charlie, he'll do right by you. Masta Charlie is your Daddy." She said more. She told Cakes how much she loved him and how special he was, but there was no more room left in his head. *Masta Charlie is your daddy*. There were other white men on the plantation; he had not been sure. *Masta Charlie is your daddy*, he kept hearing, though she'd only said it once.

Two big white men came into the cabin and pulled her away from Cakes. They put chains on her wrists and led her from the shack.

"Masta Charlie gonna get you. Masta Charlie will take the whip to y'all," Cakes told the men. The kitchen girl tried to hand Cakes's mother her things but was pushed away. Cakes watched his mother loaded on a waiting wagon. She cried but Cakes did not. Masta Charlie, he knew, would set things right. He watched the wagon take her away. My daddy will fix this, he thought as the wagon disappeared.

She was taken to a farm only twelve miles south of the Enrights', but Cakes never saw her again.

When Masta Charlie returned just a few days later, Cakes wanted to run up to him and ask, are you *really* my daddy? But he didn't.

He did tell him two men had come and taken his Mama away. Masta's face turned a bright red and his lips trembled. He stormed right to the mansion. Cakes smiled; Mama will be back any day now. Nothing came of it, though. Somehow, Mrs. Enright had won, and Masta's mistress was banished. In the days and months following, Cakes brought up the subject of his Mama to Masta Charlie as many times as he dared, but was either ignored or received some half promise never kept. Finally, he sensed that mentioning her only angered Masta Charlie, so he let it go. Besides, Cakes figured, since Masta had not helped him in this case, then surely he would send him to a school. And after Cakes became a gentleman, he could find his mother himself. He fretted over when would be the best time to ask. He was always putting it off.

The night that changed everything came about a year after Cakes's mother had been taken. It was a lonely year for Cakes, though he probably didn't recognize it as such. He had lived alone in the stables for years, but his mother had been the one to feed him, mend his clothes and mostly listen to him dream about what he was going to become. Now, Cakes kept totally to himself, having rejected one world and having been rejected by the other. Somewhere along the line, Cakes's dreams became fantasies. You're quite the gentleman now Cakes, Masta Charlie says to him and takes his bag as he steps down from the carriage. Mrs. Enright is there too, smiling along with her niece, whom Cakes figured was his cousin. His mother is there, and even Tommas. Cakes would sit in the stalls among the horses and he would dream this dream.

Now, on the night in question, the Enrights threw a big party and all the real ladies and gentlemen throughout the county showed up. Everyone was excited, even the slaves, because though a party meant more work, it also meant more food, some of which never found its way to the banquet table. The slave children would gather in the front yard, just far enough to the side not to be a nuisance, and watch the parade. That's what all the fancy carriages arriving at Enright Farms was to them, a parade. Gilded carriages, with colorful painted woodwork and bright ornamental lanterns followed one after another. The horses had special trimmed bridles and reins, and even, to the astonishment of many of the children, the slaves who drove the carriages were dressed up with white gloves and black jackets. But the stars of the show were always the women and their elegant, flowing, light-catching gowns that dropped from their waists like large bells. Adorned with flamboyant, sparkling jewelry and feather plumes sticking from their piled-up hair, they primped and preened as they stepped down from their coaches and walked with perfect southern dignity. Some of the younger children had never seen anything like them and were awed. Every now and then one of the ladies would notice "the little pickaninnies" and wave, which sent the little ones running about giggling or hiding behind the bigger ones.

Masta Charlie worked Cakes unusually hard in the stables that day, but Cakes sneaked away from his work long enough to watch the guests arriving from a safe distance. This was all very exciting for him. He knew he belonged with them. The pretty women stirred him up and he thought about Masta Charlie's niece. He was very frustrated and bewildered by the time he went back to mucking out the stalls.

When the sun was completely down, Cakes lay in the hay in an empty stall next to a fidgety, complaining brood mare who kept shuffling her feet. The merest haunts of the music reached his bed of hay and teased him. He had seen the band arrive earlier that day with their shiny, peculiar instruments and he realized what he figured no other nigger on the farm knew: that an entire world spun beyond the split rail fences of this plantation, that somewhere a man made fiddles the size of wheelbarrows, and another man taught people to play them, and still others would gather to listen to them. The siren call, like a beckoning finger, pulled him from the warm hay. The mare snorted a warning, which he ignored.

Cakes shuffled like a sleepwalker to the empty front yard. The children had returned, thrilled, to their mothers and their tiny shacks. The coachmen congregated around back with their gaudy charges waiting, talking, and eating what food the kitchen help brought out for them. Under the moonlight only Cakes's lean shadow fell across the front yard. He watched the yellow lights of the house and listened to the music. He heard women's laughter and it occurred to him that he had never heard a colored girl laugh in that lighthearted, frivolous kind of way. Every now and then a silhouette would whirl by a window and Cakes knew they were dancing. He wondered about it all. Hands calloused as tough as hide, gritty sweat sticking his shirt to his back, and smelling of horses and horse dung, he stared at the light and wondered about waistcoats, white gloves, and soft, white women smelling of that French toilet water, and eating the best part of the ham on lacy table cloths with silverware.

He wondered about being a gentleman and being worth something, and knowing things, and riding in carriages that someone else drove. And then he thought about traveling and cities like New York and Boston to the east, and he thought about the open west where, he heard, a man could do what he wanted, even a nigger. But the big cities and the open plains meant nothing really. No images could be brought up to hold them in his head, and so his traveling mind returned to the house and the lights and the laughter. It was not difficult at all for Cakes to imagine what the folk inside had to laugh about; they were inside and had everything to laugh about.

Cakes was no black to spend back-bent days baking in the fields. He belonged with his father. If he were in there now he could show Masta Charlie, Mrs. Enright, all of them that he could fit in, that he was just as white as they were. Cakes did not know anything about birthrights, but that is what he demanded. And tonight, Cakes smiled, was his opportunity to show everyone where he belonged.

Cakes ran, with his heart running far in front of him, to the shack he alone used since his mother left. He grabbed his prayer meeting suit, neatly folded away and seldom worn. He agonized over its patchwork. His finger traced around one of the patches. His mother had repaired the suit the best she could; it would have to do. He poked his head from the shack. He didn't want to see anyone, didn't want to answer any meddlesome questions, but the way was clear and he hurried away to the creek.

He could look down at the creek and see the moon and the clouds until his naked foot stepped in and the picture rippled away. He had a piece of lye soap and a brush he sometimes used on the horses and he scrubbed himself ferociously, grunting with exertion like a woman in labor, as if he were trying to wash off any bit of nigger that might remain.

Finally, he finished. He bemoaned the fact that the dirt around his fingernails would not wash away. And when he put on his suit, he was further dismayed; the jacket was too tight, the pants too short. He fretted. They will have to do, he steeled himself, besides they will be looking at me, not some old suit. He thought about the ladies, their smiling faces, and the music, and waltzed—he thought he was waltzing—back toward the house. He stopped his dancing when he set foot on the mansion's brick pathway to the front door; a sensible fear began to argue with him, yet still he walked forward, chin up as gentlemen do. At the mansion's big, double doors, he hesitated, not knowing whether to knock or walk right in. He could hear the music plainly now and the collective murmuring of people in conversation. He waited a long time, and was even able to pick out Masta Charlie's gruff laughter from the noise. Abruptly, he stepped away and went around back, deciding to enter through the kitchen and ease himself into the party.

As Cakes climbed the steps to the kitchen, one of the drivers called him to fetch more vittles. Cakes was angry; couldn't that nigger see he was a member of the party? "Nawsuh, get it your ownself," Cakes said, and was angry at himself for calling a nigger sir.

The kitchen was hot, almost suffocating, and the black women, all damp under their arms and on their backs, moved quickly preparing dishes and sending them out, stopping briefly only now and then to exchange words or to taste the food; they had tasted their fill by the time Cakes showed up. He watched all of this activity and was staggered by the amount of food. When the kitchen door swung open letting the servers bring out or retrieve another dish, Cakes could see glimpses of the party. He walked through the kitchen.

"Where in de hell, you goin', boy?" one of the kitchen girls asked, and they all stopped and looked at him.

"You don't work up heres," another one said.

Cakes straightened his jacket and looked down at the women. "Ah'm attendin' the party," he announced, smiling at their shocked faces. Cakes pushed through the doorway and into the party.

The music had stopped for the moment. Couples walked arm in arm from where they had been dancing to the large crystal punch bowl. It was too much for Cakes to take in at once, all the finery, the lights, the ladies, the gallant looking gentlemen so at ease with themselves. All of them divided into chatting groups. Cakes stood at the kitchen doorway virtually unnoticed. Masta Charlie was across the room with his back toward Cakes. The boy was frozen by it all. His determination faltered, but he couldn't bring himself to retreat either. He stood in his too-little patchwork suit and dusty shoes, with dirty fingernails, dumbfounded. Then their eyes met, his and Mrs. Enright's. She stood with a small group directly in front of Masta Charlie. Cakes didn't know it, but he'd seen her eyes, large as silver dollars, like that before, fifteen years ago when she first saw him. She didn't choke this time, but stood just as dumbfounded as Cakes. Masta Charlie noticed his wife's expression and turned to see what was giving her fish eyes. His eyes grew big, too, but they narrowed quickly and his color changed so fast it was as if someone had flicked a red light on inside his head. At that moment, Cakes realized the enormity of his mistake.

A serving girl stepped out of the kitchen with a food tray just as Masta Charlie crossed the floor. She saw what was happening. "Here's de tray, Cakes. Take it to de table," she said loud enough for Masta Charlie to hear.

"Boy, what are you doin' here?" Masta Charlie said to Cakes.

"He come to help out," the serving girl said.

Masta Charlie gave her a fierce look and she stumbled backwards into the kitchen, spilling food as she went.

"You know better'n to be here, boy, dontcha?" Masta Charlie grabbed Cakes by the hair and dragged him out of the room.

Cakes's last look at the party was of the beautiful ladies laughing at him. He could only see down after that as Masta Charlie pulled him along from the polished, shiny wood floor of the front room littered with slices of ham and turkey, to the dull, grease stained floor of the kitchen with the fleeing feet of the cooks getting out of Masta Charlie's way. Then they were outside and he was yanked down the steps. He fell to the ground, but was jerked by his hair back to his feet. Masta Charlie's fingers dug like claws into Cakes's scalp. He was dimly aware that Masta Charlie was saying something to him or at him all this time, and he heard the coachmen at their carriages laughing. "I guess I gots to get some vittles my ownself." Cakes heard. Bent over, he had to run to keep his hair from being ripped from his head. Masta Charlie threw him down on the hard, knotty roots of the fat sycamore, the one with the iron ring embedded in its bark. Cakes quivered, shaking his head violently.

Masta Charlie slowly uncoiled his bullwhip and Cakes wondered when he had picked it up. "You tryin' your best to embarrass me. Is that it?" said Masta Charlie. "What did you think you were doin' up there, huh?"

Cakes trembled and said in a small voice that carried across the yard, "You're my Daddy."

Masta Charlie leaped on him instantly, tearing the clothes from his back and beating him about the head. He tied Cakes's wrists to the ring with the tatters of his jacket.

"I been givin' you too much credit. Much too much," Masta

Charlie said. "I thought you knew the way things were, but you have no ideer, do you? This is unbelievable, but I don't think you know what you are. Tonight I teach you."

Cakes wet himself waiting for that first blow and when it came it erupted on his back, and shook him to his bones. He screamed up into the highest branches of the blood-stained tree. Masta Charlie gave him just three stripes, terrible and deep, but a lot less than what he usually doled out. He left Cakes and returned to his party. Cakes hung against the rough bark, feeling his blood flow away, convinced he was dying, unable to do anything but whimper.

In the darkest part of the night, Tommas Huntley came. *You're my Daddy. You're my Daddy*, Cakes had been trying to say over and over. When Tommas got there only Cakes's last word was audible, "Daddy."

*

When Gramma reached this point in the story, she had stopped and cupped her hands into the watering bucket. Her voice was becoming hoarse; still I pressed her to continue, wanting to know if Cakes had died then or not. But Gramma told me that Cakes survived. Tommas cut him down, carried him in his arms to his shack and tended his wounds. Cakes worked the rest of his life in the fields, died fairly young and there wasn't more, Gramma said, to his story. Except that he was one of the slaves on hand when Masta Charlie died.

More than ten years had passed since the night of the party and the plantation had hit hard times. Mrs. Enright's increasingly extravagant taste created a cash poor situation. Masta Charlie became one frazzled and erratic man and he took to beating his slaves much more than he used to until even Mrs. Enright complained he was "probably being excessively harsh".

The day he died, Masta Charlie stood in the bed of his wagon overseeing the harvest—having fired most of his overseers earlier that year—and hollered at Tommas and Cakes and any of the other slaves he knew by name. He called to Tommas and Cakes across the field of green and yellow tobacco leaves and the two, so alike in mannerisms and movement, looked at each other, rolled their eyes, and slowly shuffled toward the wagon—keeping Masta waiting and aggravated as long as possible.

"Tommas, you boys are missin leaves ready for pickin! You watch 'em," Masta Charlie said, and "Cakes, don't let no leaves fall off the wagons and get all broken up; they won't look like nothin at the auction then."

"Yahsuh," both men said.

And Tommas this, and Cakes that, Masta Charlie kept adding something every time the two would turn their backs to leave.

Tommas and Cakes gave him all the appropriate "Yahsuhs" and "Nawsuhs" and they turned to try to leave for what seemed like the hundredth time and Masta Charlie called, "Cakes!" But this time his voice was different, more like a squeal. This time Cakes and Tommas spun about. This time every head looked up from the ground, looked up from the long rows and the leaves and looked to the buck board and Masta Charlie standing in the wagon, one arm raised high, fingers spread as if trying to grab hold of the sun. The other hand, full of his shirt, gripped at his chest and he had such a look of shock as if he were looking at the last thing he ever thought he'd see. He dropped like a bale of hay at Tommas's feet.

Cakes and Tommas stared in shocked disbelief at the dying man. The blacks in the field moved toward the wagon.

"Tommas, go get help," said Masta Charlie. He drew his knees to his chest, gripped one of the spokes of the wagon wheel. "Help me, Cakes."

The slaves gathered around, utterly silent, watching the Masta die. He looked small and gristly like a skinny chicken nearly plucked. The slaves had trouble believing what their eyes witnessed. This was a bolt from above, a rare justice. For some this was the justice for which they had thrown themselves face down on the ground and prayed. They'd prayed to that God who'd seen fit to yank them from their own lands, ways, and families and place other strange men over them. The God who saw that they were enslaved, beaten and sold and used, and who they devoutly loved without question, without reservation as a young child loves her mother. This was Masta Charlie delivered to the slaves. God surely still listened to their cries, their songs. He had delivered into their hands their enemy. Masta Charlie, curled in pain, gripping the wagon wheel spoke, lay vulnerable to their mercy. Mercy he and his swift whip beat out of them when he tried to beat their spirit.

The slaves approached in silent surprise, still carrying bundles of leaves or holding their tools. This is the work of God or some strange white man's trick; it could not be, Masta lying there with no other blue-eyed gaze to hold them back.

Masta Charlie should have seen their hard faces. He looked up at them, but he could not recognize this expression. This was not the servile babbling, nor the sleepy-eyed uncomprehending faces of ignorant slaves. These flared nostrils, and narrowed, penetrating eyes were on the faces of angry men and women.

"Cakes, help me."

In Cakes, perhaps, there was some piece of his heart tugged at by the Masta's plight, some bit of him not yet melted away by the crucible heat of the field.

But then Masta Charlie said, "Help me, son."

The word Cakes had thirsted twenty-five years for cut into him like a whip. He turned his back.

Tommas stepped forward, met Master Charles Marshall Enright's half opened eyes, and spat right in his face. Another slave placed his hand on Tommas's shoulder, eased him aside, and spat too. Still another followed, and the slaves formed themselves in a single file reviewing line as if performing a ritual and spat, women and children, one after the next, on their master, who stopped breathing sometime before the line concluded.

Only Cakes refrained from the ceremony. When they finished, he took a rag and wiped the Masta's face, ignoring the dark frowns around him. "Put him back on the wagon," he directed. Then Tommas understood. He and another man propped the Masta's body on the wagon bench and slapped the horse's rear, letting the wagon jump down the trail. "Jus be surprised when yous hear the tragic news bout Masta Charlie," Cakes said and he followed Tommas out to the fields.

\*

That is all the story of Cakes Gramma Ruth ever told me. She looked at me when she finished, and I probably looked like I wanted to hear more. "That's it, Sarge. I talked the entire morning away."

"But, Gramma, how did Cakes die? Did he die trying to escape?"

"Pneumonia, when he was around thirty-five, I'd say."

"Oh." I was disappointed. I pointed to the cross. "His last name isn't really Huntley is it?"

Gramma rose to her feet and picked up her tool tray, motioning for me to get the watering bucket. As we started down the trail to the house, she said, "Tommas was one of the rare slaves who had his own last name, if he and his woman were married, I suppose it was Cakes's name too. I reckon Mrs. Enright made sure that last name was on that cross. That's probably why he has a cross in the first place. You okay, Sarge?" Gramma asked. "You look a little sad. I guess that wasn't a very happy story to tell."

I shrugged. "Things happen that way though," I said trying to sound thoughtful.

Gramma Ruth seemed surprised, but smiled at me. "Yes, Sarge, they do indeed."

Cakes's cross tilts slightly to the right above yellow flowers, sweet, gentle suns, surrounding it. Cooled and protected by the great arms of the oaks, it is nestled among markers front and back, and others just a step to the side. In the afternoon, the long shadow of his cross stretches far into the garden, overlapping the shadows of other stones, merging with them as if all were cast by a single source.

## III

## A Night for Fighting Bobcats

*June 3, 1975*
*Dear Major,*
*How are you? Fine I hope. Everything is going*
*fine here. Mama went to Louisville to find a job, so I*
*can't watch her just now, but Julie is okay. She says*
*to say she'll write you tomorrow. I go exploring with*
*Zeke and met a new friend. I help Grandpa Standard*
*fix the fence and ride on the tractor. Gramma Ruth*
*tells me neat stories. Are you coming here or will we*
*go back home? I think you should come here. Love,*
*Sergeant Kenneth Willis*

I figured the noise came from bobcats that were attacking the chickens. I sprang from my bed to my half-opened window in one bounce. Zeke's barking and the chickens' panicky squawking came through the screen, yet I could see only my face reflected in the window's glass. I located my jeans in the darkness and pushed my feet through its legs. On the floor, I felt blindly for my shoes not wanting to turn on a light and chance waking anyone. This would be my adventure. Only one shoe turned up; Zeke's barking became more insistent, and I decided bare feet were better for sneaking down stairs anyway. By now I knew which boards in the hallway and on the stairs to step over. I crept down with minimal squeaking. I was surprised to see light coming from underneath the closed door to Gramma and Grandpa's room and hoped they weren't getting up to investigate the commotion outside.

It was more night outside than it ever gets in the city with its street lamps and roving headlights; clouds covered the stars that night and I stepped onto the porch cautiously.

The chicken coop seemed buried in shadows, but Zeke still yammered away. I ran toward him, feeling cool dust between my toes and little, sharp rocks stab my feet. Zeke's furry shadow slipped between my legs startling and nearly tripping me. He ran and jumped around, grateful for the rare nighttime company. His wet nose pushed the back of my hand.

"No, Zeke, the bobcats. Where are the bobcats, boy? Will you pay attention?" I said to the distracted collie.

The chickens had settled down a bit, but suddenly, their screeching hysteria began again, and Zeke darted around the coop and I followed, scared and excited at the same time.

Something small and sleek and very busy clawed at the chicken wire. Zeke growled and the little animal froze. It was not a bobcat. It stared at Zeke and me; even in that darkness its round, black eyes glowed. And then it was gone like slippery oil squirting away. Zeke and I chased after it, leaping blindly, pell mell, into the blackness. We lost it to the night in the middle of a field sloping down and away from the house. I dropped into the grass while Zeke continued the game, barking reports to me, for a little while longer. When he returned, I heard his movement through the grass, his heavy panting, felt his hot breath and cold nose before I could see him. He settled down beside me.

The night sky was black, but moving. Great, silent clouds migrated over the fields and the hills. A cool wind rose up and I lay back in the grass watching the shape changing sojourners roll across the heavens. I felt bodiless and shapeless in the dark, part of every black shadow that bent and swayed around me. It was a feeling at once disconcerting and soothing as if one could be purposefully lost. I have recaptured this feeling a time or two since then, but never quite like that first innocent, unanticipated moment.

For a long while, I thought of nothing at all, not the Major nor Mama and Julie, not Gramma Ruth and Grandpa Standard. Then I thought about everything at once, wondering if Chief or Cakes ever lay in the very spot I lay and looked up into the same sky. I thought about the Major and tried to figure out what time it was in Germany and what he might be doing.

Zeke let out a restless whine.

"I'm with you, boy," I whispered, in respect to the night. "There probably ain't any bobcats out here at all."

It was meeting my new friend that had me thinking bobcats. Zeke and I had gone exploring on the kind of bright morning when a boy shouldn't have a worry in the world except about what new thing he might discover. We'd investigated the grove of sycamores where Gramma Ruth said the slave quarters used to be, where Tommas had paced anxiously up and down on the night of Cakes's birth, where Chief had dragged his ankle chains, creating a constant cloud of dust at his feet. I kicked through the light undergrowth, turned over a few rocks, but found nothing. Finally, with my archaeological efforts coming to naught, I picked a direction at random and started off, the newly improvised game being to see how far I could go without seeing anyone else. We wandered across vacant stretches of freshly overturned earth, past disciplined rows of soybeans and sloping pastures, staying far from the grazing cows, negotiated fence after fence, always finding, or making, a hole or low part for Zeke to squirm through or jump over.

Our uncharted course brought us to a narrow creek that broadened as it poured down hill. Bushes, brambles, and trees crowded its banks. The trees' gnarled roots looked like the legs of old men wading in the stream. Mosquitoes and dragonflies hovered and darted over the places where the running waters had been trapped and turned into green pools. Zeke and I gave each other a knowing look of agreement and pushed our way into the green congestion to follow the creek. The banks rose steeply in places making the going slow. I found a long, sturdy branch for support, a staff, making me feel very much the part of a wayfaring traveler. Zeke opted for simpler routes, sometimes diving into the creek, especially when given the opportunity to harass a frightened bullfrog. I jabbed my staff into the stream creating little puffs of disturbed creek bottom. Billowing brown clouds boiled to the surface before being swept away.

"Can you two think of anything else to do to disturb my fishin'?"

Across the creek sat a white boy no bigger than me with a bamboo fishing pole. His blond, almost white hair fell over his forehead into his eyes. He wore a pair of bib overalls held up only by a right shoulder strap. The legs of his overalls were rolled up to his knees. The bottoms of his bare feet were nearly black. He shook his head in exasperation, making Zeke and me look fairly dumb as if we didn't know some commonly held rules of the creek. "This spot is just ruined, just ruined is all it is," he said in his funny, twangy voice. He gathered in his string.

He had ruined my adventure too. My solitude adventure of the lone wayward traveler out on some unnamed quest had been interrupted. This white-haired, dirty boy had intruded just as much as I had and I was about to tell him so, but couldn't think of a way to say it without sounding silly.

He was about to leave, to disappear in the green tangle of the opposite bank when he turned back toward me as if he'd had an afterthought. "How old are you?" he asked, setting me to wonder why.

"Eleven," I finally answered padding the truth by a year and a couple of months. Eleven sounded so much older.

"No good." He shook his head again. "Eleven is just no good is what eleven is. Ya finally just about know somethin, but damned if no one will ever pay no attention to ya."

I remembered these words on my eleventh birthday and became depressed, much to my family's confusion.

"I was eleven once," he said, "No more. Do you play basketball?"

This is a strange boy, I told myself and wished he would be on his way. "No."

"Naw?" He looked surprised. "I figured all black boys played basketball, all of 'em. Guess I was wrong."

"I figured all hillbillies didn't wear shoes," I said. "Guess I was right."

I hadn't noticed he had a half smile on his face until it abruptly dropped out of his cheeks. "Where you from, cause I know everybody that lives around here." He stepped into the creek and began crossing the knee-high deep water.

I wanted to shout *sic'em, Zeke,* but Zeke didn't know sic from roll over and I didn't want this hillbilly to think I was afraid of him. I sat on a fat root nearby and tightened my grip on my staff. As he approached, I had to reassess my estimate of his size. He was taller and heavier than me. It would've been nice if I could've heard a low, throaty rumble from Zeke, watched as he faced this hillbilly with the sides of his snout flaring, showing just a glimpse of quick and ready fangs. Instead the collie had continued his bullfrog hunt, frolicking in the shallow pools along the creek.

"Watch who you call a hillbilly round these parts," the boy was saying, "Some don't like it much. That's cause they really are hillbillies." He clambered up my bank, maintaining a grip on his fishing pole and reaching out the other hand for help up. The proffered hand had only three fingers; the ring finger and pinky were gone and a mean, wide stripe of shiny scar tissue cut a swath on the outside of his forearm from his hand to his elbow.

My relief at seeing he meant no harm was offset by my repugnance. I did not want to touch that hand, instinctively loathed the feel of it. Yet I feared angering him and so grabbed the hand to help pull him up. He yanked me off my seat and I bellyflopped into the creek with a splat before I could even cry out. I still gripped my staff, sat up sputtering trying to clear my nose, feeling my butt sink into the soft, oozy mud of the creek bottom.

"I s'pose I am a hillbilly when you come right down to it." He grinned a set of yellow, crooked teeth at me. Laughing, he scurried up the embankment and disappeared.

I pulled myself up from the muck, soaked and angry, but mostly shocked. Nothing like this had ever happened to me before. The situation had been completely uncontrolled, and unpredictable and both my parents—my safety nets and protection—were hundreds of miles away (the Major, thousands). I realized how alone I was and how vulnerable. Though I didn't admit it to myself at the time, I was frightened. It wasn't the three-fingered boy that scared me; it was my own vulnerability. The creek took on a haunting aspect and I forgot about my lone traveler fantasy, wanting only to be back with Gramma and Grandpa Standard.

"Zeke," I called while climbing the bank, but the dog was no where to be seen.

I called several times, but he did not appear, nor did I look for him. I wanted to get out of that alien, green congestion as quickly as possible. I bulled my way through the vines and the brambles and stepped into a cleared field of short scorched grass where a farmer had recently used fire against encroaching weeds.

This field was not familiar. I had crossed a different pasture when my path had intersected the creek and would have to follow back along the creek further to find it. I returned to the banks desperately looking for any familiar thing, a fallen tree, a green pool, or a dip in the stream where it poured over shiny rocks. No landmark presented itself.

Everything resembled everything I'd seen before, every vine covered tree mimicked the one next to it and my fear quickly became panic. I climbed away from the creek again and into a field of young corn. I did not recognize this field either and worried that I'd gone too far and passed the path I'd blazed.

"Major," I said under my breath while surveying the unfamiliar landscape. "Major, I don't know what to do." Tears slipped down my face.

Just then something wet and covered with mud and burrs separated itself from the creek's shadowy vegetation. He barked and came bounding to me.

"Zeke, where the hell have you been?" I scolded. "I don't suppose you know the way home." He only sat and looked at me. "You are the dumbest dog." But I was relieved by just having him around. "We're trapped behind enemy lines and we have to find our way back to headquarters," I informed Zeke.

But I couldn't make a game of it. I was wet and worried, afraid to leave the creek—my only landmark—and also afraid to return to its entangling confusion. I wandered just outside the tree line in one direction then the other. A rescue would not be coming; no one knew where I had gone or where to start searching for me. This thought haunted each short, hesitant step I took.

I chewed at my thumbnail, casting about in a wet-eyed panic, not concentrating, not really searching anymore, just wanting to be in my bedroom at my window. I blamed Mama for this. She had taken me away from home to this strange place where everything looked alike and no street signs marked the turns.

My clothes dried in the afternoon sun, but now even the sun was leaving me. It turned soft and orange and easy to look at, but I could not appreciate this abandonment. Evening descended from the opposite direction and fireflies lifted into the cooler air. Bewildered and frustrated, I rooted myself to one spot, talking to a hungry Zeke, who wondered why we weren't heading home.

About a half hour before nightfall, I spotted someone coming toward me and knew I'd have to ask for directions. Then I recognized who approached. I took a deep breath and wiped my tears away.

"What you still doin round here?" the white boy asked when the distance between us had shrunk to just a few feet. "Where you from? I know everybody around here. Know 'em all. Say you ain't mad about that dunkin I gave you, is you? Shoot, that ain't nothin. That's just funnin around really. So where'd you say you're from?"

He didn't seem bigger than me now. He was just another boy again, one I did not trust. "I'm just out walking around with my dog," I told him.

"What kinda dog is he anyway? Is he a bird dog? My dog is a bird dog. Is he a squirrel dog? A water dog? Looks like he might be. Is he a gun dog?"

"He's a collie mix."

He pushed the hair out of his eyes, but it fell immediately back in place.

"I live on the Standard farm." I wondered what he would do with this information. I remained wary, though now he seemed harmless, and I needed help. Still, I did not want him to know I was lost.

"Standard. Standard? Let's see now." He snapped the fingers of his three fingered hand. "Miss Ruthie, right? Miss

Ruthie!"

"My grandma."

"See. I told you," he said jumping up and down as if he'd just won on *The Price is Right*. "Didn't I say I knew everybody round here? Yeah, I know Miss Ruthie, sure." He sounded very pleased with himself. "The way you're headin will take forever to get back. That is if you're on your way back. I know a short cut."

"Well, I don't know." I tried to sound calm. Inwardly, I promised God if this boy got me home, I would never leave my room again—if that's what God wanted—except to go down to eat, and I promised I'd always have a kind word for country folk (the term hillbilly having already been banished from my vocabulary) wherever I met them. "I'm always willing to learn a short cut," I said, "if you really know one."

"I sure do. I'll show you. I know Miss Ruthie don't I? My name is Bobcat." He offered his mangled hand again. I shook it awkwardly. "Some wants to call me BobbyCat, but it's Bobcat on account of this." He held up his three fingered hand. "Did you notice?"

I shook my head.

"My mom says most time people don't even notice cause it ain't no big deal is what she says. She said, 'Eight pins is almost a strike, anyhow.' I lost my other two fighting a bobcat that come to steal the chickens. Bobcats is 'bout the size of your dog here, but a thousand times meaner, and a million times faster. They're like a bundle of dynamite and their paws is just a handful of razors is all they is really. I come into the coop and we surprised each other and he already had two bloody, ripped hens—good laying hens— right in front of him. His hackles rise and he hisses." BobbyCat imitated the hissing and held his hands up, fingers down as if they were claws. "And he had fangs as long as his whiskers."

I asked, "What did you do?"

"I threw my egg basket at him is what. Beaned him right on the head. And he jumped right on me with those claws. I tried pushing him away and he took my fingers clean off. Took 'em as souvenirs."

"Jesus," I said awed, still trying to absorb his story. "My

name is Kenny, but I'm called Sarge," I told him, happy to also have a nickname to offer. We started across a pasture eventually coming to a double rutted dirt trail. "This is Zeke," I told BobbyCat. The collie walked between the two of us, tired from his long day. "He's been chasing bullfrogs all morning and afternoon so I guess that makes him a frog dog."

"Really? A frog dog!" BobbyCat laughed. "A frog dog."

*

I saw the stones in the cemetery first, a dark pack in the night protruding from the field; the tension fell from my body and I began to smile. BobbyCat mentioned something about how spooky the cemetery looked and I laughed. "This is a great short cut," I said. BobbyCat just nodded until we were well away from the markers.

Gramma and Julie waited under the soft, yellow, porch light, Gramma with her hands on her hips, Julie pointing the finger of accusation, the young prosecuting attorney gleefully at work.

"You're in big trouble now, Kenny," she called while I crossed the yard.

"Well, hello, BobbyCat," Gramma said when we reached the steps. "Haven't seen you in awhile. How are you and your mother?"

"Just fine, thank you, Miss Ruthie," he said.

Then she turned to me with a lot less sugar in her voice. "Sarge, you've been out long enough."

"Yes, ma'am." I kept my head down and she and I both realized her point had been made.

"All three of you look hungry, but you're much too filthy to come into my house so you're eating on the porch. Are you hungry, BobbyCat?"

"I could eat, Miss Ruthie."

"Julie, you get some water and food for poor Zeke," Gramma instructed.

The frog dog lay sprawled on the porch with his long, pink tongue hanging out.

Julie opened the screen door, then turned and mouthed the words, "Wait till I tell Mama."

I didn't care. I felt grand just to be back and I especially didn't care what Mama would have to say. I ate and listened to Gramma and BobbyCat talk about people they knew in common, each giving the other some new tidbit of gossip. Grandpa Standard came out and offered BobbyCat a ride home, but the country boy politely refused. He promised to stop by again and the last thing he said to me he whispered in my ear, "Your sister is cute."

After I had cleaned up and put on my pajamas, I came down and helped Gramma put away the dishes.

"BobbyCat is a nice boy," Gramma said, "But you keep your common sense when you're around him because he's always finding mischief. He lost two fingers a couple of years ago playing with his Daddy's table saw."

Still, two days later when I heard Zeke's alarm and the rioting chickens, the image of a hunched, hissing bobcat with a dead chicken clamped in his fangs sprung to mind. But there hadn't been any sharp clawed wildcats for BobbyCat to face nor for me, just a quick-eyed, slick weasel and the dense all encompassing night. Behind me, just the top story of the house was visible above the rise of the hill. One lonely, yellow light shone from Gramma's room. It called to me just as she would, had she known I was out in the night. I lingered in the grass another moment to watch the herd of clouds and to savor the luxury of the cool darkness, then rose with Zeke at my heels and followed Gramma's beacon back home.

Grandpa Standard was in the living room in his easy chair. I hadn't noticed him until he called out to me.

"Grandpa?" I asked the voice in the darkness while retreating back down the stairs.

He turned on his reading lamp, which, even though shaded and dim, hurt my eyes. "You been out lurkin late with that white boy again?"

Something was wrong. A harshness I had not heard before edged Grandpa's voice. His dark face showed strain. His eyes, red veined and rheumy, were only half opened. His body filled up the big recliner, made it look small; the brown plaid chair, fully reclined, seemed overburdened under Grandpa's weight. He still wore his work clothes, faded jeans worn thin on the hard working man and a white, raggedy tee shirt, yellow under the arms. His boots were still on too, caked with soft earth from the fields and as he moved, his feet soiled the fabric of the footrest.

"A weasel tried to get at the chickens," I said and wasn't sure he'd heard so I repeated myself.

He exhaled a long breath seeming to sink deeper into the chair. I smelled the alcohol.

I stood in the middle of the room and would not go closer to the man and the chair, one and the same somehow, immobile, but huge and terrifying. At first I thought he had come down to look for me, perhaps he had checked my room—like the Major use to—and found it empty, or, perhaps he too had heard Zeke and the chickens and came down to investigate. But, no, this felt different than those easy explanations. He sat in the dark alone for his own purposes. Perhaps work, maybe repairing the chronically ailing tractor, kept him late outside and weariness forced his rest here before tackling the chore of mounting the stairs to his bedroom. Then Gramma Ruth's light, her beacon which brought me out of the night was meant for him. Perhaps she waited for him still.

"I'm sleepy, Grandpa, I'm going to get to bed."

"No, no, no." He motioned for me to come to him with his near hand, waving it from the wrist, his forearm seemingly locked inextricably to the armrest of the chair. I stood my ground; his red, half eyes scared me. "Did you get him? Did you get the damned thing!"

"What?"

"The weasel, boy, did you get the damned, egg poachin'... I swear look at you, outside all hours, barefoot, chasing weasels. You're becoming a country boy. Not gonna want to go back to ol' Europe. Give you another month." He let out another sigh and the chair sighed with him. "Well, did you get the damned weasel or not?"

"No. Zeke chased him off."

"Maybe that dog's good for something then."  Between Grandpa's legs protruded the transparent, tapered neck of a bottle. I didn't notice it until he reached for it, but he pulled his hand away leaving the bottle in its nest.  "You like it around here, don't you, Kenneth... your mother calls you Kenny. Do you like Kenny better?  You'd rather be called Sarge, right?"

I wanted to go upstairs. "No," I lied. I wanted to get away from him.

I thought he noticed it was a lie; surprise momentarily opened his red eyes. "Your grandmama calls you..." he began, but let the sentence go. He tried smiling and looked with this forced smile even less like Grandpa Standard, the one I had known. "She takes you to her little cemetery with all her flowers.  She tell you all her god-damned stories?  Sorry, boy, my language. Your grandmama done told me before you came to watch my lip around the kids. Nothing you ain't already heard, I imagine."

I nodded.

"Yeah, Stephen being in the army probably has a harsh word or two.  No harm done right?"  That labored smile showed again. Sweat beads caused his dark face to shine.

I considered calling Gramma. *Grandpa isn't right*, I would say to her.

"Well, come on, what stories does she tell you?  His eyes appeared to awaken from their sluggishness.  I looked from them to the neck of the bottle to his dirty boots and back across the mass of man and chair to his eyes. I retreated a step.

"Stories about the slaves," I said and wanted to run to my bedroom and lock the door.

"She can spin a story, can't she?  Did she tell you the one about the slave who had to be lynched twice cause they botched the job the first time?  Or the fool slave who invited himself to his master's party?"

"Cakes," I supplied.

"Between us guys, Kenneth."  He cast his eyes side to side as if to verify we were alone.  "Those stories are just stories, you know, tall tales.  Just your grandmama's fancy."

"They're true," I asserted, not frightened at the moment, but angry, ready to defend Gramma.

Grandpa continued as if he hadn't heard me. "So don't put a lot of store by all them slave stories. She been wondering about the names on them stones for so long, guess she figures making things up about them is better than leaving them as just a name." His head reared up. He searched for my reaction. "Come here, boy."

Fibber, fibber, fibber. "Fib—They're true stories," I said.

"What all she done told you?"

"It's all true. Chief and Hattie May, and Tommas and everything about Cakes and Cakes's daddy and—"

"Whose daddy? Whose daddy?" He lunged over the side of the chair, severing himself from it so abruptly I was startled. His long, strong fingers gripped my wrist. The bottle, empty, fell to the carpet. "What did you say, boy? Whose daddy?"

I struggled to pull away from him, leaving my feet to put all my weight against his grip. "Cakes Huntley's daddy," I said. "I'm gonna tell the Major. Let go of me." He did let go and I dropped on my butt. Grandpa Standard bent to pick me up, but I rolled out of his reach, jumped to my feet and ran to the stairwell.

I glanced back then, but he wasn't chasing me. He just stood in the middle of the living room floor, in the middle of the night, blocking the light of his reading lamp with an empty bottle at his feet. He stared at the bottle or maybe the dirt on his boots. "Huntley?" he asked.

"They're true," I shouted and bounded up the stairs.

My back pressed against the bed's bookshelf headboard. My knees were tucked tight against me and my heart took up all the room in my chest with its frantic beating. I waited for the merest movement of the doorknob, listened for the first tell tale click of the lock before the door would separate itself from the wall. I waited, though the door was never to open again that night.

Gramma should've come to see what was wrong. Certainly, she heard our shouting. Maybe she slept. Old people can fall asleep with the lights on, I knew that. Fears of Grandpa charging into my room, and grabbing my wrist didn't materialize. "The stories are lies," I expected him to come in and say. He'd shake me on my bed. "Your grandmama lies to you and so does your Mama. Nothing you've ever been told is true." And he would grip me by the shoulders, shaking me furiously. "Everything you've ever been told is a lie. Didn't your Mama lie to you? You know it. Everything is a lie. You're a lie too."

Confusing as the night had been, with its magic, nomadic skies and absorbing blackness, with Grandpa's burning eyes and giant hands, I must've fallen asleep, but can't remember when.

The dreams of that night, though, have not been forgotten. In my dream, Cakes, just as Gramma described him, tall, light-skinned with light brown eyes walked up to Grandpa. He carried Gramma's garden tool tray, which Grandpa snatched away from him, as soon as he came within reach. Grandpa Standard sneered at Cakes and held out the tool tray for me, but I recoiled from it because the hand grasping the tray had only three fingers. I ran from them, down the hill behind the barn, down the dirt trail lined with cornstalks to the cemetery. She was working, as usual, with her flowers, kneeling before the grave of the infant Kate with her back to me as I approached. Her nimble, aged fingers plucked yellowed, limp leaves from a flowering plant, but no matter how quickly she picked, more wilted leaves appeared. This seemed to be her task. This was sensed by me somehow rather than observed. This was her lot, to pick and prune amongst the dead forever. And she would never tire nor lose speed in those deft fingers.

"Gramma." My hand reached out to touch her shoulder so gently, so lightly that my fingertips did not feel the fabric of her clothes, yet she whirled about in such a spin as if bitten on the back. Mama's face, not Gramma's, stared into mine.

"Do you want me to tell you some more stories, Kenny?" Mama asked. "Do you want to hear more tall tales?"

I pointed to the one new marker where the stone, winged cherub perched, grounded from flight. This was his lot, his trap.

"I don't know a story to tell you about baby Kate, Sarge." And it was Gramma who said this, smiling, not with her mouth, but with the little wrinkles around her eyes.

That was my dream.

I was a ball at the head of my bed, still wearing my jeans. The early light of summer had breached my room and the door remained closed. The dream was momentarily forgotten, not to be recalled until hours later. The smell of bacon frying slipped under the door with the sound of kitchen drawers rattling open. These were the smells and sounds of the Standards' morning routine and this morning they surprised me. Creeping out of my bedroom and down one set of stairs, I peered over the banister into the empty living room. Grandpa Standard was not standing there with an empty whisky bottle at his feet as I had somehow expected. In fact, upon closer inspection, all evidence of last night was gone; the recliner's footrest, worn as always, had no trace of mud.

I touched it in disbelief. It was not even damp. It must've been cleaned awfully early, I figured, and congratulated myself for the keen detective work, though that fact told me little. I walked to the kitchen as if walking through a stranger's house, not knowing what to expect around the corner, and dreading a new confrontation with Grandpa Standard. The sound of Gramma's voice bolstered me.

Grandpa Standard sat at the table, just finishing his breakfast. He used a piece of toast to force the last bit of the eggs onto his fork and finished off both together, following the last bite with a last gulp of coffee. He looked for all the world like Grandpa Standard.

"Morning, Sarge," Gramma said. "You're up a bit earlier than usual, ready for breakfast? I opened up a jar of peach preserves."

"Good morning, Gramma."

"Kenny's becoming a country boy," Grandpa said, his only reference to last night. "Morning, Kenny," he greeted me, his eyes as bright as his white teeth.

"Morning," I answered coming to the table.

He picked his work gloves off the counter and pushed open the screen door. "Clouds done rolled in," he said more to himself than to us. "Maybe we'll get some rain for once."

He strode off directly to his first chore that sat atop a checklist in his mind.

Zeke replaced him at the screen door eyeing wistfully his

forbidden territory.

Gramma scrambled eggs; her fork beat rhythmically against the bowl and I watched her move from range to refrigerator and back. Would she say anything? *Did you and your grandpa have words last night, Sarge?* Would she ask? Maybe Grandpa had told her. Probably not. I wondered if I should.

"Mrs. McEachern gave me these preserves for a couple of sacks of mustard greens. I declare, can't say who got the better deal."

Are your stories true, Gramma, I wanted to ask. Grandpa says they're not. My mouth opened to say these words, but I could not question her. I preferred to believe her in faith, like believing in Jesus. She was the adult I had decided to trust.

"Go get sleepy head, Sarge. Tell her I'm not going to be making breakfasts all morning."

"Yes'm."

Later the same day, at my window, I could see gray clouds in the low ceiling sky. Unlike my drifters from last night, these clouds were stationary and had merged together to form a foreboding dome over the world. Gramma appeared from the tool shed with her tray, the threat of rain not keeping her from her charges. She had called for me, but I made myself scarce and just endured the pull of her voice. She headed around the barn and Zeke came flashing to her.

My dream came back then, racing to the front of my mind. It scared me again for I remembered too the fright and confusion in which it was dreamt.

"I don't know a story to tell you about baby Kate," Gramma had said to me in the dream. But not just in the dream. I recalled her saying those words when I first asked of Kate weeks ago. If her stories are just tall tales, then why didn't she just make up a story for Kate?

"They are true," I said, then hollered out the window, "Gramma, wait for me." She was out of hearing range, but it didn't matter; I could catch up to her easily enough and I knew where she was headed.

# IV

### The Rumble of Old Thunder

She survived Vietnam. She had made it through the free fire zones of an embroiled America alive, but not unscathed. Early in 1970, the war meant nothing to Constance Standard Willis, Connie Willis. The bloodshed in Southeast Asia consisted of encapsulated television reports half heard, often ignored preceding the morning weather. Her priorities dominated her day: Julie, her daughter then in kindergarten; me, her handful just four years old; Stephen, her husband, Captain Willis of the 25th Infantry, Fort Hood, Texas; and her new, single level, air conditioned (two window units at each end) ranch style home (without the ranch).

Each of these priorities demanded a full measure of her attention for most of the twenty-four hours the army had allotted dependents per day. Vietnam could not compete with picking up Julie after school, and taking the neighbors' kids and us to swimming lessons on the post, and ferrying Dad to and from work, and picking drapes that would match the modern, chrome, one legged chairs in her living room. So, while the nation reeled from the depths of the dual Kennedy-King assassinations just two years prior, and the heights of men golfing on the moon, peace marched and protested itself into turmoil, and witnessed its own national guard fire on students at Kent State, Mama housewifed in her finite, insulated, ranch style world. This may or may not have been what she wanted. The fact is, she was too busy to ask herself if the role that had gradually encompassed her was her choice or not. She told me, many years of living later, she was very happy in those young times of the family, but really had no right to be. "My happiness came from ignorance, not awareness," she says.

And, I think, she is embarrassed by the woman she once was.

Deserved or not, her happiness smacked into a wall and crumbled so abruptly she can recall the very hour it happened. Dad came home just before noon.

"That alone should have tipped me off," she has said on those occasions when she's willing to tell the story and I've been there to hear it. "Your father never came home early. I must've been pretty blind for that not to have tipped me off."

She was sitting in a lawn chair, relaxing, sipping lemonade with the young wife of a lieutenant who lived next door, the sweating pitcher on a table between them. Julie was in school and I ran about the bald backyard chasing a horned toad. (I'm told I ended up face down in the dust every time my quick quarry changed direction and I tried to follow.)

"Here you are," Dad said to the two women stepping onto the patio. "Hello, Barbra."

"Hi, Stephen, we're just watching your clumsy kid," the neighbor replied.

"Hello, sweetheart, what are you doing home?"

His face tightened at the question and maybe he tried to smile. "I've got some news." Since early that morning when he had received his orders, he had thought of nothing except how he might tell his Connie. Her face was expectant, but her friend Barbra had already guessed it.

"I should be going, you two. Tell you what, Connie, I'll pick up Julie in an hour and I'll take Ken Doll with me."

"That'll be great, Barbra," Dad said.

She jogged out to me, "Come on, Ken Doll," scooped me up and left my parents alone on the patio.

I can see them standing there facing each other, though I was not there and would probably not have noted nor remembered it if I had been. Most of Mama's story I have pieced together from scattered conversations with her and Barbra, who is still close to the family. The Major supplied a few details too.

"Orders?" she asked. Military dependents live in fear of orders; indisputable, voiceless edicts from on high, less contradicted and broken than God's own ten commandments.

Already, she dreaded the upheaval orders brought: leaving her new home, taking Julie from school, and bidding goodbye to her friends.

"Damn, Stephen, where now?"

He put his hands on her shoulders, shook his head and finally said it. "Vietnam."

Now Vietnam and all the frustration, fear, and confusion the word implied became real. The war had invaded her living room and snatched her husband away. This might've been the first time we would go to live on the Standard farm, but Mama chose to remain in Killeen, just twenty dusty minutes from Fort Hood's main gate. She intended to minimize the impact of Vietnam by attempting to ignore it. Stephen would only be gone a year; she would carry on her normal routine as best she could. She probably arrived at this decision because she was incapable of considering an alternative. I am sure she feared for Dad's life, but, also, she must've been terrified of the prospect of coping with life without him, of being on her own.

My parents met in college. The University of Louisville gave the country girl her first experience away from home. The only child who'd grown up on a farm by herself, found campus life with crowded dormitories, and crowds of protestors, and the press of peace marchers overwhelming. She had stepped from an idyll where time stood still, and stumbled into the sixties where time spun madly and change was the order of the day. (*Mama says the only time the clock moved on the farm, and then rapidly, was when a chore needed doing. She called this phenomenon Standard Time.*) She wanted only to be a student and, though believing in the issues Martin Luther King Jr. stood for, she could never bring herself to join the walks and the rallies. My father was in ROTC, effectively placing him amongst the least popular on campus. They first laid eyes on each other at one of the rare parties they both happened to attend. 'She was the only girl impressed by my uniform,' Dad said. She was a freshman and he, a senior. They married. She left school. The time she spent living on her own amounted to eight months.

The family spent the weeks before Dad shipped out ignoring

or looking past the year to come. Connie and Stephen talked a lot about what they would do when he returned. Just days before his flight—to Pearl Harbor and then on to Saigon—she asked, "What if you didn't go?"

"They'd throw me in the stockade."

"For how long?"

"Connie!" He gently reprimanded her for seriously considering such a thing.

*

The airport filled with uniforms, and overstuffed, olive drab duffel bags. Couples embraced and kissed openly at every departure gate. A few desperate kisses would be the last for some. Julie and I said our goodbyes. I do not remember it. Julie has said she remembers, but did not realize at the time how important a goodbye it might have been. Barbra and her husband came along and she led us back to the car after Dad hugged and kissed us. His flight was called, but Mama would not let go of him. She knotted her fingers into his uniform.

"Connie, my plane," he said. He held her until the last possible minute, tenderly rocking her, trying to soothe with promises whispered in her ear. Still, he could not gently extricate himself. "Connie, I've got to go, sweetheart."

The lieutenant tried to pry her fingers loose.

She cried out then. The strength went out of her legs and she fell grabbing Dad around his knees. She cried in near hysterics when the young lieutenant pulled her away.

"Go, Stephen, I'll see to her," he said.

Many sympathetic faces turned to her. They knew what she felt. They wanted to scream too. And maybe she cried for all of them. The lieutenant held her up. Mascara black tears streaked down her face. Both men, maybe a little embarrassed, spoke at once trying to console her with words that meant nothing. Dad kissed her forehead. She hardly noticed. He touched her cheek to wipe the dark tears away and she slapped at his hands.

"Then go on, damn you," she wailed. "You want to go so damn bad, just go."

"Look in on her for me, Cliff," Dad said, and his friend

nodded.

Barbra, Julie, and I waited in the car, me in the front seat. When the lieutenant returned, half-carrying, half dragging Mama, Barbra jumped out and hugged her friend. Julie saw her mother crying and began crying too. Only then did Mama try to bring herself under control. She climbed in the back seat and wrapped her arms around her daughter. Barbra hugged both of them and they all cried.

I remember this distinctly. The scene is the oldest of my memories, the first page in the album of memories that gives one identity and a sense of self. I peeked between the car seats at the two women and my sister crying, hugging, and rocking in the back seat. My eyes began to water.

The lieutenant climbed in behind the wheel, started the engine, then shook his finger at me. "No, Kenny, you're the man, little brother, don't you start bawling too."

I looked to my mother, then to him, and back to Mama, held in Barbra's arms, Julie in her lap. I didn't know the lieutenant. I started crying more then than ever before or since.

"Oh, Jesus!" said the lieutenant.

Years later, it was explained to me why we were all crying that day.

Ignoring Vietnam now was, of course, impossible. But she tried and got away with it for perhaps a week. Then one day Walter Cronkite intruded on our dinner and Mama jumped for the off switch and her hand stuck there as if her arm were a cable connecting her to the television. The green light from the jungles of Indochina splashed on her face. She listened to the popcorn sound of automatic weapons fire and the abrupt punctuation of a grenade burst. She watched a soldier die from an invisible hand. He had been patrolling just two men in front of the cameraman and simply dropped into the vegetation. The gunfire increased, along with shouting and cries for the medic.

"The fighting in Loc Ninh province intensified as units from the 25th Infantry moved to counter the insurgency."

"Loc Ninh," Mama repeated trance like, "Twenty-fifth."

Her Vietnam began just like that. She watched and read

everything on the war she could, books and essays on how it started and why—not that anyone knew.  Eventually she kept a detailed notebook showing major battles, which units were involved, and the number of KIAs, WIAs, and MIAs.  Along with dutifully writing her husband every other day for the full year he was gone, the book became her religion.  The book allowed her to be with Dad, to suffer with him.  Each evening as Julie and I ate supper, she leaned forward in her chair in front of the television with her composition book, recording numbers next to strange names of places she could not pronounce or spell.  The book hurt and saddened her and pages were often marred when tears mixed with the ink.  Yet somehow, her grim, little book kept her strong by providing an intimate tie with her husband across the ocean.  She tossed it away—she claimed without a second thought—the day Dad returned.

She also joined the officers' wives' club along with Barbra in 1970.  Barbra thought it would provide distraction, friends, and maybe, some recreation.  Mama hoped it might provide some first hand information on Dad's battalion, their area of operations, and the latest stats for her book.  They discovered that, to their mutual disappointment, the aim of the club was to raise money for poor enlisted families.  Most of the club members' husbands were "over there," as they put it, but they rarely discussed the war.  Mama says, for most of them not talking about it demonstrated strength.  And officers' wives were supposed to be strong.

If any group of women defined themselves by the accomplishments of their husbands, it was this gaggle of slightly snooty first ladies.  The chief hen in the coop was the biggest offender.  Jacqueline (*never Jackie*) Braithwaite, a big breasted, silver-haired woman, wife to the battalion commander, who marked her worth by her husband's rank.  The protector of the pecking order, Jacqueline Braithwaite wore a necklace, which dangled a silver oak leaf on her plump, damp chest.  She never attended a meeting without her rank insignia.  She made a show of welcoming Barbra and Mama to the club, embracing each of them.

"It's about time we had some black representation in this group," Jacqueline said, "seeing as how so many of the families we raise funds for are black."

"I should've quit on Mrs. Colonel right then," Mama has told me, "but the club did do some good work and I wanted to be as busy as possible that year."

So she stayed, worked hard, and Barbra and she actually became favorites of the club. That is until Mama turned in her hot comb for a natural, began wearing brightly colored dashikis, and proposed the group conduct rap sessions for wives of men in Vietnam.

"We support each other informally, my dear," Mrs. Colonel —as Barbra and Mama called her—said. "I don't see a need to officially, uh, rap do you?"

Mama told her, "Our husbands patrol the fire zones and fight along the DMZ. Yours patrols a desk at headquarters. You probably don't have anything to rap about." Mama stormed out of that meeting with her sidekick, Barbra, following after her.

Unfortunately for Mrs. Colonel, the duo returned the next week. When the ladies debated over which groceries would be best to buy for the needy families, Mama suggested giving the families the cash and letting them decide for themselves what to buy. This sparked a verbal free for all with everyone talking at once, but none louder than Mama and Barbra. In the end, the families in need received their groceries plus a small check to get special items.

Connie Willis found she made a difference and there was no stopping her from then on. She drove to Dallas to attend peace marches and would've become more involved in demonstrating but, "Those people blamed the soldiers for the war and I wasn't buying any of that."

Tired of its pettiness, Mama eventually quit the officers' wives' club. (*Barbra stayed for the sake of her husband's career.*) Through Barbra, Mama learned that Colonel Braithwaite's jeep hit a mine on a stretch of muddy road between his headquarters and division headquarters. He was killed instantly. Mrs. Colonel suffered a nervous breakdown that left her all but incapacitated. "I found out then that it was necessary to have an identity totally separate from Stephen's," Mama has said, "Having your own identity seems so simple just to say it. But somehow it's more difficult than that."

*

Dad came home physically unscratched except for a scar across his left rib cage, cut by the sharpened bamboo shoot of a booby trap. "Luckily, I was exhaling at the time a rack of pungy sticks swung at me, Private Willis," Dad told me. "If I'd had a lungful, it would've got me."

I haven't any memories of the year without him or of his return. He arrived, little more than a stranger to me. Julie recognized her father and welcomed him home with a big hug, but then told him, "You seem different." He had changed, of course, and so had Mama. After the longest year of their lives, these two survivors discovered they were married to strangers. "We went through the 'getting to know' all over again," Mama said.

Four years after Dad's return, they had another airport goodbye totally dissimilar to the traumatic good-byes said at the Texas airport. The good-byes at the Frankfort airport in West Germany were different and, I think, sadder. And this time, Connie Willis boarded the plane, an act which she thought would take all of her strength. But she had strength enough to face her parents again, two people she dearly loved, but was never quite convinced she knew. And a well of strength remained for Louisville. Turning down the streets of the city in her rented car, a map in one hand, the steering wheel in the other and a sliding stack of resumes on the seat beside her, Connie realized she had survived Vietnam; she could survive this too.

She knew she was up against it. She was black. She was a woman. She'd never held a paying job in her adult life. She'd never gotten that degree. The move to Europe had put an end to night school. She scanned this short, but imposing list of handicaps each time her hand knocked on an office door then flew to her hair to reassuringly pat it into place. But I do not think she was afraid. Doggedly determined to succeed and to ignore her mother's advice, she marched from interview to interview, filing away the rejections, "Well, thank you for your time," and following the leads, "Yes, I'll give them a try."

After two weeks and over thirty go sees, Mama returned to the farm, needing very much "to see my babies" before beginning a second assault on the city. I hoped no one would hire her, then we'd have to go back to Germany and the Major.

\*

It had been raining on and off for a week, a gift to the farm and the flowers of Gramma's garden from the great clouds whose arrival I had witnessed on that dark night. The rains were gentle and nourishing at first, never lasting long and leaving wide, arcing rainbows behind. Once, after a rain, Gramma and I walked down to the cemetery. The June sun poked out and steamed the dampness from the ground. Gramma said the rising steam trails from the cemetery looked like souls journeying to heaven.

The day before Mama's return the clouds turned ugly. Rain came in driving sheets, bending the heads of the corn, scattering the petals of Gramma's delicate flowers, and sending Zeke under the porch for safety. This went on all day and into the night until I thought the sky couldn't possibly have another drop left. But the downpour continued, smacking fat drops on the roof just above my head in a rapid machine gun beat. Fleeting cracks appeared in the wall of the night, brighter, it seemed, in the country darkness. The stones in the cemetery, visible from my window because the tall cornstalks were bent under the storm, appeared vulnerable in the quick, terrifying glare of the lightning.

The television had gone out in the middle of Mannix. I had watched the picture of the befuddled technician, snarled in wires, who held up a sign apologizing for temporary technical difficulties, for about five minutes before giving up and climbing the stairs to my room and the spectacular light show at my window. When I finally went to bed, finding security and comfort under the sheets, Julie came in. She said nothing at first, just sat at the foot of the bed with her legs tucked under her. I could see her only intermittently, when the lightning strikes showed a white image of her in her white nightgown. Propped on one elbow, I looked to where she was for explanation, to hear her say something, maybe to say something smart or to tell me the trouble I was in for forgetting to do some chore. Only the pounding rain and the bold clap of new thunder overlapping the rumble of old thunder could be heard and I let my head fall back into my pillow. A bright flash filled every part of the room, white then black again just that fast.

Julie's voice said, "The rain is so loud up here."

"I like it," I said.

"You're starting to like everything about the farm. You didn't like it at all at first. You still hang around that funny, afflicted white boy?"

I had to wait on the thunder to have its say before I could reply. But Julie said first, "There's no other kids around here. No other girls and the stores are too far."

I said, "BobbyCat's not afflicted, just missing some fingers. They got chewed off by a bobcat." I had decided BobbyCat's version was more exciting than Gramma's.

"It's boring in the country."

"If you made friends with him, he could show you where all the kids live. He knows everyone around here."

"Big deal. Probably five people, max."

"He thinks you're nice, but I don't know why."

She didn't say anything else for a long time and I lay there wishing she would go away. Another lightning flash whitened every corner of my room. Julie said, "I wish Mama were here."

I listened for the accompanying thunder, counted the seconds, one thousand one, one thousand two, one thousand three, to figure out how close the lightning struck. After the thunder roar faded to a distant growl, I said, "Me too." But another flash lit the room and Julie had already gone.

*

The next morning, I sat at my window with the makings of a slingshot, a 'Y' cut by BobbyCat and I earlier in the week from the fallen branch of a sycamore. With a file, and a worn piece of sandpaper nailed to a wooden block, I shaped and smoothed the

'Y' down to the naked, white, under skin, in the process sending a cloud of fine wood dust around my room. The slingshot, thick and sturdy, felt good in my grip and already I liked it. I pictured myself sending smooth, round rocks far across pastures, and way up into the sky until they were lost in the sun. And each rock would take me up there with it to the blue part of the sky. BobbyCat promised to come by later and together we would find the very best inner tube rubber for the slingshot. "It's gotta have snap," BobbyCat said. Then we would need only a small piece of leather for the pocket to complete my new weapon.

Two, hard, quick knocks at my door sent me into furious motion. "Wait a second," I said. I popped the bottom of the screen window out and set my slingshot, file, and sanding block on the roof directly under the window sill, blew wood shavings off the sill and said, "Come in," just as I pulled the screen back in place.

Gramma stepped in my room. "You can start picking..." Her hands swiped at the air in front of her and she scowled. "What's this smoke? Sawdust! What are you up to?"

I sat stunned by her detective prowess; only the merest veil of dust hung in the room. "Declare! I never raised a boy and I don't think I would've made sixty-two if I had. It's a sure thing you won't if you chose to do your woodworking in my house again. Of all the places on a farm..." She got after me, but I saw she wasn't mad. Her face was saying, boys will be boys. "Nothing with sharp points," she said.

I shook my head. "No, Gramma."

"Let it settle, then dust and sweep in here."

"Yes'm."

She turned to leave, then stopped. "Made me forget why I came up here. The blackberries look really nice this year. Julie and you—"

The honk of a car horn interrupted her. I looked out my window at a new, powder blue Chevrolet pulling up to the house. Grandpa came running from the tool shed, in an old man's run with arms and legs swinging or dangling in slightly different directions. Mama stepped out, ran around the car, and Grandpa and she hugged as if she'd been gone two years instead of two weeks. Julie hurtled the porch steps and made it a group hug.

I felt Gramma's breath behind my left ear and a hand squeezed my shoulder. We looked down at the scene and I sensed we felt differently than those below. Countercurrents flowed in our streams of emotions. We were somehow made allies by exclusion, by the feelings that kept us staring out the window at the three who pulled luggage from the back seat of the car. My arm slipped around Gramma's waist.

"Run greet your mother," Gramma said.

I pulled my arm back feeling instantly rejected, but her eyes told me otherwise and a kiss on the forehead confirmed it.

She said again, "Go greet your mother."

I dragged down the stairs, one step at a time, still getting to the front door in time to open the screen for Mama.

"Ken Doll!" she said. I hadn't been called that in a long time. Julie laughed and I burned with embarrassment. Her suitcase dropped to the floor. "I brought you something, a University of Louisville tee shirt," she said and I saw her scanning my face. Her arms surrounded me with familiar, comfortable warmth. In spite of myself, I held to her tightly. Later, I chastised myself for that act of betrayal.

Julie kept dinner from being just the scrapes of forks against china, and Grandpa's quick, noisy chewing. She moved and bounced in her seat and talked incessantly about clothes, and television shows, and starting school in the fall. I tried not to listen. Mama did, and made comments every now and then. Gramma wouldn't stay seated for more than a minute at a time. She circled the table dishing out second helpings and removing empty serving dishes. Grandpa was silent as usual, except for his chewing. I watched him the most, but tried not to let him notice. I began to suspect he didn't remember our strange conversation at all or that he'd grabbed me. It seemed funny to me that anyone could forget something that happened so recently. Part of me figured Grandpa was pretending. Maybe Gramma didn't know he drank, I thought. No, it would have to be something more than that. He surprised me that night and I no longer trusted him so that his quiet manner now appeared secretive. I resolved to keep an eye on him.

"Daddy called twice while you were gone, Mama," Julie said. And a waiting kind of quiet followed.

Gramma stopped her orbiting next to me and in front of Mama. "Yes, Connie, Stephen called and among other things wanted to know if he should have the household goods shipped, the kids' books and toys, some winter clothes you left behind, or should he ship everything?"

Another waiting followed. Julie and I looked to our mother.

"I'll have to give him a call," she said.

"Does Daddy know where we're going to be stationed next?" Julie asked Mama.

Gramma began gathering up the dishes. "Connie," she said, "Why don't you tell them what's going on? I'm tired of secrets."

"The kids know everything."

"Ruth, let Connie raise her own children," Grandpa said.

Julie showed her confusion. She understood less of what was going on than I did.

"I knew this job hunting would be hard, Connie. You'd best talk to Stephen like I told you."

"You two get upstairs," Grandpa said to Julie and me. Mama and Gramma were resuming the argument they had the night before Mama left for Louisville. I wanted to hang around, but Grandpa's look drove us both upstairs. "And don't hide behind the banister."

I went to my room and pressed my ear to the air vent, but heard nothing. Julie came in and announced she was going to tell on me, but then joined me at the vent. "They ain't saying anything right now." We heard the kitchen door slam.

Julie ran to my window. "It's Grandpa going to the barn," she said, and raced back to the vent.

In a moment, we heard voices picked up by the vents in the kitchen, channeled through the wall's arteries to us, stretched out on the carpet with our faces pressed so tightly against the vent that we bore the impression of the grating on our cheeks for a long time after our snooping was finished.

The voices sounded hollow as if they spoke inside a cave.

"—told them what they needed to know for now, Mom." We heard Mama's voice.

Gramma replied, but neither of us could make out the words. Then they were talking at once and that was a useless jumble. Still, we strained to recognize any stray syllable.

"She said, 'Stephen hasn't done anything, but that's not the point,'" Julie replied to my questioning face.

"Who? Mama?" I whispered.

"Yes, stupid, now shhh, I'm missing it."

We heard Mama's cavernous voice say, "I can't stay just for the sake of staying, Mom. You chose that, but don't choose it for me. That's where we're different." A pause followed and then she said, "I'd have thought you'd be happy I wanted to make my own way."

"You don't—It's not the same thing," Gramma's voice came through loud and clear then faded.

"What did she say?" I asked Julie.

"She said something like, 'it's not the same, because I owe your father.'"

"Grandpa?"

Julie looked annoyed with me. "For all your experience as a snoop, you sure are bad at it." She sat up. The side of her face resembled a waffle. "Mama and Dad might be breaking up."

"No, shit, Sherlock," I said, but it scared me to hear Julie say it. I rubbed blood back into my face. "I been knowing that."

"But Mama said Dad would join us when his tour was up."

"She fibbed."

"Oh, shush, dummy. Mama doesn't fib. She just doesn't want to worry us that's all. Besides we don't know for sure. We should keep this between us for now, till we know for certain. It's probably nothing; I bet."

I was glad Julie was in on the whole thing. My suspicions had been a burden and I felt very much relieved to share them. I even considered telling her about Grandpa, but didn't. She was still Julie and would have to tell somebody something.

At the end of the weekend, Grandpa put Mama's bags back in

the car. He told her, "Next time, you call me to come get you. No need wastin good money havin a rental car just sittin in front of the house all weekend. Just a waste."

"Yes, Daddy," she said and kissed him. She kissed us all. I stood beside Gramma. I'm happy she's going, I thought, and wanted to say it aloud.

Grandpa shut the door and said something about Interstate 70 and crazy drivers. Even though he was standing right beside her, Mama didn't seem to hear him. Mama and Gramma looked at each other and, finally, Gramma smiled.

Four pairs of eyes followed the car away down the gravel road. And four busy minds worked on thoughts kept to themselves.

# PART TWO

# V

## Signs of Work Abandoned

The sky was huge, with nothing to challenge it. There were no clouds and the sun was a mighty dot, impossible to look at, high above. BobbyCat pulled the pocket of his slingshot clear back to his nose and launched a rock.

"It's in orbit with the Apollo," he bragged, stretching the truth farther than the rubber of his slingshot. "It's a hundred miles up."

A few seconds later, I heard a thump on the porch roof and smiled.

Julie came out with three bowls of blackberry pie each topped with a round scoop of vanilla ice cream. The three of us stretched out on the porch and greedily attacked our mid-day treats. This dessert was hard won. Julie and I were stabbed by thorns and attacked by gnats and chiggers that got a thousand more bites of us than we got berries from the bushes. The burning sun was on the berries' side too, and twice Julie and I retreated into the house. BobbyCat came over and helped. Surprisingly, Julie and he got along fine. Everything he said made her laugh whether he was being intentionally funny or not. She'd giggle and I'd roll my eyes. But more than BobbyCat and Julie becoming friends, Julie and I became friends that summer. Before then, she had been just my sister, some tattletale, who happened to have the same parents I did.

As we ate our pie, Julie said, "Kenny says you know everyone around here, BobbyCat. Are there any other kids our age around?"

"Shoot yeah," BobbyCat said between gulps of pie. "If junior high depended on just me showin up, they'd have to close down. That's for sure."

Julie laughed.

"There's a lot of kids. They're just a good walk away is all. I'll show y'all sometime."

I tilted my bowl and let the last bit of berry juice and melted ice cream drain into my mouth. "But we've got to finish my slingshot first," I said. BobbyCat and I licked our bowls spotless.

"Tell Miss Ruthie she don't even have to wash the bowls that was so good," BobbyCat said.

"Great compliment," Julie said. "You guys are pigs." She offered to take the bowls in.

"Ain't you comin?" BobbyCat asked her.

"Next time, when you guys go to see the other kids. We might be going to school here. Who knows!" She shrugged and went into the house.

We started down the gravel road away from the farm, beginning what would be for me a very strange and bewildering day. I heard Zeke barking and called to him several times, but the collie didn't show.

"That's okay, Sarge," BobbyCat grinned. "We weren't gonna hunt frogs anyhow." He picked up a rock and displayed it in the strangely smooth palm of his three-fingered hand. "This is perfect," he declared. "Just the right size, shape, and weight. This one's perfect all right." So as we walked we picked up more perfect shot for our weapons until our rattling pockets weighed us down.

BobbyCat remembered where he'd spotted an inner tube some kids had played with near the creek. "That was last summer," he said. Amazingly, we found the tube along the banks, half buried in silt and humus. It looked like a shriveled, black, dead thing. BobbyCat exhumed it from its partial grave, but the rubber tore easily in our hands. "No stretch left," he said.

We followed the stream until it ran under the covered bridge of a narrow road. The banks were steeper here, but the stream was now a shallow trickle just five feet wide. We climbed the embankment and followed the road.

"Your sister sounded like she didn't wanna go to school here. Don't she like it here?"

I figured BobbyCat had been thinking about that ever since we left the house. "It's not that," I said. "It's more complicated."

He looked to me to say more.

"We think our parents are going to get divorced. My Dad's still in Germany and Mama is looking for a job in Louisville."

"You think? Ain't y'all asked them? I just went up to my old man and old lady and asked them right out. I sure did."

"Your parents are divorced? What did they say?"

"Hell," he said in two syllables; it sounded like hey-yul. "They told me weren't none of my business, which is like saying yeah cause if they weren't bustin up then wouldn't be nothin a matter with just sayin so. Just ask your Mama when you get back."

"She's in Louisville. What's it like, with your parents divorced?"

He shrugged and didn't reply for a long while then said, "It ain't like anything. Sometimes it's just the same as it was cause the old man is always hanging round anyway. He don't want Ellie to date nobody. But usually, it's quieter."

"Who's Ellie? You have a sister?"

"Ellie is my mom. She don't like to be called Mama or Mom and such, says it makes her feel older than rust. They used to fight and holler all the time and Dad would win til I started helping out Ellie."

"You don't like your Dad? My parents never fight. The Major would never hit Mama. He says boys don't hit girls cause it's not fair and wouldn't prove anything." BobbyCat didn't speak. "Don't you like your Dad, BobbyCat?"

He answered, "He's all right."

We walked about two miles down the road, never saw a car, and began walking right down the center line. Over-hanging tree limbs shaded most of the way. We came to an old, rusted car, a Ford Belvedere. Only the rear window wasn't busted out. It looked diseased and in pain. You could almost see the rust eating the chrome right before your eyes.

"This pile of nothin been here for more'n two years. The owner is dead and they say the car's the one that done it. He was a chubby, funny lookin man with a big round nose that had bumps growin all over it. Folks called him Mister Malcolm. I'd seen him around a time or two. This here car played out on him while he was headin home one night. And Mister Malcolm—so I heard tell—got out and kicked it—see them dents on the driver's side door—and cursed it somethin awful. Then he stomped on home, but never made it. He was found splattered down the road, victim of a hit'n run, and they never found out who did it, even though this road is one of the least used roads in the county. Some say his own car did it.

"Get out of here." I laughed and BobbyCat did too.

"Let's see if we can find an inner tube in the old boy," BobbyCat said.

We found torn bags of garbage in the front and back seats.

"People throw the garbage in, coons rip through it." The trunk was empty except for a tire iron and jack. BobbyCat took the tire iron and jabbed it in the seam of the right rear tire and the wheel. All the tires were flat and bald. Grunting, he pulled on the iron trying to work the lip of the tire over the wheel.

I placed my hands over his. "Let me help."

"No!" he shouted and I snatched my hands away. "I can manage as good as anybody," he said.

I said, "I know."

He pulled and yanked for another minute then I tapped his shoulder. "Forget it," I said pointing to the tire. "We should have read first, tubeless tires."

"Oh, shit," he said and laughed. He jerked the iron out and slammed it into the fender. "Damn hunk of junk," he growled and swung the iron onto the roof.

"Damn hunk of junk," I shouted and smashed the jack into the trunk.

That started our frenzy. "Stack of shit!" Smash! "Piece of crap!" Slam! We bashed the car until no glass nor flat surface remained. We swung and beat, laughing all the while, until our arms wearied and our bodies were coated in sweat. We were in a wild abandon, a frantic release, feeling sinful and strong, and uncontrolled, and dangerous.

I swung, teeth gritted into a snarl, and felt the sheet metal give and the vibration jar my arms and shoulders through the muscles to the bone. The old metal tore under our pounding and I was wickedly gratified. At last, exhausted, I threw the jack, my club, into the car and fell back to the road where I lay sprawled over a yellow dash. BobbyCat climbed on top of the mangled hunk and made a few attempts at a Tarzan yell.

"Now watch," I said, still trying to catch my breath in between each word. "We'll get a block or so down the road and the car will come run us over!"

We laughed in our euphoria as we went along our way, almost skipping down the road, glancing over our shoulders only once or twice.

*

Our scavenger hunt did have a successful, but criminal conclusion. As I think back, the inner tube is the first thing in my life I can remember stealing. (*This is not counting various slices of cakes and pies from Mama's or Gramma's kitchens.*)

The narrow, little road brought us to a larger highway. Trees lined our side along with a thick confusion of clinging, climbing vines. Across the two strips of hot, black asphalt spread open air almost to the horizon where hills bordered the edge of the earth. A vast field of soybeans ran underneath the sky all the way to the distant hills. Each perfect, unbroken, green line of soybean plants paralleled the next like disciplined files of parading soldiers. At the edge of the great field, snug against the highway stood our target, a small two pump, no name gas station. The dilapidated station house had one garage bay with a pick-up parked in it and on the left side, as you faced it, a small office displaying in its window cans of oil, a pyramid of Coca Cola six packs, and candy bars. The side of the station house office shone like dozens and dozens of miniature suns. A wide assortment of hubcaps completely covered the wall, each reflecting the world a little differently like circus side show mirrors. Out front of the station, rocked a little, bald black man. From across the highway, hidden in the shadow of the trees, we could hear the slow, regular creak of his rocking chair.

"It ain't stealin if he never misses it. And he ain't gonna miss one dang tube."

BobbyCat talked me into it because I wanted to be talked into it. I wanted my slingshot and my blood was still pumped from battering the car. As I walked alone across the highway, I heard Gramma say, "Keep your common sense around BobbyCat; he's always finding mischief."

The old man watched me approach without interrupting the rhythm of his rocking. When I got up to him, he glanced away toward the pumps as if eyeing me directly would be rude or something.

"Can you help me, sir? I'm searching for a hubcap for—"

"They's around the side," he said in a dry, quiet voice and he sneaked a peek at me.

I began to shake. I couldn't go through with it. I heard Julie saying, "You're really going to get it this time." I saw the Major glaring at me. *"I'm demoting you to private."* I saw Mama with her lips all pinched up and her nostrils wide like they are when she's angry. *"Just what were you thinking about? Do I have to watch you every minute?"*

I nodded to the little man, unable to speak and backed away. The old man's head followed me around the side of the station house, but his eyes stayed down as if he knew I was bad, and he was ashamed to watch me. I'm on the road to hell, I thought, staring at the bright, silver plates. I saw myself with an exaggerated nose and lips in fifty reflections, the Pinocchio nose of a liar. Then the old man was beside me and multiplied by fifty on the wall too.

"What model car is it for?" All his funny faced twins asked me in unison.

I'd planned to say for a Ford Belvedere, for my Dad's car, that he's been missing one, and I wanted to make it a birthday present. None of this came out, just, "I don't see it!" And I fled the scene of my crime.

I raced across the highway, ripped through the vines deep into the woods. I stopped running and leaned against a tree to catch my breath, actually listening for police sirens.

"Sarge. Where are you dammit. Sarge!"

"Over here, BobbyCat."

He bounded toward me and I heard his laughter. "You didn't get me much time," he said. "But lucky the old man stayed round the side lookin at the hubcaps on his ownself. Ta da!" BobbyCat triumphantly held up an inner tube. "We can make extras in case some pop and everything. Come on, we ain't too far from my house. We can cut it up there."

I had passed caring about the slingshot. I knew my way home and considered leaving him. But my shame of being a gas station hold up man was fleeting. BobbyCat draped the inner tube around my neck as if it were a gold medal presented to me at the Olympics. Again emboldened, I pulled my slingshot from my back pocket.

"All right," I exclaimed, "We did it."

\*

BobbyCat and his mother lived in a trailer out in the middle of nowhere. The doublewide trailer, parked on an incline, had cement block legs under one side to keep it level. It rested on the edge of a natural clearing where the rock came within a dusty coating of the surface and nothing could grow. Signs of work in progress or, rather, work abandoned, could be detected everywhere. Rolls of roofing tarp were piled up to one side of the trailer's front door. More sat atop the trailer curling like a backward 'C' away from the roof, testifying to a job begun and only one third completed. The same gremlin had started painting the rough, gray wood of a nearby storage shed an absurd turquoise blue, but only half of one side had been covered and now the turquoise peeled back in brittle, potato chip sized flakes.

Behind the trailer in a semi-circle skirting the tree line the rusting, skeletons of five automobiles lay in state: a black, fifty-six Mercury with sunflowers growing beneath the opened hood and around the engine, two white rambler station wagons facing each other with grimacing grillwork, a red Ford pick-up without an engine or hood, and the burnt shell of a van nearly covered with vines and tall weeds as if the earth were slowly absorbing it.

A dog curled under the trailer in the shady space where the hill sloped away from the trailer's floor. He raised his head sluggishly. His tail beat puffs of dust behind him, but he did not move.

"That's Ranger, best bird dog these parts ever seen, really. Cept he's old and got the palsy or somethin but I won't let my old man put him down. No way. He done earned his retirement, you can bet on that."

I peered under the trailer at the sad-faced dog. Flies buzzed around his eyes and nose.

"Ellie ain't here," BobbyCat said. He picked up a battered, dirty cake pan from underneath the trailer. "You turned it over again. Then start whinin when you're thirsty." Ranger's tail patted a response. BobbyCat knocked the pan against his leg letting the dirt drop out then filled it with water from a spigot near the storage shed. He sat the pan down within easy reach of the dog, pulled a blue bandanna from the bib pocket of his overalls and wiped the dog's mucous heavy eyes. The dog passively submitted to this treatment and licked at BobbyCat's hands.

"Come on, Sarge, let's fix your slingshot."

Inside the trailer was hot, stuffy, and smelled of the last cooked meal and a faint sour milk odor. The disarray of the outside wasn't present though. Most everything seemed neat, and in its proper place.

BobbyCat cut a portion of the rubber in one inch strips. We constructed the pocket from the tongue of an old shoe. We pulled the rubber strip through slits in the leather pocket and BobbyCat tied the black band to the posts of my 'Y' with knots that only got tighter as you pulled. He stretched it the length of his arm and let go. Alive and ready, the slingshot snapped at the air.

"Let's test it," BobbyCat said. "After a nature call." He disappeared down the hallway just as a car pulled in the yard in front of the trailer.

A woman not much taller than Julie, maybe five feet tall,

climbed out of a faded, blue Corvair, cradling a bag of groceries with an unlit cigarette dangling between her smallish lips. She wore a tee shirt and tight jeans with frayed bell-bottoms nearly covering her shoes.

I waited for BobbyCat in the kitchen where we had put my slingshot together. The woman stepped in the trailer and placed her groceries on a table just to the right of the door. Her back was toward me.

"BobbyCat." Her call sounded like a question.

*He's in the bathroom, Ma'am. I'm called Sarge*, is what I was about to say. My mouth even opened to say it. But her hands crossed to either side of her waist and pulled her tee shirt in one quick motion over her head. My mouth stayed open. At almost ten years old, this was my first brassiere. (*It was my first occupied bra; I had examined Mama's brassieres from the dirty clothes hamper on earlier quests for knowledge.*) She turned in my direction though not yet looking up to see me. The dark circles of her showed through the cups and I stared unabashedly. She dabbed at the perspiration on her chest, picked up her groceries, then spotted me ogling her.

If I surprised her, she didn't show it nor did she make any move to cover herself. I heard her snicker, probably at my wide-eyed wonder and I snapped my eyes down to my feet. She walked past me into the kitchen.

"You must be Sarge, Miss Ruthie's grandson."

I mumbled something, eyeing the tattered canvas of my Chuck Taylor's.

"Tell me, she still caretakin that colored cemetery? Bet she is. So peculiar."

She put away her groceries as she talked and I peeked under my eyebrows at her white back, speckled lightly with pin dot moles. As she reached for a top shelf even whiter skin showed from beneath the bra straps. My eyes followed the shallow dip in her back that started between her protruding shoulder blades and disappeared into the waist of her jeans. "If it were me," she was saying, "The county'd have to pay me for all that work. Caretakin an all." She turned facing me again and my eyes sought the safety of the floor. "Sarge, huh, what's your real name? BobbyCat told me how he led you home the night you got lost."

BobbyCat knew I was lost? He never said a word or teased me about it. I was surprised, but just gaped at her, unable to answer. She laughed and returned to her groceries, enjoying my embarrassment. I should've waited for BobbyCat outside, but I didn't want to. My glances became bolder, lingered longer. This is bad, I told myself. But she is a grown-up so maybe it's not, I argued.

"Geez, Ellie," BobbyCat said reappearing in the kitchen. "Can't you cover up at least when we has a guest over?"

"Oh, BobbyCat, Sarge is just folks. He don't care, do you, Sarge? See more outside if you go down to the pool." She went into the living room. "And don't say I didn't warn you," we heard on our way out the trailer door. "Your daddy might be comin round this way."

"Why is it a warning?" I asked BobbyCat outside.

"On accounta Ranger," he said. He brought a length of rope and a collar from the storage shed. "We told my Daddy Ranger up and ran off. And he said, 'Well, maybe he knew his days were up. He was always a smart dog.' Anyway," BobbyCat said while fastening the collar about the dog. "Because of the injunction against him, my Daddy got to tell Ellie anytime he's fixin to come over. She says she always says okay, come on, cause if she didn't he'd come over anyways. Bring his water pan, Sarge. I'll feed him when the old man's gone."

We led Ranger into the tree line. The dog moved slowly and tentatively as if he had to test the waters with each step. His hind end moved stiffly and bent to the side as if it were trying to get ahead of the rest of him. "So we hide him until my Daddy leaves." BobbyCat tied him quickly to a tree approximately two dozen yards into the woods behind the old Mercury.

I placed the pan next to the dog who regarded me with big, black, ancient eyes. He whined and it sounded like a sigh reminding me of Grandpa Standard settling into his easy chair at the end of a day.

"Let's go shoot our slingshots," BobbyCat said and we took

off. I glimpsed back to see the dog, cradled in the roots of the tree, watch us run away.

*

Squirrels darted for cover. Birds sang of the new terror in the woods. Sarge Willis had a slingshot. I liked listening to the leaves snap and pop as my rockets hurtled through their green shadows to the blue space beyond. Everything was in season and fair game. First, large targets were selected and bombarded, the van, the shell of the pick up, even the storage shed. I got the hang of firing the slingshot easily enough and moved to tree trunks and heard with satisfaction the knock of my rock bouncing off its target.

"If you can hit the tree you want, you could hit a person," BobbyCat said, and added, "if they keep still."

I graduated to squirrels and crows and a now and again rabbit, collecting only one jet tail feather from a frantic crow for my efforts.

BobbyCat didn't shoot at the animals, well, not to hit them. "If I aimed at 'em, I'd hit 'em," he claimed.

We rapidly emptied our pockets of shot, filled them and emptied them again, and again. In this way, one of the longest days of the year swiftly passed.

We began feeling hungry around seven o'clock, but the sun still shone brightly and there seemed to be no plans for having a night time. A big, white Dodge pick-up sat next to Ellie's Corvair, jacked up high over fat, thick tires. The tailgate was missing and the bed was littered with tools and crushed pop cans and beer cans. Gray blotches spotted the truck where the surface had been repaired, sanded, but not repainted.

"My Daddy's here," BobbyCat said. He put his hand in the truck's grillwork. "He's been here long enough. Let's go in and fix some peanut butter an jelly sandwiches." We stepped into the hot box trailer. "Gettin somethin to eat," BobbyCat called loudly. His warning given, he stomped into the kitchen, and I followed, wondering why he was suddenly angry. He went through each kitchen cabinet banging one door against the next, until he found a nearly empty jar of Peter Pan.

"It's enough," he said. "She puts it in a different spot every time." He effortlessly opened the jar by trapping it under his arm and twisting the lid with his complete hand. He'd learned to manipulate anything without consideration of his missing digits. "I just don't figure her, I don't figure her at all." And I knew he wasn't referring to where the Peter Pan should be kept.

A man whose white blond hair matched BobbyCat's stepped from a back room into the hall. He wore only a pair of blue jeans with the fly gaping open. Our eyes met and his index finger placed to his lips, bisected his lean face. BobbyCat rummaged through the refrigerator, nearly in it, roughly pushing milk cartons and Tupperware aside searching for the jelly. The man crept with exaggerated stealth on tiptoes, keeping his finger to his lips all the while. In spite of myself, I grinned. He winked at me when he stood behind his unsuspecting son. His lean muscled arms descended and he pounced on BobbyCat putting him in a swift, tight headlock.

"Ellie! Thief in the kitchen. Call the cops, Ellie."

BobbyCat yelled, "Get off me, you son of—" The rest came out in a strangled mumble. Like his namesake, BobbyCat became a quick, furious ball of action. The wrestling match stumbled and rolled into the living room. "I live here. The police can come get you." The wrestlers fell to the floor. BobbyCat freed himself and climbed on his father's back and tried to pin his opponent's arm behind his back. "I got you now," he said laughing.

Ellie came from down the hallway wearing a shiny, silky robe of large, red print roses. "Sic 'em, BobbyCat!" she said and punctuated it with a delighted high, pitched squeal. "Don't let him get behind you. Watch it!"

She yelled encouragement and other instructions like that and, I guess, I watched her more than I watched the contest. She bobbed up and down on her red painted toes. Her robe didn't show her body, but suggested it, and I spied her shape, the silk sliding over it, as she moved. The vision of the bra, the mystery of her dark circles turned and played through my head and, already fantasies grew in the aroused twists of my brain. She caught me peeping. Her hand went to the bright red lapels of the robe and she eased them apart revealing the smooth rise of her breasts. My eyes jerked away, back to the grappling on the floor, before they would see too much. I heard her laughing at me, but didn't dare to glance her way again.

BobbyCat still on his father's back wrapped an arm around the Daddy bobcat's neck. "Say uncle," he demanded.

His father pulled himself to his knees with a lot of fake grunting and groaning, and tossed BobbyCat off him like a rodeo bronco.

BobbyCat fell hard and his back hit against a steel leg of the dining table. I winced. BobbyCat grimaced.

A glass on the table fell over from the impact, but I caught it as it rolled off the edge.

"You okay, sweetheart? That's enough rough housing for today," Ellie said.

But her ex-husband and her son just glared at each other. The game was over but they were not through. BobbyCat picked himself up while his father was still on all fours, and leaped on him. He brought two, heavy, fist blows down on his father's back before being shoved roughly away.

"All right, that's it," Ellie said, and she gave a weak laugh that died somewhere in the middle of the hot living room.

BobbyCat's face was tight and focused, and sweat rolled freely down his cheeks, dripping off his chin. His daddy shook a finger at him.

I grew scared for my new friend, and I think I said, "Come on, BobbyCat, let's go back outside."

But he didn't hear me or I didn't say it because he jumped at his father again swinging his fists in wild, wide arcs. Only one or two blows landed before his father struck him on the temple. Dazed, BobbyCat's anger seemed to fall from his face for the quick part of a second and then he was attacking again.

Ellie yelled, "Stop it!" and "Quit it!" constantly now, and tried to maneuver between the two.

I didn't see the blow that ended the fight. BobbyCat just

staggered backwards with his hands covering his stomach. His eyes grew wide, and the color drained from his face.

"You okay, you okay?" Ellie was beside him trying to pull up his tee shirt, but he wouldn't let her.

"Course he's okay," BobbyCat's father said. "I didn't hurt the boy. He was askin for—"

"You just shut the hell up. You're both just a couple of boys. Don't know when to stop. Just don't know when to stop. You play too rough." She stroked her son's hair, "I've got to cut these bangs," and kissed his temple where he'd first been hit. "That's going to be a bruise." Then she looked expectantly at her ex-husband. "Well, Bailey, tell him you're sorry."

The man, Bailey, sighed, wiping sweat from his face with the crook of his arm. "BobbyCat knows we were just playing," he said. "Men play rough is all that is. Right, BobbyCat?" They both looked to their son, who, still clutching his stomach, nodded his agreement. The parents seemed visibly relieved by this and the tension left the room leaving just the stuffiness and the heat.

"There you go," Bailey said. "Besides, I come up here to show y'all a good time. I got a big package of ground beef in the fridge and buns and we can grill outside. How does that sound? And you're invited, boy," Bailey said to me. "Introduce your friend, BobbyCat." BobbyCat told him my name and Bailey extended his hand. I shook it because I couldn't think of a way not to. "How do you do, Sarge. Stay and have some grilled burgers with us."

"Well, my Gramma wants me—" Behind Bailey, BobbyCat nodded vigorously. "—home, but I don't think she'd mind. Thank you, sir."

Bailey clapped his hands. "All right! Let me get this picnic goin. Soons I find my shirt and shoes. Shit, Ellie, my barn door's been open all this time and you didn't say a thing."

Ellie giggled and the two of them ran down the hall.

BobbyCat and I went outside. The wind had cooled things off a bit and the fresh air felt ten times better than the stuffy atmosphere of the trailer. I sat on the steps and BobbyCat climbed on the pile of roofing. He just shrugged when I asked him if he was really okay, and neither of us spoke for awhile. I toyed with my slingshot, pulling on the inner tube band and feeling its resistance.

"I'm going to carve my name on the handle," I told him, having thought of the idea and said it simultaneously.

The door of the trailer swung open and I jumped from the steps in order to avoid being hit. "Hey, BobbyCat, you and Sarge set up this card table in a nice spot and come back for the chairs."

The two of us set up the table and chairs, and then set up the grill and started the fire too. Ellie came out dressed in jeans and a blue shirt with the tails tied above her navel. She brought out a bowl and jars of mustard and mayonnaise, and relish.

"I have all the ingredients for macaroni salad," she announced.

Bailey came out with a lawn chair and a radio. He spent some time fiddling with his coat hanger and tin foil antenna, and finally got some passable reception. He grabbed Ellie in the middle of stirring her macaroni salad, and the pair danced to Paul McCartney and Wings' "Band on the Run". Ellie giggled all the while and tried to coax both BobbyCat and me to dance, but we wouldn't budge. She grabbed my hand, pretending to dance with me as I sat on the steps.

"I know Sarge wants to dance with me," she said, and winked and pursed her lips. "Colored boys do blush!" She laughed and jiggled back to Bailey, who danced and formed the hamburger patties at the same time. Chagrined, BobbyCat watched them dance, glanced over at me and rolled his eyes.

"Bring me a cold one, honey," Ellie said.

Bailey replied, "Comin right up, dumplin." They started calling each other all kinds of desserts like dumpling and sweetie pie, and angel cake. I came to the conclusion I didn't know a thing about divorce. I thought at the time, if this happened to Mama and the Major it wouldn't be so bad. Bailey returned from the trailer with beers and sodas, and handed an Orange Crush to me. Ellie put the fat, red patties on the grill while singing along with Olivia Newton John, batting her eyelashes, getting BobbyCat to laugh with her.

"Are these suds cold enough, sugar britches?" Bailey asked and pressed a beer can to Ellie's back. She shrieked and ran, starting some kind of impromptu tag game with the only rule I could see was you had to touch the other person with a cold can of beer. Even BobbyCat joined in and the family, momentarily forgetting me, ran in pursuit of each other around the trailer, the vine covered van, the storage shed, anywhere.

I just sat there smiling at their comfortable silliness and wishing the Major would come to the farm and we could have a cook out. I wanted to see Mama and the Major together. I pictured all of us in Gramma Ruth's garden. Gramma was telling a story. Julie stood next to Mama. I picked a flower for Mama and the Major winked at me and patted my head. The fantasy made me smile and made me sad too.

The pop and sizzle brought me back to reality; the grill was engulfed in orange, spitting flames. "Fire! Fire!" I shouted.

Everyone converged on the scene. BobbyCat and I poured our sodas on the fire. We all shouted warnings and instructions, and squinted with our hands in front of our faces to block the heat, crying from the smoke. Bailey tried rescuing the hamburgers with a spatula, but the two he managed to retrieve were dry, black lumps.

"Is that the meat or the charcoal?" BobbyCat asked and everyone laughed, keeping their humor.

Ellie tried blowing the fire out, nearly getting her hair singed. "Well, least we got macaroni salad," she said. "And I think there's some hotdogs in the freezer."

Doused with Strohs and Orange Crush, the fire was brought under control.

"BobbyCat, you and Sarge check the freezer for—" Bailey began, but he didn't finish. His eyes stared past us. I turned to see what he saw.

Ranger sat on the side of his tortured haunches, a long white cord trailed from his neck to the dust behind him. His big, black, sad eyes peered quizzically at our commotion. The tilt of his head asked, 'What noise is this? What's going on?'

The four of us were quiet for a moment, the kind of quiet that comes when everyone wants to talk, but doesn't know what to say. Ellie and BobbyCat eyed Bailey, waiting for his reaction.

Ellie spoke first. "I am stunned. Look who found his way home after all this time."

"Bullshit," Bailey said.

"Bad dog, Ranger," BobbyCat said to the dog. "You were supposed to stay put."

"Shut up, BobbyCat." Bailey went to the dog, who eased himself down to his belly. "Dog's much too old to be scolded by a young turd like you. Too much goin on over here, had to come check it out didn't ya, fella? They been tying you up in the woods when I drop by, haven't they, boy?" The man rubbed the dog behind the ears and I could see in the gentleness of his touch a deep affection. "Ol' Ranger." Bailey stood up turning to Ellie. "You lied to me and you got him lyin too." A finger stabbed toward BobbyCat.

"We don't want you to hurt the dog is all, Bailey," Ellie said.

"I shoulda figured lyin... got him lyin too. Just like you lie about everything. BobbyCat's a boy, but you ought to know—" Bailey grabbed the front of Ellie's shirt. She flinched, tried to pull away, and the shirt tore. She slapped ineffectually at his arm. "Just like you lie about who's been in your bed." He jerked her toward him.

"Leave her alone," BobbyCat said.

"You stay outta this. You done more than enough, startin a fight when you know we's just playin, and lyin—"

"You're a fine one to talk about lyin," Ellie said. "Ever body from Owensboro to Louisville knows about you and Amy Stetson."

"Stimpson."

"Simpson, Stimpson, I don't care how you say it, damn you." She slapped at his arm again, this time freeing herself.

"I told you it weren't true, Ellie. You can't say the same though, you cheatin slut."

"Don't call me that in front of these boys, you asshole." They glared at each other for a long time. Slowly, Ellie seemed to shrink from the wife and mother, pass the teasing flirt, to a little girl no older than BobbyCat or me. She pouted, dropping her gaze to the hard, dusty ground. She reached for Bailey who stepped back. "We were doin so well, just like a family ought to. Let's not spoil it with name callin."

"I can't now. Can't pretend with you no more today, Ellen. Sometimes I can forget what you done to me. It's amazing, I can't figure it, but sometimes I actually forget what you done, what I saw, and I come on over here. But most of the time I can't do nothin but remember cause it's like a giant hand grippin me by my brain." Bailey wiped tears from his eyes and took a deep breath then forced it out to fight against crying. Men don't cry, the Major had told me. Bailey waved a hand through the air letting it fall back to his side. "It's gettin late," he said.

For the first time, I noticed evening had finally arrived; the sky was purple, dotted with the glow of fireflies, and full of the complaints of frogs and crickets.

Bailey said, "I'm goin now. Ranger's comin with me."

"No!" BobbyCat shouted and jumped on Bailey. BobbyCat tried scratching him, but Bailey caught his wrists and pushed him away.

"Stop it, BobbyCat," Bailey shouted.

The boy kept pressing, determined to win this rematch. "Ellie, he's gonna kill Ranger. Help, Ellie. Help." Now Ellie jumped on Bailey's back and they both pummeled him.

"Sarge, save Ranger," BobbyCat yelled.

I snatched up the rope immediately. "Come on, boy. Come on, Ranger." I pulled on the rope. Ranger's sharp yelp of pain froze us all. "I didn't mean to hurt him," I said.

Bailey shoved his family away. Ellie and BobbyCat fell to the ground. Ellie ran into the trailer and Bobbycat scrambled to Ranger's side kneeling next to the dog who began licking the boy's arms.

I let the rope fall from my hands.

"You didn't hurt Ranger, Sarge," Bailey said, standing over BobbyCat. "He's an old dog with a lot of aches and pains."

"You can't just kill him, Dad." BobbyCat stroked the dog.

"Grow up, boy. You're just puttin him through some messy

hurtin is all you're doin."

"If the boy wants to see that damn dog rot to the bone then leave him be." Ellie stood in the doorway of the trailer with a rifle leveled right at Bailey.

"Dammit, Ellie, put that away," he said then waved his hand as if to dismiss her. "Sarge, " he said squatting down next to BobbyCat. "BobbyCat an' me an' Ranger used to go huntin out by Charter Lake. You remember those October mornings, BobbyCat? The early morning frost made the grass white and stiff and you could feel it give under your boots. We'd shiver against the cold. Kept reminding ourselves it was bound to warm up. Who was more excited to be out in the wilds? Weren't me or you, I'll say that. It was Ranger, just a rippin and a runnin. Wouldn't wait til I put the tailgate down fore he'd jump out the truck—that's back when I had a tailgate. Always figured the dog was gonna hurt himself doin that.

"And when I got off a shot, Ranger would stay right at my left leg, but I know he wanted to take right off, you could see it in his legs like tight springs. He'd look up at me, right in my face. Bring it back, boy, I'd say, but he'd be gone on the first word out my mouth. Never chewed a bird up either. You loved the water too, didn't you, Ranger? This dog would go anywhere to bring in your kill."

Bailey was quiet inside his thoughts for a moment. Ranger's head slipped down between his front paws. "Never chewed up a bird," Bailey repeated. "Brought them back the way he found 'em. Ranger loved to run, BobbyCat. Damn, that's all he was, a quick blur of red through the tall grass. Now he can't no more, not just cause he's old, cause he's hurtin. He's hurtin bad, son."

Tears ran along the creases of BobbyCat's nose and he bit at his lower lip to stop it from trembling. He stood, went to Ellie and took the cradled rifle from her arms. He brought it to Bailey.

"No, BobbyCat," I shouted.

He ran back to the trailer, and pushed past Ellie, who followed him inside.

Bailey slung the rifle over his shoulder.

"Don't, Mister Bailey."

"Go on home, Sarge." He bent down and gently scooped the dog into his arms.

"Don't." I shouted, and began to run.

I ran as hard and as long as ever I had before. I found the road and kept running. My lungs burned and I pushed harder, wanting the pain. And though I ran hard and fast, I could not outdistance the abrupt shatter that caught up to me, or its echo following after, through the trees.

## VI

### Hattie May's Lap

My flight ended at the cemetery. I bounded over the short fence and allowed myself to crash onto the garden's soft, grass carpet. The ground relieved me of my weight, which seemed heavier than my muscles could bear. It rose to cradle me just as your own bed does when you drop on it at the end of a long, tiring day. I cried, though the Major had told me men don't cry over the little things as women do; men had to be stronger. More tears fell despite my attempts to dam them. Getting a cut or a bruise was a little thing, I knew, but was Ranger a little thing? I decided I did not care. I wallowed in my sadness and anger. I remember feeling hurt and hateful.

I wiped my eyes with the back of my hand. I would have to wait for them to dry and clear before I could go on in. My tears stopped, but a dryer, deeper hurt remained. "Why can't we all just go back to Germany?" I asked the stones around me. They could not answer. Each, still and dark in the evening, waited for what it could do. I crawled to my favorite spot in the garden, Hattie May's stone, and placed my back to its warm smoothness, still warm with life because the sun had set only a little while ago.

Bright, night flowers appeared in the sky. The longer I gazed upward the more stars would twinkle into being. A slight breeze blew through the garden and around the gently assenting heads of Gramma's flowers. Their sweet fragrance surrounded me and the spirit of Gramma Ruth's garden began to work its magic on me. I thought of her stories of Tillie, and Chief, the proud Wolof General, and lonely Cakes.

Then, in front of me, a shadow separated from the dark

cornfield across the trail. The large shadow moved heavily, and unerringly toward me. The starlight gave form and features to my company, a large woman, not really fat but big of frame. She wore a kerchief over her hair and a drab blue dress, it seemed in the night, stretching over large, hanging breasts and wide hips, ending frayed at the top of her unlaced boots. She walked like a man and her hands were as big as Grandpa Standard's. I knew exactly who she was.

"Boys or men folk, black or white, they all come to Hattie May least once, usually more," she said. With a grunt, she settled down next to me. "Child, why you cryin? You thinkin this here plantation needin another pond or you want to make a river to float back to the homeland? Hattie come with you then. It's all right you cry then. But don't cry cause what they done. Don't do no good, that. Hattie knows.

"You cry over the cur? The Masta had to put him down. The Masta, he feed the dog, he work the dog. He give it water and food, and work each day of its life. And the dog hates his Masta, truly. Listen to Hattie. But the Masta say, 'Good dog,' and the dog wags his tail like a fool. One day they will come to put down Hattie May. They will know when. Hattie don't know when. She don't know any better than to cling on to the last, uh, huh."

She started humming. She hugged me and I could feel the vibrations of her deep, inside sound.

"Ah, you cryin over the Major and your Mama. Hattie understands. The Masta split my Mama and Papa, but yours split them ownselves. Ah. Masta came down to the quarters one day when Hattie just a girl and say to my Papa, 'Boy, come on with me.' Papa been trying to straighten out some snarled up string to fish with and he hands it to me, say, 'See what you can do, I be right back.' But slaves can't say what they gonna do. They can't say see you tomorrow, or we gonna fish the pond this afternoon 'cause it ain't up to them. Papa go off with the Masta and Hattie never see him again. Just like that. Me standin there diggin knots from a string and my Papa goin away forever.

"Your Mama and Papa want to split, that's a shame. Hattie don't know why. But least, they want to do it. When you free you can make good decisions or bad, ah. Might be for the best. You'll still get to see the Major. You can go visit wherever he be. Oh, the hot, dusty days Hattie wish she could come and go as she please. Hattie'd be a walkin woman, that's right. Hattie would walk the whole land, if she could, cross every damn field, and wave to the people when they look up from the cotton and the tobacco. Just to come and go. Masta used to say, 'It's too late to free the nigger. He wouldn't know what to do or how to behave himself. Slavery's the best thing for him now.' Hattie don't know about that. But, oh, just to come and go. Take to the trail til it run out. Even if it don't lead no wheres. That's all Hattie ever wanted."

Hattie put her arm about me. Now we both leaned against her marker. She touched my cheek and lips. Her hands felt rough.

"Did Hattie tell you she once had a boy? Spencer Hayman the third, Young Spence. He was more Hattie's boy than the mistress'. See Hattie and Mrs. Hayman both have babies at the same time, but Hattie is young and Mrs. Hayman showin gray hair. Hattie used to catch her snippin away at it in front of her mirror. Hattie have Liza Blue and back in the kitchen in three days but the Mistress, she all sickly actin and moanin for a month til the Captain finally had enough of it and boot her from her bed. By then it was too late. Hattie done been nursin both babies. Sometimes at the same time. Ah. To see young Hattie with a white baby and a black baby, both just nursin away. See now with Hattie's milk in him, that baby was Hattie's and weren't nothin they could really do. Mrs. Hayman got steamin hot to find Hattie been nursin the heir to the plantation. But the Captain say to her, 'What did you want me to do while you been lying around. I can't nurse him.'

"Young Spence grow up lovin Hattie and playin with Liza Blue. See he had Hattie's milk in him in the beginnin when it counts the most. He run errands for Hattie, bring her catfish all the time, kiss Hattie on the cheek and say, 'I'm going to save my money and buy your freedom, Hattie May.' Hattie would tell him she's lookin for that day. Young Spence was Hattie's boy. When he fall from the tree, he run to Hattie May's lap, yes. Mrs.

Hayman is so jealous. When the Captain bought Young Spence his first rifle, he run to show it to me before he show it to her and she seen this. Ah. But weren't nothin to be done. Hattie the best cook and maid she got, yes. And Young Spence hate her if she got rid of Hattie.

"Used to be the house slaves would have a party when the Haymans would go visitin. We'd have it out back so no spilled food or drink would give us away. 'Sides you know niggers, we might break somethin and there'd be hell to pay, yes. Tillie and Hattie and the rest of the girls would go into Mrs. Hayman's closet and put on her best dresses. Yes, we would. And fuss somethin silly over who got which one. 'Now, Hattie, you knows Ah looks better in yellow. It flatters mah figure, don't you think,' Tillie would say an' prance about with her hands a'flutter just like the mistress, and try to walk all proper with her back straight. She had us laughin and fallin down. Oh, but those dresses, with their bows, and fancy lace. Hattie never felt anything like them. We couldn't wear the shoes on account the Mrs. had such dainty feet. So, we'd gather up the hem of those ball gowns and run barefoot out to our party. We'd eat pig feet and turnip greens, and dance to the fiddle or to our own singin', but we wouldn't dance on the ground for fear of gettin the dresses soiled. So we clears off the tables after the eatin and dance on top of the tables, whirlin about and kickin, yes. We got caught once, by Young Spence. He tell us to put those dresses away and clean everything up. He hollers when he says this and looks just like his Papa. All the niggers was afraid for days they was goin to get the beatin of their lives. And if the Captain had ever found out, we woulda'. Hattie weren't feared for a minute though. To ease the rest of them's fears, Hattie tell them how Young Spence is her boy, an' how he kisses her cheek and say, 'I'm saving my money to buy you free, Hattie May.' The Captain and the Mrs. never found out.

"But there come a day when both the Captain and Hattie stand on the gallery wantin to cry. By then we both knows cryin don't do no good. Young Spence came home from schoolin with this New York girl. Not a body on the plantation like even a little bit of her, not the nail of her baby toe. But Young Spence is struck hard, he can't smell nothin but her air. The day he came home with her, he didn't even come in the kitchen and say hello to his Hattie May. Hattie gettin on by then and wants to ask him if he done saved enough money to buy her free.

"Hattie got her bad news before the Captain got his. After dinner, Young Spence calls Hattie in from the kitchen and say he got an important announcement. This is it, Hattie thinkin', just to come and go is all, Lord, just to come and go. 'Hattie May, you're just as much a part of the family as anyone else,' Young Spence start off sayin, but he's lookin at the New York girl. Hattie's feelin so proud right then. But my smile drops right to the carpet when Young Spence announce he and the New York girl gonna get married. She turns to Hattie May and shows her hand with the ring that say she's promised to Young Spence. Hattie knows she seein her freedom sparklin on that girl's china white finger. Mrs. Hayman runs from the room cryin, but Hattie just turns about and heads back in the kitchen. Later, we find out Young Spence gonna go live in New York. That was the Captain's bad news cause now he got to leave the plantation to his daughter from his first marriage. She married Charlie Enright. The mistress wouldn't come down to see Young Spence off when the time came, so it was just the Captain and me on the gallery. Young Spence say to me before he leave, Hattie's gettin old an' be better off stayin on the plantation. Hattie don't look at him. White people think they know best for the black people. They say, Give me liberty or give me death. And they say, Live free or die for themself. For the blacks, they say, oh, they better off this way or that. For blacks it just depends, you see. He kiss my cheek, but Hattie wipe the kiss away." Hattie rubbed at her eyes. I could see them glistening in the starlight. "Hattie knows better than to cry, so what is this?" she asked.

"Liza Blue and her children lived to be free, Hattie, to come and go just as they please. Gramma Ruth told me so."

"Ahh, yes? This is God's reward for Hattie May."

She hugged me fiercely to her, buried me in her embrace and rocked me back and forth. She sang a song, low and sad, without words. I suppose it may have just been a moan, but it soothed and calmed me and gave me peace.

I absorbed the smell and warmth of her, and for a short time slept in her arms.

*

"Sarge, we can't stay out here all night. It's time to be going in."

I looked into Gramma Ruth's face. We helped each other up and headed home. We held hands.

## VII

### Ghost in the Garden

I awoke early as a retreat from my dreams. My emotions and worries churned while I slept. Awake, I could control them—a little. At my window, I witnessed a soft, silent dawn.

The morning mist, stranded clouds, covered every drop, dip, and depression on the farm, softening the lines which define one thing from the next, blurring and blending the landscape. The hill on which the house and barn, coop and shed stood had become an island surrounded by a white, vagrant, sea. The heavens had descended to whisper close to the cheek of the earth. Little stirred, perhaps a rabbit on the edge of a field or a cock taking measured strides across the yard. They and their brethren in the brambles and the coop kept a quiet veneration as if aware of their proximity to the God, who filled the air like the mist, touching everything and leaving with everything a part of Himself.

Gramma Ruth appeared in the middle of the yard. She must've been standing on the porch for a while because I hadn't heard the squeal of the screen door's spring nor the slam of the door closing. Her attention was focused out in the cornfield it seemed, which the mist obscured from my view. She seemed to linger there indecisively. My curiosity was piqued, never having seen her hesitate over anything. I rubbed the sleep from my eyes, dressed quickly, and ran to join her. By the time I stepped outside, she stood at the trail that began behind the barn. I caught up to her.

"Are you going to the cemetery this early, Gramma?" I whispered feeling somehow it only proper to do so. I could hear the birds' song now, cheery as usual, sounding irreverent this morning.

Far down the trail, a bit past the cemetery, idled Grandpa's tractor, unmounted. Smoke, darker than the low-lying haze, rose from it like curls of breath in winter. The engine grumbled sleepily. Gramma and I both contemplated it, wondering about its motionlessness. She started down the path. I tailed her a step behind.

"Biscuits and honey are in the kitchen, Sarge," she said without regarding me. I did not get the hint.

Gramma spotted him first and stopped. I looked to her and followed her gaze to the cemetery. Grandpa Standard, veiled in mist, faced the tiny, stone cherub perched on Kate's marker, both as unmoving as the other, engaged in silent conversation. I had never seen him there before. The fields and the chores had been forced to wait. Grandpa Standard had halted time and the normal course of the morning with his presence amongst the stones. Hat in hand, head down, the man who scowled at the mention of the garden, who claimed the stories of the souls lying there were just tall tales, posed as reverent as a deacon, as solemn as a mourner.

"Charles?" It was a question asked of her own senses. She stepped forward, slowly at first, then quickly, wanting, I think to run. Instinct told me not to follow. But, abruptly, she stopped, drew herself up. Grandpa had turned about, returning to his tractor, his place, pulling down his hat as he went.

The tractor belched forward and bounced down the trail.

At length, just when I thought she would not move again, Gramma came back up the path, walking past me as if I was not there.

# VIII

## Slinking Low with Luther

I'd sometimes slip under the porch with Zeke. He liked having a guest. Zeke had his own cemetery under there, I think. Shallow pits gave evidence of hundreds of buried bones and who-guess-whats. Zeke's digs—forgive me—were cool and private. The frog dog wasn't so gracious a host as to share a ham bone with me, but he never begrudged a nice, shady spot either. While I preferred the view at the window of my own room, everyone knew to look for me there.

With Zeke, I could be away without going anywhere. They could look for me and call from the porch and say, "Now where's that boy got off to this time!" All the while I would be as near to them as their own feet. The underside of the porch had walls of latticework covered with vines, and thick, squat shrubs, a cool, dusty, and perfect hiding place. Hiding became very important to me. I would hide even—and this was usually the case—when no one searched for me. Then I could mysteriously appear just a bit late for dinner or supper or for bedtime. Under the porch wasn't my only hiding place, but it gave the best vantage point. Between the boards of the flooring, I could spy on who wanted me and how mad they were getting. I could count the number of times Julie stamped her foot. I'd shush Zeke not to laugh and cover my own mouth too. I'd show late to supper, sweaty and dirty. "Don't think because your Mama and Papa aren't here, you're going to get away with devilment or bad manners," Gramma would say.

Grandpa Standard might ask, "Where you been, Kenny?"

"Just around," seemed to satisfy him or a dumb look and a shrug.

Julie, of course, promised to give Mama a full accounting. I'd give Julie the finger as soon as Gramma looked away.

I took to hiding the day after I came back from BobbyCat's place. That morning I crawled under the porch looking for Zeke and accepted his invitation to hang out for awhile. I told no one about my day with BobbyCat and his parents. Too much had happened. My mind needed time to sort through and catalog all of the events of that full day. Most of what happened, such as stealing the inner tube, or beating the abandoned car, or seeing Ellie in her bra, I could store in a pouch in my mind, like the one I had for my marbles. Then take them out to examine while at my window some evening or while under the porch with Zeke.

The remnants of that day would not be easily put aside. I wondered about BobbyCat and Bailey fighting, and what it meant to be a divorced family. I knew I did not want to be a part of one. I wanted to cry about Ranger, but didn't anymore. The fly-harried, sad-eyed face of that dog lingered with me. I tried to figure out why BobbyCat had given his father the rifle, why Bailey had done it. They both seemed to love the dog.

Vaguely, I understood they had acted in the dog's— everyone's—best welfare or so I came to believe they thought they had. I saw only Ranger's face, thought of Zeke, and remembered the rifle shot that had, at once, filled every space of the woods with its sound.

The rest of that first time hiding under the porch, I spent telling Zeke about Ranger, and what a good hunting dog he'd been.

\*

Days later, Gramma and I witnessed Grandpa Standard's early morning visit to the garden. This new mystery replaced concerns over BobbyCat, Ellie, and Ranger. What had compelled Charles Standard to stop his work and pay respects to Gramma's ghosts? Grandpa had not gone to see Hattie, nor Cakes, nor Chief. He'd stood squarely in front of baby Kate's marker.

I didn't have to know Grandpa to realize the rarity and strangeness of this event. Gramma's face told it. She usually said what was on her mind, but on this misty morning she'd said nothing, even hesitated to go down to her own garden. When she walked right past me on the trail, I watched her return to the house. I saw the tractor head further and further down the trail until it was engulfed in mist.

I peered again at the cemetery, wondering what they saw that I could not see. I knew it concerned only grown-ups, just as everything else going on around me lately had been labeled hands off, adults only. The garden had changed, not because the mist muted the colors of the flowers. I knew the mist would lift or burn off, but the mystery, left behind by Grandpa, would remain. Not solely from curiosity did I wish to solve the puzzle, but because I knew the grown-ups did not want me to.

So I went spying. Inspired by reruns of Secret Agent Man, I went on the prowl for information. While Gramma and Julie snapped beans on the porch, and listened to Grandpa and a neighbor, Mr. McEachern, talk about corn prices, I slipped upstairs to my grandparent's room.

They had a big bed with a huge, old headboard, which stood three quarters of the way to the ceiling. Their tables had white marble tops, veined with black, and wood carved into animal claws for feet. Two electric space heaters with their cords wrapped about them sat at the foot of the bed waiting for winter use. The brown carpet had some darkly colored design on it, most of which the bed covered. The bureau used by Gramma had a colony of dusty perfume bottles all clustered to one side. Some had atomizers, some were opaque bottles, others, oddly shaped crystal. No two seemed alike. None of them appeared even a quarter empty.

In the middle of the bureau on a white, oval doily rested Gramma's brush, full of her hair, and a scattering of bobby pins. On the other side of the bureau in a dull, brass frame stood Mama in her navy blue cap and gown with a gold tassel dangling at the side of her face. She smiled without showing her teeth. She looked so young, only barely like my Mama. Her hair was straightened and turned outward into stiff curls just past her shoulders. The latest school pictures of Julie and I, still in the cardboard holders they came in, flanked either side of Mama's picture.

At the top of a mirror, which ran the length of the bureau, wedged by a corner into the mirror's frame, hung a cracked photograph of an old black couple, much older looking than Gramma and Grandpa. I could not see it well, so I pulled it down and carried it to one of the windows. The old man wore a suit, and looked uncomfortable in it. He held his chin up, obviously a proud man, and though he looked so old that he most certainly had to be feeble and brittle with age, he seemed strong and capable. The woman wore a scarf on her head, hiding all her hair except a few strands in front of her ears. The man had white hair and a thin, white moustache. The most striking thing about the photograph was the woman's silver eyes. She was, of course, blind from cataracts, or nearly so, but I did not know this then and gazed, fascinated, at those large, milky eyes.

Much later, I learned their names were Grainger and Mary Browning, a couple who had raised Gramma Ruth for a portion of her childhood. I ran into a little trouble returning the photo to its place. The cracked and frayed edges would not easily slip under the mirror's frame. Knowing I'd be caught for sure if I could not replace it, I panicked and forced it under the lip of the frame. The thin cracks across the photo deepened. Also it wasn't exactly placed as I'd found it, but I didn't dare try to improve on my handiwork. "They won't notice," I said, unconvinced.

I went over to the tall chest of drawers belonging to Grandpa, the true focus of my investigation. An old, two drawer shaving mirror perched on top of the chest. The mirror's glass reflected dully and looked as fogged as Mary Browning's eyes. I picked up a shaving mug from in front of the mirror. The stand's surface let go of it reluctantly; it made a soft, breaking sound when I picked it up, leaving behind a dry, soap ring for a footprint. The bristles of the brush in the mug were frozen in old soap and dust allowing me to hold the mug by the handle of the brush. I replaced it on its ring. Nothing else sat on the top of the chest. I opened the shaving mirror's little drawers. The first was empty except for three pennies and a pearl handled pocket knife with a broken blade.

The other drawer rattled as I slid it open. It held two, old lighters, neither of which would light, a pocket watch without a chain—I thought it was neat—another pocket knife, this one with a wood casing and two broken blades, a small amount of change, a tie pin with a gold "S" on it and a silver fountain pen.

I thought the pen was neat too. I wanted to take the watch and the pen just to look at them for awhile. I wondered if either one still worked.

I shut the drawer. A few seconds later I opened it again, took out the watch, and slipped it into my pocket. The other drawers contained just his clothes, nice shirts with collars that he never wore. Two closet doors waited for my inspection, but my time was running out. If I got caught in one of their closets, no excuse would be good enough.

I opened the nearest door expecting to walk into a dark closet and stepped into another small bedroom. The narrow room had one window, a small bureau and a single, post bed. A pair of Grandpa's jeans hung over the foot of the bed. On the bureau lay fingernail clippers, a brush, a brown medicine bottle without a label, a dog eared John Deere catalog and Mama's wedding picture in an ornate, white frame.

I'd seen this photo before with dozens of other family pictures under the glass of Gramma Ruth's coffee table in the living room. Before I could snoop further, the spring of the front, screen door let out a warning squeal for me. I beat a hasty retreat to my room, but no footsteps sounded on the stairs. I wanted to go right back to search the little, secret room—a secret to me at least—and, too, I knew I should return the watch.

Behind my own closed door, I pulled the gold timepiece out, awed by its intricate hands, large roman numerals and porcelain face. The crystal was only slightly scarred and still clear. Five fifteen, the watch insisted. I wondered how long ago that five fifteen had been. The watch went back into my pocket. I wanted to examine it some more before returning it. It probably held no clues to the mystery of Grandpa and Kate; I just liked it. In the evening, I took a plastic sandwich bag from the kitchen, placed the watch in it and buried it under the porch, supervised by Zeke, who found my activities very puzzling.

*

A few days later, BobbyCat showed up while I swept the porch. We exchanged "Hi's". I kept sweeping. Zeke came from under the porch to greet BobbyCat, who took longer to pet him and scratch behind his ears than he had before.

"Did you carve your initials on your slingshot?"

"Not yet."

"It's a good idea, it is, really. I might do it too."

Gramma, wearing her grass stained apron, came out on the porch. "Keep the broom down, Sarge. Just sweeping the dust into the air doesn't accomplish a thing. Might as well have Zeke fan it with his tail."

"Yes'm."

"Howdy, Miss Ruthie."

"How are you, BobbyCat? Looking forward to school?" Gramma managed to smile at BobbyCat and frown over my broom handling at the same time. "Why don't you boys come down to the garden with me? Sarge, you're more useful there than around the house."

I didn't argue with her, setting the broom aside immediately. BobbyCat brought her tool tray and I carried the watering bucket. We followed Gramma down the trail, not speaking much to each other. I wondered if he still thought about Ranger. I didn't know what to say to him.

"How is everyone?" Gramma said entering the garden. BobbyCat and I looked at each other. "Not near as hot as I've seen it," she said.

"No, ma'am it ain't, not really it ain't," BobbyCat said, thinking Gramma had been talking to him.

She went right to work, breaking up the soil around the zinnias. I began picking wilted flowers and yellowed leaves from wherever I saw them. BobbyCat followed me around or, rather, his whisper followed my ear, telling me how weird and spooky graveyards were and how he'd seen this movie on Midnight Madness, "where this vampire comes outta the grave with a wooden stake in his chest, but he could still move on accounta' they missed his heart when they did the hammerin."

I told him, "There's no vampires here."

"How do you s'pose they could miss his heart?" he asked.

Gramma worked on the side of the garden where the markers were only flat, rust colored rocks standing on edge. None of these little stones had writing on them. Gramma Ruth stopped her work and began pulling one of the stones forward. I ran over and pushed from the other side.

"Keeps wanting to fall over," she said, grunting.

With my foot, I pushed earth against the back of it and that seemed to do the trick for awhile.

"When your grandfather and I first came here most of the red stones had fallen over. We were very young, younger than we thought we were, and had such plans." I could see the years falling away in Gramma's eyes. They weren't focused on the stone nor me nor anything in that present.

"Especially your Grandpa, 'We're gonna do this, Ruth, and we're gonna do that, Ruth.' To his credit he built this place up just like he said he would. We'd been walking all about the farm. Charles's chest pushed out in front of him. Rooster strutting his yard. He told me what's going to be where. We stopped right about here. 'This'll just be part of the cornfield,' he said, looking out over the fields with dreams in his eyes, 'No one comes out here to visit these graves.' And all the while he was saying that, I was busy propping up these stones. He saw me, shook his head with his hands on his hips, then came over and helped." She looked at me now. "Just like you came over and helped, Sarge."

I thought about asking her then about Grandpa's mysterious visit to Kate's marker a week ago.

BobbyCat walked cautiously around the mass grave. He nearly tiptoed, probably scared he might awaken any vampire whose stake wasn't placed just so. "Reckon no one knows, since there ain't no name an' all, who's buried here, huh, Miss Ruthie?" BobbyCat lightly touched the stone Gramma and I had just straightened.

"Luther is buried here, BobbyCat."

In surprise, BobbyCat peeked from under his white bangs at Gramma, not daring to ask the same question I didn't ask when similar information was first imparted to me.

"Luther was a thief," she announced. Her eyes shifted from BobbyCat to me. I thought about the watch buried under the porch; my heart raced.

"Luther stole from anybody. But mostly he stole food, chickens, hams, melons, anything he could light his quick hands on from neighboring plantations. A slave who found his spool of thread missing would cast a suspicious eye at slick Luther. Then that very night, maybe, there'd come a knock at his door and Luther would be standing there with his big mouthed smile and part of a ham or something for him. You couldn't hate Luther for too long."

Gramma, BobbyCat and I huddled around Luther's marker like campers at a fire. The rough facets of the red stone made an old, dull flame in the sunlight. The warmth of this fire radiated a feeling kinship between the sleepers and myself, a bond stoked by Gramma. It felt natural and comfortable and I did not question it. Once faceless and nameless, the sleepers were now my heroes. They were my ancestors, given substance by Gramma.

Gramma Ruth told BobbyCat and me about many of Luther's adventures. This Robin Hood slave had experienced harrowing close calls, eluding detection and capture by the fat of his shadow. As it turned out, Luther and I had something in common. He too buried his booty. (*When Gramma mentioned burying loot, I knew she must've known about the pocket watch, but she continued the story without a blink and I started breathing again.*)

Luther would return from his all night forays usually just before early morning roll call. His family and friends would shuffle slowly from their shacks; dragging their feet, they'd pretend not to have heard the slave driver spit their names, bringing the driver's ire down on themselves all in an effort to buy Luther more time. He'd bury his goods nearby to be retrieved later, and waltz into slave row, smiling broadly, winking at his conspirators.

Luther, loud mouthed and bragging among his own kind, could become as silent and ethereal as his own crouching shadow. Nature had built Luther for stealth with an ebony body to blend with shadows, a wiry, nimble frame to slink around corners, and alert, active eyes able to discern, as Gramma said, "a black cat in a coal bin on a moonless night."

Julie and Zeke joined us somewhere in the middle of Gramma's storytelling. We listened attentively, enthralled by Gramma's tales. When she finished, we thanked her.

BobbyCat said, "You sure can spin a yarn, Miss Ruthie."

She and Julie went back to the house together.

BobbyCat began discussing what we might do with the rest of our day. He wanted to hitchhike to town to play the new pinball machine at Twenty-Four Hour Carol's. I just shrugged. He could see I wasn't in the mood for pinball.

"My treat. I got some quarters off of Ellie's dresser," he said. "Well, what do you want to do?"

"I know a mystery, a real good one, too, I think," I said to him before I even thought about saying it. I walked over to Kate's stone then gazed up the trail. Gramma and Julie were long gone. I whispered anyway. "Gramma knows about Luther and he don't even have a name on his stone."

"This place is haunted, ain't it? That's the mystery ain't it? I knew it."

I told him he'd been watching too many spooky movies. "The mystery is here," I said pointing to the baby angel then lowering my finger. I whispered again, "Gramma knows about everybody buried here except this little baby named Kate."

"I got no use for dead people, none at all." BobbyCat kept glancing around. He genuinely seemed nervous. I could see he would be no use to me in solving the puzzle. "You ain't thinkin 'bout diggin nobody up, is you? Ghosts don't take to that sorta thing. An' Miss Ruthie would have you stripped of your black hide for sure. An' if I helped I'd be a little, white throw rug in a corner somewheres is what would happen."

"Never mind, BobbyCat," I said, but I was disappointed in

him.

We had to shoo Zeke away a few times, something I always felt bad about doing, but if we went hitch hiking he could not come along. We hit the road, a narrow, cracked highway which led to town, eventually, after rounding every hill or farm it came near. We hiked on the road's rocky shoulder, sometimes on the road itself when the shoulder played out for a stretch. I followed behind my friend, not feeling too enthusiastic about going. BobbyCat kept his thumb perked up and hanging over the pavement even with no car in sight.

"My daddy says if you want to get picked up you got to walk like you really wants to get somewhere." BobbyCat walked backwards now to talk to me, but still displayed a thumb to the empty road. "Daddy says you look suspicious if you ain't walkin. I always walk, I do. Never stand still. My daddy says people want to give you a ride, you just gotta give 'em no reason not to is all."

High overhead the sun bore down on the road and us. There were long stretches through open country without trees for shade. I was getting tired of hearing Bailey's advice on hitch hiking. I thought that BobbyCat sure did quote him a lot, considering last time they were together they'd gotten into two fights. I had never hitch hiked before. I recalled my parents had forbidden me to ever try it. "You never know who you're getting in the car with. They could be kidnappers," Mama had said. I smiled realizing this opportunity to go against them had been my only reason for coming along.

A few cars and trucks zipped by us. BobbyCat would stick his thumb toward them as they passed as if trying to hook the brass ring. When a green pickup rumbled by us, he began to shout and curse and stomp about. He kicked at rocks and generally acted like a lunatic. "That was the McEachern's actin' like they don't know nobody!" he said. "Can't even give a body a ride into town an' you know that's where they's goin."

"Maybe they're going someplace else."

BobbyCat looked at me as if I'd told him pigs can fly. "Naw, it's just that some people put on such airs. That's what it is, really.

An' Mr. McEachern owes my daddy for two days of well diggin. Daddy was s'pose to dig the whole thing for him, but wanted some pay for the first couple of days an' tight ass McEachern says he'd only pay for a finished job. My daddy tells me, if Old Mac ain't gonna pay for two days he know he ain't gonna come across for the full thing so he quit."

We stood along the road awhile, BobbyCat seething, me surprised at the extent of his temper. Now neither one of us felt like playing the new machine at the truck stop.

"Some people got airs," he repeated.

I just nodded, poking at a rock with the toe of my sneaker. I thought it best not to say anything to him for a bit.

"Let's go over my place for awhile," he said, "fuck pin ball."

"And Old Mac too," I said just to be agreeable.

"Yeah, fuck Old Mac too!" He ran away from the road and I raced after him.

*

It took a half hour of tramping through the woods to get to the Baileys' trailer. The only thing changed from my last visit was the increased amount of vines and weeds covering the dead cars. Ellie's Corvair was parked out front.

"What is she doin' here?" BobbyCat said upon seeing the car. "She's the one who said she wanted to work days."

The idea of seeing Ellie Bailey again excited me. I felt just a bit ashamed. I hoped she wore only her bra like last time. Since then I'd had various fantasies involving Ellie and always she wore just the bra and her tight hip hugger jeans. In the fantasies, which always left me feeling guilty, (*Ellie was, after all, my friend's mother!*) she would be cooking dinner for me in the kitchen of her trailer.

I'd be sitting at a table in the middle of the kitchen watching her go from sink to cupboard to stove. (*In reality there was no room for a table in their tiny kitchen.*) She'd set a hot plate of food down in front of me saying "Careful it's hot." (*I always liked that touch, "Careful it's hot." It turned me on for some reason and I thought it a very clever piece of double entendre.*) She leaned over me when she said this and the softness of her brassiere-covered breast would lightly graze my cheek. That would be more than both of us could stand, evidently, because I would jump up from the table upsetting my chair and she would give me this ferocious, very unmaternal hug. My face would be pressed into her cup-covered bosom. She'd cry my name, or moan it, "Sarge, Sarge," over and over again. I'd be rubbing up against her now, then a few moments later pull down the bra and watch her dark nippled breasts pop free.

My fantasies didn't go much past that. At that age there were still gaps in my knowledge. But Ellie had awakened a desire for discovery. I looked forward, very much, to seeing her again.

BobbyCat entered the trailer with me following close behind. He mentioned something about lemonade and oranges and then called out, "Ellie, what are you doing home?" He went into the kitchen.

I stood in the ring, the small, living room which previously hosted the Bailey/BobbyCat wrestling match.

"Shut the fuck up," I heard followed by shuffling up the narrow hallway. When she saw me she said, "Sorry, Sarge, didn't know we had a guest, but Mr. Bobby Bailey been given a lot of lip lately." She wore a dull, washed out, purple tee shirt, no bra this time, and jeans. She was sock footed, but the socks were threatening to come off, making her toes look long and crooked. Her hair clung limply about her face and she seemed tired or drunk or both. She'd brought an odor with her, or rather, I hadn't noticed it until she shuffled into the living room and I spotted the homemade cigarette she pinched between her thumb and finger. I knew what it was immediately. I'd seen some high school boys in Munich passing one around.

"I know what I smell," BobbyCat said jumping from the kitchen. He reached for the joint, but Ellie held it away from him.

"Not with the grief you been given me, no sir. Act like a body can't be sick from work, Jesus H. Christ."

BobbyCat bit his lower lip, obviously regretting what he'd said. "Did you call in?" he asked.

"Yes, I called in." She brought the joint to the pucker of her lips and inhaled. Her chest rose. Her nipples poked against the tee shirt, giving me fuel for a whole new set of fantasies. I think I inhaled and held my breath along with her.

"Can Sarge an' me each have a jay? One apiece? Come on, Ellie."

Ellie giggled, then laughed. Her red eyes watered. "Give Sarge grass? I swear Miss Ruthie and all her kin would hunt me down an' shoot me like a dog." She laughed some more.

I thought of Ranger from her remark. I watched BobbyCat's face for a reaction, but all I saw there was scheming and a funny desperation that kept his eyes locked on the joint no matter where Ellie moved it.

"C'mon Ellie," he whined.

"Not good for a young boy." Ellie smiled, enjoying teasing her son. "Make you grow titties," she said. "Did you know that, Sarge?" She reached out and pinched my chest right on the nipple. "Colored boys do blush!" She laughed, not realizing she'd made that discovery before.

I grinned and crossed my arms high up on my chest. I didn't care if she gave us the joint or not, but I was curious and figured smoking a reefer would make up for not getting to hitch hike.

"Just one then." BobbyCat kept up his whining and Ellie just laughed and blew smoke in his face which he tried to inhale, which made her laugh more.

"Okay, quit bein a big baby." Ellie dug into a front pocket and produced another, slightly crumpled joint. I couldn't figure out how it had survived intact in such close quarters.

"All right!" BobbyCat snatched it from her.

"Where's your manners?"

"Thanks, Mom." BobbyCat emphasized 'Mom'.

"Welcome, son." Ellie giggled.

BobbyCat and I drank water from the kitchen faucet then dashed outside with the joint and a book of matches.

"C'mon, Sarge, let's take this trip in the van."

We climbed into the back of the vine covered van which sat ensnared with four other rusting wrecks behind the trailer. The van had been gutted out and nothing but the front two captain's chairs remained. I sat in the dusty, ripped driver's seat and gripped the steering wheel. Fat, dark green leaves of old, king-sized weeds and white splotches of bird splatters obscured the view through the wind shield. The dust in the van made me sneeze. Little spiders marched across the speedometer. A hole in the floor right under the clutch gave a view of the oil soaked ground beneath the van.

"This is neat," I said.

"Yeah, my home not far from home," BobbyCat said. He struck a match, but didn't light the joint, just watched the flame fade into a thin curl of smoke. "I'm plannin to put a mattress in here or a sleepin bag, I'm thinkin really. Cause sometimes I can't stand goin' inta that goddamned trailer. Sometime I go in there an' I think the air is gonna turn inta poison an' gag me. I swear I do." He lit the joint and dragged off it. He squinted as he handed it to me. "Here, it's pretty good."

I didn't take it right away. My parents hadn't specifically talked to me about drugs, but I knew they disapproved. Mama would be angry, but she was in Louisville, having abandoned me to the farm. I took the joint gingerly, maneuvered it so that my thumb and forefinger pinched just the paper skin as Ellie and BobbyCat had done. I didn't want to embarrass myself. "It's been a long time since I had a hit," I said in my best casual, sophisticated air.

"Yeah, right," BobbyCat said, "Well, don't pull a lung full til ya start coughin an' pukin your insides up. Just suck in a bit, just a bit and hold it in."

I did. My insides came up anyway. My lungs felt as if they'd been stirred with a hot, dirty poker. Tears raced down my face and I shook with big, hacking coughs.

"Yeah, must've been awhile," BobbyCat said.

I thought I still held the joint, but looked through watery eyes to see him toking on it again.

By the time I was ready for a second hit, less than half remained. I had a far less violent reaction the second and third time.

"I don't feel different," I complained to BobbyCat. I was

disappointed.

BobbyCat squeezed my arm with his three-fingered hand. "Yeah, you feel the same to me too."

We both laughed.

I grabbed the wheel again and pretended to drive. We bounced in our seats, evidently the road was bumpy or the van's shocks were shot. I turned left, we leaned right. I turned right, we leaned left. BobbyCat supplied the squealing noise of our tires cutting the turns. Left, right, left, left, right, we swayed, almost falling out of the seats, and laughed. One of us got mixed up and we bumped heads. We laughed some more.

"Step on it!" BobbyCat shouted. He made some wailing noises which I couldn't figure out right away. "It's the county mounties. They musta smelled the pot as we drove by. Oh, shit!"

"Oh, fuck," I said and it felt good to say, so I said it again, "Oh, fuck," and giggled. I floored the gas pedal. "Errr! Errr!" I supplied the sound of the engine racing.

"They're gainin'! An' look," BobbyCat said pointing at the windshield, "it's raining birdshit!"

I tried to make louder Errr's, but was laughing too much. BobbyCat raced to the back of the van and opened the door. "Pa kow, pa kow," he said shooting a loaded finger at the cops. He staggered back to his seat laughing. "They got me," he cried. "These are some fast damn growing weeds," he said looking out the window. "They kept up with us the whole way."

I hadn't realized how hot it had been in the van until we finally climbed out. We were hungry. BobbyCat hadn't eaten all day and his stomach was growling. I hadn't eaten since breakfast and by now it was twilight. We went into the trailer to search for food. Ellie had gone back to her room and fallen asleep. BobbyCat checked the refrigerator and the cupboards, turning up nothing edible.

"Pot gives you the munchies, you know. I sure hope we didn't just get high off the grocery money," he said into the refrigerator on his second survey.

"Gramma set a pot roast in the sink to thaw this morning," I told him. "She usually puts carrots and potatoes with it. You can slip a fork through her roast. It's so tender."

"Jesus."

"Yeah, and, of course, there's rice and greens, and biscuits."

"Oh, shit," BobbyCat said slamming the refrigerator door closed. He put an arm about my shoulders. "How do you s'pose a body can get invited to one of Miss Ruthie's sit downs?"

I shrugged. "You got to know a member of the family, I guess."

"Right on, Sarge! Let's go." He flew out the trailer's door and over the steps with a whoop.

"Ain't you gonna tell your mom where you're going?"

"Pot roast!" he exclaimed.

\*

Despite our hunger and BobbyCat's enthusiasm, we did not run the couple of miles to the farm. The high from the pot had dissipated, leaving both of us, I think, to churn in our sobriety. We were quiet for a long while, walking around the trees, avoiding the trails for some reason. I thought about the boy, two or three years older than me, who walked a couple of yards ahead. I admired his independence, and self-assurance, even the way he talked back to his parents. He reminded me of Huckleberry Finn. (*I hadn't read the book, but must've seen a movie about Twain's character.*) BobbyCat did not let his parents hurt him; he fought back. I wanted that for myself. I told myself if I were in BobbyCat's situation, I would act as he did. In point of fact, I had already chosen the BobbyCat career path. He lived without regard to the clock or rules. I wanted that freedom. Our circumstances were really not that different. Ellie and Bailey were divorced. Mama and the Major, I was convinced, were getting divorced. Ellie left BobbyCat to fend for himself. She didn't seem to care where he went or what he did. My mother didn't seem to care what I did. The similarities scared me and the only person to blame seemed to be Mama. She had taken us from the Major. She had left us on the farm. I didn't remember the Major and her arguing as BobbyCat said his parents constantly did. I thought everything was fine even while Mama helped me pack my suitcase for our visit to Kentucky to see her parents. Not that, I said to myself, everything was fine. I just didn't perceive any problems. Mama and the Major. I thought of them as a set, a constant, not people, and certainly not people with problems of their own. Together, they anchored my world and protected me from the real one. Not until the quietness of that drive to the airport had I suspected that something was wrong, really wrong. Not until the airport had I known it.

What was going on? I did not think I had done anything wrong. What was Mama doing to us, and why? Perhaps BobbyCat had never had to wrestle with this problem as I had. He had grown up more quickly, realizing long ago that his parents were just people.

I had a big advantage on my country friend. Gramma Ruth, my ally. I trusted her and no one else. The Major was too far away and Grandpa too full of mystery. And my Mama. "My Mama didn't even call us this week," I told BobbyCat.

"She's lookin for a job right? Wish she done took Ellie with her, really." BobbyCat stopped on the edge of the woods. A field lay before us and the open purple sky. Across the field that gently sloped up away from where we stood, lay the McEachern farm, small with distance, looking empty with dark windows. BobbyCat kept his eyes trained on the house and barns and silo. "Ellie's got men problems around here. Damned if she don't bring them on herself, my daddy says. Course he would. Wish we had another joint, don't you?"

"Who do you like better? Your Mama or your Daddy?"

"What would it matter, Sarge," he said glancing at me momentarily then returning his eyes to the farm. "Can't sell one off or nothin."

"What are you looking at? What's out there?"

"That's Old Mac's place. Ain't nobody there, I'm thinkin."

"So?" I could guess why he eyed the McEachern place, but I thought if I made him admit it aloud then, maybe, he couldn't do it.

"He owes my daddy over a hunnert dollars for that well

diggin.  An' he owes us a truck ride.  C'mon, I want to check it out.  I don't see his pickup nowhere about."  He started across the field in full view of the purple sky and the owls, crows, and gray squirrels who hid behind the tree tops' leaves.

"What do you think you're going to do?" I asked, not moving from my spot.

He turned to face me, but walked backwards away from me. He held his palms out.  They looked very white in the gathering, evening darkness.  "I'm gonna look around is all, really.  If you're too chicken shit, then stay right where you are."  He turned toward his objective, but then spun about again.  "I'm just curious is all. I'm gonna scout it out."

"Like Luther," I said, but I didn't think he'd heard me.

"Hell, Luther would steal and Miss Ruthie thought he was a cool guy."  He headed determinedly across the field now, his back and shoulders daring me to follow.

The farm stood quietly, seemed to fairly wait for us, looking like blocks of dense shadows in the lesser darkness.  Across the field, between us and the farm, stretched a fence coming late to my vision, growing from obscurity to dominate the field like a great brick wall around a football stadium, or a stockade fence belting an old west cavalry post.  It was actually just cage wire, and overgrowth, four feet off the ground, not at all a strong enough fence.

I ran after BobbyCat, but slowed to a walk still several feet from catching up to him.  I thought I would just look around, despite what BobbyCat decided to do.  My heart revved with the same fear and excitement it had the day we'd stolen the inner tube. I didn't want BobbyCat calling me chicken shit.  Chicken shits could not survive parents abandoning them.

BobbyCat came to the fence, and negotiated the rusting strands with liquid ease.  He'd moved so quickly, I failed to see how he had done it and stood baffled by the obstacle for some reason.

Down the fence, a shadow, almost perfectly a part of the dark, hunkered low by a reclining fence post.  A black arm waved once for me.

Luther. I could discern him from the shadows of the trees that lay across the field only when standing inches from him. Stripes of scars like the tattoos sailors wear, crisscrossed his bare chest and arms. He showed me a brief, white fire smile.

"Luther!" I whispered.

He leapt like a panther onto the lazy fence post then bounded over the top wire to land soundlessly on the other side. I did likewise, then the two of us sprinted to catch up to BobbyCat. Suddenly, I was no longer afraid, or only a little bit. This felt like adventure now; forbidden and dangerous, dark, Luther doings. We came to the first barn. BobbyCat walked around it, but Luther flattened himself against its rough, scratchy wall. I followed his expert lead.

BobbyCat looked back. "Ain't nobody here, you know." But his low whisper said more to me than his words. He gazed this way and that in the middle of a triangle whose points were the barns and the house.

Luther crept to the edge of the first barn staying as tight against it as its old paint. He knelt in the weeds growing along the wall, feeling their stems crushed under him. His eyes flicked, assessing the situation. No pickup truck in the bald part of the yard next to the house where Old Mac, evidently parked it, no lights, even on the porch. Luther placed an index finger to his lips, smiled behind it, and beckoned me to follow. He darted to the second barn, a quick glide, reminding me of the slick, chicken thief Zeke and I chased several nights ago.

"Sarge, where ya goin?"

Luther disappeared into the other barn. The door, off its track, leaned against the barn to one side. I followed after the master thief. BobbyCat's shadow slipped over mine. Starlight pitched black, elongated images of everything to the back of the barn.

"What's in here?"

Luther'd already cased the place, finding nothing but the same kind of stuff Grandpa Standard stowed in his barn, the same clutter, the same moldy hay smell.

"He's got two milkin cows in the other barn," BobbyCat said.

"We oughtta let 'em loose. McEachern'd have a fallin down fit is what would happen. Damned heifers prob'ly wouldn't wander too far off though."

Luther glared at BobbyCat. He thought the white boy talked too much and was too loud. Luther knew if we were caught, BobbyCat's punishment wouldn't be as bad as it would be for us niggers. Luther feared BobbyCat's loud ways would get us the whip for sure.

BobbyCat walked deeper into the barn. Luther crept to the doorway, breathing the fresher outside air, squatting just out of the moonlight.

During one of his expeditions, Luther had wormed his way through the tiny window of a curing shed. As soon as he pulled his shoulders and chest free of the little opening, allowing his lungs to expand, he inhaled the sweet smell of curing hams and hickory smoke. Inside, he'd nearly cried at the sight of so many haunches of meat, hanging by rawhide thongs from the rafters like ripe peaches in an orchard. His mouth watered. When his lips parted spittle flew out from the back of his throat. He wiped his chin with the back of his hand, entranced by the amount of food dangling above him.

He had known hunger many times. The portions of meal and peas doled out by the overseer never filled the empty ache in his gut. He figured that, as a boy he'd been hungry every day of his life.

Luther remembered the day Captain Spencer Hayman stood on his back porch and tossed a steak bone, still raggedly dressed with plenty of red meat, to his dog. Luther had raced the dog for the bone, across the yard with all his young speed. He ignored Captain Hayman's gruff voice and the angry growl of the speeding dog, and stretched out like a diver going into a pond for the bone. The race was a tie. As Luther grabbed the bone, he felt it nearly yanked from his grasp by the dog whose bared teeth clamped hard to one end of Luther's prize. A tug of war ensued. Luther pulled. His sole focus became the bone. His hunger urged on his efforts. Luther did not know if the Captain had remained on his porch to witness the battle. His concentration spiraled into a sharp single mindedness as pointed as the dog's. However, a distraction blunted his resolve, leaking in faintly through his ears. He heard laughter. He turned to see the white children of the manor laughing, pointing at him and slapping their legs, having to lean upon one another to keep from falling down.

Humiliated, Luther eased his grip and the dog jerked the bone away. Luther watched the dog lift its head in victory and saunter off with the prize. The children laughed more than ever.

Whenever Luther, the man, thought back to that day, he became bone-shaking angry, not because he had wrestled the master's dog for a bone, but because he had let the white boys and girls, whose opinions of him were already fixed and locked, shame him into letting go. He vowed to his roaring stomach that night never to let go again.

So, silently, he cried at the sight of all those hams. And he smiled thinking of the tummies he could fill with hot ham back at slave row because of his skill and daring. Luther wondered if he could carry three, though even two would be a burden, violating his rule never to take more than he could swiftly carry.

Yet Luther had already broken one of his strictest rules, never linger at the scene of the crime, steal and run. In fact, he had completely forgotten this rule until the creak of the shed door instantly reminded him. The door opened just enough at first to allow yellow lamplight to stream through and the gray-blue barrel of a musket to poke in.

"Who's in here?" Luther heard. "Ah'm fix ta put a ball in yo hide."

Luther leapt straight up just as the door swung fully open. He grabbed one of the wooden beams the hams hung from and pulled himself up into the rafters away from the light. Now crouching on all fours on the narrow beam above the hams, Luther could see the man, rather he could see a ragged, broad brimmed, gray hat and a pair of hunched shoulders, cautiously enter the shed. The musket led the way, seeming to stick out, from Luther's vantage point, from just under the hat like a long, iron nose.

The lamp swayed in the man's nervous hand making the black, bulbous shadows of the hams swing to and fro on their thongs. The man went to the little window Luther had squirmed through and stuck his head out, peering in one direction then the other. He muttered to himself. Luther could not hear him plainly. His knees began to hurt from bearing all his weight on the narrow, hard beam. He feared he would lose his balance.

"Jes try'n take me hams," the man said and began a furious whisper and Luther realized the man was counting. Only the hams themselves, the lamp's weak light in the smoky shed, and the brim of the man's hat were saving Luther from discovery. The man seemed to count over and over, never satisfied or unable to arrive at the same number of hams with each count. He circled, the light, the hat and the musket moving around the shed slowly.

Luther trembled on the beam. It dug into his hands and knees, shooting pain through his tensed arms and legs. Every muscle wanted movement, cried for relief. He would have to move soon, if he still could, or he'd fall from his perch to the waiting musket below.

But the old man (*Luther had determined by the farmer's voice he was old*) would not leave. Something, a noise? Scuff marks at the windowsill? Maybe just his own farmer's stubbornness told him he had an intruder. He would not believe the inconclusive evidence of his own eyes. He would not leave. The count finally satisfied him and he quit circling. He stood in the middle of the floor directly underneath Luther then eased himself to the ground to sit with his legs crossed. He rested the rifle across his lap.

Luther figured the man wasn't leaving any time soon. He began to slowly stretch himself out along the beam. He slid his hurting knees and feet backward and his hands forward, fighting to maintain his balance. Inwardly, he cursed the man with the old musket and he cursed himself too for being so foolish.

Luther, he told himself, you in it now. Dey gonna whip de skin offa you til you no mo' a nigger. And then Luther wanted to laugh, wondering with his skin gone what would he be then. A long splinter sliced deeply into his palm as he slid his hand forward. He gritted his teeth against the pain. His eyes remained trained on the rumpled hat below. Finally a bit of relief came. He stretched out on the beam, evenly distributing his weight. His wounded palm continued to pain him.

Dis white man gonna hang you up like one of his hams, Luther, he told himself. Far from his own plantation, he began to worry about the time being wasted. He had to make roll call. He thought of untying a ham and dropping it on the farmer's head. He liked that idea because then he could take the ham and run. That would be a tasty ham indeed. But he feared the man would hear him working on the tight knots, plus he feared that with his wounded hand he might not be able to manage it at all.

The man below removed his hat to wipe at his brow. Luther tensed. He had felt safe with the hat between the man and himself. Please don't let him look up, Lawd, Luther prayed. The man had dirty brown, long hair with only a bit of silver on the sides. He appeared not to be as old as Luther had supposed. He flirted with the notion of leaping upon the man, but too many reins held him back. The height worried him; he might hurt himself in the fall before he could hurt the man. His bleeding and swelling hand placed him at a disadvantage too. Plus the noise it would take to simply gather himself up for the leap might alert the pig farmer. The farmer would only have to turn his rifle upward and Luther would fall right into the blast. Still with all these arguments dissuading him from action, his desperation would have pushed him to it if not for one final barrier.

The man below was white. He could lie to a white man, steal from one definitely, but could not touch one and much less hit one. Luther felt shame. He had always wanted to fight one, had bragged to his fellow slaves that if the overseer ever set aside his whip and pistol, he could take the measure of him, beat him soundly.

Stretched out on the narrow beam, Luther faced the truth that he had been lying to himself. No daring set him apart from the other slaves. He only skulked, and bent, and hid better than most. He could not fight this white man. If the man got a good look at Luther, he could hunt Luther down, search him out even if he managed to escape that night, he could even insist that the Captain kill Luther. So if they fought, it would have to be to the death, and Luther could not manage it, even in his head.

The pig farmer put his hat back on. He fiddled with the lamp on the ground in front of him by wiping the built up black carbon off its glass. He patted the shiny stock of his rifle. He obviously expected the intruder to return that very night and intended on being present to greet him.

Luther watched him. He was conscious of time moving, not in minutes and hours, but in the darkness he could see through the window. The sun would be rising soon, slowly, yes, but rising against him, rising to make him late for roll call, rising to show the pig farmer the thieving nigger who'd been right above him all along.

After awhile, Luther noticed the man had not moved. But he noted it dimly because Luther himself was falling asleep. He caught himself once, as his mind had almost slipped away. The prospect had sent his heart racing and shocked him back to alertness. Luther had spent a long, tiring day in the fields worming tobacco before going on this expedition. The sun had been hot and the rows of green leaves miles and miles long. He had not gotten enough to eat, had in fact, given a portion of his noon day meal to a pregnant slave girl who had not moved quickly enough to the chow line to get her own meal. Luther had been mad at her because, usually, expecting girls received the biggest portions.

His hunger prompted this foray though he was tired at the outset of it. Now his weariness caught up to him. Sleep stole upon him as furtively as he stole upon chicken coops in the night.

The impact woke him up. He heard a muffled, brief cry right before or right after the crash and knew, somehow, despite his initial disorientation, it had not come from him. He looked up at the empty beam that had been his hiding place and saw wildly swaying hams. Then he felt the potato bag lump beneath him and scrambled to his feet. The pig farmer lay unconscious next to his crumpled hat.

Luther would laugh, jump, and howl until his cheeks and ribs hurt later over the fortunate and funny outcome of his dilemma. To most, he would tell how he'd jumped the white man and knocked him unconscious with the stock of his own musket. He would tell this lie so often that in his old age he confused it with the truth. To a few close cohorts, he would tell the truth like a confession and his telling of it was not funny at all.

He leaped upon two hams, let his weight snap the rawhide thongs. Steal and run. With this second chance, he did not violate his rules. Except that as he slipped out the doorway with each arm encircling a ham, he glanced back at the farmer and the musket, both untouched by him.

I squatted next to Luther at the open doorway of the barn. We waited on BobbyCat to finish his search. We both grew impatient with him. Luther and I remembered the rule, never linger at the scene of the crime, steal and run.

"Hey, Sarge, check this out," BobbyCat called.

"Shhh! Shush!" I said probably louder than he had called me.

"Well come on back here then."

Luther and I shrugged our shoulders and went back to BobbyCat.

He'd found two fishing rods and reels, expensive looking ones, and a tackle box full of fuzzy, fake fish, plastic mosquitoes, and red, rubber worms. "Too neat not to keep," BobbyCat said.

"You can't," I said. "You said you were gonna just look around."

"McEachern owes my family."

"I know." I waited awhile before saying anything else. He played with the rods, pretending to be pulling in a monstrous catch from somewhere in the back of the barn. "It's just that—" I hesitated, worried about his quick temper. "It ain't right and we could get in trouble," and I quickly reminded him again, "you said we were gonna just look around."

"We ain't gettin in no trouble cause we ain't gettin caught. Didn't you hear Miss Ruthie today? Luther stole all the time. He didn't get caught; she talked him up big, Miss Ruthie did."

"But Luther only stole food."

Luther didn't say anything. He stood behind me like he was my shadow or I was his.

"What do you think I'm gonna catch with these, Sarge? Mink coats? Look at all these lures."

I dropped to one knee and reached toward the box. I wanted to pick up one of the fake fish, but worried about the hooks. I couldn't see them clearly. Then, suddenly, I could see them all, every barbed hook and every blind-eyed lure. The entire barn filled with light as if lightning had flashed nearby. But this light remained, and grew brighter.

"Shit, McEachern!"

Two burning headlights charged the barn. The only way out was to run directly at them. I shut the tackle box and snatched it up. BobbyCat yelled for me to run. I seemed caught in the light for a moment, but Luther shoved me forward. I shielded my eyes with a forearm and raced with Luther and BobbyCat to the barn's entrance and the headlights of Mr. McEachern's pickup. I thought we were going to be run over.

"He's gonna hit us!" I shouted. But even as I said it, I heard the truck's brakes squeal and the tires sliding in the dirt. BobbyCat went to the left. Luther and I went right, grazing the bumper of the truck as I exited.

The truck's door flew open. A big, snarling man leaped out.

"Come here, you thieving son of a bitch."

I ran between the two barns and down the hill. I could hear the man's rapid, train engine breathing right behind me along with his heavy footfalls slapping after me. He wasn't shouting now, needing all his air just to breathe. I ran in a panic. The fence Luther and I had jumped grew nearer. Luther sped yards in front of me. I felt a hand fall on my shoulder, grabbing a fistful of my tee shirt. I screamed and fell forward, breaking his grasp and tumbled down the hill for several feet.

The box crashed and rattled but my grip held. I managed to gain my feet without loss of momentum and raced away parallel to the fence into the woods. I glanced back to see McEachern bent over, hands on his knees, gasping. I'd caught up to Luther now. We ran through the woods for several minutes before daring to stop. When we did, I thought about going back to see about BobbyCat.

I supposed he'd made a clean escape with rods and reels, since Old Mac, who ran pretty good for an old man, had decided to chase me instead of him. Luther grinned at me and winked. For him, not getting caught meant victory.

He trotted away from me, looked back long enough to wave and see me hold up my hand, then slipped away into the blackness beneath the trees. I remained in that spot in the safe darkness for awhile sitting on the tacklebox. I didn't want it, didn't know why, when gripped by the truck's lights, I'd grabbed it.

Just as my heart finally calmed down and I'd gained control over my breathing again, I heard a voice and the soft crackle of footsteps in the woods coming toward me. I froze. Between the narrow, black tree trunks, I spotted BobbyCat's shiny, blond hair. He'd already spotted me, and was saying something about close calls, quick feet, and what Old Mac owed his daddy. I left the tacklebox there for him and took off after Luther.

*

"You're late again, Sarge," Gramma said.

Grandpa Standard, Julie, and she sat at the dinner table in the middle of their meal.

"Kenny, don't you know to come when you hear people calling your name?"

"I didn't hear you, Grandpa."

Julie said, "I'm going to tell Mama."

I put my hand close to my chest where only Julie could see it and gave her the finger.

"I'm going to tell her about that too," she said and went to buttering a biscuit as if my fate had been decided and she could now return to her meal.

"Someone is going to mop the porch tomorrow, clean out the coop, wash Zeke, he's starting to stink, and, let's see, I might as well get something out of this, mop the kitchen too, Sarge." Gramma looked at me to see if I had even the slightest protest.

Julie giggled.

"Yes, Gramma," I said.

"Now wash up for supper and be quick. You're a mess. There's burrs all over you. And here's some good news, your

Mama will be here tomorrow, phoned Charles to come pick her up."

"So if you want to drive in to Louisville with me you're gonna have to get up early, same as me, to get your extra chores done."

I headed upstairs. "I don't want to," I told him.

I did get up early, as Grandpa had suggested, but when he drove away to get Mama I continued mucking out the coop. I chased out the hens, collected the eggs, raked out old hay, feathers and droppings and hosed the floor down. BobbyCat, I figured, was probably at a lake or stream somewhere casting his line far out into the water. I tried to decide what I thought about our robbery. I balanced the inarguable wrongness of it against BobbyCat's justifications. "He owes my daddy anyway," BobbyCat had contended or something like that. By the time I'd completed putting fresh hay in the coop for the hens to nest in, I'd decided I really didn't care one way or the other.

Once Luther had been called down about his thieving by a slave preacher from another plantation who was allowed to come to the Hayman plantation about once a month to give the blacks there the good word. The Negro preacher would always have to give his sermons twice, first to the Captain and then to the slaves. He had to get Captain Hayman's okay for everything he said. Even then, an overseer would be on hand at a discreet distance to make certain the sermon the preacher delivered to the slaves was the same one he'd given to the master. "Don't mention Moses," the Captain would tell him. "Slaves get riled up when they hear about them Jews fleeing Egypt. No Moses." So the slaves wouldn't receive messages of deliverance just calls to duty and sacrifice, plus a lot of the Ten Commandments.

While referring to commandment number eight one day, the preacher had pointed a finger straight at slick Luther. His reputation, amongst the blacks at least, had spread to neighboring plantations. Some slaves on these plantations had been falsely accused and severely punished by their masters for missing chickens, hams and melons. "Thou shalt not steal! The Lawd done said. It's a sorrowful wrong. Goin 'gainst the word is to suffer damnation. Do you understand, Brother Luther?"

Luther was angry that the preacher had singled him out, especially with a driver listening not too far away. He stood and flashed a smile at the congregation. He waved his hand around him to indicate the slaves who watched him now.

"We slaves, preacher man. De God who wrote dat was talkin to free men not slaves. Slaves ain't got no rights. An' when you ain't allowed rights, you can't do wrongs."

Gramma said what Luther meant was since he was suffering such a grievous wrong, nothing he did could tip the scales against him. He could not be held responsible because he had not been given responsibility for himself. "You wouldn't hit Zeke for making his mess in the kitchen if you didn't let him outside, would you?"

Somehow, while moving the chairs off the porch in order to mop it, I applied this bit of Luther philosophy to my situation. My crimes were not my fault. None of this would've happened if Mama hadn't abandoned the Major and abandoned me. I had no rights, how could I do wrong? Like Luther, I could not. Along these rational lines, by the time I'd filled the cleaning bucket, I'd just about absolved myself of guilt.

I slapped the porch with the heavy, soaked mop sending water running away in every direction until channeled by the cracks in the floorboards. I heard the pickup truck grinding up hill, but I kept my eyes on the soapy water. Grandpa had returned with Mama so soon? Don't look her way, I told myself. I pushed the mop across the boards. Just say hello and keep working like you're real busy.

Gramma came out to the porch drying her hands with a dishtowel. I told myself, don't let her make you give Mama a hug this time. Gramma said, "Well, hello, Mac, now how am I lucky enough to get a visit from you?"

My heart raced up to the same number of r.p.m.'s it had when the headlights had snared us in the barn the night before. Now my head jerked up.

"You're using too much water, Sarge," Gramma said.

Mr. McEachern climbed out of his pick up leaving the door wide open. He walked to the edge of the steps. He wasn't smiling and I saw Gramma's smile fade too. "Ain't no social call I'm 'fraid, Miss Ruthie," he said.

Gramma went to the edge of the porch, but didn't step down. I couldn't see her face. I squeezed the mop handle.

"I got robbed last night, Miss Ruthie. They took all my fishing gear. One of the rods Claire just bought me for my birthday. Only used it once. Cost her dear, I'd bet."

I didn't know what to do. I didn't know if I should keep mopping as if the matter did not involve me, or if I should stop and listen casually as anyone would listen to a story of a neighbor's misfortune. I wasn't sure what casual listening looked like. Do you nod? Or just say, Hmmm?

I thought about leaping the porch railing and skying out of there, but that is simply an inarticulate form of confession. Maybe right away I should've blamed BobbyCat; everything had been his idea. In the back of my mind I could hear my mother saying, "If BobbyCat said jump off a cliff, would you?" Thus destroying the blame-the-other-kid defense. In the end, I sort of moved the mop with timid half-strokes while eyeing first Old Mac then Gramma and back like a spectator at a tennis match.

Gramma said something about how sorry she was to hear that, then told Old Mac that Edie Spelman thought someone had broken into her boy's trailer just a week ago. She shook her head. "Crime's everywhere."

"But I know who took from me, Miss Ruthie." Old Mac's pink face grew darker. I could tell he was having difficulty saying what he'd come to say. Now he glared at me and his lips tightened under his white moustache.

I dropped my eyes to his hands, wrestling with each other in front of his stomach.

"What are you thinking, Carlton McEachern?" Gramma said. Her voice rose. "Maybe you better say what brings you here."

"Now, Miss Ruthie..." I think he looked toward me for help. He wanted me to be less of a coward than he was. He wanted me to admit it, but I was much more of a coward than either of us knew. He waited, saw I would not speak.

"Your boy here, Ruthie, 'long with Bob Bailey's boy from down Route Four, stole my fishing gear from my barn."

"Not Kenny," Gramma said immediately, adamantly, so much so I was at once ashamed of myself. "Kenny is a good, well behaved, young boy, brought up right."

"You ask him."

"Do you have some proof for me, Carlton?  Or are you supposing?"

"No proof. You ask him." He pointed at me, angry now and no longer timid. "I came to you, Ruth, cause I knew goin to those poor trash Baileys over yonder weren't gonna do no good. But I knew you'd do right by me. I ain't callin no sheriff's office. I just want the rods and reels and my tackle box. Had everything in that tackle box."

"You saw my boy do it? You saw Kenny?" Gramma reached back for me and pulled me along side her as if to give Old Mac a better look. "Be careful now, you know we all look alike."

Her fingers dug into my arms.

"Now see, Ruth, that ain't called for. You know it. I ain't never been like that. See, y'all always have to bring that into it to hide behind. Now I admit it was dark, but it was him. He runs with that one handed, white-haired boy don't he?"

Not releasing my arm, Gramma looked me directly in the eyes. Her eyes were bright and fierce, but I saw faith in them too. Faith in me. "Sarge, did you do any stealing with BobbyCat?"

I was going to tell the truth until I saw her eyes. She trusted me. She was ready to tell Mr. McEachern to get the hell off her property and take his damn lies with him. I did not want to let Gramma down. I shook my head.

"Say it."

"No, Ma'am."

"Do you have anything belonging to Mr. McEachern?"

"No, Ma'am." I said this more forcefully, I thought, since it was actually true. I looked to see if she believed me. I realized right then, I needed very much for her to believe in me.

"Mac, there are other boys in these parts."

He didn't say a word at first, just eyed me, tried to get me to at least admit silently between him and me that he was right.

I wouldn't give him that. "I haven't been over your place, Mr. McEachern." I sounded, I thought, very innocent even, maybe a bit sympathetic.

Gramma put her arm about my shoulders.

"The Standards ain't no better than the Baileys," Mr. McEachern said. He kept shaking his head all the way to his truck and probably kept on shaking it as he drove down the trail.

Gramma looked at me again, briefly, when dust all but obscured the exit of Old Mac's truck. Her eyes were different and totally unreadable. Her arm fell from my shoulders. Without a word she returned to the house. At that point in my life, I'd never felt lower nor more disappointed in myself.

*

I was under the porch when Mama returned. I saw her, or rather her legs since Grandpa had parked so close to the house. Her black high heels went up the stairs followed by Julie's sneakers and Grandpa Standard's roughed up work boots. I'd been inspecting the pocket watch. It no longer worked, was no more a timepiece than any other antique. I wanted to return it, undoing the one sin I could undo. I placed it back in the plastic bag and re-buried it, determined to restore it to its proper resting place as soon as the coast was clear.

They went inside. Through cracks in the floorboards, I saw Grandpa trying to keep the screen door open long enough to wrestle Mama's bloated suitcase through. Julie came back out five minutes later calling my name. I enjoyed ignoring her. I enjoyed letting Mama wait. I crawled over to Zeke and scratched behind the collie's ears. After Julie gave up, Mama came out.

"Ken doll!" she called. I rolled my eyes.

I heard Julie say from inside, "Mama, he doesn't like to be called that anymore. Call him Sarge."

"Sarge? Oh, yes. Hope he didn't hear me." She laughed. She was in a good mood. "Sarge!"

I remained Luther quiet.

I missed something by staying out there with Zeke. I came in the house during the aftermath. I'd expected everyone to be at the table getting ready for supper. Gramma would be checking the stove while Mama handed Julie the forks and knives in order to set the table. Only Gramma was in the kitchen, though, washing a saucepan in the sink, paying more attention to the pot than seemed necessary.

I walked by her to peek into the living room. Grandpa sat in his recliner in front of the television. The set was on. I could tell by the gray-blue light brightening and dimming on his face and in his eyes. The volume was too low for him to possibly hear it. I saw the TV light shift in his eyes. He'd glanced at me then returned his eyes to the set.

"I don't know what you're becoming," I heard Gramma's voice from behind me. I turned around, but she still faced the sink and the little kitchen window. "I know you hear people when they call. You know better than to not answer up. Could be they call you for something important." She said this flatly, without anger or frustration. She continued to scrub the same clean pot.

I didn't say anything. She had not asked me to say anything. For a moment all I could hear was water in the sink and the low drone of the TV.

"Your mother is up stairs. Of course, you know this too. Do you think it might be nice if you went up and said hello? She's got news for you."

I didn't move. Mama had caused this. Her news had ruined supper and sent Grandpa to his recliner and the TV. It would not be good news.

Gramma turned away from the sink, leaving one hand in the water, the other, she wiped across her apron front. "I declare I don't know what you're becoming," she said again and seemed to wait for a reply, but I didn't know what she wanted.

She's starting to believe Mr. McEachern, I thought. I began backing away from her. The thought that Gramma Ruth might know I lied to her terrified me. I backed out of the kitchen and fled up the stairs. Mama's door stood half-open. As I crept by it, I could see her on the bed examining some papers with the end of an ink pen dangling like a cigarette between her lips. I slipped by without her noticing, heading toward my room until Julie came bounding up the stairs.

"Mama, Kenny is here," she announced.

I glared at her.

"Don't worry," she whispered, "I didn't tell her what a jerk you've been. I just say I will to get you to act right. Go say hi; she's got news. She found a job."

"Kenny?" Mama called. "Is that you? Come here."

No more postponements were possible. My shoulders slumped. Julie called me a jerk again and went to her room. I went into Mama's room about two feet within the doorway and stopped. Papers lay in a fan on the bed around her. Her lips still held the pen until she saw me and let it fall to her lap. She held her arms out to me, but I didn't move. After a moment, her arms fell back to her sides. Her attention seemed to return to the forms displayed in front of her.

I knew I'd hurt her.

"Just wanted to make sure I still had a son. I do don't I?" Her Afro was gone; she'd straightened her hair. She must've noticed me looking at it. "Part of your mother's new look," she said, patting her hair. She sighed. "All these forms. Number of dependents, number of deductions... I thought they were the same. Health, catastrophic medical... I'm a little lost. Julie told you I found a job didn't she? I'll be working in the registrar's office at the University of Louisville. I can take night classes myself. Employees get four free credit hours per semester, I think. First, I have to fill out the rest of these insurance and benefit forms." She smiled through her complaining, obviously excited about having a job. I didn't want to be happy for her. "They are so complicated and too important just to fill in anything. All these little, demanding boxes!"

Just ask them right out if they're getting a divorce, BobbyCat had advised me. "You and the Major getting divorced?" I asked. I crossed my arms, maybe held my breath. I'd actually asked. I braced myself for the answer.

Mama looked up from her papers and looked at me hard,

studying me in order to decide something. "Come here," she said.

I came to the edge of the footboard, still out of her reach.

"Kenny, I don't know," she said.

This was not what I expected. How could she not know? It was up to her; she had left the Major.

"Even grown-ups don't know what they want or what's going to happen all the time," she said. "I was trying not to tell you or Julie until we knew something for certain. Your daddy loves the army—"

"It ain't the Major's fault."

"No, it's not. Don't think we can point the finger at anyone for this mess, Ken Doll. Sorry, Sarge, right?"

"We could have stayed in Germany 'til you figured it out. The Major's all by himself."

"Things weren't good there. I'm not sure how I can explain this." She took a deep breath. I waited for her. "I don't know what you're old enough to understand, young man. Like I'm not old enough to understand this fine print." She placed the forms she held on a stack with some others.

"Let's see. When I was a girl, Sarge, this farm made up my whole world for a long time. And in that world was your Gramma Ruth and Grandpa Charles and all our animals, we had more animals then, and not a whole lot else. I had a quiet childhood. For two years in grade school I was the last kid on the school bus. The driver was this skinny, little, white woman named Shirley. I don't remember her last name, but I can still picture her bouncing up and down behind the big, black wheel of that bus. After dropping off the other kids, and just she and I were on the bus, she'd dig into this wicker basket under her seat and bring out a cup cake or a brownie for me. I enjoyed talking to Shirley very much. She was a sweetie. After Shirley and I had gotten to know each other awhile, she started asking me about my family life and about Mama and Papa. I think she wanted to know if they were good to me, or bad like some parents are.

"'Constance,' she said, 'I usually only see a little picture of you in my rear view mirror, but I think its an accurate picture. Looks to me like you're being squeezed real small. You look to me like a girl under a lot of pressure. And it sorta seems to press down a bit firmer the closer we come to your farm.' That's when I really started to think about what I'd been feeling. See I used to pick berries with Mom, and fish with Dad and he'd take me to the movies in town now and then, but Mom wouldn't come along. And me and Mom would go shopping, but Dad would be out in the fields. Never the three of us. I got one or the other, never both. I can't say how I came to know it or Shirley came to see it, but I was under pressure. I came to think of myself as the glue that held the family together. I thought Mama and Daddy stayed together only because of me. I figured if I wasn't a good girl and didn't do everything just right, one of them would leave. I used to dread going to school because while I was away something bad might happen that I wasn't there to prevent. And I dreaded coming home because all the burden of keeping my family together would be heaped on me again. I finally went away to college. Nothing happened. They've been married forever. I don't know what I sensed, what scared me. They don't show each other much affection, never did."

Mama and her talk had been wandering away from me. She seemed to have drifted into a past she'd not considered in a long time. Then her eyes focused on me again. "I didn't want you and Julie in that kind of situation or anything like it. Real or not. Understand?"

I nodded because I knew she wanted me to.

"I think you do!" she said. "Now you're a sergeant, right? And sergeants don't have to worry about things that haven't happened yet."

I suddenly felt too old for my parent's games. I wasn't a corporal nor a sergeant or anything like that. But my nickname was already stuck to me by then. It seems in all the misunderstandings between my parents and myself, they assumed I was younger than I really was.

"I know you don't like being cooped up on this farm, Sarge, but that's taken care of. I found an apartment in Louisville near campus. Well, not too far. We're leaving here this weekend."

I took a swipe at the papers on her bed, sent some of them

floating to the floor.

"What do you think you're doing, young man!"

"You didn't ask if I wanted to come to this farm. You didn't ask if I want to leave. You didn't ask if I wanted to divorce the Major. And then you go off and leave everybody."

I started to cry which made me angry because I didn't want to. "You think I'm stupid. But I ain't. You're gettin a job and an apartment because you're gettin divorced just like Ellie. If I know that how come you don't?"

I ran to my room and slammed the door shut despite her calls for me to come back right this minute, and her shouts about raising my voice.

After I'd been in my room a few minutes, a soft knock came to my door. I did not answer it and whoever it was did not knock again.

*

Since, at this point, I had lied to, hollered at, or stolen from every adult around, I planned to stay in my room the eight years and two months until my eighteenth birthday then just saunter unfettered away. It was a glorious plan with just a few shortcomings. I set the plan to motion and endured my self-imposed solitary confinement all the way to eleven o'clock the next morning. Hunger would've driven me out anyway. I'd missed supper the evening before, but, at my window, I saw BobbyCat and Julie in the back of Grandpa's pickup. I had to find out what was going on.

They sat on opposite sides of the truck bed pushing against each other with their feet pressed sole to sole in some silly struggle. Julie giggled. I couldn't figure how those two got along so well. Their game ended when I ran up to the truck.

Seeing BobbyCat gave me an idea. I would have to steal the fishing gear from him. Luther and I. I'd return it to Mr. McEachern then tell Gramma the truth. I couldn't bear facing her with my lie strung out like a spider's web between us. With just two days left on the farm, I'd have to move fast.

Julie said, "Mama's going over to K-mart to get some things

for our new place. She's going to drop BobbyCat and me off at the library. We—"

BobbyCat interrupted her. "We went down to Miss Ruthie's garden lookin for you. Where you been all morning?"

Julie playfully hit BobbyCat on the top of his head, the result being he grinned as if the smack was a kiss. She said, "No we didn't! I knew you were laying low in your room til the heat was off. Won't do any good. Mama's going to swing away on you 'til her arm gets tired. She told me she had to cool off because anything she did now wouldn't be legal in most states."

"She did not."

Julie smiled. Trying to get me to squirm brought her such pleasure. "BobbyCat told me you guys' secret."

"BobbyCat!"

"The one about the baby Miss Ruthie don't know a story for," he said quickly.

"Oh."

"How many secrets do you have?"

"Just the one," I said.

"Yeah, just one," BobbyCat laughed. "Get in, Sarge. Come with us."

I shook my head. With BobbyCat gone, it would be the perfect time to steal the fishing gear back and make things right with Gramma.

"We're going to the library to find out about Kate," Julie said.

"Kate ain't in no book," I said.

"The librarian will know where to look," she said. "Wouldn't it be great to be able to tell Gramma a story for once?"

I climbed into the truck.

Mama stepped out of the house wearing red framed sunglasses. She gazed up into the dull sky and put the glasses in her purse. "Everyone ready," she said. Just as she pulled the driver's door open she pointed a finger at me. "Later we're having a talk, young man."

On the way into what passed for a town in that county, Julie and BobbyCat put on a show for me. Julie, as Mama, spanked BobbyCat with one of her sneakers. He, in turn, in the role of

Sarge, howled, squealed, and whinnied, and otherwise feigned pain. "Ohh! Mama! I know I got a lip on me, Mama! Ohh! Whatever I said I didn't mean it!" Julie spanked away. "What I mean, Mama, is I didn't mean for you to hear it, Mama!" When they were exhausted from fun at my expense, BobbyCat said, "Truth is I'm gonna miss you guys, I am really. It's gonna be a sorrowful situation." And he turned away from us for the rest of the trip in.

The first librarian had silver hair twisted and spun in a tight bun, which looked like a silver, inverted cereal bowl on the top of her head, but not the exact top. The bun drooped lopsided and BobbyCat kept pointing to it and laughing every time the poor woman turned her back. This did not put her in a helpful mood. She finally said, after closing an old book on county history, the library didn't hold such information and we should try the coroner's office.

Julie, undeterred, sought out another younger and friendlier looking librarian. Though she wasn't that much taller than Julie, she would bend to even eye level with my sister everytime she spoke.

"Bobby Bailey in a library," she said to BobbyCat. "Will wonders ever cease!"

"She teachers over at the school sometimes," he told me later.

Julie told the young librarian all about Gramma's garden and all the stories Gramma knew.

"Well, where did your grandmother find out about all the other... the other residents," she asked.

Julie shrugged. The lady looked at me and I shrugged too. Julie said, "I want to know about Kate because it would make a good school project." She turned to me and winked and I thought she wasn't so bad a sister.

"Well, we'll have to go to the County Office of Register of Deeds. Marriage licenses, birth and death certificates are kept there."

"Where's that?" I asked.

"Just across the street," she said and led us over there. To the bifocaled man behind the counter of the County Office of Register of Deeds, the young librarian said, "It's all quite a mystery because no last name is on the marker." She was caught up in the secret too by now. "Let's see, we know her first name, Kate. Year of her death, 1931. She lived just a week, poor thing. And given the type of cemetery she was laid to rest in, she was probably Negro." She said again, "poor thing," and shook her head.

"No problem," the man said and disappeared into a room in the back. It must've been a problem though, because a long time passed before he came out again. The young librarian said she had to get back to work so we thanked her for her help.

The man re-appeared finally. "Not much to tell kids. "Kate died ten January in thirty-one of crib death it says. Just five days old."

"What's crib death?" Julie asked.

The man looked at Julie and said in a soft voice like maybe the voice he used for his own daughter, "Oh, honey, the baby didn't hurt or nothing. Sometimes babies just go to sleep and don't wake up. No one knows why. It don't happen often, though."

"What was her last name?" I asked.

"Father's name's not listed. Mother's last name was Wolfork. Can't make out the first name. The records are old, worn, and we had water damage three years ago. Kate's last name is Wolfork."

"Wolfork," I repeated. Somehow, right then, it made me feel better to think Kate had a last name. She had belonged to someone for awhile.

BobbyCat said, "I don't know any Wolforks around here, Mister, you?"

The man shook his head.

Mama was waiting for us across the street when we stepped out of the county deeds office. She told us to climb into the cab because it looked like it might rain. Julie sat next to Mama. I sat at the window with BobbyCat between Julie and me.

Mama asked us what we were up to at the deeds office.

Julie asked, "Mama, do you know any Wolforks around here?"

"Sure do," Mama said, "You do too. Your Gramma Ruth's maiden name is Wolfork."

# PART THREE

# IX

## The Road to Damascus

This is my grandfather's story. Long ago, he told it to his young girlfriend Ruth, who, a lifetime later, would relate it to me. For the sake of understanding him, I tell the story now. I have considered it often.

In 1928, Bismark Standard took his Power of the Holy Ghost Revival Show on the road. He brought his youngest son, Charles, with him; the older boys, Ash and Junior, remained behind with their mother to take care of the farm. Bismark, a sharecropper, raised green beans, corn, and mustard until he stumbled "down the road to Damascus" one afternoon while plowing his fields. He had literally tumbled over his plow and into that end of the mule by which it gets its other name. "I had been startled by a voice so clear I could not refute it," he later told his family, and abandoned both plow and mule to the field and ran to his home and his Bible.

The Power of the Holy Ghost Revival Show traveled the narrow backroads amongst and over the foothills of eastern Kentucky and western Virginia, stopping in minute, black communities along the way—sometimes playing to just one or two families. Bismark and Charles journeyed in a creaky, short bed wagon, made by Bismark and Ash, and drawn by two shaggy, hard working, farm horses. The wagon bed carried the revival tent—a patchwork of canvas and burlap sacking—the stakes; the altar, also made by Bismark; a six foot, white cross, which Charles would plant at the tent's entrance way; Bismark's long, white cotton robe made by his wife, Mercy; one large canvas bag serving as luggage for both man and boy; and a sack of horse feed.

The most precious cargo rode on the bench, between father

and son, a red leather Bible with a broken brass latch. The book —that particular copy at least—often carried in a cotton sack, contained undeniable power. While it sat on the bench near his leg, Charles half expected to see it burn through the sack like his mother's iron through a shirt when heated red hot and not given its due attention. He always unpacked the Bible last, recovered it first at the end of a show, and handled it with fear and awe.

"The holy words in this book have the power to change a man's soul," his father would tell him, "strike you blind and send you down your road to Damascus. Praise Jesus!"

At fifteen, Charles had no desire to be struck blind nor to have his soul changed. He wasn't sure just what a soul was, but he felt comfortable enough with the one he had. Nor did Charles wish to venture to Damascus. He little enjoyed traveling with his father and did not wish to journey to a place as far away as Damascus. (*He knew it was far because he'd never met anyone who claimed to be from there.*) Consequently, Charles approached the book and its well-thumbed and ruffled pages with trepidation and fear if not plain terror. For years it was the only book he knew existed and he could testify to its curious power.

\*

Before he could read or understand the concept, or was allowed to go to school, he bore witness to the book's sway over his father. He'd watch his father hunker over the pages set between the unsteady lights of two candles for long hours, reading a verse aloud every now and then, without warning, in a booming voice that startled everyone in the room. The book transformed a stern, but kindly father, who fretted constantly over the crops and the bills, into an evangelical elocutionary; harsh, and ever ready to condemn.

On rare occasions Junior, and sometimes Ash, could escape their father's tirades by remaining late in the fields or fleeing the house just before the mood would fall on Bismark. But always Mercy and Charles felt the full brunt of righteous wrath and flecks of spittle that sprayed from the angry man. He would stalk from wall to wall, seeming, to Charles, to double or triple in size, shaking the flapping pages of the good book at his family, threatening them with its power.

"The wages of sin is death, Romans the sixth, the twenty third. The unrighteous shall not inherit the kingdom of God, first Corinthians the sixth, the ninth! I cannot save you. But with the Holy Ghost you can save yourselves!"

And Mercy would offer a soft spoken, well timed, "Amen."

Charles would nod vigorously and clasp hands right on the spot, but if he prayed for anything it would be for his father to calm down and let them all go to bed.

Lying awake in bed after a particularly long and harrowing sermon, Charles watched his oldest brother slip open the single bedroom window and climb back into the house.

"I didn't think he ever gonna finish tonight," Junior said closing the window after himself. "I could hear him in the outhouse, an' clear to the shed so I went down the trail, stoppin ever five or so feets." Junior laughed. "You know I heared him all the way clear to the pond!"

Charles asked Junior how he knew to get out of the house, how he knew one of their Papa's sermons was coming on.

"You ain't figured that out yet, boy?" Junior laughed again.

Ash was wide-awake now too, and joined in. "I done been knowin that. Just can't seem to get away quick enough though."

"I shouldn't tell you. Cause if'n we all get away, he's sure to come huntin us then. See, tonight was look like the well might be goin dry. See an' befo that it was Mr. McCutchan sayin' he gonna be givin less for green beans this year."

"An' fo' that," Ash offered, "that dang mule took sick for a spell."

"See, boy it's weight," Junior said at last. "The weight of you an' me, an' the mule, the weight of that cracker McCutchan, and the farm, the weight of the whole world. Just watch it build right on Papa's shoulders. You'll see it an' know when to clear out."

Charles often thought about what Junior said, not truly understanding it all. He knew his brother wasn't entirely correct, though, because he had not mentioned the power of the book.

That Bible held the blame somewhere on its thin pages, amongst its narrow columns and tiny words. He promised himself he would one day come to know the power of the red leather book or he would destroy it.

His mother would not comment about the book's effect on Bismark's behavior. Once, when Mercy and Charles were alone in the house, he told her how scary he thought his father's preaching seemed. "Only the unrepentant need fear the word of God, Charles," she replied. "Your father is concerned with our salvation."

But this is what she said in the light of day. During the evening sermons, her face, her eyes revealed the fear she had as her husband paced wildly in front of her, shaking his Bible as if to shake something from it or dispel an evil in the air around him. The pages would flap like a panicked bird snatched in mid-flight. And Charles knew she, too, was frightened of that book.

Charles had not expected his mother to say anything more than what she had. Mercy was a quiet, almost mousy, woman who rarely scolded or praised or made any sound, a laugh or a cry, without being conscious of how it would be received by those around her. She had her own demon of which Charles learned and this kept her introverted and within herself.

She loved her sons. Charles was certain of this. The boys often competed for her affections, especially Ash and Charles. Her love came through her hands. She squeezed Charles's hand in hers when the family would say grace before supper. She would ruffle his hair playfully or, when he was worried, touch the side of his cheek and briefly smile in a way that said to Charles, *between you and me everything is going to be all right*. When he shared these secret moments with his mother, he worried less about what the book said, or what his father had divined from its pages.

Mercy was the third of seven daughters born to a beleaguered, Maryland man who was desperate to marry them away. Her courtship with the much older Bismark Standard lasted nearly three months with both the father and the beau cajoling her toward marriage everyday of it. She relented and agreed, wanting as much to escape the family and her crowd of chatty sisters as her father eagerly desired to see her go. The day after her wedding the couple set out for Kentucky and she immediately missed the closeness of her sisters. But she had married also out of a sense of duty to the family. Her absence gave them one less mouth to feed at a time when money and jobs were scarce. So she did not complain about her lot—marriage to a man she respected, but did not love—nor did she protest the move, which she was belatedly informed of on her wedding day.

Mercy, the quiet sufferer, came to believe complaining to be selfish and evil, and to silently endure a gift and a virtue. In this way, she consoled herself on the bleak and isolated plot of land Bismark sharecropped. Five years after the birth of her last son, the illness, nameless and mysterious, came upon her. She mentioned the shakes to Bismark just once, after she had lived with it a full year and had tried every remedy learned from her mother or hearsay. The shakes, as she named it, frightened her. She wanted to see a doctor.

In the days before the voice spoke to Bismark in the field, she might have been given a chance for a visit to a doctor. But concerned with the loss of money and time a doctor's visit would make, Bismark said, "Let's hold off and see how it goes. Sound like it might be just one of those woman thangs."

His answer made her embarrassed that she had brought it up to him. She promised herself not to mention it again unless he did. He never did.

So Mercy Standard endured the illness that gave her body uncontrollable tremors and grew more vicious and lasted longer with each episode. (*In the wake of Bismark's sermons, she came to believe the illness her personal curse. Like Job, she would demonstrate her patience.*) The shakes might attack her at anytime, beginning with a shiver, as if she'd been suddenly exposed to a chilling draft. She was usually alone in the house with the men out working or, if not, she found ways, more clever than they had to be, to dismiss herself from the room. At its worst, the illness violently shook her body, sent her in and out of consciousness, denied her control of her water, and caused her to bite her tongue. Warned of the onslaught of her curse while in bed, the small woman would slip from the sheets and Bismark's back so her shaking would not disturb his sleep.

One night Charles crept from the bed he shared with Ash, having heard a soft, steady rapping. He went cautiously to the back door, holding in front of him the wavering light of a small oil lamp. No one waited at the door. The unabated sound lured him into the kitchen. The tapping came from the other side of the closed pantry door. The sound lacked urgency. The monotonous persistence was not a request for release or attention. It was not a chief activity, but the by product of another action. Its odd, unbroken regularity reminded him of the tapping of a woodpecker he'd heard while on early morning trips through the woods. This mystery frightened him only a little. Likely, some animal had gotten itself caught in the pantry. And when Charles recalled his father had placed rat traps in there, the answer to the mystery became clear; some small animal had been snared and its twitching limbs were beating against the pantry door.

Thus fortified by the soundness of his deduction he laid a hand on the pantry's doorknob. Keeping his light high in front of him, he pulled the door open and thrust the lamp into the cold darkness. His mother lay in a jerking curl on the floor in a puddle amidst upset bottles of preserves and pickles. Her quivering knee had been making the rapping at the door. The twin odors of vinegar and urine filled Charles's nose.

"Mama?"

Mercy seemed on the edge of consciousness, perhaps aware of the light revealing her, but not its source. She looked up from her spasmodic knot and Charles stepped back when he saw the blood and spittle bubbling over her chin. She thrust a shaking, open palm at him as if to warn him off. He stepped back again, still amazed and in shock. Long moments passed before his wits returned. He dashed to the sink and pumped water on a cloth, mindful of the noise he made. Instinctively, he'd decided not to call his father for help. He knelt down beside her, held her up— she only trembled now—and wiped her face. He asked her in whispers what was wrong.

When Mercy's full awareness returned she felt the familiar

embrace of her rocking chair. Near the stove, it was the warmest spot in the house. A blanket covered her. A single, low light sat on the cupboard near the pantry where Charles finished mopping the pantry floor.

"Broken pickle jar," he said, seeing her watch him. He asked again what was wrong.

She stood, wrapped herself in the blanket and clutched it tightly in front of her. She went to Charles and caressed the side of his round, lamp-lit face. Nothing was said. Charles's only answer was her touch and for the boy who adored his mother it was enough. She left him to clean up the pantry and he made quick work of the task, armed with the secret the two of them shared.

Their relationship changed after that night. Charles appointed himself his mother's protector, a role he found comfortable, satisfying and zealously guarded. He watched her at the dinner table, and while she filled the lamps with kerosene, and mended clothes in her rocking chair. He remained in the house on Sunday afternoons when previously he would've been fishing at the pond or trying to tag along with his brothers when they went to town. In the fall and winter to follow since the mother and son shared their secret, he helped her through three more bouts with her curse.

Each time, he would hold her tightly to him, trying to absorb her violence, often inadvertently slapped and clawed. The boy would cry for his mother at these times because her metamorphosis from the quiet and benign to the frothing, unthinking animal frightened him. She never saw his tears though, for he would recover before she did. She, in turn, drew strength from her son and felt an unexpected relief in sharing the knowledge of her curse. She told him this one day as he helped her clean the ashes from the stove. Charles was thrilled. He touched her face, leaving a gray, black track of char on her cheek and, briefly, he kissed her lips.

*

On that early, spring day in 1928 when Bismark heard the voice and fell over the plow, Mercy suffered one of her attacks.

She had served her family a breakfast of gravy, biscuits, and ham and returned to her room to make up the bed when the shivering started. The men were heading out for a long day's work. Junior and Ash led the way and Charles followed his father through the doorway. He thought he heard his mother's voice faintly call his name. He wasn't certain; his mind had tricked him before as he lay awake in bed on vigil, listening for her call, a tapping, or some quick noise that didn't belong to the night. His mother's voice had caused him to pull in his fishing lines or to drop the hoe in the middle of the field, though reason told him he was too far from the house to possibly hear her. He'd raced home anyway, his name floating at him as a haunting plea.

When he heard her that morning, or thought he had, he looked to his father who kept walking, apparently hearing nothing. This is the power of our secret, Charles thought, it allows me to hear her when no one else can. He stepped backwards into the house then rushed to her room. Mercy stood in the midst of her tremors by the bedpost. She held tightly the blanket she had been spreading on the bed. It shook in her clutches like a shapeless beast trying to twist away from her. Charles closed the door behind him and crossed the room to his mother's side. He grabbed her just as her legs gave way beneath her. He couldn't hold her. They fell across the bed, Mercy's body jerking beneath Charles. Her mouth made harsh, clucking sounds.

"It's all right, Mama. I got you. I got you, Mama," Charles repeated knowing she did not hear him. Tears rolled from his eyes onto her cheeks tracking down to the corners of her mouth.

They continued to wrestle like that in a shuddering hug for long minutes. Charles fought against her tremors, knowing nothing else to do, feeling her body jerk and quake under him. The box springs beneath the mattress squealed at the abuse. He tried soothing her by humming in her ear. The unpredictable snaps of Mercy's head made this impossible, but the humming was more for himself just as a scared man whistles when walking at night. Charles sagged with exhaustion when the kneading grip of the curse finally left Mercy.

He lay next to her, close enough to see her eyes still twitching behinds their lids, and pulled in deep breaths of air full of the smell of her. He examined her peaceful face then kissed her once and then again, first tenderly on her forehead and again on her nose. He kept one arm wrapped about her waist, feeling, from her body to his, the rise and fall of her chest become steadier and steadier. He did not want to relinquish her, break the warm bond that held them together, but finally he did and sat up on the bed in time to see the narrowly opened bedroom door being pulled shut.

In the early evening of the same day, Junior discovered the mule and plow alone in the field. The mule had traveled scarcely ten yards on its own, plowing one erratic furrow perpendicular to the rest. Junior returned the mule to the shed that passed as a barn, fed and watered the perplexed beast, and returned home for supper. Charles scrutinized Junior's face when he stepped through the door just as he had Ash's and his father's. Bismark had returned from the field earlier than usual, while the sun still shone overhead. When Charles scanned his father's eyes searching for a hint of knowledge of the secret he and his mother shared, he thought he saw something there. But Bismark brimmed to the eyes with his own secrets and Charles could not be certain.

Bismark had gone straight to his Bible and poured over it, his nose just inches from its tiny words, as close as the human eye could focus. In this rapture, he remained until Junior came through the door and the entire family was present. Bible in hand, he told them about "the miracle in the field," and what the voice had told him to do.

Junior glanced to Ash and Charles "What happened?" He mouthed the question then whispered to Charles, "I didn't see this one comin. Some bad thing musta happen. A big one."

Charles stiffened. Maybe a draft had closed the door, he thought, if not, wouldn't whoever had discovered them have spoken up? The wind closed the door. Again, he eyed each face around him.

"The Lord has directed me to be about his business." The Bible flapped through the air. "Sin, I have seen, is everywhere. Everywhere!"

The fear that his father might know the secret worried

Charles to no end; everything would be ruined. He might even turn the power of his book against them, changing their souls.

Mercy showed her usual, joyless smile, simply worn for her husband to express her tacit agreement. She said, "Amen."

"The Holy Ghost told Philip to preach to the Ethiopian eunuch. Acts the eighth, the twenty ninth. The Holy Ghost directed Simon Peter to tell the gospel to Cornelius, a Roman centurion, Acts the tenth, the nineteenth. If we all would but listen, we would hear the plan the Holy Ghost has for us."

Charles had not told his mother someone had been at the door, that another member of the family knew the secret that should have been theirs alone. He watched her nod at her quickly pacing husband who, at the moment, was not even looking her way.

"Amen," she said.

"The Holy Ghost stole the light from Paul's eyes." Bismark ranged from wall to wall, cornered. "Sent him to Damascus, and now, the Ghost has commissioned me in the Lord's army. I must travel throughout the hills of Kentucky and reveal to those who can not see the power of the Holy Spirit of Christ." And he glared directly at Charles when he said, "For evil is everywhere."

"Praise the Lord," Junior shouted jumping to his feet. Ash immediately joined him in a chorus of hallejulahs and amens. They lifted their hands and faces skyward, laughing in their hearts at the revelation that their father intended to be away from home for awhile.

Charles's subdued relief lived only briefly because Bismark next announced he would be taking his youngest son with him.

*

Mercy had actually approached Bismark and suggested that maybe one of the older boys might be better help for him on the road. She had worked herself up to it. First, she convinced herself Charles should stay home and, perhaps, continue school. But he should be near the farm. Then she pretended to believe her older boys, either one, deserved to get out and "see different things."

She discussed this with Charles and he waited for her to bring it up to Bismark. Finally, she did on the evening before they were to depart.

"The Ghost has laid it on my heart what to do and how to do it," he told her. And Mercy Standard, already wrestling with one curse, knew not to argue with the Ghost.

The day of the departure arrived. In front of the small, Standard home, the packed wagon and the nervous team waited. The horses bit at each other. Mercy and Junior came outside in the early morning's chilly mist to see the travelers off. Ash remained in bed, refusing to be roused from sleep any earlier than necessary. His father had not yet gone, but Ash's holiday had officially begun. Bismark clambered aboard the wagon. Already triumphant, he glowed with energy, checking the tethers and patting the holy cargo sitting at his side. He and Junior again went over a list of chores Bismark expected to see done when he returned. Junior probably began figuring this would not be the vacation he'd originally envisioned.

Mercy said goodbye to her husband and her youngest son, kissing each in turn on the cheek. Charles resented the equitable treatment. He searched her eyes for special acknowledgement of the keen sorrow their parting caused. No covert glance came his way as balm for his wound. She did nothing to indicate she felt as bad as he did.

Who will look after her now, Charles wondered regretting—a little—his selfish decision not to tell Junior about their mother's sickness. He climbed onto the wagon and sat next to the white sack, which held the Bible protecting its thin pages from the morning damp. The sack barely touched the side of his leg, yet he pushed it away against Bismark's thigh. Bismark called to the team flicking the reins at their rears. The wagon lurched forward; the crusades had begun.

*

Some of those remote farming communities peppered throughout the Kentucky hills welcomed the Standards, and others gaped at them curiously as if they were the tattooed man and the dog faced boy from a circus side show. Quite a few mothers herded their children into the tent, grateful for the opportunity to give them "some fear of de Lawd". The men would cross their arms and eye Bismark suspiciously. "Are you an ordained preacher?" they would ask.

"My license comes from the Holy Ghost himself," they would hear and the wildness of the light in Bismark's eyes would kill any of their prying right on their tongues. In the beginning, the tent went nearly empty and the congregations, scant handfuls, would dwindle as Bismark's belligerent sermon carried into the night. Charles, envious through and through, would watch the men, heads down solemnly, back out of the tent or the cleverer children worm their way under a tent flap as their mothers stared at the pacing, stomping preacher in front of them.

The women, who would remain for the entire sermon, Charles figured, did so out of fear of God. They probably knew about the soul changing powers of the book and had little more desire to be struck blind than Charles did. He also guessed that anyone else who stayed until his father's robe clung to his sweaty back and his voice grew hoarse, did so because they had done something particularly sinful that week or maybe that very day. Those people could be counted on for a little offering for Charles's hat when he passed it around—fresh tomatoes or cobs of corn were more likely than a nickel—and left relieved of guilt, feeling they had been punished enough for whatever transgressions they may have committed.

The people sat on crude benches, planks nailed to wood stumps, made by Charles and whoever he might find to help him or they brought chairs of their own. Charles would watch them enter quietly, eye him and the pulpit and take a seat. This was after having their hands squeezed by Bismark at the entrance way. The women would remove their men's hats and scold their children into behaving. There would be some laughter about what silly thing happened yesterday at the catalog store or some hushed snake-like hissing about you know who and where she was spotted Saturday morning. Bismark would wait at the pulpit until the last word was cut off in embarrassment and swallowed. The offenders hung their heads. And Bismark let the silence convict them.

The book's power shamed these strangers, made them behave like children caught at the cupboards. The first word out of Bismark's mouth let them off the hook and they looked up again relieved. They would exhort him in the beginning, hands waving in the air and beseeching God to bring down his power and Jesus to bring down his mercy. A few had brought their fiddles and tambourines, but the instruments remained silent unless jostled on a restless lap.

Bismark chastised and finger pointed and told these simple, farm folk—worthless sinners—that the path they trod led to damnation. Charles saw his father lose them. Their attention wandered. They heard, but no longer listened. Furtive whispering began. The men backed out; the youngsters crawled away if they could. Bismark railed on, sweating, expending huge amounts of energy, looking to Charles after the sermon just as he would after a long, hot day in the fields.

When Bismark's voice gave out, Charles passed his hat before anyone else could make their getaway. The revivals ended quietly, the folk escaped in silence and did not return the next night. Bismark would wait though, in the white robe Mercy had made for him. Charles would begin loading the wagon, not allowed to strike the tent until his father nodded and resigned himself that no one would return or, having heard tales of the angry preacher, dare venture in his direction. "It is a long way for some to walk. Maybe I should send you round in the wagon," Bismark would speculate on those second nights. But he never sent Charles on that mission. "These people are poor in spirit," Bismark finally concluded and Charles would pull up the tent stakes.

They moved on in the morning, the cycle repeating itself. The wagon bounced down narrow roads and strained over hills. They rode in silence, the father and the son, the thoughts of each a complete mystery to the other. Charles began to understand just how huge the world really was.

Despite himself, the unique newness that spread open for him around each bend in the road, like a fresh sheet snapped out by his mother for his bed, excited him. Whether it revealed a vast field or a tiny community of shacks with smoking tops nestled in hills, or the majestic blue and purple Appalachians in the distance ringing the edge of the world, or just another wooded hill to climb, Charles saw the wonder in it. Sometimes he dreamed of leaping from the wagon and racing away from the man, the book, and the Ghost, plunging across a great, bright field with the tall grass whipping at his legs.

In that space breathed freedom, no ties, no gospels nor testimonies, no chapters nor verses. His dream never concluded. He only knew he ran with all the strength of his legs and lungs and did not tire. But out there in the middle of the field, when the wagon and the horses were just dots trudging up a hill and the man in the robe could not be seen at all, Charles would remember his tormented mother shaking and crying his name. Only then, in his dream, did his pace falter and his chest begin to heave. And he would spin about in the very center of this wide openness realizing, at the last, he didn't know where to go or what direction to take. The wagon had long since disappeared, but Charles heard its creaking and the horses' monotonous clopping. He would open his eyes at these sounds and find himself sitting next to the man and the book.

Usually, it was not long before they found another small pocket of black humanity off a trail from the main road. They were sharecroppers, and miners. They were poor and had dirty, barefoot children who ran about laughing and playing games. After Bismark introduced himself to a few of the families and asked if they were in need of spiritual uplifting—he knew they were in need, he just wanted to ascertain if another preacher was roundabout—Charles would pitch the tent. The two would usually eat with one of the families. Some seemed truly honored to have a holy man at their table. Most gratefully shared what little they had with the Standards. Charles often felt guilty taking the food for many of these people were poorer even than his family. He also wondered if the women, who smiled and spooned the butter beans and greens onto his father's dish, would feel betrayed later the same evening during the sermon when Bismark accused them and everyone of "foulin God's air with their cussin, gossipin, and lyin."

"What if nobody wants to feed us?" Charles once asked.

"Then we shall shake the dust of the town off our boots," Bismark replied.

Charles did not understand, thinking, we'll still be hungry, dirty boots or clean.

*

The crusades lasted nearly three weeks before the pair completed an erratic circle through the Kentucky hills and headed homeward. Charles began to smile at last. He promised himself he would not go on another trip no matter what it took to get out of it. Besides, it should be Ash's or Junior's turn next. He thought he might pretend to be sick or maybe just hide in the woods in back of the house until his father gave up looking for him. But also Charles hoped Bismark would give up his preaching. The man seemed weary, his voice, now harsh and scratchy, had nearly played out. And no new souls had been added to the "roll that's called up yonders." Perhaps he will quit, Charles thought, and we can stay home and I can look after Mama.

Two days by wagon from home, Bismark picked up a white haired man who rode on the buckboard with him, relegating Charles to the back with the tent. The white haired man talked constantly and Bismark just nodded, wanting to save his voice and Charles listened not at all until his ears picked up the words "gatherin field." Charles caught his breath as the stranger spoke of a vast field where people came from "all abouts" to socialize, play games, and eat on the last two days of every month.

"An' dats to where Ah'm goin ta see mah son an' his new boy dats named fo' me," the white haired stranger told Bismark. At the direction of the stranger's pointing finger, Bismark turned off the main road down a wheel-rutted trail. He called encouragement to his tired horses. His voice sounded strong; he seemed invigorated. As Charles suspected, his reunion with Mercy would be delayed.

A few miles down the trail, the white haired man tried to get Bismark to hurry the tired horses. He leaned forward in the wagon and bit at his fingers. He rocked himself from side to side, and

Charles feared the man might rock himself right off the wagon.

"My boy, Grainger Jr. got a good farm, best in dese parts better'n many white folks'. Dey don't begrudge him none on account he work hard an' he help dem too. Ah woulda stayed, but mah wife's mama, truly mean spirited woman, took sick so now we live in Lexington, Mah wife thinkin' her mama gonna die any day now an' didn't want me ta come heres, but Ah say, nah, she gonna live on account heaven don't want her an' de devil couldn't take de competition." The man laughed and didn't seem to care that Bismark did not. "My boy got a nice, nice farm. We real close on to it now."

In his anxiousness, he began to point out any familiar thing to the Standards, a fence, or trail, or a field where he and his son had cleared a stump or thinned corn long ago. "Y'all can stay wit my son's family tonight, an' tomorrah we go to da gatherin field. You can set yo' tent up, Reverent Bismark. Catch a whole lot of souls wit one snare."

His son's house was actually two, narrow, yellow shotgun houses—so called because by the way they were constructed, one room behind the other, a man with a shotgun at the front door could shoot straight through. The houses were joined in the middle by a tin roofed causeway forming an 'H'. A healthy field of corn came up to almost the back door of the house. The outhouse stood in the front yard twenty yards from the front steps. A thin, dark skinned man stepped from the house as the wagon pulled up. Squeaky springs slammed the door after him. He remained on the top step, shirtless with his hands pushed into his pockets, saying something about travelers being welcome at his table until he saw his father behind Bismark and let out a whoop. That was like a signal because instantly a flood of children, yellow, brown, and black came pouring from the house.

"Is this a school?" Charles asked.

The white haired man climbing down into the reaching arms of the children just laughed. "What's dis fussin?" he said to them.

Grainger Jr. stood back between the children and his father. His arms were wrapped about his thin, smooth chest and he was obviously delighted. "You know the ones here that's ,your grandchildrens, an' your new grandson is in the house with Mary. The rest keep showin up an' Mary won't say no to nobody."

In the gang of squealing, bouncing children—some of who did not even know the old man—Charles spotted a pretty, brown skinned girl with long hair and almost golden eyes. Ruth. She hugged the white haired man, then whispered in his ear.

"But you done heard all mah stories, child," he said and she looked disappointed.

Even while she pouted, Charles could not take his eyes off her. Her skin was smooth and her face bright. He thought her the most beautiful girl he'd ever seen. He stared, stupefied, until she noticed him and shot her eyes angrily back at him. But, unembarrassed, Charles continued to stare until the girl stalked away.

"If we stays here tonight, Charles," Bismark said, "We might have to sleep outside. These people probably ain't got a lot of room."

"I don't mind," Charles said.

*

At the crowded table, over small portions of greens and turnips, Charles tried unsuccessfully to be furtive with his glances at Ruth.

"Sorry it's so hot in here, Reverend Standard," Grainger Jr.'s wife, Mary, said. She stood with her baby, Grainger III, on her out thrust hip. She was amused by Charles's keen interest in Ruth, the oldest girl. She'd taken Ruth in three years ago.

"Normal, we eats outside in the summertime, but the bugs been so bad lately," Grainger Jr. said.

"Jes' burn some green wood," old Grainger said, "De smoke'll drive 'em right off."

"Drives me off too is de problem," Mary said. Around the table everyone laughed except Charles, who wrestled with all new, and very powerful emotions, and Ruth, who suffered under the constant gaze of the traveling preacher's strange, silent son.

Abruptly, Ruth jumped from the table and stuck her tongue at

Charles. He looked down at the small heap of boiled leaves on his plate. "I'm going to take a plate to Tree while there's still some left," Ruth told Mary, who nodded at her.

Ruth used her own dish and spooned out more greens, onions and turnips onto it. She then disappeared into the darkness of the connecting hallway. Charles gulped down his food, fidgeted for awhile as everyone else talked about the gathering field, and finally, slipped from the table to follow after Ruth.

The adjoining house, away from the kitchen and the long dinner table and the noisy chatter of a dozen children, was dark and nearly quiet. Charles crept through the connecting hallway and into the house where all the sleeping was done. Each 'room' had walls of quilts or sheets suspended by ropes from the ceiling. Charles went to his right, toward the front of the house seeking the golden-eyed girl, but it was empty except for small cots or lumpy mattresses on the floor. Clothes hung on wooden pegs along the wall and shoes sat in small boxes and shelves. Even with just the dim, tired light of twilight outside the windows, Charles could see the wear in everything, the frayed blankets and the worn, thin soles of the shoes, and the repaired and repaired again mattresses. The clothes evidently circulated from child to child until the stitches could no longer hold them together.

The room in the very front of the house had a double bed though even its mattress sagged in the middle. The walls here were covered with pages from a Sears catalog and a pitcher and bowl, white with blue flowers, sat on a bureau under a mirror. Mary and Grainger's room, Charles guessed. But Ruth was not here so he ducked around each quilt partition to the back of the house, hearing talk and laughter from the kitchen as he went by the connecting hallway. A heavy, dark red curtain separated the room in the very back. Charles eased behind its folds and into blackness.

"What are you doing here?" Ruth's voice asked.

"I can't see."

"Then go away, boy." Her voice came from beneath him, from the floor.

"Ruthie, behave," said an old voice as slow as molasses, as

heavy as a filled bucket.

Charles gasped, startled by the bodiless words from the dark.
"Is there a light?"

"Ruthie, you don't has a lamp lit?" the voice in the dark,
sounding as old as the dark, asked. "You gwine ta end up likes
Tree. It's night. Ah knows its cool face."

Ruth said, "I can see your stories better in the dark, Tree."

Charles's eyes slowly adjusted. Pale splinters of light from
outside snuck through cracks in the walls near the ceiling. He
could make out Ruth now, sitting on the backs of her legs upon the
floor. Still, he could not discern the source of the old voice.

"Go away, boy," Ruth repeated.

But Charles would not leave. Boldness didn't keep him there
just behind the curtain. He stayed because to go would be to
return to that hot kitchen and noisy children, and his father and his
sermons, and his fears about his mother. This didn't form as
conscious thought in his head, rather he felt these problems as a
constant, nagging pressure. But for the moment, the curtain, and
the girl and her dark closet that spoke to her had shut out Charles'
problems. So he stayed even though the girl had said, *go away,
boy*. And this time the voice had not scolded her on her rudeness.

"My name's Charles," he said to the girl and the dark, fearing
and fascinated by both equally. In the quiet that followed, he
could hear the breathing of the voice and the effort that went into
pulling in each lung full. He could smell the turnips and the
vinegar on the greens Ruth had brought. Then he heard the sound
of chewing and swallowing, and knew the dark to be somehow
human.

"Tree is least over a hundred and ten years old," Ruth said.

Charles smiled to himself, accepting this statement from her
almost as a present. She had consented to his company. Though,
at first, he wasn't sure he believed what she'd said; no one lived to
be that old.

"I'm fifteen," he said, and sat down on the floor a yard from
her, as close as he dared to get. He wanted to know her. He
wanted to know how she came to be raised by Grainger and Mary.
(*One of the boys at the dinner table had filled him in on who were*

*brothers and sisters "for real" and who were not.*) He wanted to know why she'd stuck her tongue at him, and why she came into a back room to visit an ancient man she could not see. None of these questions he asked.

"Why do you call him Tree?" He pulled his eyes from her to look in the direction she looked. A dark pile propped against the wall moved nearly imperceptibly. The waning light would not betray it. But Charles thought he could see the ancient, black skin of this man's hands and forearms and part of his face, skin as wrinkled and craggy, dry and scarred as the bark of an age-old tree. His face appeared as if it had been carved from black wood, not by the hand of man, but by the erosion of time and the winds of many storms. Two shadows pooled where his eyes should have been, looking like the dark knots on a cut plank.

"Thank Mary." The shadows formed a black hand, which held out an empty dish to Ruth. She took it and placed it beside her.

"I named you. Didn't I, Tree?" No answer came. "You are gonna tell me a story, aren't you, Tree? Old Grainger came back, but he won't tell me a story. All the children won't leave him be."

Charles watched the girl wait. He hoped she'd glance his way, but she did not. During the stillness of the girl's patient waiting, only Tree's breathing could be heard. Something in the heaviness of his breathing gave weight to the dark.

Tree hid in the shadows; they emanated from him. He exhaled the blackness with each labored breath. He had gathered it around him as protection. The shallow pits that once held his eyes condemned him to darkness; so perhaps, he sought shadows in order to put himself on equal terms with everyone else. But maybe the family had put him back here away from the light and the kitchen table. Maybe he was wrapped in black not by his own choice. Perhaps, like his skin, it had been hung on him and then made a thing to shun and fear, something to hate and beat on. The scars on his skin showed it. He had been a victim to his blackness all his long life, defined by it and answering for it. And there hung just as densely about him the must of antiquity.

Ruth claimed he was one hundred ten. Yes, at least. He had

always been one hundred ten. He was the ornately carved, claw-footed antique sitting amongst attic dust. No, older. Dark had always been. Dark lived long before divine decrees on the existence of light. His seamed and creased face had weathered the ages. He had been blinded by all he had witnessed. In his sight, loved ones had been chained, branded, and lynched. Tree had, Charles was to learn from Ruth, buried every member of his family. Tree had seen too much. He had blinded himself.

Charles said, "Mr. Tree, tell us a story."

No answer came. The two waited in the hot, sticky dark like acolytes before an old god.

"Come on," Ruth said to Charles and took his hand. This new thrill immediately erased his disappointment at not hearing the old, black man speak. Ruth led him to a side door he had not noticed before and they stepped outside as the last little bit of twilight faded. Momentarily it seemed bright compared to Tree's room. Charles noticed a rope strung from the far end of the house to the outhouse in the front yard.

"That is for Tree. He guides off the house, then the rope to get to the outhouse."

Charles nodded.

Ruth seemed to notice they were still holding hands. She gently pulled hers away. "He didn't want to talk tonight. He's like that at times. Just wants to be left alone."

"Probably wants to go to sleep," Charles said.

Ruth shook her head. "Not at night. He likes night best. He'll sit outside here and whittle a top from an empty thread spool or he'll go down the rows of corn and thin 'em or weed 'em. He can work his way up and down the rows without getting lost." And she whispered, taking a step away from the door, "I think Tree is fraid of getting lost."

Again, Charles simply nodded, trying to get used to the idea that he was alone with her and talking to her.

"Don't stare at me anymore, all right?"

He nodded again and stammered an apology while looking at her bare feet.

"Over there, Grainger is digging a new hole to sto' potaters and turnips for winter." She pointed to a black mound of fresh earth several yards to the side of the house. "I told Tree bout it. He's terrified he'll step into it one night."

She fell silent for a time and Charles began to wonder if she might not be just as nervous as he. "We found Tree some five miles down the road one morning sitting in a tree, hugging against it. Grainger said Tree was scairt cause he didn't know how far down down was. Some one had pulled him up in that tree. Can you imagine that? Pull an old, blind man up into a tree. There is low devils on this earth. Anyway that's why we call him Tree. Wish he'd told a story tonight. I want to hear a story or a secret."

"My mama's sick an' only I knows about it," Charles said and saw the girl frown. "It's a secret, " he hastily added wanting to gain her interest. He told her everything, realized he'd wanted to share this with her from the moment he saw her. He told her about Bismark's Bible shaking sermons and rages in the house and how he'd heard a voice out in the field while plowing.

Ruth asked him if he believed his father had heard a voice.

Charles shrugged. He told her how he'd discovered Mercy in the pantry shaking, how he thought he'd open the door and see a trapped weasel or something.

Ruth listened while he told of his mother's shaking fits and how he tried to stop them. He even told how someone must've been snooping on him and his mother, and might know the secret. She seemed surprised with the boy's candidness; they had met only a few hours ago.

Charles wondered sometime during the telling if he might not be making a big mistake. And he wondered what the girl would think of it all. But he trusted her without really knowing her. Maybe, he thought, he trusted her because she alone had brought supper to Tree and without a lamp had shared his darkness. He figured she could be trusted to share his secret. Then too, it is the very nature of secrets—their exclusiveness—to share them. They are useless if kept to oneself, and they are better if shared with someone special.

Charles wanted Ruth to be someone special. Tears welled in his eyes as toward the end of his story he began to falter. "I got to get back home an' see how my Mama is doin. She needs me." He saw that the girl didn't know what to say and that she probably felt awkward and embarrassed for him. He felt foolish. He turned to walk away from her, but she took his hand. She offered no words of comfort or advice. Nor did she look at him. Hand in hand, neither of them knowing what to say, they walked about the yard, amongst the fireflies, until Mary's voice called Ruth in.

# X

## Brother Chancy Walks

All the talk could not have prepared Charles for the Gathering Field. The Gathering Field burst at the seams with people and excitement as if one hundred family reunions had convened at once! Wagons and Fords, Packards and mules crowded its edges. Folks had brought tables and chairs and blankets, plates of chicken, and roast pork—a lot of the cooking was done right there. Trucks pulled up with their beds loaded with watermelons and all the children jumped and squealed and climbed over the green mountains. Everywhere there was movement; the field as crowded with as many laughing black faces as with blades of grass.

The women spread tablecloths, and sat out heaping plates of food, eyed each other's clothes, laughed about this and that, and gossiped relentlessly. The men sat on the running boards of their trucks or the tailgates of their wagons. They smoked, passed bottles, eyed the women, told off color jokes and couched their gossip between talk of crops or of what the white folk been up to. The young men only eyed the women. Hair slicked back and devilment in their eyes, they maneuvered through the crowds and around the wagons on the prowl. The Gathering Field was the best place to meet girls from the farthest reaches of the county. A lot of marriages—and affairs—had started as encounters at the Gathering Field.

The old folks sat in chairs in circles, sipped corn liquor, made gapped toothed smiles and counted who amongst their friends had not returned, cursed their own creaking joints, and faced their own mortality. The immortal children had no such thoughts. They gave the field its movement and excitement. They raced about, laughed and cried, stole melons and cakes. They played walk-the-cans with large tomato cans on their feet with strings attached to the cans held like reins in their hands. The awkward giants stumbled and rolled over each other in dusty clouds.

Charles played with the oldest of Grainger and Mary's children, though he noticed other boys near his age did not play the games. Ruth played, when not helping Mary with food or with the youngest, and so Charles played too. In the early evening, after he'd helped Bismark pitch the tent on the edge of the field, he joined Ruth and the children for a big game of tag. More than thirty kids held hands in a great ring chanting, "Tisket a tasket, a green and yellow basket. I wrote a letter to my love, but on the way I lost it." Charles stood opposite the circle from Ruth. The boy next to him tried squeezing Charles's hand hard, but Charles was much stronger and the boy yelped in pain. The girl, who was *it*, skipped along the outside of the circle with a balled up white sock in her hand. When the chanting ended, howls of laughter began.

Charles noticed Ruth nodding at him. Delighted, he nodded back. All the children in the circle laughed and jumped. Ruth's nodding became more urgent. Charles looked down at his feet. The balled sock had been placed next to them and the little girl was more than half way around the circle. As he snatched up the sock, he thought how embarrassing it would be for the oldest boy in the ring to be made *it* by a little girl. Already, Ruth laughed with the other kids. Charles charged around the ring. The children laughed at him over their shoulders. Their faces blurred as Charles sped by gaining ground on the shrieking girl with the flying pigtails. He almost caught her. Just as she made the haven of his spot in the ring he'd tagged her with the sock.

"I'm safe! I'm safe!" she yelled.

Charles could've argued the point, but even the adults who'd been watching were laughing. The boys his age pointed and laughed and went their way. He wanted to quit, but knew how bad that would look. He had the sock; he was *it*. The chanting began anew and, embarrassed, he skipped around the circle. Then he thought to place the sock at Ruth's feet and searched her out. She was no where to be found and must have quit the game right as the little girl had taken his place. Quickly, he left the sock at the feet of a boy he knew he could outrun. He quit the game too, right after making it back to the ring.

*

The population of the field only grew as night approached. Lamps and fires looking like grounded stars were scattered throughout the field. Now the children slowed down a bit. Bottles and jugs were passed more freely. Husbands snuck away from their wives, and wives from their husbands. Charles knew Bismark would want him at the tent, but he didn't want to abandon his search for Ruth. He asked Mary where she might be, but the woman began shaking her head before he'd finished the question.

"I shepherd the young'ns til they get too quick or too uppity," she said. "Ruthie hep me for awhile, but I can't speck a young woman ta hang about. I do the best I can."

Charles kept searching, pushing his way into one group after the other. Something about her quick absence disturbed him, as did Mary's description of Ruth as a young woman. He had not had a girlfriend before, had never really given much thought to getting one. But he knew he wanted Ruth. He wanted to hold her hand again as he had the night before. He walked up and down the entire field searching for her. He was convinced he saw every tan, brown, and black face there. Frustrated, he headed toward his father's tent.

People had filled the tent. Though many at the Gathering Field had already sampled the sermons of the angry Reverend Standard, word had not passed quickly enough. Bismark stood at the tent's entrance. Charles avoided his face, already knowing the look, the scowl, he would find there. Just as he was about to enter the tent, a car drove up, winding its way around wagons and a group of chatting people who lingered near the tent. The long, bright automobile reflected, seemed to magnify, any torch light or campfire around it. Entranced, children chased after it, each begging vehemently for a ride. The driver wore goggles, looking as if the bottom of small soda bottles had been affixed to his face.

The car pulled to a flashy, abrupt stop next to the tent now displayed across the field by the car's headlights. Ruth sat in the passenger seat laughing at something the goggle-eyed man had said. He reached over and squeezed her shoulder and Charles saw that she seemed not to mind this at all. Then she turned, noticeably angry, not at the driver, but at the children whose curious hands touched and tested everything within reach on the car. She slapped at their hands. The driver only laughed.

The driver was Elmore Langley, said by all to have "done well for hisself" as part owner of a produce distribution operation. The man's prosperity had made him popular and caused him to be regarded as the single best catch by all the black women in the county, many of whom had attempted to seduce him with potato casseroles, and sweet yams drowned in butter and sugar, and steaming plates of deep fried chicken or catfish.

"Mr. Langley's own pots don't know what a stove is," went the joke. Indeed, the women threw themselves his way hoping he'd reach out and catch hold of one of them. But the elusive Elmore would let woman after woman slip by even though quite a few dropped their dresses in his company. These attempts to appeal to either of his appetites gained a woman only a temporary status in Elmore's affections, though still quite enviable. Women would speculate about the number of days the current girlfriend could hold on before a rival unseated her. "Girl, Norma couldn't keep him interested fo' even a week." Those who spoke of their relationship with Mr. Langley in terms of months did so with deserved pride. Elmore accepted the flood of feminine attention with reserve. He laughed at their bickering amongst themselves.

He also took in stride the menfolk's hostility hidden as it was in glad-handing and backslapping. None of the men particularly liked him, but none were willing to get on the bad side of such a well-to-do black businessman.

One of the most popular Elmore stories concerned a near fatal scheduling conflict. Elmore had accepted his current woman friend's offer to come over to his house and fix his Saturday evening supper. He had also agreed to Mayella Tucker's offer to bring him a Sabbath Day supper. It should be noted that Mayella was a member in good standing of the only congregation of Seven Day Adventists in the area, who, of course, celebrated the sabbath on Saturday. Elmore, to his credit, smoothed out the situation as best he could, promising both women he would sample each of their fine cooking. The threesome sat down to a large spread at Elmore's table. The ladies argued over who would tuck the napkin under Elmore's chin, turned their noses up at each other's dishes, and eyed each other like boxers in a ring. The dinner was doomed when Mayella nudged her cornbread closer to Elmore while pushing her rival's plate of rolls out of reach.

The lady friend promptly placed Mayella's "prize winnin'" pork chops at the far end of the table. Mayella put the woman's peach cobbler on the windowsill "to let it cool off a might, honey" then gave it a bump with her hip sending it hurtling into the front yard. Passersby reported seeing pigs' feet and pork chops and cornbread, bowls and plates come flying out of every window in the house. Finally, Mayella came flying out the front door and over the porch steps. The girlfriend came bounding after her, wielding a butter knife. Screaming, they disappeared across a field. Elmore was doubled up on his porch—in one of his fancy suits—laughing hysterically.

Elmore was one hip cat. He worked in Louisville and Cincinnati. He wore gleaming processed hair, slicked back over his head except for one rakish curly lock, greased into submission, which hung in the middle of his forehead. He was in his mid-thirties, a round man just beginning to show a belly from too much good food. Recent gossip said his current interest had broken all records for number of days holding on to him. And if she'd ever fixed him a decent meal no one could say, so the mean gossipers figured she kept his attention through other wiles. It was scandalous because she was much too young for him, the girl living at Mary and Grainger Browning's house. "Why, she jus' sixteen if she a day."

Elmore Langley pulled off his goggles and smoothed back his hair with the tips of his fingers.

Charles walked over to the passenger side of the long Packard with his hands digging for cover in his pockets. The driver seemed so much older than Ruth. He had hopes—which he knew were silly—that the man was her father or an uncle maybe. Ruth smiled at Charles and introduced the two; Elmore as friend, Charles as new friend.

"Hey, cat," Elmore said and held out his hand. Charles shook it out of politeness and gained some confidence from the fact that his hand was bigger than Elmore's.

"We've been good timin, Charles," Ruth said. "This is Elmore's new car. We've been everywhere and it took no time at all."

"You was gone the whole day."

"Isn't this the prettiest car you've ever seen?" Ruth asked.

Charles shrugged. He had not seen that many cars.

"It'll stay pretty if these kids keep their grimy, nose picking hands off of it." Ruth made another swipe at one of the children. Charles could see she deliberately missed. Elmore laughed again.

"Come riding with us, Charles. Is that all right, Elmore?" She didn't look back to see Elmore's fleeting grimace, but Charles caught it. "The night is cooler when you're driving around."

Charles was ready to accept Ruth's invitation when he heard Bismark's voice from within the tent. The service had begun. "I'm supposed to help my Dad."

Ruth said, "Do you have to?" Elmore said, "Another time then," both at the same time.

"I have to pass the hat. Stay with me," Charles heard himself say. "After the sermon, we could listen to Tree."

"Tree?" Elmore frowned.

"Let's go listen to the preacher, El. Might do you a world of good."

"Might do you a world of good," Elmore mimicked and poked her in the side with his finger.

Giggling, Ruth pushed his hand away.

"Girl, I done heard ever'thing preachers have to say. Thing is they have nothing to say that coloreds need to hear. That's why we ain't done a thing since slavery."

Ruth waited for his answer, ignoring the comments she had not asked for. "Elmore..."

"Okay, Ruthie girl, let's take a peek." He cut the car's engine and turned off the headlamps.

Charles led them into the tent. He walked down the narrow aisle between the seats and the tent's side looking for a spot up front for the two of them to sit. The tent was hot and smelled of people who'd been out in the sun all day now jammed together in one spot. Never had he seen the tent crowded before.

He found a spot for Ruth at least, but turned around to discover they had followed him only as far as the entrance way. Elmore hovered slightly behind Ruth with his hands on her shoulders. Charles noticed a lot of necks craned to spy on the couple. He is too old, Charles thought looking at Elmore and Ruth, I wish I hadn't told her me and Mama's secret. He took up his usual position on the ground, in front, off to the side.

Bismark read out of the book. He read gently. This caught Charles's attention; his father's usual ranting, he had learned along this trip to tune out. But now Bismark spoke almost quietly and those gathered in the hot, little tent strained to hear over the murmuring and stray laughter that filtered through the canvas from the rest of the Gathering Field. Charles wondered if this reserve from his father came from his hoarse throat or maybe the large crowd made him nervous.

Bismark turned the pages of the book, but did not need to look at the words. The people listened, nearly motionless, some swatting at worrisome flies, a few holding fiddles or tambourines on their laps. Charles marveled at the power, which brought them to the tent when good corn liquor passed from hand to hand outside. He did not understand it nor his father's part in it. He looked to the book, to his father, and then the crowd—wishing he could see Ruth from his seat on the ground—and his eyes returned to the hysterical book—subdued now—that had flapped and waved in front of him so many times in the past.

"Verily, verily, I say unto you all," Bismark quoted without reading, "He that believeth on me, the works that I do, shall he do also. An' Jesus promises here, whatsoever, whatsoever ye shall ask in my name that will I do."

A woman in the back said, "Amen." And Charles almost
came to his feet thinking of Mercy.

Bismark said, "I'm gonna pray for a healin' for my voice
tonight. An' I knows the Lord will do it. Don't I? I jus' read it to
y'all. He didn't say I'll do this and that. Or if'n I'm not feelin
poorly I'll do this and the other thing fo' you, maybe." Bismark
paused and sporadic calls of encouragement came from the
congregation. Bismark whispered in his grating voice, "He said,
whatsoever." And he actually smiled and looked Charles's way for
a split second and repeated, "He said, whatsoever!" and the last
word roared from his mouth and boomed through the tent.

"Praise de Lawd!" some shouted, and, "Sweet Jesus," or
"Gowan now, Rev." A few stood and waved their hands skyward
at something on the other side of the canvas ceiling.

"The Bible says we can do all things through Christ.
Philippians the fourth, the thirteenth. If'n you believes in the man,
sweet Jesus, and you do don't you?"

Everyone rapidly nodded. "Yes, yes, yes!" a lady cried.

"Then you has to believe in His book." Bismark held the
book up and shook it at the congregation. The old, castigating
Reverend Standard began to re-emerge. He shook his fingers, and
flapped the book and strutted about the pulpit. *Strike you blind
and send you on your road to Damascus*, he would soon be telling
them.

Charles looked down at the ground already tuning out his
father's fanaticism and feeling embarrassed this time because Ruth
would see what kind of preacher Bismark was. But someone
interrupted Bismark before the spiritual tides swept him too far
away. A little, wiry, tan colored man with scruffy, uneven hair
and denim overalls faded to white at the seat and knees, rose to his
feet from the middle of the congregation.

"Ah want a healin" he said. Charles heard him plainly, but
every face turned toward the man questioningly as if he'd spoken
French. "Ah want a healin, Rev'rent," he repeated.

At that moment, Charles heard an engine start. He stood long
enough to see Ruth and Elmore had sneaked out.

"You said Jesus say whatever, Rev'rent. Ah been draggin mah left leg behind me fo' five years. Cain't git no good wuk. Couldn't keep my family fed decent. Heal me likes you did your voice."

"Sit down, Chancy," a man near the little man said, but he was shushed by those around him.

Now the faces switched quickly back to Bismark. The sharecropper turned preacher gently rested his Bible on the pulpit. "Praise God for your courage, brother..."

"Chancy, Ah'm called."

Someone giggled; more shushing ensued.

"Brother Chancy, come forward. Healin is what we's here for. Somebody say, amen."

Many people said, "Amen."

Chancy stepped around the makeshift pews, his left leg following after him. The tent remained silent as he made his way to the pulpit. He took one short step then a pause for his bad leg to catch up. Everyone silently watched his slow progress. Only the scrape of that one foot along the ground could be heard. Chancy limped right past Charles, who saw both strain and determination on the little man's face. Before he made it to the pulpit, Bismark jumped in his way, challenging him.

"Do you believe, Brother Chancy? That Jesus is the son of the Almighty and that He's your personal savior?"

Chancy nodded.

"Say it!"

"Ah believes, Rev'rent," Chancy said. The congregation began to call encouragement to Chancy. "Ah believes what you said bout Jesus an' what he say bout so whatever."

Charles saw a new look in his father's wide eyes he had not seen before. He thought Bismark may have been frightened. Bismark cried out, "We are gonna heal you in the name of Jesus!"

A woman began singing, "Lift him up" and others joined her.

Bismark began praying. He asked Jesus, as if He were in the tent or maybe just outside in the Gathering Field, to touch the hip of Brother Chancy. He told Jesus a healing now would win over a lot of corrupt souls. Then Bismark beseeched all true believers to stretch their hands toward Brother Chancy who leaned in Bismark's arms. Even Charles, caught in his father's fervor for the very first time, stretched his arms toward Chancy. "Jesus said, 'Rise up, stand forth in the midst!' Luke the eighth, the sixth. We claim a healin tonight in the name of Jesus!"

"In the name of Jesus," the believers responded.

Then it seemed to Charles that Bismark struck Chancy in the left hip with the Bible and the crippled man went crashing to the ground in front of the pulpit.

There were gasps and prayers and a few who turned their heads so as not to look upon the fallen man. Charles let his tired arms drop to his sides.

Bismark, in his flowing robe, towered over the man on the ground. He thumbed through the Bible, but settled on no page in particular. He said, "Rise up, stand forth in the midst!" Sweat poured from Bismark, soaking his robe, clinging it to his chest and back.

Everyone waited. Chancy sat up. He rubbed his left leg then gazed up at Bismark. Bismark signaled for him to rise, but he would not.

"Somethin don't feel right, Rev'rent. Ah best sit a spell. Mah leg—"

"Rise!" Bismark shouted.

Charles went over to Chancy. Gripping Charles's arm, Chancy pulled himself to his feet. Bismark immediately stepped several feet away.

"Let go of him, Charles. Come here, Brother Chancy." Bismark held out his hand. "And his limb was restored, whole as the other. Luke the tenth, the sixth."

Chancy's face twisted and he began to whine. For a long moment all his weight bared down on Charles. Bismark's outstretched hand waited. The people called Chancy. "Faith," they reminded him. His right foot stepped out. His left followed. And then, in full sight of all the eager faces, his left foot took a shaky step of its own of maybe two inches.

"Praise Jeee-sus!" a woman screamed.

Chancy quickly recovered his weight over his right leg.

Charles followed, hand out to catch the man.

"Get away, Charles," Bismark said, "he doesn't need you."

Chancy made another miracle step, this time putting the left foot fully in front of the right. He gasped. "Lawd in heaben!"

"Arise and go your way, your faith has made you whole. Luke. Luke the... the someteenth or other." For a moment even Bismark looked shocked.

The fiddles began to play, the tambourines jingled. No one sat. They danced and sang and jumped and waved their hands heavenward. Chancy struggled to Bismark, four more steps with one foot in front of the other each time. The tent flaps were thrown open and word quickly spread. Many in the Gathering Field knew Chancy and they knew a miracle had just occurred.

His father basked in the glow and praise. "You got a line to de Lawd, Rev'rent Standard," they told him and touched his robe. But Charles eyes were fixed on the source of the power, the book.

They gave Chancy a seat in the midst of the dancing congregation. Everyone hugged him. Charles dashed around filling his father's hat with coins that rang like the tambourines.

The revival had its own momentum quite beyond Bismark's ability to control it. The dancing, clapping and singing spread like a contagion out of the little tent and across the field. People came to the Reverend Standard with all manner of physical complaint and he laid hands on as many as he could, but no dramatic healing such as Chancy's occurred again that evening.

Chancy left while the celebration continued. The little man had cried and said he wanted to show his wife what had happened. People said Chancy's wife had left him because of his inability to support her and the children. "She goin ta see how ever'thing is dif'rent now. Ah'm gonna strut. She gonna see. Ah mo' walk right through de front do'." A friend gave Chancy a ride in his truck to see his wife.

Charles placed the offering money in a secret place beneath the buckboard of his father's wagon. He stood between the horses and idly scratched their manes. The trip—the hills—had worn them out. Charles, too, wanted to go home. He thought of the miracle and he thought of Ruth. What a story he would have for her. But she'd ridden off with Elmore in his shining Packard. Charles wondered how Elmore had got his hair that way, and if he used a hot comb as women did. He wondered how Elmore could have so much money. When Charles climbed into the wagon to get some sleep, he dreamed of walking hand in hand with Ruth amongst the fireflies, and then, finally, drifted off to sleep with the wailing of fiddles praising God in his ears.

*

He expected it to be morning when he awoke. When Bismark nudged him awake, it was still dark. The revival had ended. The Gathering Field was quiet. Many folk had gone home, those who lived nearby or those who could spend no more than a day away from their jobs or their crops. Others slept in the field under blankets. The field looked dark and lumpy.

"There's been trouble," Bismark said. "The man who got touched by Christ. Jus lettin you know case you wonder where I got off to."

"Come on, Reverend," someone called. In the night, Charles couldn't tell from where, but near a trail that led away from the field, two Ford pickups idled, their lights showing a fence of tree trunks in the woods ahead.

"I'm comin too," Charles said and followed after his father to the trucks.

Bismark climbed into the cab of the nearest pickup. Charles clambered into the back trying to avoid stepping on the legs of the five other men who already sat there. The truck groaned as the driver slipped it into gear and then lurched forward after the other truck. Charles bounced uncomfortably. Every bone or joint that came in contact with the truck bed hurt. He felt as if he were being pummeled and wondered how the other men took it in silence.

"You shouldn't have come along, Charles."

Charles looked at the man who'd spoke, but the night and the mosaic shadows of the trees covered him.

"It's me, Grainger."

Charles felt relief, for some reason, that someone he knew rode in the bed with him. "Mr. Browning, what's goin on? What happened to Chancy?"

"Yo' daddy shoulda let his leg be is what happened," another man answered and Grainger Jr. told the man to shut up.

They bounced down the road a few miles with no one saying a thing. Charles noted how the trucks quickly covered distance the wagon and team labored hours over.

"Naw, its dat wife of his. Ornery woman," one man said as if continuing a conversation that had been going on in the men's heads. "Majin turnin him out after he come all dat way to show her his miracle. What's her name anyway? Ah don't think Ah ever liked her."

Grainger said, "Ah bet she ain't tol him to throw it back in town when de town got nothin but white folks in it cause all de niggers is at de Gathurin Fields."

"Chancy do like to put it away."

"Ah bet they put him in jail," the closest man to Charles said.

"Depends," Grainger said, "depend on if he scuffle wit somebody or wit jus a po' cracker." The men fell into silence again, leaving Charles to fill in the pieces.

There was no town, but the place had a name nonetheless, Fat Creek. Fat Creek had as much as a town, one tavern—serving whites only—two churches—neither *officially* serving whites only—a drug store, owned by a man who'd made it a point to welcome any and all customers, a smattering of small houses, and a county jail house that sat between the tavern and one of the churches. Folks thought the jail's location was mighty appropriate.

When the trucks pulled into this crossroads and up to the jail house, only the light from the sheriff's offices and one or two houses showed. The trucks stopped directly in front of the jail. For a moment no one moved. Charles heard talking from the cab and presently the driver, named Macon, Charles learned, and Bismark stepped out. Both trucks began to empty.

"You stay, Charles," Bismark said.

The rest of the men were climbing out of the trucks when a voice barked, "Hold it there." The jail house door opened catching all the men in the light that streamed out. Two white men came out on the small stoop carrying rifles. "Don't nobody move a pinky," the foremost man said.

Grainger, who was half in, half out of the truck swung his leg over and jumped to the ground.

"Who was that? Is that you, Grainger? Boy, you want someone ta put a bullet in that head of yours, don'tcha?" The click of the rifle's hammer being thumbed back sounded very loud. "Has every nigra man in the county loss his good sense? What are y'all up to? What the hell do y'all think you're doin?"

Macon and Bismark stepped forward. "Not lookin' fo' any trouble, Sheriff," Macon said. "We heard Chancy may got himself in a scrape, Sheriff. You knows Chancy. We come to take him home."

"All y'all come ta' take one little drunk home?" the man behind the sheriff said.

The sheriff turned and glared at him until he lowered his head and mumbled something no one heard.

"Then you saw him tonight, Sheriff? You know bout him havin too much to drink in celebration?" Bismark asked.

"Didn't say I saw him. Chancy is always drunk or on the way to it, and who the hell are you?"

"My name is Bismark Standard."

"He's a travelin preacher, Sheriff. We had a revival tonight," Grainger said walking over to Bismark and Macon.

The sheriff lowered his rifle and came down from the stoop. He was a big boned man with a cascading moustache that covered his top lip. His deputy kept his rifle trained on the men. "Macon, Grainger, tell the travelin preacher here how I always been fair to the coloreds," the sheriff said, then shouted, "Ain't I!"

Macon rapidly nodded, but Grainger did not respond.

"You thought I had him in jail?" the sheriff asked. "Y'all all come to break him out? Is that it? Is this a jail break? Why, I think I'm in my legal rights to shoot you all, right now."

"We hopin you had him, Sheriff," Macon said. "We knows you would treat him fair."

"That's right, dammit. I always have. So I don't deserve y'all stormin my jail. Any of y'all got guns? Best hand them over."

The sheriff looked from man to man, each of whom either shook his head in response or said, "No, suh."

"Well, then, go on back out to your field. Chancy ain't here. He got in some kinda scuffle, but he ain't here."

Grainger said, "We heard it happened behind Fat Creek Tavern..."

"Some of the boys in the tavern said Rosemary brought some drinks out to him an' he tried to put himself off on her."

"Then what happened, Sheriff? We heard there was a fight?" Bismark asked.

"Don't know nothin bout that."

"But the back of the tavern is right next to your office," Grainger said. His impatience showed. "Didn't you see nothin?"

A man standing near Charles muttered, "He sure saw us pull up an' come runnin out wit his gun awful quick."

"Naw I didn't, Grainger, dammit." The sheriff rubbed down his moustache and looked back at his deputy. He was clearly exasperated. He's trying to decide something, Charles thought. The sheriff said, "Why don't you boys go on back out to the field."

"Who told you bout the scuffle, Sheriff? We'd like to talk to them."

The sheriff eyed Grainger for a long time. No one moved. Behind the hills in back of the jail and church, silent lightning flickered. "They was jus some boys comin from the tavern. Didn't check to see who they was," the sheriff said, but his voice had temporarily lost its bark. The sheriff turned his back and remounted the stoop. "Never done a thing gainst the colored," he said to the deputy.

"What did you see tonight, Sheriff? Nothin at all?" Grainger asked. "A man mighta been beaten up right under your window."

"Now that's it, Mr. Mouth. I'm gonna start arrestin for vagrancy, an' unlawful assembly in jus one minute."

One by one the black men backed away and returned to the trucks. Bismark grasped Grainger's arm and pulled him along. Gathered around the tailgate of the truck Charles rode in, the men discussed what they would do next.

"Sheriff is free wit de lies tonight," Macon said. "Someone go round back of Fat Creek an' try to see Miss Rosemary or Dupree, her bartender. He stay back of dere wit her sometime if de truth be tol. Ah speck he de one who got word to me tonight an' tol me what was goin on anyway. Wait til we ride outta heres so de sheriff don't see you."

"He ain't in a witnessin mood no how," someone said.

"S'pose we should go talk to Chancy's wife too," Grainger added.

Everyone suggested someone to talk to or someplace to look, so after driving the trucks away from the jail, the men split up on their individual searches. Most were a long time reporting back.

Charles sat on the truck's running board with his feet in the dust of the road. He should've been sleepy, but was not. The men's urgency kept him tense and fully awake. When two of the men returned with rifles, he began to understand the graveness of the matter. No one speculated as to what had happened to Chancy, though Macon said he doubted if the little man had tried anything with Rosemary, a white woman and "not particular pretty at dat." Macon had gone to see Chancy's wife. "She say he was there. Said he seem to be walkin better, but she didn't care cause he'd had his chance an' she weren't puttin up with him no more."

"She's why he wanted the healin," Bismark said.

The men dispatched to see Rosemary returned last. "She wouldn't even come out or open her door. Said she didn't want no mo' trouble round her tonight. So we looks around her backyard. We didn't see no blood or nothin like that. But we seen tire tracks, new ones. Someone had drove a car in back of there."

"Lawd, help," Grainger said.

"We fixed to ask Rosemary bout them, but she holler for us to scat."

Macon said, "They done took off wit him." He looked at the men gathered, even Charles. "We got to go as a group. All of us." The men nodded.

They sped down a black road too narrow for two-way traffic. It had rained out there recently and the branches that hung low over the road would strike the top of the truck's cab and shake rain water in fat drops on the men who rode in back. It was very dark along that road and the truck's headlights seemed to do little to push the blackness back. The road became bumpier and the trees closed in tighter. Men grabbed the brims of their hats so branches would not snatch them away. Charles wondered if the drivers knew where they were going. They bounced along recklessly. Trees scratched and swiped at them from the blackness. Just when Charles was certain the truck would bound over some great, invisible chasm and smash into the trunk of a sturdy tree, they came to a stop.

"Turn dem around," Macon called out his window to the other driver. "Let's be pointin in the way outta here."

If, after accomplishing that, the men struck out on a trail, Charles could not be certain. He followed the shadow in front of him and held his hands up, like playing blind man's bluff, to ward off the springy, little branches that whipped at him. The walk was not far, but the going was slow. The undergrowth tried tripping them or, where nothing grew, the wet, clinging earth pulled at the soles of their shoes. At some point the moon came out making the going a little easier. The men were quiet except for low muttered curses now and then. Sometimes Charles could see their grim faces, crisscrossed with the shadows of branches from tree filtered moonlight.

"They's been here," someone whispered and pointed to where scores of footprints had trampled the ground into little pits and mountains.

Not long afterward, they arrived in a moon lit clearing. Only one tree grew there, not quite in the center. The tree, huge, old, and fat, cast a shadow that stained the ground around it black. The tree had massive tentacles that curled away from the trunk. The greatest of these had a diameter nearly half the trunk's size. It spanned far from the tree, running almost parallel with the earth some twelve feet up, before turning skyward. The long, ragged fruit which dangled from the elbow of this great arm was Chancy, his own arms tied behind his back and his chin severely pulled up by a fat noose, so that his distended neck appeared to be a foot long.

"A portion of your mercy, Lord," Bismark said.

The men's greatest fears had been realized.

"God damn it," Grainger said. Charles noticed the man looked at his father and said again, "God damn it."

They walked quickly out to the tree, not wanting to see their friend hover there in the shadow for another moment. Charles stared at Chancy. He imagined the terror of his last moments as a murderous mob pushed and dragged him across the clearing to this tree. Charles lowered his eyes to Chancy's feet, the left even and correct with the right, both seemingly ordinary, neither looking crippled nor the repository of recent miracles.

Macon said as if having read Charles's mind, "Why would de good Lawd heal his leg an' then let dem break his neck."

Bismark began to pray and someone stopped him, saying God had done enough for Chancy that night.

With the help of the others bracing his calves and ankles, one man stood on the shoulders of another, cut the rope, and eased the body to the ground.

Grainger regarded the body, then looked to the enormous, ancient tree. "Niggers been danglin like apples off dis tree all my life an' all my daddy's life," he said.

"Least we could make dem lynch someplace else," Macon said. "Ah could bring back hatchets an' axes. My place ain't too far from here."

"Go, Macon," someone said.

"Should we take Chancy's body?"

"Not yet," Grainger said. "We gonna give Chancy the pleasure of seein dis tree come down."

The black men waited in the silvery blue moonlight on the damp ground. For awhile they spoke of who they thought did it, and who they knew just had to have done it. They spoke of revenge or of telling the law in Frankfort. But all this talk slowly died away because each of them knew it as idle and silly, and these were practical men.

With dawn less than an hour away, Macon returned with two heavy axes. He and Grainger took them up first. The blades bit into the tree's hard, armored skin. They snarled as they swung and grunted with each echoing impact. Others spelled them, stepping forward to take the axes from their hands. Bismark and Charles took turns. Charles gave all the strength he had to the task.

"I kept seeing Chancy in my Daddy's tent, crying because he could walk again," he later told Ruth.

Each man's frustrations, fears, and outrage flowed from him into the blades of the axes. Some groaned with each stroke and wiped away tears with their sweat; they cut at the meat of this tree's history with each loud whack. The sun rose to the sound of this chopping, which ranged far across a sleepy countryside.

## XI

## The God of His Father's Book

Charles did not notice that the team had turned down the familiar trail, which led to the Standards' home. His concentration focused at the tip of his index finger as it inched from word to word. "What does verily mean?"

"It means, what I'm about to say is the truth." Surely, Bismark took pleasure with his youngest son's interest—at last— in the Bible, but remained in shock over the matter of the little man, Chancy. Bismark had lost his patient after successful surgery. "The Lord moves in mysterious ways," he said to Charles more than once during the trip home. Charles opened the book on his lap and delved into the mysteries for himself.

"Did Jesus really talk this way?" he asked. Bismark seemed not to have heard him. He guessed his father's mind still held thoughts of his only successful revival at the Gathering Field or the chopping down of the hanging tree.

Chancy was not the first dead man Charles Standard had seen. When just seven or eight, he and Ash had called on a neighbor who regularly bought apples from them. They had found the man dead in his front room. Later they heard he had died from stepping on a rusty nail and neglecting to treat the wound properly. Charles had not thought deeply about the man's death, other than thinking a little nail a peculiar thing to kill a big, grown man. His apple customer was dead and that was that. At fifteen, he could analyze Chancy's death and was not shocked by it as much as by the irony of it. The man had been hung, lost his life, on the very evening he thought he had regained control of it.

Two great, precious pieces of knowledge were imparted to

Charles on that early morning at the hanging tree. No one told him these truths. He had observed them. They presented themselves to him so clearly he could neither dispute nor deny them. The first and most profound truth was that man does indeed have a soul. He had been unable to pull his eyes from Chancy after the men had taken his body down and laid it beyond the tree's shadow in the moonlight. The body had lain there like a bag of potatoes or a sack of feed. Something was missing from it quite beyond the ability for movement.

Charles had observed Ash asleep, Ash, who slept like a stone, and not seen the absence that Chancy's body had.

At the revival, Charles witnessed Chancy's desperation, which enabled him to stand in the crowded tent, in the face of the wild preacher's tirade, and his determination as he pulled himself to the pulpit, and Charles saw Chancy's hope that had opened his face with joy at being healed and started his tears to flow. The frustrated little cripple, who could not earn enough to keep his family, who'd lost his pride along with his ability to hold a job, had left the tent vowing to strut.

All of that. All of the pain and hope and frustration and determination, all of that, had been the soul of Chancy. The body lying like a sack contained none of this. This had been his soul and it had fled. When this inviolate truth occurred to Charles, he turned his eyes away from the body.

The second piece of knowledge came shortly after dawn when Charles pried the axe from a man's hand, for none of them would easily surrender it, and began his turn chopping at—railing against—the hanging tree. It had felt like battering against steel. The vibrations shot pain up his arms and he almost dropped the axe. In front of these men, that would've been his greatest embarrassment, so he gritted his teeth and swung again and again. The truth revealed to him then was the reality of being a black man.

Because you are black, this truth said, you may be lynched, because you are what you are, at best the law will do nothing against you. Because you are black, sweet revenge is a sweet dream. And because you are what you are, you must rail against trees. But also the truth said (*and this it whispered*) because you are what you are, you will take up the axe, never drop it, and let go of it reluctantly. And Charles did his part. Pieces of the tree flew from its wound and he kept fighting until the axe was taken from his hand.

"Did Jesus talk like this? Verily and thou?" he asked again.

"No," Bismark said. "The men who wrote the book talked that way." Then Bismark nudged Charles. "Look up, boy, we're home."

The house came into view over the roll of the bean field. The pull of familiar things tugged at Charles. The team felt it too, quickening their pace. Charles could only think about seeing Mercy then, and the short ride around the field to the house seemed longer than all the rest of the trip put together. Junior came out of the house as the wagon pulled up in front of it. Junior did not smile when he greeted them.

"Well, you're alive, we was beginnin' to wonder. You said you'd be back way before now." Charles could see his oldest brother was angry.

"Where's everybody else?" Charles asked.

"Damn, look what you done to the horses. "They look worn to hide and bone," Junior said. Bismark told him to watch his mouth, but he seemed not to care. He began unhooking the tired horses.

"Where's Mama?" Charles asked, jumping down from the wagon. "She all right?"

"She's inside."

Charles headed for the front door purposely not hearing Bismark's call to help unload the wagon. Something had happened. He knew the moment he stepped inside. Plates of partially eaten food remained uncollected on the dinner table.

"Mama?" Charles asked.

Something had burned on the stove top and had not been cleaned off.

"Mama?"

A dirty pair of Junior's coveralls was draped over a chair in the front room; the curtains in the kitchen were closed on a bright summer day.

"Mama!"

He dashed to her bedroom and found the door closed.

"Mama, I'm home," he said.

The doorknob would not turn.

"Got a lot to tell you, Mama," he said and tried pushing on the door, becoming frantic with his fear. "Met a man older than the night, and Mama, he was as dark as it too." Charles laughed. "You sleep?" He began banging a fist on the door. "Mama, I'm home."

"What's all this?" Bismark came up behind Charles. "Quit that racket, boy."

"Mama won't come out."

Bismark pulled Charles out of the way and called for his wife to open the door.

"She's got the sha—" *She's got the shakes*, he almost said. "Maybe she's sick."

Bismark gripped the knob and drove his shoulder against the door. It burst open and banged the bedroom wall. Bismark caught it as it bounced back. "What's wrong, Mercy?" he asked.

Mercy sat on the bed, her legs drawn up to her chest. She did not shake nor tremble, as Charles had expected. On the contrary, she posed quite still, her head down, her lips pressed in a kiss on her knees. She did not acknowledge them. Said not a word. Her stillness scared Charles more than her shaking fits.

"What's the matter, Mercy girl?" Bismark asked. "You feelin out of sorts today?"

Charles tried to push past his father into the room, but Bismark spread a big hand on his chest and shoved him back. "Go help Junior," Bismark said. "I'll see to your Mama." He stepped in and closed the door behind him.

Charles stared at the closed door. His father had usurped his place. He laid a hand on the door knob. He should have been the one in there, not his father. He'd never wanted to leave her in the first place. "Can I come in?" he asked. "Can I come in?"

He heard Bismark's definite, "No."

"What's wrong? Please, can I come in?"

"You heard me, boy. Go help Junior. Find out what Ash is up to."

Charles heard a whimper from his mother. He turned the doorknob. "Mama, can I come in?" He began to ease the door open. "Mama?"

The knob flew from his grasp. Bismark towered in front of him, as angry as his sermons. "I said, no!" He shoved his son away so violently, Charles left his feet before crashing to the floor.

Charles gasped for breath. He rubbed his breastbone, which felt crushed by the impact of Bismark's open palm. Bismark slammed the door shut. Charles went to Junior right away and found him with the horses. He'd put feed bags on them and now brushed one down.

"What's the matter with Mama?" Charles asked only to be ignored. He stepped up to his brother and slapped the brush from his hand. "Forget the damned horses. What's wrong with Mama?"

"You should know," Junior said.

Charles did not understand, unless Junior knew the secret. But Mama's current state seemed to have nothing to do with her shakes. He thought maybe he'd get faster answers from Ash. He asked, "Where's Ash?"

"Gone. That boy's gone from here," Junior said and suddenly struck Charles in the face. "This whole family is sick."

Charles fell back against one of the horses, which snorted and tried to get out of the way. Charles staggered and felt another blow slam into his right temple.

"I beat the shit outta Ash, now it's your turn." Junior struck him again in the neck and then in the face.

Charles swung back, fanning the air, yelling for Junior to stop. His lip split and blood rushed into his mouth. Then came a heavy blow to his stomach and he saw the blood fly from his mouth and he fell in the dirt and hay. Pain burned in the center of him and bile rose up to his mouth.

"I'll get back up," he said and wiped blood from his mouth with the back of his hand. "Let me catch my breath."

"Don't bother. Sit and choke. Ash say he gone on to Harlem. Colored capital of the world." Junior glared at Charles, his hands still tight, ready knots. "Colored police, an' colored clubs, a nigger in every window. Maybe you should go there too."

Confused and in pain, Charles managed to ask, "What did I do?"

"Ash said all this afta I kicked his ass. An' that was after I pulled him off of Mama. He was tryin' to do somethin wicked. Wicked."

Charles's mind reeled. He could see the anger shake his brother.

"She screamed an' screamed for me. An' I come runnin' an' there's Ash. With his hands on his Mama. An' Mama is cryin. He knowed he tried to do a bad thing. At first I jus looks at him. I cain't believe it, you know? Jus cain't. He said he was sorry. But he was jealous. I said, 'Jealous?' He's real mad at Mama an' jealous. I tol him to explain hisself cause afta I finished wit him he weren't gonna be able to do no talkin. An' that's when he said he'd seen you an' Mama together on her bed."

"Oh, Jesus, oh." Charles couldn't think, not at first. A terrible thing had happened because of the secret he'd tried to keep. It was a misunderstanding, a mistake. It was his fault.

"Mama ain't said five words since it happen. She don't do nothin. Nothin all day."

"Jesus, Ash is gone?" Charles cried, but Junior had no pity for him. Charles got to his knees and then to his feet. His lip still bled badly. "Hit me again," he said.

And before Junior went to complete the unloading of the wagon, he obliged.

*

Bismark never learned of Ash's attempted misdeed; Junior told him Ash, who never liked farming, simply ran off, tired of chores and wanting much to see what life stirred in the big cities of the north.

Bismark took the news hard. "When Ash returns, we'll kill the fatted calf," he said. "I'll put a jeweled ring on his finger and put on him the finest robe in the house." But his son never returned. And no one ever learned what became of Ash Standard.

Charles, after the beating Junior gave him, feared to go into the house, feared facing anyone, wondering what they knew and what they thought, especially Mercy. For the next few days, he took to staying out late, sleeping in the front room or the shed, and getting up and about before anyone else. He did not try to see Mercy and contented himself with only glimpses of her from discreet distances and vantage points. He assured himself over and over, he had not done what Ash had believed he'd done. He remained innocent of that particular sin. But he wore a heavy coat of guilt nonetheless, knew himself to be guilty of a great wrong.

He had caused this tragedy. That knowledge ate at him. He prayed on it. Often he went to the book for answers. He asked God for forgiveness. Bismark had always told him God pardoned all who sincerely asked for it. But no relief came along with the Lord's absolution and he slumped, weighed down with the burden.

On one day, he sat on the edge of the woods, his back against the rough bark of a tree and read his father's book, struggling over the words, sounding them out to himself and understanding less than half of it. When he glanced up, yards away, he could see Mercy in back of the house hanging laundry on the line. He wanted much to help her, but did not move from his spot, did not dare. Somewhere in this book, he knew, would be the way back to her.

He wished also that he might see the girl Ruth again, tell her what happened. He could tell her without fear, he sensed, and she would listen and she would hold his hand. He allowed his mind to wander in this fantasy awhile before returning his concentration to the conundrum of the book. In a moment, a noise distracted him from the pages. He looked up to see his mother standing over him, but appearing, still, small and vulnerable. He hated himself for bringing her pain.

She squatted, tucking her dress between her knees, putting her eyes level with his. She took a deep breath before she spoke; he could tell she had worked herself up to this. "Durin my—my shakes, Charles, we never did what Ash... what Ash said."

Charles could not tell if she were asking or saying. "No Mama, never. No, Mama." Tears came to his eyes.

He saw Mercy smile and felt instantly a portion of the relief he had prayed for wash through him.

"It was Ash's wrong, not yours." And Mercy reached out and lightly touched the side of his face.

Charles felt the promised forgiveness lighten him. He brought his hand up to hold her fingers against his cheek, but Mercy pulled her hand away. Her warm smile, though, still shone. Without another word, she rose and returned to her chores.

They picked green beans the very next day; the four of them spread across the field under a bright, unconcerned sun surrounded by the monotonous roundelay of thousands of grasshoppers. Mercy hummed to herself, but it carried across the field, heartening Charles and, surely, Bismark and Junior. Junior picked up a heavy stick and brought it to Charles.

"Here, boy," he said holding out the stick.

Charles frowned, not understanding.

"Mama told me you was only tendin her cause she felt poorly an' Ash took it all wrong. You never did hit so hard, so use this." He shut his eyes, prepared for the blow.

Charles took the stick and dropped it to the ground. Playfully, he gave Junior a soft punch to the stomach.

Junior opened his eyes and shook his head. "Is that the best you can do? Ain't I taught you no better'n that?" He slapped Charles's hat off. The two brothers began slapping at each other's hands and laughing loudly.

Mercy grinned at them.

"Stop the horseplay," Bismark shouted. "We gots lots to do an' no time to waste on foolishness," and he added, "We're short handed as it is."

There were no more sermons. Bismark ceased his belligerent, remonstrating, book shaking, preaching, sparing his family the long, uneasy evenings. None of them knew why he had stopped. Charles thought his father "all preached out" by the tedious road trip. Then, too, he figured it may have something to do with what happened to Chancy. The hanging had put Bismark off balance; in his view of religion, the relationship between God and man, Chancy could not be accounted for.

Junior had an explanation for the disappearance of the sermons. "He got no fight left," he told Charles. "Them sermons of his was how he hollered back, fought back, not at us, but at the whole worl'. Don't know why he give it up. If it's cause of what you say happen on y'all trip or cause of Ash. But he don't know the half of Ash's leavin an' we best keep it that way. No mo' of his damn preachin," Junior said. "You'd think I'd be happy bout that."

Charles asked Bismark one evening if he would ever take the team back on the road. His father said he did not know what the Holy Ghost had in mind for him. "But maybe we'll go back to the Gatherin Field from time to time."

This was the answer Charles wanted to hear for he longed to see Ruth again. He did not like being so far from her when Elmore and his Packard were so near. But the season of the Gathering Field was to come and go without Bismark once taking his robe from the closet.

Fall came. It sought to empty all it touched. That's how Charles described fall—not in those exact words—to Ruth once. He saw the season empty the pond of ducks and geese and empty the woods of its lushness and lay bare the fields of all the farms around. Even the sky emptied its dense blue and bright foam clouds, revealing its stone case of muted grays. Things got further apart in the fall. The season lacked the congestion of life and growth summer spawned. He could see further, through the nakedness of woods and across the barrenness of fields.

Ash's absence affected the family more keenly in the season of emptiness, and they became, despite themselves, a quiet family, not much interacting with their neighbors or with each other. Charles, in between the gospels or the letters of Paul, would dream of visiting Ruth, discovering, in his fantasies, that she had eagerly awaited his return. He knew the timing for a visit was wrong now. His mother, normally quiet, turned even more so. She, and Bismark too, jealously hoarded their remaining sons and the question most frequently asked of Charles was the whereabouts of Junior. Let either of them tarry at the pond or in the shed for too long and a parent could be found standing silently in the doorway gazing across the fields.

Charles knew also he could never leave for Fat Creek while he still kept the secret of his mother's recurring sickness. Once considered an exclusive treasure, the secret burdened him now. He understood that Mercy still feared the critical judgement of her husband and his Holy Ghost. But Charles had gotten to know the book and no longer feared it as he had.

Mercy remained wary however. When she told Junior that Charles had helped her when she felt poorly, she had not mentioned the shakes. The affliction embarrassed her, caused her to lose control of her water, bite her tongue, and thrash about like a madwoman. She would control it herself, or, secretly, suffer under it. Charles would never, could never betray her trust even if it meant he could never leave her. Yet, on the occasion of her next attack, he finally felt free of his obligation and could dare to make a trip away from home.

The family was in the kitchen, the men at the table, Mercy at the stove, on a morning in October. Bismark and Junior planned to go into town and see Mr. McCutchan as he had requested. The Standards had been one of Mr. McCutchan's most productive tenants that year and Junior bet the landowner meant to put more acreage under their care. Having made breakfast for her family, Mercy cracked two eggs in her black, iron skillet for herself. Charles went to the stove at that moment to get another biscuit. The two egg yolks, round, gold eyes protruding from a black face, had come alive. They quivered with life and shifted from side to side in the pan as if looking this way and that.

Mercy could not set the pan on the stovetop. She fought to control her arm. Charles pulled the skillet from her shaking grip. She looked at him and he saw her panic taking control of her.

"Mama, I can't find that clean shirt you left out for me." Charles set the skillet down. "Help me find it."

Mercy managed to nod. Her body tightened, her hands became fists, as she fought to retain control long enough to escape the kitchen.

Charles's quick excuse had not been necessary. As he followed Mercy out, he heard Bismark, say something to Junior about pennies and bushels, oblivious to Mercy's presence or absence.

She could not make it to the refuge of her room. The curse shook her control from her. She went out the back door instead, nearly falling over the steps, but Charles caught her. He helped her down the steps and guided her to a spot against the house where no one could look out on her from a window. He made her sit. Her head banged against the side of the house and he leaned her forward. He whispered repeated assurances that she did not hear. Then he left her.

He raced back into the house and into the front room to pluck from his father's desk the red leather covered book. "Strike you blind and change men's souls," his father had told him. Charles had witnessed its power. Grabbing the book had not been the inspiration of the moment. Ever since he saw Chancy's left foot proceed in front of his right, the scheme had been with him. He'd read the book in order to understand its power, to use it as Bismark had. Clutching the book to him, he dashed back to his mother's side. She lay in a quaking ball.

Charles knelt next to her and frantically paged through the book. Where was the passage? He'd forgotten it. No, it was John; Bismark had read from John first.

Charles flipped to it, tearing pages in the process. "Hold on, Mama. Jesus is going to heal you. The book says in John, chapter fourteen, verse twelve, 'Verily, verily, I say unto you, he that—that believeth on me, the works that I do shall he do also.' And Jesus say, 'If you ask anything in my name, I will do it.' See Mama?"

Charles flipped more pages. "Jesus be with us, heal my Mama." Then Charles found, in Luke, the verse he thought most applied to Mercy. "An' when the woman saw that she was not hid, she came tremblin—tremblin, Mama—and fallin down before him. She declares unto him before all the peoples for what cause she had touched him, an' how she was healed immediately." Then Charles closed the book and tried to push it into her hands, but they would not take it, so he held it against her. "Faith," he said as the Gathering Field congregation had, "Faith."

Finally, the shakes began to subside and Charles grinned. "I healed you, Mama," he said. He had done it right. He hadn't read it as clearly as Bismark, but a thrill had flushed him, the power of the book, and God and the Holy Ghost, and sweet Jesus, telling him in no uncertain terms the curse had been lifted from Mercy. And this time when Mercy came to, she saw her son crying. He told her what he had done, that she was free and healed and could be always happy now.

She looked at the book in his hand and wiped the tears from his face. "My sweetest son," she said and she hugged him there, on the ground, behind the house.

*

It took four days for Charles and Charley-horse, the horse named for him, to journey to the Brownings' home. His anticipation grew the nearer he came to his destination, so that by the morning Grainger opened the door to his knock, he could barely contain himself. Everyone, except Ruth, who was no where to be seen, ran up to greet him as if he were a lost member of the fold returning, as if he were Ash come home. Mary hugged him. The children, recalling a fine playmate, pulled on his arms and the sleeves of his shirt. Charles felt a warmth at the Browning home and a bond between the family and all its orphan charges that he did not feel at home, except between he and his mother. He looked around Mary and over the children's heads for a glimpse of Ruth. "She ain't here, Charles," Mary answered to the expression, that must've shown on his face.

"She gone to Louisville to visit, she say," Grainger told him. "Her friend took her."

"Mr. Langley?" Charles asked.

Grainger nodded, obviously not pleased with the situation.

The news had fairly crushed Charles, but he tried not to show it. All the paths of his fantasies had led to Ruth. She had been centermost in his thoughts during his trip. He and Charley-horse had gotten lost twice along the way, but Charles remained inwardly proud of himself for having successfully negotiated the journey. The nights alone in the woods inspired a little apprehension, yet the trip had actually been enjoyable. He had never experienced solitude for such a length of time. He came to understand the value of time alone. His dreams contained no such solitude. He spent the hours and the miles dreaming of Ruth and going over all the things he would tell her about his mother, and Ash, and Chancy and the hanging tree. But Elmore had taken Ruth away.

Mary whispered in Charles's ear, "Hold here a few days. She be back. You see."

So Charles stayed with the Brownings and waited for Ruth. He made himself useful to Grainger about the farm and helped Mary in the house. At night he slept on the floor upon the blanket he'd brought with him in one of the "rooms" with four other boys amid a chorus of breathing and snoring. His first night there, he crept to the back of the house and peeked behind the dark, red curtain into Tree's room. He inspected the darkness behind the curtain, letting only his head protrude into it. He could see absolutely nothing. "Hello, Tree," he said.

Though the Brownings and their clan were great hosts, generous and full of humor, the days there dragged by intolerably. On the third day, Charles knew he should begin the trip homeward. Down to only one son with them, Bismark and Mercy, he knew, would be beside themselves with worry. In his mind, he saw Mercy keeping a vigil for him at the window. He told Grainger he intended to leave in the morning.

"You are a hard workin man, Charles," Grainger said. "You welcome ta' come on back an' try again anytime."

Charles nodded. A surge of pride infused him for Grainger had called him a man and at that moment he realized he was a man. He felt very strong. Grainger was dazzled by the amount of work he got out of Charles that day.

Charles was determined to get a glimpse of the one hundred ten year old man before he left. Around noontime of that third day he slipped away from his tasks and went back to Tree's room. He silently moved the curtain aside. The space allotted to Tree was a lot smaller than he had thought. Tree lay on a narrow cot covered with a thin, white sheet. His breathing sounded less heavy than before. Only his head, black and bald, was visible. His eyes were closed, but the lids were sunken in for there were no eyes behind them. He looked shrivelled and dead, but he did not have the absence Chancy's body had; a soul still languished there.

"Come way from there." Charles felt a hand on his shoulder and turned to see Mary standing behind him. "Is you spyin' in my house, Mr. Standard?" She beckoned him away with a finger, picked up the naked Grainger III, who wobbled at her leg, and led Charles into the kitchen.

Charles began his apology, though he wasn't certain of his wrongdoing. Mary waved him off.

"You ain't done nothin, Charles," she said. "It's dat old man, so damn peculiar. He'd have a conniption if he knew someone was lookin in on him. An' den he threaten ta' leave again, like he got some place to go." She shook her head. "Ever time we tried to, you know, let him be part of dis family he raise a ruckus, have none of it. He old an'...an' funny." With her free hand she tapped the side of her head. The baby watched her and tapped the other side.

"Ruth's the only one who can get away with lookin in on him. Guess cause she do mo' listenin than talkin. She say he told her dat he don't wanna know anybody anymore. Ah don't get dat. Not at all." Grainger III grabbed his mother's nose. "Naw dats mine. You gots your own nose," she said to the baby and walked out of the kitchen with him.

The night before his departure came. Charles tried not to think of what a waste of time the trip had been. He tried to look forward to going home. Just before the Brownings turned in for the night, Charles went out to the small yard where Charley-horse was kept and brought him an apple.

"It will be good to be home," he told the animal, who blinked at him. He thought of how good it would be to see Mercy now that she was cured. With pictures of home enticing him, he even allowed himself to entertain thoughts of Ash's return. Perhaps his brother had already come home. They would not speak of what happened. That would be best, and, in time, it would vanish from memory and so never have happened at all. With the entire family there, and Mercy cured, and Bismark's harassing sermons a thing of the past, home would be a good place to be again. Concentrating on that scenario, hoping it along, Charles did not hear someone walk up from behind him.

Ruth said, "What are you doing here?"

Charles turned with a start. Whatever he'd planned to say to her first, burst like a soap bubble in his head and he stood there silently for a long moment.

"I told Elmore to drop me off down the road a spell. That car of his would wake the children an' there'd be no getting 'em back to sleep for an hour. Besides it's a nice, cool night for walking." And then Ruth added, "Even better for horseback riding."

They rode across open fields on a clear, bright night. Ruth's arms encircled Charles's waist. Something of magic pushed the shadows from beneath the trees for them as they rode by. Some work of gentle sorcery kept the pair warm though the night chill misted their breath. They crossed fields at a clip, laughing at the wind and at each other. They rode—seeming to Charles to fly—for several miles. The cold wind in his face and Ruth's warmth at his back intoxicated him. He laughed. How worth the trip and the wait this moment was! She laughed too, because he did, and because they were young and because for that night nothing could reach them, no doubts or troubles, no man or God could touch them.

Charles sobered long enough to think of Charley-horse and the young couple climbed down to walk the animal. Charles slipped the single blanket from his horse's back and draped it over Ruth's shoulders. In time he remembered all the things he yearned to tell her. The words spilled from him.

He told her everything that had happened to him with a detailed honesty that ought to have been embarrassing. Ruth listened. She sometimes asked questions. Tears came to her eyes when he told her of Chancy and how it felt to chop down the hanging tree. He told her candidly about Ash and his mother and his hopes for Ash's return. Ruth told him he did not have to tell her all these things, but Charles said, "Yes I do." Charles told her how he had healed his mother just as Bismark had healed Chancy. He looked for her reaction and Ruth turned her face away.

"I've seen days not this bright," she said.

"Don't you believe in healin?" he asked.

In the middle of a wide and level field, Ruth took the blanket off her shoulders and spread it upon the ground. She knelt on one edge of it, then held out a hand for him. Charles let go of Charley-horse's reins. The horse wandered only a few feet away to nibble at the grass. Slowly, reluctantly, Charles put his hand in Ruth's and allowed her to pull him to his knees facing her.

"Are you scared?" she asked. "You are a strange boy."

"I ain't a boy," he said.

Ruth placed his hand upon her leg just above her knee. Charles could feel the firmness of her leg through the fabric of her dress. "You can kiss me." She leaned toward him, her lips slightly parted.

Charles gave her a swift peck on her lips, snatched his hand back and came quickly to his feet.

Ruth seemed surprised and then angry. "Naw, you still a boy," she said.

"Get up from the blanket," he said. He told himself he was angry with her, but knew that to be a lie. She had surprised him. He had not expected this at all and was not prepared. He was angry, actually, with himself for acting like a boy. She had called him one. He had gone from a man back to a boy in one day.

She stood.

Charles collected the blanket and walked over to Charley-horse. He made a show of re-covering the horse's back, taking much longer to do the simple task in order to buy time to think. "A empty bean field out in the open ain't no place for... it ain't the right place," he said without turning around to face her. "No tellin who's peekin out—"

"Yeah, I always peek out on a bean field around midnight myself. Though I don't see no house to peek from." Charles heard her giggle.

He turned to her. "Not just yet, okay?" he said.

She nodded.

At that moment he began to wonder if Elmore Langley in his Packard would say, not just yet. He began walking, holding the horse's reins. She followed a few steps behind. After a minute or two he stopped for her to catch up. He bent and laced the fingers of his hands together, offering her a step up onto the horse. She put her boot in his hands and he hoisted her up. Before resuming the walk, he looked up at her and all the stars that shone just above her. "Don't you believe in healin?"

"I don't know if you'll like my answer, Charles," she said and bent nearer his face. "Yes, I believe in healings. An' I also say the moment you get home you grab your Mama an' take her to a doctor. A good, white doctor in Louisville if you can. I bet I can get a friend to drive the both of you."

"Elmore?"

"Yes, Elmore. An' if your father tries to get in your way you take that book of his an' slap him across the face with it."

Her words stunned Charles. He thought she knew how things were, had listened to his stories and understood. He had allowed himself to think that she believed as he did, though now he could not figure why he had thought that. He did not make a reply; she'd given him a lot to think about.

In a few minutes, he remounted and they rode back to the Brownings. Only Charley-horse made any noise, the pounding of his hooves, the swish of his legs through the grass and his snorting at the night air. The young couple did not laugh as they had on the ride out. They'd made the mistake of stopping, allowing the world and its problems to catch up with them.

When they reached the yard where they stabled Charley-horse, Ruth slid down the animal's backside. "You asked me what I thought, Charles," she said.

He answered, "I know."

"Are you still leaving in the morning?" she asked and he nodded. "I'll be up to see you off. You are coming back to visit me again."

He shrugged saying, "Yeah, I guess so."

"That wasn't a question, Charles," she said smiling. "Next time, write first. Make sure, I'm here."

Charles jumped down from the horse. "Because you might be out with Elmore Langley?"

"Might." She threw back her long hair and grinned mischievously. "Two boys, one girl. I like the odds on that. If you don't, change them." She spun around and ran to the house.

The trip home was not as relaxed or comfortable as the trip to the Brownings had been. Charles was disturbed. Things had not gone as planned at Fat Creek; he'd only been able to see Ruth for one night and that night had been confusing. Matters he thought settled, definitely were not. The closer he came to home, the closer he came to having to make some important decisions, the first being whether or not to take his mother to a doctor and the second, whether or not to go see Ruth again.

He finally admitted to himself that he should have taken Mercy to a doctor months ago when he first discovered her on the floor of the pantry. She'd told Charles how she'd felt the one time she'd asked Bismark if she could go see a doctor. Mercy, Charles knew, still lived in fear of the book, and maybe God, but definitely Bismark. Charles contemplated the book that could inspire both hope and fear.

The book had seemed Mercy's only hope. And, secretly, Charles was not convinced his mother's illness was physical. Perhaps these fits were products of her mind. A doctor could do nothing then, only Jesus could. Calling on Jesus had been a step of faith requiring total belief. If he were to take Mercy to a doctor his faith could be questioned; it would be as if he doubted God's power. The book was clear on this. As Charles rode home, it occurred to him that even considering a doctor meant he held a portion of doubt. He tried several times to shake it from his head and resented Ruth for having planted the seed.

Ruth. He could not figure her. And he tried from every angle. Nor could he figure his feelings toward her. She was nothing like Mercy. What kind of wife could she make? She openly dallied with the disreputable womanizer Elmore Langley. Yet, she seemed to like Charles too. She had wanted to kiss him. When Charles thought of her on the blanket in the middle of that wide field, he flushed with embarrassment and burned with regret. Next time, he promised himself, without immediately realizing that his decision to return had thus been made, he would grab her up in his arms, kiss and hold her and tell her how he felt—as soon as he himself knew.

But intruding into this passionate image drove Elmore Langley and his shiny car and shinier hair. After kissing Charles, Ruth would jump into Elmore's Packard and they would roar away, leaving Charles in a dust cloud. Ruth seemed too head strong and irreverent. "Slap your father with the book," she had advised. "You can kiss me," she had said.

The first night of his return journey, Charles wrestled against admitting he'd dearly love to do both. The next morning he reproved himself.

Ruth might be a bad influence on him. She had cast doubt where no room for doubt existed.

Before remounting Charley-horse, he knelt in the wet, morning grass, praying first for greater faith. He also asked that his newfound friend, Ruth, be given faith. He waited on his knees, not for a reply, but because he sensed his prayer was unfinished. He had another request to make of God, something, evidently, he felt he could not get without the Almighty's help.

Again, Ruth. She had stirred him, excited him, had him turned inside out, and bewildered. He beseeched God for her love; he asked God for her, admitting to his creator, before he had admitted it to himself, that he loved the golden-eyed girl.

As he spoke he shuddered. The same thrill he'd experienced when praying for his mother raced through him bringing confidence with it. He was young and in love for the first time, feeling like the captain of a ship and like a drowning man.

The morning sun's first rays fell on his face like the laying on of hands by a mighty prophet, empowering him, completing a communion with the Lord, and sanctifying his prayer. "Thank you, dear Father in heaven. Amen," he said. He finished the journey home with renewed hope and confidence. How silly and weak he had been to listen to Ruth. Soon she would come to see the power of God for herself instead of trusting in white doctors from Louisville, and soon, also, she would be his wife. We will have a family like Grainger and Mary's, Charles decided. He played with this fantasy over and over again as he rode along.

*

The extra land Mr. McCutchan gave the Standards to farm had not been cleared, not completely anyway, so a long winter of work lay before the family if they expected to plant in the new acreage come spring. They pulled stumps and cut thickets of tough, dark stemmed weeds, Charles working as hard if not harder than the other two men. As they worked, they spoke little, and Mercy, who brought lunches of cornbread and ham to them, said even less. Work usually heartened this family, infused them with purpose and ambition, so that they would discuss what new thing might be bought with the extra dollars the new land would bring in, new livestock or an ice box, maybe both. But no one offered any such speculations this season. The family just methodically went about their tasks.

Charles was grateful for the distraction the additional land caused. In this way, the days passed quickly, though full of sweat and strained muscles, leaving only the nights to deal with.

A few days after Charles's return, Mercy asked him if he'd been able to "spend time with the Browning girl. But I don't reckon that's her last name."

Charles told her how Ruth, whose last name, he told her, was Wolfork—she'd given him the name and her address on a piece of paper before he left—had been to Louisville with a friend and he hadn't been able to spend much time with her.

"If I was a young man," Mercy said, "I don't know as I'd traipse so far to see a girl that goes galavantin around in fancy cars wit older men."

This surprised Charles because he had not told Mercy about Elmore Langley. Then he remembered Bismark had been present when Elmore and Ruth drove up to the revival tent. Mercy also surprised Charles because that was the most opinion she had offered anyone in a long time.

Once, when they were alone in the house, Charles asked her if her shakes had come back.

"Naw," she said, "Not yet."

"They won't, Mama. Faith. You'll see."

She looked down and away from him, seeming almost to cower, but she nodded and whispered, "Amen."

Several weeks passed and the majority of work on the new field had been completed. Charles began to talk of another trip to Fat Creek. The first objector seemed always to be Mercy.

"Field's not done," she'd say or "Lot needs doin round here." And Bismark would add, "We're short handed til Ash comes home." So Charles forced himself to wait.

He wrote Ruth a letter, trying to explain why he could not yet come to see her. He sat at Bismark's desk with a pencil in hand for long hours without getting beyond the words, "Dear Ruth." Finally, he went to bed, and after a full day of work, returned to the desk and the task the next evening.

He approached the writing of the letter as he did a stubborn, old tree root needing removal. He gripped the pencil, wanting to bring brute force to bear on the paper, to somehow squeeze the words from the pencil.

Charles's education had been spotty. Bismark had frequently kept him home to work and writing had never come easily to him. In Charles's mind swam all the thoughts and feelings he wanted to share with Ruth, but they could not flow through the pencil. Behind him, Mercy, in a straight backed chair, repaired a pair of his jeans by lamplight. She seemed to Charles to be always near him in the evenings. He thought about asking her to help him write the letter; Mercy had a fair hand with such things, but her attitude toward Ruth was clear, so he struggled alone. On the third evening of trying, he completed the letter, and placed it in an envelope very much dissatisfied. It said little he had wanted to say and what was written was so badly done, he waited another three days before mailing it.

Charles turned sixteen. Mercy and he celebrated the event with a small, chocolate cake. Junior had left to visit a girlfriend. She lived only three hours away, but the ease of Junior's exit, nonetheless, grated on Charles. Bismark, tired to the bone, had fallen asleep upon his open Bible at his desk.

It was warm in the kitchen where mother and son sat across

the table from each other, though from outside, cold winds could be heard sounding like wraiths against the house. No lamps in the kitchen had been lit; darkness did not come gradually in winter as in the summer, but fell quickly and usually caught Charles unaware.

Mercy had left the wrought iron door of the stove open. The glowing embers provided a soft, and slowly dying light. On the table between them sat the cake and they both used it as a place to put their eyes rather than on each other. At one time, Mercy's attention alone would have been enough for Charles, but now his frustration showed even when he tried to hide it. Mercy saw it, Charles knew, though he'd wanted to be happy for her.

She took his hands, so much larger than hers. "All my boys growed," she said. "I guess a mother ain't s'pose to ask for more'n that." She smiled at Charles, but for some reason it made him feel sad more than anything else. "I thank Jesus for that," she added. "All three growed."

"Mama, you're all right now, you know. I wouldn't leave otherwise. But I wanna go visitin Fat Creek. The Brownings is nice people."

Mercy let go of her son's hands and passed an index finger across the top of the cake, then put the chocolate tipped finger in her mouth. "Me an' sweets. I know I best be leavin 'em be." She stood up.

"Mama?"

"Jus don't worry bout that other boy. Girls worth havin don't fall in love wit pin stripe suits and chrome fenders."

"Bumpers," he said. She turned to leave and Charles called her back. "Mama, the Holy Ghost is gonna protect us all, you'll see."

"Sixteen," she said and headed out of the kitchen. At the doorway, the little woman paused, but did not turn around. "Soundin jus like your daddy." Charles heard her voice say. "Got the same fears."

*

Snow had fallen through the night just east of the Standards' place, just enough to disguise the trail and its treacherous holes and ruts as an evenly paved, hospitable road of white. Concerned that Charley-horse might misstep, Charles dismounted and walked the horse; they plodded along slowly. Though the sky was gray, the sun had come out and its reflection off the ground's thin crust of snow and ice was blinding. There seemed to be no comfortable direction in which to look.

Charles's lips and hands and feet were cold and growing numb. It was, of course, a bad time for a trip across country on horseback, but his eagerness to see Ruth had fogged his judgement. And, too, he had not written Ruth to tell her he was coming, running the risk that she might be away again, perhaps with Elmore Langley. At the moment, however, Elmore did not worry Charles as much as the weather did.

It had been mild at his departure from home, but a few miles down the trail, he'd run into the slippery snow and falling temperatures. What the night would bring worried him to no end; still, he refused to turn back. His only plan amounted to hoping just as he'd run into the bad weather, he'd find better conditions ahead. Under the mist of his breath, he beseeched God to help him make it through.

Horse and master found sanctuary from the increasingly harsh wind just off the trail in a densely packed stand of pines. A good hour maybe two remained before nightfall, but Charles could go no further. He and Charley-horse had worked so hard for just a few miles. In the hills, drifts evened out the draws between the slopes and trudging through snow, knee high in places, had been tiring and painful.

Charles kicked his boots against a tree trunk, trying to get feeling and circulation back in his feet. This only served to bring bursts of pain to his toes, which he thought was better than feeling nothing. Later, he plowed the snow by dragging a foot along the ground to clear a circle for Charley-horse to graze in.

The horse only stared at Charles, seemingly perplexed over the mistreatment it had received that day. The young man did not bother to clear a spot for himself, but sat on an exposed root that rose from the snow like the hunched back of a big snake.

Charles watched the wind pick up restless snowflakes from the ground and off the tree branches and swirl them into an angry, white swarm. He tried to think of Ruth rather than turning back for home. Somewhere in the tumble of roiled snow, he heard a distant voice calling his name. He worried he could no longer trust his mind to discern the real from the imagined. His father had told him just such things happen to men stranded in the cold. For a moment he thought God himself called. Perhaps he thought he was finally on his road to Damascus, the bright snow had been sent to indeed blind him and the cold, to change his soul. He heard his name called three more times as clearly now as his father claimed to hear the voice of the Holy Ghost.

The shape of a man on horseback congealed through the powder laden winds, treading across the flat brightness toward Charles. Slowly, familiarity came to the curve of the man's shoulders, how he held his head, even the look of his mount.

It was Junior. He dismounted as he came into the protection of the tree stand.

"I ain't goin back," Charles said. "You get to see your girl. If I don't go now, no tellin when Mama and Dad will let me go again. So you can turn right around an' head home." Charles didn't move off the natural bench he sat on, folded his arms and gave his brother his best defiant look.

Junior nodded.

Charles noticed how drained and weary Junior seemed.

"Uh, huh," Junior said. He rubbed at his frosted eyelashes. "Papa be takin Mama to the doctor, but... she fell, I guess. We was in the new fields, Papa an' me an' she didn't bring us no dinner. "An' you know, we wondered about... we wondered about that so I came home early. She done hit her head, Charles, bad, against the stove. I can't figure how she done it. Cause it look like her head hit more'n once."

Charles screamed. He threw himself into the snow at Junior's feet and screamed.

The brothers stopped by the doctor's first, but the portly, big eyed, black man sent them on home. Charles did not climb down from his horse.

"I'm sorry, son," the doctor had said to him, patting his leg. It occurred to Charles then, that everyone had conspired to test his faith, Ruth, Junior, and this doctor. They were deceivers, and gainsayers. He must ignore them and hold on to his faith. If he did this, if he could manage it, Mercy would be at her stove or in her rocker when he got home. "Wash up," she would say, "cornbread's near done." Charles did not remember any of the journey home, except his tears freezing and breaking on his face and the vague shape of Junior's back leading him along.

Charles smelled hot, candied yams and fresh bread as soon as Junior opened the door to their home. *She's at the stove*, Charles dared to hope. But in the kitchen sat Bismark with two women Charles vaguely recognized. One went to hug him, but he stepped quickly back.

He looked to his father whose face was buried in his hands. Before Bismark on the table, between his elbows innocently lay the book, open, showing damp, spotted pages. Charles went around the small gathering to his mother's room, hesitated at the door only long enough to remove his hat and gloves, and then slowly pushed it open a crack. He saw his father's bureau with the shaving mirror on top, then the foot of the bed came into view, then Mercy's booted feet lying upon the bed.

He opened the door no further. He stood there, saw her boots and the hem of her best dress and tried to recall the last time he had seen her wear that dress, but could not place the day or the event.

His faith had not been strong enough. Into the crack of the doorway he whispered, "I'm sorry, Mama. Forgive me."

\*

In the months to follow, Charles made frequent trips to the Brownings' in Fat Creek. And when his brother and he got their first truck, an aging, black Ford pickup, Charles became a fixture in the Fat Creek area. He could be spotted many times along the road with head and arms under the hood of that truck, sometimes with an impatient Ruth behind the wheel waiting for his signal to "try it again, but don't flood it." More likely would be the sight of the three of them, Charles, Ruth and Elmore having a picnic along a creek or sailing kites in the middle of a field, seeming to passersby to be a trio of friends.

Elmore Langley drove them north to the Ohio River one evening months after Mercy's death. He parked in a secluded spot close enough to the river to hear it slap lazily at the shore, close enough to smell it and all the living and not living it carried away.

Charles climbed out of the car immediately and pushed through the brush and tall weeds to the river's edge. He broke one of the basic rules of the Charles-Ruth-Elmore game: never leave the other guy alone with the girl. On this evening, he thought just of Mercy. He looked at the liquid stars swimming on the river's beveled surface. The river seemed always the same, but altogether new with every moment. He wished he could throw his grief into the waters, watch the current bear it away from him along with the silt, the drift wood, and the carcasses of dead animals.

Despite the noise of the river he could hear Ruth and Elmore talking, not every word, but enough. Elmore was impatient; there was still time to see a show. Ruth's voice was light yet firm. He could not make out the words, but the tone sounded like a mother gently coaxing a young child to wash his hands. Ruth was always very tactful with El. He said he understood the cat's mother had died—months ago. He asked if she had given something to Charles. What was she waiting for? And how could she like those wild flowers as much as the bouquet of roses he'd given her? Charles had picked a handful of tiny purple flowers for Ruth that morning. He did not know what they were called. Elmore was asked to be understanding; she only wanted to cheer Charles up. He heard a car door open and in a moment a rustling through the brush behind him.

"Is the river pretty?" Ruth asked. "Oh, yes, it is."

Charles turned, looked at her briefly, but had nothing to say. It hurt to talk.

She came up very close to him and placed a hand on his arm.

"The river makes me think of going on a long, long journey somewhere, I don't know. New York or some place, maybe some place exotic." She looked down stream. "I wonder where it goes. Hey!" She shook his arm as if to wake him. "I want to cheer you up. Let me. It's time to be happy again. I've got something for you."

He hadn't noticed she'd had one arm behind her back until she brought it around, displaying a small box in her opened palm. She smiled, waited for him to take the gift from her.

The pocket watch inside ticked like a heart. It was gold plated, had large roman numbers and a porcelain face.

She explained why she bought it for him. He didn't have one. He could tell her when she should be ready for a date. He could tell her how long he had to wait for her to get ready. She laughed. "Don't you like it?"

"You can't afford nothin like this."

"How do you know? I could've saved up and—"

"Saved what? Elmore paid for this."

"See how you are? I saved and scraped for that." She looked away from him across the river, her smile gone. She said, "I just wanted to cheer you up."

Charles put the watch in his pocket and let the box drop. He grabbed Ruth roughly by the shoulders, pulled her against him, and kissed her awkwardly, pressing his face too forcefully against hers.

She fought away from him, touched a hand to her lips and looked at it for blood. "What's got—"

He heard a car door slam. "C'mon," he said and grabbed her hand. He pulled her along the shore.

"What are you doing? Where're we going?"

Soon they were both running. He pulling her. They jumped over fallen limbs and the heads of buried rock. He'd leap an obstacle and she had to quickly gather her legs under her to hurtle it too. They fled recklessly. He heard her laughing. She asked if they were leaving Elmore. Did he know where he was taking them? She didn't seem to care. She was with him now.

They were forced to stop when the bank became too steep

and the larger trees came right down to the water. Charles stopped and Ruth tumbled into him, laughing until she saw his face.

"Well, you brought us here. El is gonna have a fit."

Charles dropped to his knees, letting his hands slide down Ruth. Then he clasped them in front of him. He looked up at her, his eyes begging.

"Charles?"

"Pray with me, Ruth."

"Pray? No. Get up."

He repeated himself. "Pray with me."

"Get up." She reached for him. "Tomorrow's Sunday, we'll go to church."

He asked again. The small roots and rocks under his knees began to hurt him.

She stepped away, shaking her head. He was being silly. She mentioned Elmore's temper.

He watched Ruth walk away from him until he could not see her, but heard her answer Elmore. Yes, they were coming.

Charles stood up. He had to brush wet dirt from the knees of his trousers.

**PART FOUR**

214 / O. H. Bennett

# XII

## Rain and the Angel Wing

*"Your Gramma Ruth's maiden name is Wolfork."*

Mama thought it might rain and had Julie, BobbyCat, and me pile into the cab of Grandpa's pickup with her. It only sprinkled that afternoon. The sky turned a shallow, pale gray reminding me of Germany for some reason and a trip the Major had taken the family on through the dark woods of Bavaria. The strange lands and their peculiar people never frightened me. I felt safe with the Major and Mama.

The old pickup bumped and rocked over the road home. The truck seemed to find and bounce in every crack and chuckhole from the library to the farm. We were shoulder pressed to shoulder inside. Vapor edged the windows. We seemed to be sharing the same warmed over breath of air. I felt pinned like a bug in an insect collection. No one had punched holes in the roof of the truck so that we could breathe.

I kept my face within kissing distance of the passenger side window. Rain drops landed in perfect randomness on the glass, then streaked sideways across it like tiny, clear comets. Outside, the green land and the gray sky blurred, mingled at tree top level. I did not see it well. I put my hand on the window crank.

"No, honey, don't let the rain in. It's not that bad in here, just make sure the vent is open."

I rolled the window half way down, letting warm raindrops sting my face.

The truck suddenly screeched to a stop. We rocked forward with our hands instinctively reaching in front of us.

"My packages!" Mama said, jumping from the truck. She

rescued sacks of odds and ends she'd purchased at K-Mart from the back of the truck.

"This is the juiciest secret ever," Julie said to BobbyCat and me.

"Don't tell nobody," I said. She asked why not, but I did not know why not.

Mama passed the bags to us until we were all loaded down. "Things for the apartment." She spoke as if she were out of breath or maybe just in a hurry. "Some things in here I don't want getting wet." She did not ask again why we'd been at the County Office of Register of Deeds. "Julie, the apartment is on the third floor." She started the truck forward.

I turned my face again to the passenger window. I was suffocating. Mama was saying, "Which is what I asked for. Easy to get out of in emergencies, but too high up for most burglars. A high school is five blocks away."

Julie asked, "We're going to be there when I'm ready for high school?"

I looked toward Mama, could not see her behind BobbyCat and K-Mart bags.

"Oh, well, I don't know, sweetheart," she said.

When Mama turned off the road and down the long, gravel trail leading to the farm, I almost opened my door and burst out of the truck. I could no longer tolerate the ride. I was convinced I had not breathed for the last mile, even though I'd rolled the window completely down. I would've done it too, baled out like a pilot from a crippled plane, but the trail rose two to three feet higher than the field it stretched across and I was afraid of the fall from a moving truck. The rain had not reached the farm. The pickup still woke up dust behind us. Mama braked the truck at the side of the house. I threw the door open, let the sacks fall from my lap, and flew out of there.

"Help with the bags, you jerk," Julie said.

I ignored Zeke, who came from his place to greet me. I leaped the porch steps, landing only when safely behind the door of my own room. I sat at my window.

It occurred to me that I might have jumped the gun. "I don't know a story to tell you about Kate," Gramma had said. There are different Willises, different Smiths totally unrelated, maybe, maybe different Wolforks too. *Maybe Gramma does not know.* These thoughts offered no consolation, no niche to place hope in.

I recalled the day I'd asked of Kate; how Gramma Ruth had rested her hand upon the cherub so gently, like a caress. She knew. If she'd lied about Kate, what about Luther, and Cakes, and Hattie?

"Your Grandma's slave stories are just tall tales." Grandpa Standard had tried to warn me.

Julie and BobbyCat stood in the front yard talking. Zeke circled them. What had the librarian asked? "How does your grandmother know about the other residents?"

I had shrugged. I had accepted the stories on faith, as part of Gramma Ruth's special magic. BobbyCat waved in the direction of my window. He was saying something. I shoved the glass up.

"I'll be back around before you guys leave," he hollered and waved again.

I brought my hand up. The country boy headed down the trail. Part of me, a very large part, wanted to go with him. He seemed very free. He had no beliefs to trap him, believed in no one who could disappoint him. I tossed away my plans of stealing back the fishing gear. It no longer seemed an important thing to do.

Zeke and Julie both watched after our friend for awhile, then the collie trotted away, leaving my sister to spin about in the middle of the yard until she spotted Grandpa. Her mind burst at the seams with "the juiciest secret ever". She sped across the field to Grandpa Standard. She would have to tell him what we'd learned. Perhaps she thought he would shed more light on the story of Kate before she asked Gramma about the baby with the same last name.

Julie had been asleep the morning Grandpa paid homage to the stone cherub. She did not know Kate was as much a haunt for him as she must've been for Gramma Ruth. I can imagine when Grandpa saw Julie racing to him through the tall grass with her ponytails flying behind her, he actually forgot for that moment about ghosts. His eleven year old granddaughter, a part of the present and the future, may have cheered him, given reason to his efforts and hard work, forced a smile for her sake that soon fit well on that old face.

Julie collided into his legs and the old man managed to lift her just off the ground and spin her once about. I heard them both laugh, the sound coming late and faint through the screen of my window. They held hands, marching together through the grass. Julie's constant chatter mixed with that of the crickets. Grandpa Charles was nodding to her words that I could not hear, but could easily guess at. I'd been sitting on my bench, but rose to my knees, not certain of what I anticipated until I saw it.

Grandpa froze in mid-step.

From that distance, I couldn't have possibly seen the look on Grandpa Standard's face, yet I remember the shock and astonishment of it just the same. Ghosts, he learned that day, filter up through the soil and the past to roam across the present.

He glared at his granddaughter. Julie continued to talk, not understanding, I suppose, the reaction Grandpa had given her. I made out plainly one word she said, Kate, twice, three times.

Grandpa Charles let go of Julie's hand. She talked faster now, trying to explain something to him, how she'd learned Kate was her aunt, or why she'd looked up the information in the first place. She probably felt nervous there under his eyes; her voice waned until I could not hear even the sound of it. She probably guessed, right then and there for the first time, that telling him had been a bad mistake. She had forayed into the forbidden territory of the secret world of grown-ups with terrible results.

Grandpa said nothing to her, though, later, Julie said it looked as if for a moment he might. She confessed to me that in that moment she was deathly afraid of him. I thought back to the drunken man I'd had the late night talk with and nodded my understanding. But Julie's moment of confrontation with Grandpa passed quickly when he turned and stomped away from her.

My sister stood there perplexed and confused. She told me she thought she ought to "apologize or something," but was too frightened to follow him. She called to him, but he would not turn around. I watched the old man shrink across the field until swallowed whole by the stand of sycamores that grew where the slave quarters used to be.

I went to the phone in the upstairs hallway and called the Major. The German operator spoke English, but I knew enough German back then to have gotten by. His phone rang. "Answer, Sir." It rang. "I want to go home, Major." It rang. The sound of it made me more desperate. "Please, Major, I want to go home." I let it ring. The operator came back on the line. I slammed the receiver down on the cradle. I sneaked out of the house and squirmed under the porch without being detected. I hid out with Zeke.

*

I was curled around Zeke. His abrupt movement woke me. Thin stripes shown on the ground where the porch light seeped through the floorboards.

"Is your name Sarge or Charles?" Gramma's voice asked. Zeke had gone to her in the middle of the yard. "I wasn't calling you." She scratched behind the collie's ears. "What? Is that where he's been?" She bent low as if she could peer into the darkness under the porch. "Come from out of there, Sarge, I declare. Go inside, get something to eat."

I wondered if she really knew I was under there or was she just guessing. I thought I'd wait and see if she insisted or came nearer. But she seemed to dismiss all thought of me after that.

She straightened up. "Charles," she called. To the collie, she said, "I don't suppose you know where he is too." She went to the barn, "Charles!" with the dog bouncing around her. "Trade you in on a blood hound." She joked with the dog, but the foreign accent of anxiousness tinged her voice. "Charles, you in the barn? Supper."

I crawled from under the porch. Light sprinkles immediately dotted me. I let them land on my face. When I gazed skyward, I could see nothing, no moon nor hint of it, no stars nor the lesser dark which separates one cloud from the next. The blackness, sifting wetness down on us, was impenetrable and complete.

Gramma exited the barn, continuing her search. It was not so late. Chores had compelled Grandpa Standard to persevere past supper before. The fields had talked him out of dinner and kept him later than this without Gramma mounting a search for him. Only once before had I observed in her such keen interest in his whereabouts. The house lights' influence barely reached the barn and the shed. Gramma moved about in inky shadows. She seemed not to notice the rain, which picked up for a furious practice run then tapered off again.

I don't remember what I thought then, if anything. I sat on the bottom porch step observing Gramma. It occurred to me, I'd only known her for a summer. A day before, we seemed to have a bond welded over a lifetime. We had taken our refuge amongst the same visions. We had mutual friends and were allies against those who could not see what we saw. Now seeing her head crane into the tool shed, she again was a stranger. She was again the eccentric gardener I'd first met pruning amongst stones and talking to air.

"Charles?" She headed around the barn to the trail that led to the garden.

Mama came outside. I didn't look her way; her voice fell from above and behind me. "I forgot how dark it can get in the country. It's like being blindfolded. I never minded the dark myself. A night like this makes everything go away, makes it all invisible. Not a thing to worry about. I used to go around playing blind man's bluff all alone. Just to see if I could make it from one place to another without my eyes. I'd close my eyes if it wasn't dark enough. My hands would take the lead, I'd drift after them all wrapped up in the dark. I'd spin around and around like a mean top, get myself good and dizzy first." She laughed.

"One time I thought I was heading from the coop to the house and ended up in the middle of the field standing in a nasty, smelly cow pie."

I did not laugh with her.

"You're not very happy with me right now are you?" She stepped down from the porch. She clutched an umbrella and held out one hand, palm up as if asking the sky for a spare dime. I don't think she expected a response from the sky or me.

"Oh, it's going to pour any second now. Have you seen your grandparents? Julie said Daddy was upset and Mom's gone looking for him. I don't know what's going on. She's going to get drenched."

"Gramma went to the garden."

"She's going to get drenched," she repeated. Mama headed across the yard into the dark.

"Who do you like better," I asked her, "your Mama or your Daddy?"

She froze in mid-step before turning around to face me. I could feel her glare, though I could not see her face well. "Things aren't going well for you these days and you've chosen to make them worse for everybody with hard headedness and bad manners. Well, fine. I had to find a job and a place for us to stay. Your precious Major—I think I've been through every damn door way in Louisville. I'm trying the best—"

We both heard Gramma's faint scream and looked to each other for explanation. I jumped to my feet. I believe I heard, "Stop!" and "Charles!"

"Mama?" My mother cried.

We raced toward the garden. We heard Gramma's voice again, "Stop it!" Zeke was barking, then snarling.

"Mama! Mama!" The blackness was no longer her childhood friend. Something was terribly wrong and the night protected this wrong, hid and enhanced it, kept us from it. We were two, panicked, blind mice plunging after the third. Mama fell. I could not tell where she was. "Keep going," her voice said. I ran on and heard her footsteps behind me.

"Gramma!" I hollered.

Zeke cried, a high pitched yelp of pain. Rain started driving down like hard nails. I jumped the garden's fence, spotting it only as I nearly tripped over it.

"Gramma, where are you?" Now I was playing a desperate version of Mama's blind man's bluff game. I thrust my hands wildly about in front of me.

"I'm over here, Sarge. I'm all right." I followed her voice and my hands soon found her on the ground. Zeke was hovering over her, getting in the way.

"Mama, what happened?" Mama came up from behind me. I could hear the rain bouncing off her umbrella. She stooped and sheltered her mother with it.

"I'm all right," Gramma said again. "He broke off her wing. My little baby's angel wing. Help me find it."

"Who? Daddy?" Mama asked. She called for him, "Daddy! Daddy!" Nothing could be heard above the hard pelting rain. "What happened, Mama?"

"I came down to talk to the old fool. He had a tire iron. He wanted to tear down my baby's marker."

"Did he hit you?"

"No, he just gave me a shove when I got in his way. Old fool's been drinking. The angel's wing, help me find it, Sarge."

Mama said, "No, Mama, we'll find it in the morning. A piece of the marker? It'll be here in the morning." She tried to help Gramma up, but she pulled away.

Gramma and I began questing about on our knees for the piece of stone. "Help me find it."

"We're getting drenched," Mama said.

I was soaked. The ground turned into a sponge beneath my knees. My blind hands slapped and smacked the ground around me. Water splashed in my face.

"Help me find it," Gramma kept saying. I feared Grandpa would come back. In this darkness, he could be standing just two feet away, glowering at us with the tire iron descending from above his head. My probing hand might land right on his boots.

"It's Kate's," Gramma said, "Help me find it."

Rain thumped on my back, and scurried down my arms, and dripped off my chin. My fingers combed through a bed of collapsed flowers. I thought I'd found the cherub's wing for a moment, but my hand closed around a whiskey bottle. I threw it away. The hard rain masked the sound of its landing.

"I've got it," Gramma said. "I think it's in one piece."

"Good, let's get out of here. We've probably all caught our deaths."

My eyes must have adjusted or one sliver of moonlight wormed its way around the clouds, because I could see both women now, actually, just the dark shape of them. They huddled beneath the protection of the umbrella. Zeke led the way and he appeared none the worse for his role in the incident. As we came up the trail, nearing the barn, we heard Julie calling for us. She sounded frantic. Mama answered, "Everyone's okay, honey."

"Zeke can come in tonight, Sarge. Dry him off in the kitchen," Gramma said. She clutched the angel wing to her chest. With Mama's arm about her shoulders, she seemed old and helpless.

We walked across the yard. Julie's silhouette waited on the edge of the porch in front of the light. "Have you seen your grandfather?" Mama asked.

"Uh, uh," Julie shook her head. "Is Gramma okay?"

"Yes. Let's all get inside and get dry, please," Mama said We climbed the porch steps in a wet mass.

"There he is." Julie pointed.

Grandpa Standard splashed across the yard like an errant night phantom, running like Luther, to his pickup.

Mama and Julie called to him, screamed at him through the downpour. He made it to his truck. Its bright eyes opened. The engine raced. Grandpa Standard drove off into the rain and the night, like a criminal trying to flee the scene of the crime. The truck tore away, slinging rooster tails of mud behind it. It disappeared, the sound of its fury beaten down to nothing by the torrent.

*

A pool of water formed on the yellow linoleum around my feet. I shivered, as much from fright as from being soaked to the marrow. I latched the screen door while watching the wind driven rain stampede across the porch. I was becoming more frightened instead of less. No one said anything. He was out there somewhere, wildly swinging his tire iron. He had more than one reason to be angry with me. Plus I had stolen from him. My imagination took hold. He would return in the night, his eyes red from whiskey, water dripping from the crumpled brim of his hat. As I lay asleep in bed, I would hear only two, brief, inadequate warnings: the drip of water on the floor as he stalked to my bedside, and the urgent, rapid whistle of the tire iron slicing down.

I shut the door. Everyone looked at me.

Gramma said, "No need to slam it, Sarge. And unlatch the screen so your grandpa can get back in when he returns."

I froze. I must've looked as if I did not understand what she'd said. I looked from her to the door and back, but made no move.

She pushed by me, opened the door, unlatched the screen and silently shut the door again. She had not relinquished the angel's wing. The chiseled fan of feathers resembled a large seashell. It nestled closely to her. I wondered how she could want Grandpa back in the house.

Zeke shook himself, flinging water away in all directions. That seemed to shake everyone out of their questions and speculations and back to the kitchen and each other. I grabbed the dog. Gramma sent Julie, the only one of us not standing in a puddle, to find an old blanket to dry Zeke with. Mama told me to take off my shoes and tiptoe to the bathroom.

"Ring out your clothes, then take a bath," she added. "Might as well put on your pajamas."

"Zeke is hurt," I told her. I noticed he favored his front right leg. Soaked as he was, Zeke smelled, and looked emaciated. His resemblance to Lassie was only physical and slight at that, but he had taken a kick or a hit with the tire iron on Gramma's behalf and I was proud of him. I realized his deepest loyalties belonged to Gramma Ruth and that was okay. I could not take him to Louisville with me. He would not like the city. I knew, too, the dog would hate the master that did not let him come and go as he pleased.

Mama did not examine him. "He's fine. Go on upstairs. Tell Julie to bring the mop too." She wanted me out of there; I could tell. Questions for Gramma poised on the tip of her tongue. She eyed Gramma even as she spoke to me. I wanted those answers as badly as she did and hesitated to leave.

"Go on," she said. "Where do you get this new defiance

from?" She began fumbling with the buckle of her belt.

It was a race to get my sneakers off before her belt cleared her last pant's loop. I won and scurried up the stairs, grumbling and shedding water the entire way.

I don't believe Mama received the answers she wanted that night. When I came out of the bathroom, the house was quiet. I faked taking the bath, a routine deception on my part. I'd leave the door slightly cracked as I ran the bath water so Mama could hear it. I'd wait the appropriate amount of time, wet face and hands and be done. Normally, I faked baths because I just didn't like getting wet. But that night, I didn't want to be in the tub when Grandpa Standard returned.

I went downstairs. Only Zeke lay on the kitchen floor. His tail beat against a cabinet when he saw me, but he didn't bother to even raise his head. I peeked into the refrigerator, not really looking for anything. I should've been ravenous. I had not eaten all day. Now, I was too nervous to eat, too curious to think about it, too disappointed to care.

I shut the refrigerator door and returned to my room. It wasn't near bedtime yet. The night's events had keyed me up. I hunkered down by the vent in my room. No voices chambered there. No sounds floated up to me. I went to the window, could see nothing through it, except a million rain mites driving madly into the porch roof. A knock came at my door and Julie slipped in and turned on the light.

Mama must've told her what she knew of what happened. Julie looked on the verge of tears. "It's because of what I told him," she said. She seemed scared and in want of company.

"You always have to tattle tale," I said. "You never shut your big mouth."

She sniffed. Tears rolled down her face. I immediately felt bad about what I'd said. My words had never bothered her or meant anything to her before. "You're a jerk," she said, and left me to be afraid all by myself.

The night and the rain had a pact; they would go on forever. They would hide some things and wash the others away. I dug under the sheets of my bed and waited for them to expend themselves and go away. And I waited to hear the heavy boot step on the porch, if I could, signaling Grandpa Standard's arrival.

I did not sleep during that marathon night. I outlasted it, cowering in the corner of my bed. At one point, I wanted to go hide under the porch, but could not summon the courage to leave my bed. What if Grandpa came back just as I opened the kitchen door? So I waited in bed, alone in my sweaty fear, afraid not only of Grandpa Standard, but of everything, the rapid thumping of the rain that once lulled me to sleep, the night, that had once let me be a part of it, even the familiar shapes in my room unsettled me.

None of my friends came to hold the vigil with me, not Hattie May, nor Cakes, nor Chief. I could not conjure them because I no longer believed whole heartedly in their existence. With the pillow and the sheets pulled against me, feeling utterly alone and abandoned, not understanding the nature of my fear, I gritted out the night.

I remember exactly the sweet, silent moment the rain gave up, know the moment a hint of light came to my window breaking the back of all the great dark that remained. I survived the night and the rain and specters of Grandpa and the aloneness. I was exhausted.

The first sounds of the morning were so normal I did not trust them, the quick whip sound of Gramma mixing batter, the squeal of the screen door opening, the cackling yawn of the rooster. At the window, I saw Zeke adding to the already saturated earth. Warily, I put on my clothes. I wanted to feel relieved. I tried to tell myself everything would be okay; after all, this was to be my last day on the farm. But as I dressed, I realized the night and the rain had been wrongfully accused, and much of my fear remained.

I scouted the downstairs from the top step. I remembered the morning after Grandpa had confronted me in the living room, how everything had been swept cleanly away so that I doubted, at first, if my night of chasing imaginary bobcats had actually happened. There could be no cover up this time. I took one step down then glanced over my shoulder to make certain no one lurked behind me. I was stepping into the deep end and did not want to be pushed. My foot was about to test the next step when I heard the crash that froze me in place, clutching the railing. Without having to see, I knew Gramma had dropped her mixing bowl. Her scream followed the crash.

"Connie! Oh, Connie, your Daddy!"

Mama burst from her bedroom. I saw her face, we saw each other's, mirroring the same fears. She banged down the stairs with her robe trailing behind her like a cape. I followed her down, through the kitchen, over bright yellow, spilled eggs and ceramic shards, and out to the porch.

"Oh! Connie." Gramma headed down the porch steps. She stopped to look back at her daughter. Tears rolled freely from her eyes.

"Mom?"

Gramma began to run. Mama and I looked in the direction she headed.

Down the trail, on the very edge of the property where the mailbox waited at the roadside, rested Grandpa Standard's overturned pickup. He had flipped over where the trail rose maybe two feet to meet the road. The truck pointed away from the house. He'd never made it to the road.

"Maybe he's not in there, Mom," my mother said. "Ken."

I hurtled the porch steps, easily sped by Gramma and raced down the narrow gravel road. The truck looked peculiar turned upside down with its rusty muffler and oily underbelly exposed to the sky.

I recall thinking if I ran wide of it, took to the field instead of running straight at it, I would sooner be able to tell if Grandpa Standard was still inside. I jumped off the trail. The soft earth immediately grabbed one of my loafers and pulled it off my foot. I left it and kept running.

What I don't remember thinking about during my quick sprint was life and death and what I would find when I got to the truck. I understood the urgency of the situation that had compelled Mama to send me, the fastest of us, down the trail. But death was not on my mind. I had only thought of death in terms of the sleepers in Gramma's garden. Their deaths had happened long ago and were easily and naturally acceptable. No one I knew living had ever died. So I was not thinking about it as I pulled my feet up from the muck. I just raced right toward it. Grandpa would either be in the pickup or not.

I stopped for a moment when I saw him. I cupped my hands to my mouth and called back to the house, "He's in the truck! He's in the truck!" I saw my mother disappear into the house to call for an ambulance. As I continued my sprint, I realized my other shoe too had been pulled off. I ran on to the truck, not noticing, initially, the red taint of the mud near it.

Grandpa lay in an awkward twist on the ceiling of the cab with his legs trapped between the steering wheel and the seat above him. I wanted to close the two yards at most between us. But I didn't. Blood pooled around him, rich, bright, and as thick as syrup. It stained the seat, speckled the dash, and seeped along the cracks in the windshield. The blood flowed out of the truck where rain had mingled it with earth and I saw it soak into the socks on my feet.

"Are you alive, Grandpa?"

A deep, violent gash blazed from above his right ear to the top of his head. The hair on his head was soaked red. I extended my hand. I wanted to put it on his chest to feel for a heartbeat, but then Gramma was there, bending into the open driver's side window. She pressed a hand right onto the gash on his head.

"Help me, Sarge," she said, "We don't want to move him too much, but we have to get his legs down."

"Is Grandpa alive?" I asked her two or three times while I helped her free his legs and straighten them out. Grandpa lay half in and half out of the truck. He made no sound, not a grunt nor a moan. His clothes were wet from rain that had found its way in the cab or from just the dampness of the morning. I only touched his legs and they felt cold. This is what it is to be dead, I thought, coldness and blood. I knew people needed their blood to live and figured Grandpa could not possibly have any left.

"Give me your tee shirt," Gramma said. I pulled it quickly off. She folded it once and pressed it to Grandpa's head wound. "Now run to the house. Bring blankets. Tell Connie to call Mac; he lives closest." I must not have taken off fast enough. The blood both attracted and repulsed me. "Run, boy!" Gramma scowled at me.

I ran, but met Mama and Julie halfway up the trail. Mama already had blankets, and Julie carried water in a pitcher and a wash cloth. Mama ran by me. "Daddy," she was saying.

Julie stopped in front of me, holding out the pitcher. Her mouth hung open and tears flowed freely over her cheeks. "It's because of me," she said.

I took the pitcher from her. We stood there facing each other on what should have been a fine, bright morning. Mornings on the farm after a rain usually smelled so clean and sweet, and this was supposed to be our last day on the Standard farm. I wanted to say something comforting to her. I didn't want her to feel so bad.

"How bad is he hurt?" she asked.

I wanted to tell her this wasn't her fault, that what had happened last night had been between Gramma Ruth and Grandpa, had brewed between them for a long time, that Mama had even seen it when she was a little girl.

"It's because of what I told him," Julie repeated, "Is he going to be okay?"

I wanted to say, yes, do not worry, it's not your fault. I stepped backward away from her, offering neither words of consolation nor a look of understanding. I brought the water to Mama, leaving Julie on the trail between the house and the wreck. The closeness I had felt toward her for the good part of that summer had vanished. I do not know why.

Through their tears, Gramma and Mama worked quietly, quickly and efficiently. They covered him with two blankets, felt his limbs for breaks, wiped away blood from his eyes and mouth. Gramma told him softly and repeatedly that everything would be all right. When Mama had done all she knew to do, she began to curse the ambulance.

"What is keeping them?" she asked. "I tried not to sound black on the phone."

Gramma said, "You should've called Old Mac. I told you to call Old Mac."

"No, you didn't," Mama countered. I thought they were about

to argue. I ran out to the road to await the ambulance.

Waiting slows time down whether it's for a light to turn green or to buy a ticket. Waiting on an ambulance virtually freezes the mechanism of time. I stared down the road, strained my eyes and ears for the first sign of it. Gramma kneeled in the cab of the truck, hovering over Grandpa with Mama right behind her. Julie remained on the trail, afraid, I guess, to come closer to Grandpa, maybe afraid someone would blame her. I watched her and the empty road, and the overturned truck still dripping water. Mama went to Julie and hugged her, and I'm sure she said what my sister needed to hear at that moment.

We heard the siren; the wail cut across the field before the flashing ambulance raced into view. "They're coming. I see them," I called and jumped from relief.

The white station wagon with the rotating red light on its roof pulled right up to the mailbox, and two white men in blue uniforms leaped out. They each carried bags and kits and asked a lot of questions. Mama answered them.

"We found him this morning, but he's been out here all night."

One man took Grandpa's blood pressure and said some numbers to the other man.

"No, he hasn't come to," Mama answered.

One of the men gently moved Gramma out of the way.

"No allergies that I know of."

They put a needle in Grandpa's arm. The needle trailed a tube leading to a transparent bag of clear liquid. They laid the bag on Grandpa's chest.

"Yes, we think he'd been drinking."

The other man flung my T-shirt away. He orbited a roll of gauze around Grandpa's head, around and around, layer after layer, each swelling red.

"Turned sixty three this year."

One of the rescue workers retrieved the stretcher from the station wagon. They counted in unison, 1, 2, 3, and eased Grandpa onto the stretcher. He still made no sound. They dragged Grandpa from the cab, lifted him and carried him to the ambulance. Gramma and Mama followed. "Only one," they were told. Gramma climbed into the back of the wagon with the help of a medic.

"I'll be right there, Mom," my mother said, "As soon as I get a ride."

The ambulance turned around, nearly going off the road itself, and screamed its way back to the county hospital. Gramma was inside, bent over Grandpa, holding his hand. That was the last I saw of them for several weeks.

## XIII

### The Brief Biography of Kate

That first apartment in Louisville was small, and noisy, and tight.  The shouts and the blare of car horns bounded and screeched from the streets and heavy coughs and curses resonated from the thin walls.  In the first few days we added little to the noise and the movement of the city.  We were insular, each with a different reason for guarding the quiet.  Mama woke and went to her new job.  From work she went straight to the hospital an hour and a half away.  She drove a used Ford Maverick bought with money the Major sent.  We saw very little of her.

In the days before school started, Julie would walk to the library and bring back stacks of books.  She scanned oversized volumes with bright, colorful pictures of foreign countries, and women with red dots painted on their foreheads.

I stayed in my new room, a closet compared to the one on the farm, or watched television.  A lot of kids my age played around the garbage cans and clotheslines of the apartment complex.  I would meet them soon enough in school, and was in no hurry to get to know them.

During this time, Gramma stayed at a retirement home near the hospital with a friend she'd known for years.  She hired BobbyCat to feed and water Zeke, and watch over the place while she was away. I thought that was funny, but I was told the country boy was very conscientious about his duties.

The summer ended.  I started fifth grade.  A new way of life had begun the moment I walked into the little Louisville apartment with Mama and Julie.  My determination was to resist it as much as possible.  I began by skipping classes almost immediately.  I forged Mama's signature on the notes teachers sent home with me. When I skipped classes, I would wander about my new neighborhood, going out further with each excursion.  I wished I was back in Germany, or in Gramma's garden, or even on a tractor ride with Grandpa Standard.

One evening, three weeks into the new school year, Mama returned from the hospital with the announcement we would not be going to school the next day.

"Tomorrow's Friday and I'm sure one day missed won't hurt. We're going to try to be of help to your Gramma," she said, "Your Grandpa is coming home tomorrow. You'll finally get to visit him."

Julie jumped up excited. "Did Grandpa wake up?" she asked.

"No, honey, he hasn't woke up."

Julie asked, "Then why is he leaving the hospital?"

Mama tilted her head up to keep the tears from falling out. "Just pack a bag for three or four days," she said.

The farm's welcoming committee consisted of BobbyCat and Zeke, both of whom were sitting on the porch when we drove up. The frog dog seemed genuinely happy to see me. BobbyCat told us ambulance drivers had carried Mr. Standard inside a half-hour ago. Mama and Julie went directly in.

"Come on in," Mama said, holding the screen door open.

"In a minute," I told her.

The pickup, with its crushed cab, sat by the barn. Friends of Grandpa Standard had righted it and towed it there. BobbyCat and I wandered over to it. The blood inside was brown and dry like a scab. I told BobbyCat what had happened, that Grandpa had tried to knock down Kate's marker.

"My daddy been in two accidents on accounta he been drinkin," BobbyCat told me. "He says a third one would finish him. He says he ain't gonna drink nothin stronger than beer if he's gotta drive."

We compared notes on school. BobbyCat was impressed that I'd skipped more classes so far than he had. "Did you ask your Mama how come your granddaddy took a tire iron to that tombstone? He's gonna be haunted for doin that."

He's already haunted, I thought. "Julie asked her. She said Grandpa was drunk and it wasn't any of our business. I think she's still figuring it out herself."

"Guess what!" BobbyCat ran his mangled hand along the dents in Grandpa's truck, gazing at me only through the far edges of his pale eyes. "Miss Ruthie offered me a job helpin her tend the farm."

"I heard."

"She pays okay too. Trick is she said I had to give back Old Mac's fishin gear." Now his eyes returned to meet mine. "Wonder how she found out about that?"

"Mr. McEachern told her."

"Oh, shit! Really? Do they know about you too? What did they do to you?"

I shrugged. "They ain't had time to think about it, I guess." We were silent for a time, inspecting the dry blood on the truck's ceiling, and just kicking our feet in the dirt. I told BobbyCat he wouldn't like the city, but that raised no comment from him.

"Are you going to do it?" I asked. "Return Old Mac's gear?"

"Guess so. I can use the money more than I can some fancy, old fishin rods really. Maybe I'll sneak 'em back at night, leave 'em on his porch. Sides, Miss Ruthie thinkin she'll have Old Mac come harvest for her." BobbyCat climbed on the hood of the pickup. "Remember that car we beat up?"

"Yeah." I smiled. "I remember."

"Gotta go," he said suddenly and jumped to the ground. "Ellie's been sick lately. I gotta look after her. Truth is I'm going to be a big brother." I must've looked surprised; he laughed.

When he left, I snuck under the porch to retrieve the watch, still encased in its protective baggy. I had loot to return too. This became an important act. I could be done with them when I returned the pocket watch, Grandpa and Gramma Ruth, and Kate, and the garden. I'd become entangled in their concerns, only dimly acknowledging I had thrust myself into the situation. Somehow I felt returning the watch would allow me to walk away. Gramma and I would be even then. We would be square.

I did not know, having just turned ten a few days ago, that I'd set foot on a new path I would walk for many years. This circuitous route steered me clear of confrontations and responsibilities. No one need place faith in Sarge Willis for he would be out, or late, or tied up elsewhere. And he, in turn, would have faith in no one. Years and years have slipped away. I have only recently realized that I had the ability to circumnavigate through crowded seas and not get wet by anyone else's emotions or problems. On the day before my grandfather died, I knew only that I needed to return his watch.

*

I waited until the smell of supper faded from the kitchen door, and the new, autumn sun had nearly set, before entering the house. I wandered around the farm awhile with Zeke, thought about going down to the garden, but did not. With everyone preoccupied and turned inward, I could get away with this tardiness.

I slipped through the kitchen. I heard talk along with the little, buzzy, quick voices of the television from the front room. I crept up the stairs undetected. No light showed from beneath Grandpa Standard's door. I braced myself. I turned the doorknob slowly. There was no chance of awakening him. He had lain in his wrecked truck too long, had lost too much blood. Still, I went in cautiously.

In the room's weak light, I could make out his shape in the middle of the huge bed, and his dark face and arms amongst the white sheets. His breathing was shallow, almost inaudible, but as I stared I could see the slight rise and fall of his chest. A thin bandage wreathed his head. This man could not coil and strike at me.

"I've got your watch, Grandpa. I only wanted to look at it." I pulled open the tiny drawer of his shaving stand and fished the timepiece from my pocket.

The door to the small, side bedroom opened and Gramma Ruth stepped out. "I'm glad you finally decided to visit your Grandpa. I told Connie not to make you do it. It's good that you came." She moved to the side of the big bed and turned on one of the lamps.

The man on the bed didn't look like Grandpa Standard. He

was too frail.

"I just wanted to return the watch."

Gramma eased herself down on the foot of the bed as if she feared waking him. She kicked off her shoes and drew her legs up under her. She looked to see if she might be causing Grandpa any discomfort, hoped, perhaps, she might see him grimace. His face remained dark and blank.

"I hoped you would. I knew you'd been in here, Sarge. Mary and Grainger's picture had been moved a bit. When I first noticed that, I just figured you were being your usual nosy self til Mac come by. Then I took a look around to see what might be missing. Put that off awhile, checking the room. Made me feel real, well, low. Made me feel low. I owe Mac an apology don't I?"

I think she thought I would begin to cry and apologize, and, maybe, beg her forgiveness. I said nothing. I was about to place the watch back where I'd found it, but she held out her hand. I gave it to her. I wanted to leave then, my mission was accomplished.

She examined the watch. "He would've given you this if you'd asked. Lord knows he never used it. He didn't like it. Claimed I bought it with a friend's money. My friend, not his, Elmore Langley." She laughed softly and looked at Grandpa. "You were right, I did.

"I was real disappointed in you that day, Sarge."

I hung my head, momentarily ashamed and defensive. Then I said, "You told me you didn't know a story about Kate. You said all your slave stories were true. Grandpa told me they were tall tales."

"Did he?" She looked caught for a moment. It was her turn to look away from me. "Yes, Kate is my daughter. You guessed that, right? But she didn't live long enough to have a story. Julie told me what you two found out. I didn't tell her what it meant. Guess I owe it to you though. And as for my stories..." She said nothing for a long time. I grew impatient. "Sit here," she said. She scooted over and patted the bed beside her. "A boy should know about his grandpa. I'm going to tell you about yours."

There appeared to be no way out of this except to run. I gave it serious consideration. I wanted to escape her old eyes, which seemed to look into me, read my mind. My inability to secret my emotions from her made me uncomfortable. And it angered me that I was being judged when she too, by my witness, stood equally accused. I wanted to run.

Grandpa's presence increased my anxiety. His stillness suggested tension. The accident had not subdued some inner part of him. I did not want to come within reach, though Gramma patted a spot for me on the bed. If she could see through me, she missed completely, the fury beneath the white sheets and black skin of Grandpa Standard. She would not sit so near him if she'd seen it, for his mute passion was as much directed at her as it was at me. Maybe what I sensed was only that he wanted, finally, to speak, to offer an explanation or an apology.

Why this occurred to me, I can not say. Much of what I perceived may have filtered from boyish imagination and guilt. Yet there were reasons for the dread and the heaviness.

Impatient Death waited in a dark corner of that room. Beneath the tall headboard which reared up like a marker awaiting an epitaph, lay the culmination of a lifetime of experiences, joys and anguishes, now bottled in an inarticulate coma. Gramma sensed, at least, his desire to communicate if not his belligerence, for she was offering to testify on his behalf, to tell his story.

I reluctantly went to the edge of their bed. Recalling how I felt then, I am amazed I did not run. Certainly, I was capable of such disobedience. Perhaps curiosity alone forced me forward. I think also I hoped something in what Gramma might say would set everything right, explain away my disappointments, even bring my parents together again, and allow me to believe in her fairy tales. I climbed upon the bed, letting my feet dangle above the floor. My back was to her and I sat within inches of Grandpa's feet, an untenable position.

Her stories usually began like a plunge into a cold pool, but she waded into this one. "When I first met your Grandpa, he was fifteen years old," she began, "traveling around with his loud talking father who thought himself a preacher man. I was just a year older. Didn't like either one of them at first. Can't recall why, Sarge, except they both had this look. Their eyes stayed on you too long for one thing, and, I don't know, but they both looked haunted. I don't mean by ghosts like in the movies, Sarge, but like they were hiding something or hiding in it." She paused. "Like you and your escapades with BobbyCat."

She seemed to wait for a comment from me. I remained silent. I felt surrounded.

"Maybe I didn't notice the look at all but only imagined it later, after I learned more about them. Anyway, Charles did not hold his secrets long. Not back then.

"When I came to live with the Brownings, Grainger and Mama Mary," she pointed to the photo over the bureau, "you've already met them, I used to love hearing the stories Grainger's daddy used to tell. He use to just go on so! He'd say, 'Ruthie, Ah had de big Papa possum dead to rights, wit my barrel pointin straight fo his heart. Mister Possum plead wit me not to shoot him an' he'd tell me a good story in exchange. Ah say to him, Ah don't know on account a lot of chilun back home gonna be comin to de table. But Papa Possum gets ta beggin, sayin, please! please! an' Ah say, all right, what's your story? Now y'all listen up an' let me know if Ah made a good deal.' Then Old Grainger would tell a story fanciful enough to make us forget there would be no meat to eat with our greens that night.

"When Old Grainger left for Lexington, we found Tree and so I had a new storyteller. I'll have to tell you about that old, gentle man one of these days. He's a story all to himself. Weren't any TVs back then, Sarge, and we didn't have a radio either. We entertained each other with stories and games. Did you know the Brownings had fourteen children by the time I left? I know where four of them are now, just four... Dora, Little Mary, who ain't so little, and—listen to me, Sarge, I'm supposed to be telling you about this man here." Gramma laid a hand on one of Grandpa Standard's unmoving legs. "When he and his daddy showed up with Old Grainger, I wanted to hear a story, but the young ones kept Old Grainger busy, and Tree only spoke when he felt like it, so Charles took it upon himself to be my storyteller." She chuckled softly to herself.

"So he told me all about himself and his family. I don't mean their address, how old his brothers were, and what crops they grew. I mean secrets, about his father's voices and his mother's shakes, and who thought what, and things that scared him. I didn't know what to say to him or what to think. What's the matter with this boy, I asked myself over and over. Why does he need to tell me these things?"

She let me in on the secrets, telling me about Bismark and Mercy and the Power of the Holy Ghost traveling show. She weaved his story in rich detail as she had her slave stories. I became apprehensive. She told me fare normally not considered digestible by ten-year-olds. She painted troubling images, the ranting father badgering his family with a Bible, Mercy's cruel illness, the lynching of Chancy. I don't believe she was being harsh. By the time Gramma Ruth turned ten, she had probably lived events similar to the ones she described to me. So I'm sure she saw little harm in the telling. And, certainly, the storytelling served to help her retrace history, to straighten out facts in her mind, maybe uncover a clue to how things came to be as they were.

Hunting for me, Mama peeped in for a moment, letting the harsher light of the hallway stream in. But she did not quite break the spell. Gramma gently sent her away and continued Grandpa's story. I used that moment to slide down from the bed. I brought over the chair at Gramma's bureau, placing it just outside the soft net of lamplight, and knotted myself into it.

I tried to imagine my grandparents as young people, the man lying before me as a youth on his knees, having fallen in love, praying for the hand of Ruth Wolfork. Each time Gramma revealed some new thing about him I would glance toward his masked face as if some corroborating evidence might be found there. I felt closer to him.

"He shared every feeling, every odd notion that flitted through his head. He told me how he felt about our first date. It wasn't a date at all, not like the ones with Elmore Langley, but Charles considered it one. He'd traveled all that distance from his home to see me but I was touring the big city with Elmore. Going to fast parties. Dozens and dozens or hundreds of people squeezed in one room and still finding space to dance. Dancing in each other's laps. The floor would vibrate beneath your feet and when you first pushed your way in, the air was so smoky and hot you thought it had been all breathed away. That is until you became part of the whole living, bumping process, and danced and drank." She waved an arm in the air and shook her head from side to side.

"Sarge, the women laughed so loud, over the music, jazz just like wine, hmmm. Those city girls would wonder. To be so black and be so green too. Cause Elmore was handsome. My dresses were beautiful. Elmore held me on the floor..." The party, with the press of dancers all around Elmore and her, must have continued to revolve in her head and I don't think she realized for a time she had stopped describing it.

Moments later she said, "I came back home and felt sorry for you." Her eyes didn't leave Grandpa. "We went horseback riding in the middle of the night. A fast, wild ride. I loved it. Funny. You know, I mean peculiar. This boy letting me in as he had. Deep in his head and his heart. So deep I thought I might suffocate under the covers of his secrets. All that about poor Miss Mercy, and the red leather book that scared him. And then, after telling me all that, still be too timid to kiss. On this beautiful night, in the middle of an open field, with every star ever lit shining down on us, I laid out the horse blanket, but he would not join me. Too many of his daddy's sermons in his ears maybe. Oh, but if you'd known I'd just spent the evening fighting off the advances of Elmore Langley...

"I know you hate for me to mention Elmore." Gramma crawled on hands and knees up the bed, looking like a little girl for a brief moment. She settled next to him and lightly rested a hand on his chest. Then I realized she wasn't resting it; she was checking. That same hand went to his face, gently caressing and touching. "But you never hated him as much as I came to. And I never hated you, Charles, oh, no." Gramma inspected his bandage. Her fingers toyed with the sparse hair remaining on his head. While she did this, she hummed or moaned really, just like Hattie May. "No, baby," she whispered.

I had been forgotten. In the dark, out of the soft, feeble lamp light, I had become invisible. Gramma saw only her husband of forty-five years lying next to her. A driving need to speak to him tunneled her vision. The present fell away and I fell with it. Whatever she had originally intended to tell me had been forgotten. Only the two of them were there for her, Charles and Ruth, in a past of which I could not be a part. I remained in the darkened theater, aware that I did not belong. Now, I was peeping in.

"I'm going to have to believe you hear me, Charles. In near fifty years... Is it fifty years? You'd think the opportunity to say this would've come up a time or two. Plain fact is it hadn't. So I got to believe you hear me now.

"Where was I? Hmm?" She smiled at him. "Oh, yes, Mr. Elmore Langley. Wonder what happened to him? I don't spend too much time wondering that, cept I hope his sins caught up to him," and she added, "like ours did to us. Elmore couldn't understand why I liked your wild flowers as much as his roses or rides on Charley-horse as much as rides in his Packard. He could see where my heart lay; why couldn't you? You know, I think that's why he chased me up and down every hill in Kentucky, cause he saw I wasn't willing to give him much more than the time of day. I let him give me things though. When you're young you see the ribbons on the gifts, but miss the strings. That high seditty boy could've had any girl in the county. Probably did, what you say? They just ran after him like fools and asking each other, 'How does dat young Wolfork girl dat lives wit de Brownings hold on to a man like Elmore?' By not trying to hold on, sister hens, I should've told them. He asked me once what kind of game I thought I was playing, Charles. Yeah, just like that. He said, 'Charles Standard and I don't like it. It ain't cool to nobody.' He was talking about how I made us into a threesome. See I wanted you along with Elmore and me because I didn't plain trust him all the time and because I just wanted you along. Elmore was supposed to be my fun time. He was parties, and new dresses, and houses with electricity. He played jazz while you hummed gospels."

Gramma Ruth fell silent for a time.  The conversation
between her and Grandpa continued on a level I could not get at.  I
squirmed in the chair.  She stared into her husband's face, maybe
giving him his say.

"We were young," she finally answered.  "Why do we blame
old folks for the mistakes of young ones?  But I enjoyed our
lakeside picnics.  And the attention of two men.  I felt pretty and
right smart.

"I thought I deserved it.  Spent the first part of my life being
shuffled off from aunt to grandma to cousin to uncle, one relative
to the next.  No one wanted an extra mouth to feed.  Except Mary
Browning.   I taught myself how to survive; she taught me
everything else.  She was a big-hearted woman, said she loved
making babies and having babies.  But she'd work you hard too.
In between helping the neighborhood women deliver another
Browning baby, I wiped more butts and runny noses, mended
more britches, picked more greens, rolled more biscuits, washed
more plates than... than I care to remember, I guess.

"Charles, I'm not complaining, mind you.  I was the oldest
girl.  They needed me like I needed them and that felt good for
awhile.  I'd sit out on the front stoop in the morning, and from
there you couldn't get a good look at the sun for all the trees, but
you could see the light peeking through them like finding the gaps
in a fence, and I'd plait the little girls' hair.  Swat them on the butt
and say, 'Next!' Kit, and Eulene, and Janey, Dora and Little Mary.

"One time plaiting Janey's hair, she asked me, 'You my
Mama too, ain't you?' Little girl thought she deserved two Mamas
when I never had one.  I answered quick, 'Uh, uh, Janey, don't ya'll
put that on me.' Hurt her feelings the way I said it, but I didn't
care.  They needed me all right.  That family gobbled me up
quicker than they did evening supper.  I started wondering who I
was, and when was going to be my time.  Didn't want to wear my
fingers to bony nubs on a dirt farm in the middle of the hills.  Then
came the desirable Mr. Langley, and later on, Mr. Charles
Standard, both showing an interest in Ruth Wolfork.  Up til then,
my only fun had been listening to old time slavery stories by Tree.

"I'm just trying to explain, Charles.  Why... trying to explain why I went off with Elmore to Cincinnati. That was a few days after we buried Tree. Elmore said he'd take me up to Cincinnati to cheer me up. I waited all day for him to come by. I wore this shiny, yellow dress and my first pair of sheer, silk stockings and I had a big, yellow bow in my hair just to the side." Gramma touched the side of her head, feeling the stylishly extravagant loops of soft silk that had been there long ago. "All bought by Elmore. I was a sensation. The dress went above my knees. Grainger thought it was scandalous. But you couldn't tell me nothing! I knew I was looking sweet. Wouldn't let the children touch me. Finally went down the trail a bit to get away from them. To get away from that look Mary was giving me too. I kept smoothing my stockings, hoping I still looked fresh. Evening came before I saw a pair of headlights coming down the road. I ran toward them til I heard that rackety trap of a truck of yours.

"You didn't hardly stop it before you jumped out. Never seen you so excited, Charles. 'Ruth, Ruth! I got it!' You were just shouting. You spun me around and around so fast all the tree tops whirled together like a phonograph record. We were so dizzy, falling against your truck was the only thing that kept us from falling to the ground. I don't know if you knew how tight you were holding me, but that felt good.

"You didn't have any breath left when you said, 'I got it Ruthie. I got the land. Our land.' Then you kissed me. Must've been holding back, or practicing with someone on the sly because I didn't know you could kiss like that. It was my turn to be out of breath. Elmore drove up without my noticing. I don't think you noticed either, cause we were still kissing until we heard his car door slam. Guess, even though I could feel your body tense up against mine, I still didn't expect any trouble.

"Elmore said something like, 'I don't know if I like this too much. My good friend Charles kissin on my girl.' I felt your hand trying to hold me close, but I took a step back, just a short step. I told Elmore I was congratulating you for getting the farm you wanted. He asked me if I was ready to go, but he stared right at you. I told him, 'Charles is going to have his own place. Isn't that great, Elmore?'

"He pulled off his driving gloves and applauded. 'Very smart, Charley,' he said, 'What we Negroes need more than anything else today is more dirt farmers. Now I know you can argue a case for more train porters and boot blacks, but I gotta go with sharecroppin dirt farmers as the new spear heads of Negro society in America.'

"Elmore stepped up close to us. I grabbed your hand; it was fisted as hard as a rock. I told Elmore to shut up.

"He didn't hear me. Just kept talking, which, besides making money, is what he did best. 'And I suppose, Ruth,' he said, but his eyes were still on you, 'You're thinking of going off with Charley boy to his mud hole and live a nigger's life with him, a life no one respects not even yourself. You'll give him babies and wipe noses and rear ends til you can't tell one from the other. But that'll be cool cause it won't really matter.' He knew what to say, knew how restless I'd been. I thought he'd read my mind.

"You said... what did you say to him? 'I can make a good home for Ruthie,' or 'a good life for Ruthie.' Something like that.

"He laughed. And I was mad at him, and if you'd said just then, come on let's get out of here, I'd have taken hold one of those big hands of yours and let you lead me away... I would have. But you didn't say anything, just stood there smoldering like a lump of coal, burning from the inside. You standing there made me think you thought, deep down, Elmore was right. Elmore started talking about my dress then. I suddenly wished I wasn't wearing it, so that he couldn't use it against you. He said, 'Doesn't Ruthie look beautiful in that new dress, Charley? Ruthie, I swear, you're breath taking. You're the type of girl that should always be wearing pretty things, lace and bows, and silky, slippery little things. Can you get her dresses like that? Where did we pick that one up at, sweetheart? You did notice her dress, didn't you, Charley?'

"But you'd been too excited about your new farm to notice. You looked me over good then. I could see you hated that I was wearing that dress. You hit him. So quick, I didn't see your hand, just Elmore's head flop back like it'd come loose and about to roll right off his shoulder. He dropped to his seat right in the road and you were on him like bark on a tree. I tried pulling you off, telling you to let up, but you kept swinging away. I don't think Elmore could fight worth a damn, not men anyway. I managed to grab one of your arms and pull you off him. Then you turned so fast, gripped the top of my dress and ripped the strap. I remember you said, 'Why you got to wear his things? Don't you know how it looks?'

"Elmore jumped up. He said, 'Naw, nigger farmer, why don't you tell us? He had a pistol in his hand, a little, shiny one that looked more like a piece of jewelry. He jammed it into your ear. 'Let her go,' he said. But I didn't wait to be let loose. I jerked away and climbed into Elmore's car. I believe I said something smart like, 'Don't shoot him, Elmore. You might make us late to the show.' Yeah, I said something sassy like that."

Gramma covered her face with her hands and exhaled into them. I froze, not wanting this intermission to bring her out of her past. But that was impossible. She'd dedicated herself to telling Grandpa this story, and though it seemed an ordeal as her voice weakened and grew hoarse, she kept talking, pausing only to swallow or to gather pieces of her memory, making a critical search sometimes for the right words.

"Was that you behind us for awhile on the way to Ohio? We saw headlights following us, but they fell further and further behind til they were as faint as stars. All the way to Cincinnati, Elmore talked about how Negroes dreamed too small cause they didn't think anything of themselves. He also had to hold a bloody handkerchief to his top lip most of the way up there. 'Big dreamers become big people,' he said. He asked me if I wanted the best in life or if I just wanted to have babies like Mary. I watched the headlights behind us grow so tiny they disappeared.

"In Cincinnati, he took me to this all colored bar, and we listened to a big woman in a red dress sing blues, and we drank gin. And I started feeling better, you know. When it got late, he said he knew about this party we could go to. We drove through town, but didn't find a party. Instead, we went to the apartment of a couple he knew. He and the man sat in the living room drinking. The woman and I went into their bedroom. I took off my dress and she mended the tear for me, though I told her I could do it. While I sat in my slip on the edge of her bed, she told me Elmore was a great catch. If I treated him right, life wouldn't be too hard. I didn't say much to her; I just nodded.

"He left me with his friends that first night. Went off and wouldn't tell me where. Charles, I don't recall their names, his friends, the couple. I didn't like them. He drank too much and her hands were always all over him. She'd cup a hand to his chest and say it felt as soft as a titty. They laughed over anything. Sheila. I think her name was Sheila. But it doesn't matter. She reminded me of my mother, although that's silly since I never knew my mother. I suppose she reminded me of the cruel, little stories my aunts used to tell of my mother. The four of us went out the next night and the next and I was glad they went along, though I don't think I thought about why I wanted them along. Elmore bought me more dresses and matching hats and shoes. We went everywhere coloreds were allowed to go. The lights, and the people, their clothes, my clothes... the city so different. People didn't spend their time putting up green beans, and mixing cornbread, and mending slippers so worn out the only thing left to them was the stitches from the last mending. These people laughed, saw all Negro revues, saw movies from the balcony... Grainger and Mary worked at life. The city colored didn't work at life, they lived it. Least, that's how I thought about it at the time. And though, none of it seemed real to me, looking back and all, I really figured I'd discovered the good life, something Mary didn't know about. But then came the catch.

"The catch was the first time I had to go to bed with Elmore. We came back to Sheila's place from a nightclub, but Sheila and her husband—I guess he was her husband—decided to stay longer. It had all been arranged, I think, because they didn't show up til very late and Sheila's man usually called it a night first cause he had to get to work early. Elmore made it clear what he wanted as soon as we stepped through the door. I told him, maybe it's time he took me back home. I didn't want to leave, mind you, I just figured if I could change what we were fixin to argue about I could put him off a little while longer.

But he wasn't allowing any stalling that night. He grabbed and kissed me, started kissing down my chest, so I pushed him away. I said, 'You don't own me, Elmore Langley.' And he said, 'I own those shoes. Give them here. And I own that hat. Give it here. I paid for those stockings you're always playing with. Give them back.'

"I tried to head to the door but he gripped me by the arms and rushed me into the bedroom. He... he threw me on the bed, face down, and put all his weight on me. His knee dug into one of my arms and I thought it was going to break. He said, 'This dress, I believe, is mine too.' He unbuttoned it down the back, and I couldn't move to stop him. Then he turned me over and pulled the dress off me. He stood up and shook the wrinkles out of the dress, folded it, and laid it across the back of the chair. I sat on the bed crying like a fool. Elmore didn't care a wit. He said, 'Take off whatever else is mine.' He waited. I cried and started taking everything off. My hands were shaking. It took a long time. I cursed him and threw the under clothes at him. He caught them and tossed them on the floor. And when the only thing I had left was what I was born with, he came at me and took that too.

"I didn't put up a fight with him after that. We'd sleep together almost every night. He'd climb on me and work himself out and I would lie there. Sometimes, if I forgot who I was and who I was with, it would feel good for a bit. Sometimes, I'd think of you, baby. I remember laying there once while he took care of himself, breathing in my ear, and I looked off to the side at a pair of shoes he'd bought me. I tried to decide what outfit I had to match them, or if I really did like that color.

"He began to lose interest in me quick. He'd complain in front of his friends that I didn't know how to love a man. Sheila once told me she couldn't figure how I'd been able to put Elmore off for as long as I had, but that now it was time to be real good to him. She'd talk to me as if we were sharing sisterly confidences, but I figured Elmore'd put her up to it. He started flirting with other girls at parties and more frequently he'd have 'some business to see to' and leave for a long time.

"The night I snuck away from him, I went rummaging

through his pockets for bus fare with his snoring all loud behind me. I'd already packed my bag, had what I was going to wear rolled in a bundle under the bed. I dressed quiet and slow. Not that it mattered; his mouth made all the noise. I went through his wallet, took some, not all. I came across that pretty, tiny pistol of his. It had a soft, white handle that even I could only get three fingers on. I pointed it at him. His head pressed into the pillow and his legs and arms curled to him like a baby's. But Elmore wasn't really to blame, I'm thinking now... The dresses, the cars, the shows turned my head—I don't know. Anyway I never let my finger go near the trigger. It was too late for shooting him. I laid the gun beside his head on the pillow with the little barrel staring him right in the eye. I hope he woke up to that hello.

"I rode the bus, then hitched a wagon ride here, your new farm. Then I came to your door.

"When I was a very small thing, I woke one night to the sound of bumping like something dragged down stairs, but that isn't right cause there were no stairs in the shack I was in. And it wasn't a single sound that woke me, but a lot of loose noise that slowly nibbled me awake. I lay on a tiny, skinny cot not knowing when my sleep had stopped and my wakefulness had started, and I listened for the next bump or knock, the next hint to what was happening to me. Because I was frightened and I knew something terrible was happening. I got up and went to the door and my hands trembled on the knob and I remembered then, a warm presence had visited me while I slept, had hunkered over me like a ghost and whispered warm, tickling breath into my ear. I was scared, knew everything was dreadfully wrong. The door opened, creaked from my hands.

"In the outer room sat a large, naked man on a stool. His elbows were propped on his knees and his head rested in his hands. He was looking out a window, up at the night sky, I imagine. This man wasn't my daddy. I got no reason for being sure of that except my memory of him is too quick for him to have been my daddy. He turned slowly on me and his eyes were so dark, I could not see them. 'Little Slip,' he said, his voice was unsteady and I thought he was going to cry, 'she done left both of us.' That was the scariest moment of my life. I was abandoned, emptied and filled with nothing but fear. Standing in the dark with this strange, naked man, staring at the front door, the door she must have just disappeared through, and not daring on my life to open it. My scariest moment, up until I climbed the hill and stood at the door of your cabin.

"I hope you hear me, Charles. When I knocked on your cabin door I'd already missed a month. I was late. Damn. Took forty-five years to say that. And you can't get me off the hook now can you?

"Lord, wake him for just—" Gramma waited, looking lost for a moment. "Where?...the door," she said. "The door opened. We stared at each other. You'd been smart to hit me, throw me right down the hill. But, uh, uh, you wrapped your arms around me and practically dragged me inside, kissing me all over my face. I loved you more than ever right then, Mr. Standard. I'm trying to remember what you said, Charles. 'Just like I prayed.' I think. Cause I recall thinking, no, not just like you prayed.

"But I knew I was safe then. Everything was fine. We married. All the children were there. Grainger made us jump the broom, and all the while I thought I'd gotten away with something. No one had to know I already missed a month. Worried quite a few days, you'd meet up with Elmore. Why didn't you ask me what happpened in Cincinnati? Maybe you didn't want to know, no more than I wanted to tell. I couldn't have told it back then anyway. Cincinnati became my nightmare. I hated that city, its clubs, theatres, shops. I hated Elmore and his friends. I burned all the dresses. Did you know that? While you were out in the fields one afternoon, I put dress after dress into the fireplace, the shoes and the hats, watched the lace curl up tight, turn black and float up the chimney. That left me with only one reminder.

"Before I began to show, I told you we were going to have a baby. I put my best face on. I went over and over in my head just how to say it, to be excited, to put it just right. I told myself to mention money, you know, bills as if finances were the only worrisome thing we had to wrestle with concerning the baby.

"You used to worry over money just like your father did.

Mention money, I thought, that will distract him, and act excited. Never did occur to me to tell the truth. I'd think, what does it matter who fathered the child? Charles loves me. Why should it matter? Something inside had the answer all while I asked the question. Something whispered to me, 'A great deal. It would matter a great deal.'

"When I went out to you that morning in the field, with the knee high, tiny cornstalks all around, and you already done worked up a sweat though the sun was still cool, I smiled and we kissed and I could see pride in your eyes at what you'd accomplished in the field, and the confidence you had in your hands' ability to shape our future. You stood very tall, like a lord, over your land. I thought I said it just right, 'I hope you're going to be happy, baby.' I bounced on my toes; everything was going to be all right. 'We're going to have a baby.' I laid the lie right out there. Sowed it into the ground like another row of corn, stretching long and high between us."

Gramma tilted her head up and took a breath. She straightened her shoulders before looking again at Grandpa and resuming her story. "Everything became risky for you in that moment. I saw the uncertainty on your face, and it never really left. Suddenly the crops depended on if you could get enough rain and enough sun, and the harvest depended on how many men you could hire to help us pick, and how much you had to pay them and the house you wanted to build depended on whether or not the bank would give you the loan. You became vulnerable in that moment. Someone had let you down. Either me or the God of your father's book had let you down. I can't say if you believed me then. I don't think so. Was that surprise or suspicion I saw on your face? But the suspicion grew, just like my belly did, til it swelled up as much as I did.

"When the snows fell and the ground froze, and the wind cut around and through the cabin, shutting us in with just each other, you couldn't take it anymore. I used to lie in bed thinking, what if the baby looks just like Elmore. And I'd see Elmore laughing at the both of us from a crib. I wanted to pray this would come out okay for all of us, but praying was your domain, not mine. Well, it used to be your domain. Near my time, you finally had to ask. I was sure you would, but it surprised me just the same. 'Who's the daddy?' you asked, 'Is that my child?'"

I gasped aloud, but Gramma did not hear me. One night talking to a slightly drunk Grandpa Standard, I had mentioned Cakes's daddy. He had heard Kate. My heart thudded.

"I was sewing some heavier curtains for the windows," she continued, "and you came right out and asked. How many days did we argue? How many times did I almost tell you the truth? Don't tell him, Ruthie, I thought, he'll leave you like your Mama did. But you left anyway. I saw you ride off on Charley-horse. On cold nights like that one, the truck wouldn't even think about starting. I said, he'll be back soon. The snow was too deep and treacherous, and it was too cold to stay out long. After awhile, I'd go to the window, gazing out for you. Getting worried sick. I should have just worried about myself. As far as everyone figured, the baby wasn't due for another month at least. Mary's visit was still weeks off. Me and the baby knew better. She was ready to be born any day. And only to spend a snowed-in week with me. Tiny thing, fingers so small. Kate was so delicate, you see." Gramma's hand covered her mouth and her tears flowed.

"Much too fragile for this hard, old world. Not like Constance, she cried loud in the delivery room. She was a fighter from the get go. Not Kate though. You told me the doctor said maybe something was wrong with her heart. Just too tender."

Gramma sat up, pushing herself away from Grandpa, glaring at him now. "Charles, if you knew... how could you leave me like that? I had no one's hand to squeeze. When that first wave of pain hit me, I said, 'Oh, no! Not now.' I called out your name. I went to the window. Been alone and snowed in two days by then. The next pain brought me to my knees before I could get to the bed. I cried, 'Mama Mary, Mama Mary!' I recalled the time Mary took me with some of the other women over to Mrs. Hamey's. Her baby tried to come in the world sideways, then feet first. Mrs. Hamey's labor dragged over two nights and a day and she went hysterical from the pain til her husband barged in with his sour mash—which she forbid him to keep in the house—and poured it down her throat. Even then her body would twist and arc, and four grown women had to throw their weight against her to keep her down. They eventually had to cut her to get the baby out and one woman said, 'She's ruined for a man.' Thinking about that just scared me more. But in between the pain, I found myself. I wrestled the mattress off the bed and dragged it over to the fireplace. I didn't know how well I'd be able to move after the delivery and I wanted to be close to the fireplace when it needed more wood.

"And too, I was scared I might fall from the bed. Guess I kept seeing pictures of poor Mrs. Hamey. I gathered blankets, and food and water, and a lamp, and I cursed your name with each contraction—cursed Elmore's name too. I wadded up the corner of a quilt, stuck it in my mouth and bit down on it. I pushed, and beat my fist against the mattress. I thought I would die from the pain. Each time the pain would let go of me I'd look to the door. But no one came to rescue me. God it hurt. It hurt even more to endure it alone. But when Kate came out, I knew instantly she was worth it. Such a miracle. I was alone in that cabin, then I wasn't alone at all. I named her Kate. Charles, I glanced around that cabin; Kate had no father. There's the real truth that's been eatin at you. So I held that little girl to me and told her I was her mother and her father. 'Just me, Kate.' She seemed perfect. Just a perfect, little bit. I wouldn't leave Kate like my mother had left me... like you'd left me.

"I washed her in warm water. I nursed her just some. I kissed her all over. Kate and I were the only people in the whole, wide world. Every hill, mountain, and ocean had frozen and fallen away in the snow, leaving Kate and me by the fire in that warm and cozy heart I had made for us. You know, she was born with a head of hair, so fine like soft down or velvet. I think she would have looked something like Julie. Oh, but too much a perfect, little soul for this world. Right at my breast, she quit nursing.

" 'Now you can't be filled up already, ' " I said to her. She... she was maybe four days old, but I had lost track of the days. Not one separated itself from the next while Kate was on the earth. I held her to me, her skin against mine, realized I did not feel her heart beat."

Gramma shouted, "Kate! Kate!" Her curled hands grasped the air before her face and shook the infant she saw there. "Kate! I shook her and called to her. I put a damp rag on her face. I spanked her bottom. I shook her again and called her name. But couldn't wake her back up. She wouldn't... she wouldn't wake up. My little angel. I said, 'Aw, Kate, it was going to be all right. We weren't going to worry about what they said about us. Let their tongues wag all they want. It was going to be just fine. You and me, Kate.' I just held her for the longest time. Didn't tend the fire. Didn't care. I was going to let those miles and miles of cold just blow in on us...

"I don't know how much later you showed up. The mattress and I were back on the bed. Charley-horse was on the other side of the room, too cold outside. 'The doctor was here,' you said, 'the baby's gone. I guess you know that.' I spotted the little wooden box on the table. You said, 'The ground's frozen. We'll have to wait. I'm gonna put her outside.'

"I pointed my finger at you, and even that took effort. I was surprised by how weak I felt. 'Where were you? You abandoned us. You didn't want Kate to live. We could've gotten her to help. God damn you. Your God damn you,' I said, 'You abandoned us.'

"And I decided never to tell you the truth. My pay back for you leaving us. But there were so many times I wanted to talk about it over the years. We've stayed together with love and guilt. And you never believed me anyway." Gramma crawled backwards, away from Grandpa Standard and stood watching him on the opposite side of the bed from me. She looked cold, mean, but this appearance passed after awhile. "Or, maybe, you believed me and doubted yourself. Is that where all that faith went?"

I hoped she would not rediscover me. I had sat in the chair, as still as the chair, for nearly three hours with my legs tucked tight against me. Only now did I become conscious of their hurt, but I would not move.

She asked, "What good would busting up my little girl's marker do? I didn't put Standard on the stone." She waited as if listening to her husband's answer. "Yes, I know the little girl would've died anyway. Yes, we had Connie. And built this farm up from mud. The good times outnumbered the bad, Charles. I just wish I knew you knew that." She walked around the bed and retrieved the pocket watch from where she'd left it. Near the lamp, she turned it over in her hand before gently setting it on the bedside, nightstand. I saw her hand go under the lampshade to turn off the light, but then she straightened, paused a moment, and left the room, closing the door softly behind her. Leaving me with Grandpa Standard to say goodbye.

*

I remember his hands more than his face. Is that strange? I recall his face, too, the dark seriousness of it, the repetitive furrows of his brow, the way he bit his lower lip when considering the best way to tackle some chore. But his hands were the most animate. His character and ingenuity manifested in his hands.

They deftly loosed knots, readily snatched up pliers and wrench and mastered them, gripped tractor wheels, or dug into the husk of an ear of corn, shelled a pea pod quicker than I could snap my fingers, lightly floated over the grain of a warped door in need of planing, wormed into the inaccessible crevices of tractor engines, slapped mosquitoes with deadly accuracy, and assayed the soil with a gentle squeeze. His hands held true life lines, etched into the leather of his skin. His history could be read there without palmistry. The toil and grind of his days were told in smoothed over scars, rough, white capped callouses and badly mended, slightly crooked fingers. Never did I see his hands as clean as yours and mine get everyday. Always there seemed to be a line of dirt beneath his nails. His hands were big and strong, scarred, and knew nothing but work, had forgotten how to clasp in prayer. They moved through their daily rigors with a surety derived from repetition. They are working now, if that place they find themselves has anything "runnin rough" or "needs tightenin". It's just that I can't picture them idle, or laced across his chest. If Charles Standard made it to that perfect place in the afterlife, then it must have some imperfection, something that breaks down regularly, just for him.

## XIV

### A Mother and Child Reunion

I spent most of my high school years with the Colonel. Mama sent me to him in desperation, a last ditch effort on her part. After I grew to a certain man-sized height, she could no longer do anything with me, though she kept trying. She would ground me for some violation, and I, staring her straight in the eye, would get my jacket from the front closet and walk out the door. The Major turned Colonel and I lived in Ft. Ord, California and then in Ft. Gordon, Georgia.

I was fourteen when I first arrived in Ft. Ord. My father had a speech ready for me, and I got the impression he had rehearsed it. "People who resist discipline are, usually, the ones who need it the most," he said. "You've been giving your mother and sister a lot of problems, but your days of pranks and high jinks are over."

Pranks and high jinks? It sounded as if I'd been sneaking around giving everyone hot foots, or shaking hands with a joy buzzer, instead of skipping classes and getting caught smoking grass in the boy's room. I laughed when he said this and he'd thought I was laughing at him, so we started off on the wrong foot. It didn't matter much anyway. He was a very busy soldier, and it ended up that we didn't spend a whole lot of time together. Just as Mama, on numerous occasions, had tried to warn me, he was married to the Army. I continued my 'pranks', but I never fell in solidly with a click or gang, preferring always to be alone. The Colonel gave me a car for graduating from high school. I promptly drove off the next day from Georgia to Kentucky, without telling him, never to return. I was to turn eighteen that year and I think, we both considered that his job was done.

On that sunny and sober afternoon, I drove straight to the Standard farm from Ft. Gordon. I steeled myself for miles, after my near accident with the semi, and wanted much to see my Gramma Ruth.

She wasn't there. The farm reminded me of the ghost towns of the old west. It radiated that same aura of abandonment, as if everyone, bent with despair, had fled, leaving it to just eat on itself and erode. Certainly, the absence of Charles Standard's industrious hands could be seen in falling fence rails, tall weeds amongst the crop, peeling paint on the house.

I walked around. The only sounds I heard were the crunch of dirt beneath my feet, and the vacant sound of a squeaking hinge somewhere being played by the wind. I don't know where Gramma was on that day. Perhaps a neighbor had stopped by and they'd gone shopping. I didn't know, nor did I dwell on it. I, in fact, found some relief in being spared the confrontation. I hadn't known what I would say to her had I pulled in front of the house and found her on the porch picking the stems out of a sack of greens. I might not have stopped, simply driven around the house and out and down the road. I couldn't think what it was I might want to say to her. Her absence afforded me the luxury of returning on my own terms, to look here and there without explanation or apologies.

I stooped in front of the house and peeked under the porch. It was not the elusive hiding place it once was, for the shrubbery in front had thinned with age and, in some spots, disappeared completely, exposing my shady, dusty study.

I had a wistful hope of seeing Zeke crawl from under there with his nose dulled with dirt, wagging his tail with joy at seeing me. But I'd learned from Julie that the old frog dog had already completed a full life of trees, fields and bones. Still, I waited a bit to see if I might see him crawl from under there.

Knowing it was probably locked, I didn't try to go into the house, but stood in front of it and tried to take it in all at once to compare it to the black and white photographs I had stowed in my memory. My eyes centered on the window of the room that had been mine, had, I realized just then, felt more like mine in that one summer than any of the rooms with toy soldier wallpaper and airplane curtains that Mama had created for me.

I remembered my first country sunset, observed from the window of that room. I'd seen the broad strokes of painted sky and witnessed life and life beyond life. I heard Zeke playing, grumbling, and the wind in the barn, a curious wind that ran through each and every row of corn and gave the living leaves animation and vitality.

Just beyond them, holding on to the last, soft rays of the sun stood the magical, ominously attractive stones. The spirits of those lying in humble state made the stones glow, I believed then, or convinced myself to believe. My grandmother, gardener of flowers and souls, had made me believe in something just when I'd given birth to skepticism. But the new beliefs had not lasted long, overshadowed by the revelations I was to learn. In fact, I stayed away from the garden after learning the secret of Kate. I did not know what to think of the whole thing. I had learned more than even my youthful curiosity wanted to know. In subsequent weekend visits to the farm with Mama and Julie, I avoided Gramma and her garden as much as possible.

On that sunny day in 1982, alone on the farm, I thought about going down to the garden. It occurred to me; Gramma Ruth could have been down there. I slipped my hands into my pockets and stood in the yard, wanting to get caught by her. I told myself to go down the trail, find her, listen to her stories and who would care how true they were, these stories she'd probably learned from the ancient slave she'd named Tree.

The thought of seeing her made my heart beat fast, just as the thought of looking the Colonel directly in the eye and shaking his hand scares me, or the thought of hugging my mother frightens me. I could not be sure what these expressions of affection meant, and if they said anything to me, I would not know how much of it was true. Less disappointing and so much easier, I had discovered, to just avoid them. I climbed back into my new car and drove down the trail, slowing at the spot where Grandpa Standard had overturned his pickup, then headed to Louisville.

\*

Last year, I sat in the back of the church pews at Julie's after-the-fact wedding. Somewhere up front, my niece, Kate, squirmed in Gramma Ruth's lap, lending scant attention to the ceremony convened to grant her social legitimacy.

I had planned on staying away from the wedding, and gave some half-true excuse about work. But Julie called, begged me to come, though I was certain my presence wouldn't be that important to her. She refuses, as she puts it, to let me dangle alone by a frayed cord, so we both endure the ritual of her invitations. "We'll see," I tell her. "Okay, we're counting on you," she will say. And we both know better.

She told me the Colonel would make it to the wedding after all. Seems a gentleman friend of my mother's, I never met the man, was scheduled to give Julie away, but the Colonel decided at the last minute that he could attend.

The morning of the wedding, I woke early, though I usually sleep in Saturdays. I completely forgot about the wedding; it had slipped to the side of my mind during the night. I read the paper, and drank coffee in bed, and got the urge for a drink. I mean I actually went to my kitchen, opened a cabinet and hung on to its door trying to think of what I wanted. I laughed when I realized I was searching for a bottle. My high school plunge into alcoholism is far behind me, but echoes of it, invisible web lines tied to my wrists, will attempt to puppeteer me from time to time. Usually some reason accompanies the impulse. And that is how I remembered the Colonel would be in town and that my sister was getting married.

I went for a drive in the opposite direction of the church. I drove over to the Indiana side of the Ohio, parked, and walked down to the riverside. The dirty, brown water flowed sluggishly, and I watched it carry along the elongated, twisted toes of an uprooted tree, and I wondered what I was doing there.

I recall being cold that morning for I had left my apartment without taking a jacket, but I stood amongst the rocks and tall weeds long enough to see the tree root get hung up along the shore line where the river splashed foamy, white suds over it.

No answers presented themselves to me. My mind didn't seem to want to work on answers. The chilly wind, which flowed along over the water, chased me back to my car. I decided to go back home, maybe read a book, but then I thought, perhaps I'd get that drink after all. But I was too afraid to actually stop somewhere and buy a bottle, so I drove around, up and down streets until I passed in front of the church Julie was being married in. I sat down in one of the empty pews in the rear just in time to hear the vows exchanged and see the bride kissed.

The photographer arranged different sets of relatives for pictures. He told who to stand with whom and everyone seemed to surrender themselves to his direction. Several pictures of the bride and the groom, and the bride and the groom with Kate were taken. I didn't know my new brother-in-law well. We'd met, we'd talked, but I don't remember having any kind of impression of him. I remained in the back behind the encircling crowd of friends and on lookers.

One photo grouping featured the bride and her family. Gramma Ruth again held Kate, who wanted nothing more than to grab hold of the colorful ribbon that dangled from the wide brim of her great grandmother's hat. The baby's name had been a gift from Julie to Gramma Ruth. I don't know if it had the effect Julie had wanted. Certainly, Gramma Ruth was touched by the gesture, but it could be she wanted her Kate to be the only Kate. Anyway, despite Mama's and Julie's requests and demands that she come live with them in her advanced and enfeebling years, she adamantly refused and lived alone on her farm, dutifully continuing her stewardship of the flowers and the dead in her garden.

The photographer kept cajoling his subjects to close up tighter, and finally the space between the two parents of the bride disappeared. Mama kept glancing sideways at the Colonel. I didn't blame her. I don't think she had seen him in over ten years before their daughter's wedding day. He looked very handsome, and, I thought, reserved.

His brass buttons shined like yellow lights and ribbons as colorful as Gramma's garden adorned his chest. His eyes stayed locked forward, probably trained on the lens of the camera, undoubtedly keeping his concentration on the task at hand. I guess I studied him the most that day. He represented the most mystery.

I waited to see if he would catch his wife in one of her sidelong glances, but he did not. Julie glowed as a bride should, and the day seemed to be a very happy one for her and I was glad for that.

These were the people I loved. The photographer and I held a frame around them, and both of us suspended the moment in our way. I had never seen them all together like that before. I would have liked to have pushed my way through the gathering to them, congratulate Julie and kiss her on the cheek, shake the Colonel's hand, hug Mama and Gramma, and, even hold Kate, but I couldn't. It would've all just started up again if I had. "Where have you been this time?" "This is how you show up to your sister's wedding, in jeans?" "When are you going to show some responsibility, Sarge?" "What are you running from?" I did not want to risk diminishing her day, so I backed away and left.

*

Today, Julie and Mama are expecting to see me again.

"You will be there this time, Sarge? No joking," Julie said.

"I've never been joking," I told her before hanging up the phone.

But the day has arrived and I've again not made it to my destination, the place I am expected to be. Julie, hugging her daughter to her, will sort through the crowd searching out my face. When she fails to spot me, a bit of the tattletale left in her will make her turn to Mama and whisper, "I can't believe Sarge isn't here. Where is he?"

Mama's reaction will be as if she did not hear Julie at all, for she will have been hunting for me too. Finally in exasperation she will say, "I long ago gave up worrying over his whereabouts. He's a grown man now."

But I think I am in the right place. Though, this morning I set out my suit, shaved, dressed, and had every intention of being at my mother's side, this is where I wound up. I think I am in the right place, in a small corner of a cornfield by a garden sprinkled lightly with thin, chalky stones and rusty red, cracking rocks all hailed by the pom-poms of daisies, sunflowers and irises. And in no way am I alone. The family of souls who reside in the garden wait with me. They press at the fence, hearing the familiar, soft steps of Ruth Standard approach.

My mind did not conjure up the spirits gathered here today. My imagination has been crushed beneath the reality of a great pyramid of days. The spirits' presence can be keenly felt, radiating like the sun's heat in invisible waves washing through and around the trees, the fields, the stones, and me. This is all the evidence I need of the truth of Gramma's stories.

When she first came by here, surveying the land with her proud husband, her first act was to prop up the fallen stones, to show respect, to keep their dignity intact. She did not fabricate the spirits that compelled her to do that. They were already here. Any believer, who has ever entered a temple of his worship, has felt what she must have felt. And if a story's veracity can be judged by the sincerity of the teller, Gramma's stories were true. She believed them. She even spoke true when she told me she knew no story of Kate she could tell me. I see that now with the crystal clarity of hindsight.

They are all here. Cakes Huntley wears the suit his doting mother made for him. If his trousers fall a bit short, I cannot tell. He stands tall, anxiously awaiting Ruth, looking every inch the gentleman. Near him is Chief, wearing lion skins and the ornate headdress that marks him as the warrior general of a great tribe. In his proud, arrogant stance, his head is up, and his feet wide apart. No manacles bind his ankles. Luther has slipped to the front of the gathering, smiling broadly as if he is up to something. Hattie May waits with a bundle in her arms. Tommas is here, and Tillie, and Mark Littlejohn and so many more.

Finally, we see her, Ruth Standard, with her grass stained apron, walking down the trail as she has a thousand times. She is happy.

She smiles and her whole face gets into the act; even the wrinkles around her bright eyes curve upwards. As she walks into the garden, the circle of souls falls in around her. There is hugging, and laughter that I hear carried on the wind. Everyone makes room for big, ponderous Hattie May, who steps up to Gramma Ruth. Hattie hefts the bundle over her head, and turns this way and that for the entire gathering to see. They dance, and jump. They clap, and holler. And I hear the tiny cry of a baby just before she is reunited with her mother.

Up the trail, another figure approaches, at first, more ill-defined than the rest. In a few moments, I recognize her. It is my mother, dressed in black.

"I thought you might be here," she says.

The rising air whips at her dress, the wide brim of her hat and the netting covering her face, making the outline of her seem to waver, giving me the impression she is allowed to be here only at the mercy of the wind, which could blow her away like black dust at a whim. She walks up to me and lifts the net away from her face. Helpfully, the wind blows it over the back of her hat. Her make up has run, leaving streaks on her face.

"You came out here looking for me?"

I feel her eyes on me then she gazes at the garden, and I wonder what she sees there.

"No. Maybe. But I was looking for my Mama too. I had a feeling she might be here. You know?"

"Yes."

"She said to bury her body next to Daddy's." Mama pushes her hands into the deep pockets of her dress. She seems to shiver. I bring an arm up to hold her, hesitate, then pull it back. "But she liked it here so much. Mama finally told me about my half-sister, Kate. A big scandal it would've been, in those days especially. I know the whole thing was a burr between Mama and Daddy, but, I think, they still loved each other an awful lot." She begins to cry again.

I suddenly wished she could see what I see, the souls dancing in a ring around Ruth and Kate. I wish she would say something, point to it, know that everything is all right.

"I don't think Mama told me as many stories as she told you. But I heard a few. I asked her how she could know all these facts about these people and she said she learned them from an old gentleman, an ex-slave, named..."

"Tree."

"Yes, Tree. When she lived with the Brownings. I didn't believe her. I said, sure, Mama and how did this Tree find out about these people? The farm used to be a part of a plantation, you know. She said, did you ever think Tree might've come from this very plantation?"

I look at Mama. "Did he?"

She smiles and wipes tears and make up away. "That's what I asked. Your Gramma laughed and said, maybe he did."

We both look to the garden awhile, and its congregation of flowers and souls. I sense I want to say something to her, but I don't know what it could be.

"The things I see when I'm here, Sarge. I have double vision. I can see things as they were when I was just a little farm girl, when this was my entire world. All the fields seemed to stretch way over the curve of the earth. Now they seem quite small and humble. I look around and I can see it both ways. The old and the new. The old barn and the one that stands now. But not so much has changed."

She glances around, frowns momentarily, then the frown disappears as if the answer has presented itself to her. "I guess I'm the one who's changed. Not what the eyes see, but the eyes themselves. We grow up, hopefully, and the way we see things change." Her hand clutches at my arm. It is an almost desperate gesture, followed by a run of tears. "Julie is busy these days with her new family. Ken Doll, I think I'm going to need someone around... Family. I know you like being on your own, and I know you need your own space. But I thought, we could try to get along; you could drop by, say hello."

I wrap my arms about her and hug her fiercely to me. "I'll be there, Mama," I tell her.

When I return up the trail with Mama, our arms about each other's waist, I risk one more look back at the garden. Serenity is there. Just under the harsh blow of the wind, which races unrestrained across the empty fields, the laughter of fiddles plays.

To learn more about us visit our web
site at
www.laughingowl.com

Laughing Owl Publishing, Inc.